Julie Bozza

Writ in Blood

LIBRAtiger

Published by LIBRAtiger 2021

ISBNs
    Paperback: 978-1-925869-28-6

libra-tiger.com | juliebozza.com

Dedication

To Bryn,
the very best sister and writerly chum,
always my "without whom".

TABLE OF CONTENTS

ILLUSTRATIONS

Anyone can be a barbarian; it requires a terrible effort to remain a civilized man.

Leonard Woolf

Chapter One:

Fear No Ill, But Follow Me

Llano County, Texas;

November 1877

"The bravest man I ever met?" John Ringo echoed. His audience of one loved a dramatic pause, so John frowned up at the chilly blue arch of sky, making a show of pondering though the answer was sitting astride the horse just ahead of him on the trail. "That would be," he finally replied, "my friend Mr. Gladden here."

The Texas Ranger riding beside John glanced at the oblivious George Gladden and then his gaze swung back again, keen on the scent of a story. "How so?"

"He and another man rode into a town once, intending nothing more than visiting a store for supplies, and the place seemed peaceful enough, so they dismounted. Which was when shots rang out—"

"An ambush!"

"Yes, sir." A grin quirked John's mouth despite the sad story, and he took a moment to contemplate Private Davis's soul. Unlike the drabness or firmness defining the other lawmen, the soul of Mervyn Davis was like one of those handsome white clouds on a perfect spring day—huge yet nebulous. In contrast, George Gladden's soul looked much like George himself, though comfortably shabby and worn around the edges.

"What happened?" Davis prompted, even more eager than usual.

"The other man was hit twice or thrice in a moment, and his horse was spooked so badly he couldn't remount. But Mr. Gladden—even as he himself was shot—helped his friend onto his own horse, then scrambled up after him, and they made their escape…" John sighed. "For a short while, at least."

Davis contemplated this, before asking in a hushed voice, "Was the friend Moses Baird? Is that when he was killed?"

John nodded, though he was staring up at the infinite pale blue again. It wouldn't do to start getting into too many details and incriminating himself. Not that he had been there that day, but he had been part of the group that sought justice afterwards. John Ringo lifted a hand and let the rattle of the iron shackles make his excuses for him.

Undiscouraged, Davis asked, "What about Scott Cooley? What was he like? Was he brave, too?"

"He was a gentleman and my friend," John replied in honest yet distant tones that served to put an end to the conversation for the present.

The party continued on. It was late afternoon, and they were drawing close to the Colorado River. There were twelve of them: seven Texas Rangers including their leader Corporal Warren and the ever-curious Private Mervyn B. Davis; the sheriff and a livery man from Llano County; and three prisoners, George Gladden and John Ringo, and a cattle thief named Ed Mitchell. George and John were polite, of course, but they didn't associate much with Mitchell, except during the cold nights when the three of them huddled together under their scant blankets shared for warmth.

All was quiet once Davis quit talking, or as quiet as it ever got with the gentle rhythmic thuds of the hoof-falls on the trail, and the occasional jingle of harnesses and jangle of shackles. Maybe too quiet for John, and he should have let Davis continue to distract him, because thoughts of Scott Cooley brought thoughts of death, and the autumnal sumac glowing crimson in the westering sun didn't help any.

Scott had died suddenly in June 1876, while traveling—died of poison, they assumed, there being no signs of violence and no better explanation. Since Moses Baird had been shot to death after that ambush in Mason County in September 1875, there had been constant retaliations back and forth, a life for a life, and it had gotten so that if a man had any sense of honor or loyalty he could hardly avoid being drawn in. The Hoo Doo War, it came to be known as, and it had seemed righteous at first, to take up arms when the law failed—but then where would it end? Jim Williams had been killed by a mob in September 1876, which was no doubt considered justice by some, while others would see it as vengeance. Either way, John Ringo had earned himself the same fate. He wondered if anyone would be left to seek justice for him.

Death was everywhere, whether violent or not. Not long after Scott

Cooley had been killed, John's mother Mary had succumbed to the consumption that had also taken his younger brother Albert, back in San Jose, California. That left his three sisters living there alone, though they were all grown up now and doing well enough, taking over the running of Mary's boarding house. While working as a cattleman, John had sent them money regularly, but he'd spent the last few months imprisoned or being escorted from one jurisdiction to another, so he'd been in no position to earn anything honestly. He pondered on what they'd make of it if they could see him now, trapped in iron and guarded by seven Rangers. Would they assume him innocent? Demand an explanation? Or want nothing more to do with him? Their parents had abhorred mob violence after all they'd witnessed in Missouri, so John couldn't imagine his sisters understanding let alone approving of the path down which he'd turned.

Such thoughts weighed on him for the hour or two remaining of that day's journey.

As the sun began setting and the sky turned gold and then purple, the party made camp among trees on the riverbank, with the Rangers breaking up an old fallen oak for firewood. John sat on the ground with his back to George, close so they could lean against each other, prop each other up after a long day's ride, and share some warmth. "All right?" John asked with his head resting back on George's shoulder.

"All right," George confirmed with a sigh. The party was heading to Austin, where George was appealing his murder conviction, and whatever his hopes for that outcome there was no denying George was enjoying the freedom of the open air while he might. John, whose own murder charge had not yet been tried in court, could empathize.

Soon they were eagerly eating their standard camp fare of fried bacon and bread, and washing it down with coffee. Then, as the party began settling for the night, the prisoners were hobbled with more iron, and the three of them lay down together—it was George's turn in the middle—with one of the Rangers taking the first shift keeping watch, firelight glinting off his rifle. John stretched out tall from head to toe and then turned in to huddle close to his friend, getting as comfortable as the shackles on wrists and ankles would allow.

For a while John lay awake. He was cold but also hungry... so hard and hungry... and alas George wasn't that rarest kind of man who'd bestow such favors, even if they weren't in such unfriendly circumstances. John sighed, and huddled closer, grateful that George would allow even so much despite knowing John's nature. Eventually John warmed up enough to drift off…

To be woken in the small hours by a shriek.

It might have been an animal but somehow John knew it was a man. Perhaps its source was the primitive part of a man. Hoarse, shrill, terrified.

He lifted his head, startled and wary. But he lay alone, the blankets beside him empty. Corporal Warren, who'd been on watch, was dead—sitting with his back to a tree, his rifle still clutched in his hands and his stark cold face staring up at the sky.

John looked around further, but couldn't see what had caused this—unless it was the missing George Gladden and Ed Mitchell, but surely such violence was too cruel a deed for either of them, even if they'd been desperate to escape, and why wouldn't George have taken John with him? The chilly bright light of the full moon revealed the other lawmen sprawled dead on their bedrolls—except for Mervyn Davis who screamed again, lying near the fire, taut and quaking as if racked by nightmares. John cautiously got to his feet, still unable to fathom what on earth had happened.

His shackles slipped off as he rose, and he was astonished to see the other two sets of shackles discarded a short distance away—by the side of a deep pit. "George?" he whispered, and in the unnatural silence his friend would have heard him and responded if he could.

John glimpsed a creature in the corner of his eye—a man appeared just beyond the firelight—though how could John not have seen him already when he had swept a searching stare all around? A beautiful man, with golden hair brushed back from a high forehead, and simple black clothes, and bare feet, untroubled by the cold. He returned John's gaze steadily, with nary a flicker when Mervyn cried out in terror once more.

Then he turned away with a heavy rustle as of feathers fanning a hot breeze, and he stepped beyond the nearest trees. John followed before he could lose the sense of his presence, for those bare feet left no tracks on the ground.

The two of them were beyond reach of the camp when the creature turned toward John once more, this creature in the guise of a man, the most utterly beautiful man, smiling. None of which was reassuring, for he was tall, and behind him wings hid all the ordinary things, shifting restless, rasping against the highest leaves and branches. Somehow, despite the dark wings, there was a glow of light, though it might have been nothing more than the creature's own warm beauty. Another distant scream sounded from the Texas Ranger, the lawman sworn to protect his prisoner, able to defend John against all—except this one.

"What do you want?" John whispered, throat too dry to voice the question.

The smile widened, though whatever there was of humor in the expression was cruel. "What do you believe we want, Johnny Ringo?" A measured voice, both sensual and threatening. "What do you feel is wanted of you?"

John let out a breath that might have been a laugh had he the nerve for it. "Surely my soul already belongs to you."

The brow rose on that bold and simple face. "Does it?"

"Surely…" What did a fellow have to do to reserve a place in hell these days? John had known his fate was sealed ever since that morning he and Jim Williams rode to James Chaney's house and shot him dead right there on his front porch after he'd invited them in for breakfast. Which was justice undeniably earned by Chaney having lured George Gladden and Moses Baird into that deadly ambush, but it was also undeniably a sin that could never be washed clean. "After what I've done…"

"But there it is, you see," the demon said, gesturing with one large, elegant hand. "There's your soul. You have it with you."

John glanced behind him and, yes, his poor soul clung to his shoulders by a thread or two. It resembled nothing more than the tattered gray silk lining of his jacket, having fallen from grace what felt like a lifetime ago. "I thought I'd lost it," he murmured. But this flimsy thing was of no import. John Ringo said to the spirit that stood over him, "Take this soul, if that's what you want."

"What would you ask of us in return?"

How to answer that? John had the capabilities to achieve, he was certain. His wits, hands and eyes were all sharp and clever, and he'd always learned quickly. He'd done well as a cattleman and now, when needs must, as a gunman. But he also knew there was something else he was fashioned for, something as finely crafted as this lean body of his, but of the intellect instead. The strange thing was that he had no idea what. Would this creature tell him, if John could ask in the right way?

Eventually he tried, "Tell me what I was made to be."

Laughter, and the wings stirring, bringing with them the hot winds of hell. The air shimmered as if they were out in the desert, and John glanced around wondering if the dry leaves littering the ground and the old fallen branches might combust.

"Why, you were made to be nothing more nor less than you are. What more *should* you be?" Such a boundless, melodious voice. Such rich humor. "Do not forget that your skills have already released a soul. No doubt you believe that credited my Father's account." With a respectful nod of acknowledgment.

John was half pride, and the rest was horror. Not that Chaney, that treacherous son of a bitch, deserved anything other than hell, him and his fifty pieces of silver—but John felt queasy. He remembered the blood blooming through the towel that shrouded Chaney's head… before forcing himself to shake off the thought.

"We already owe you a favor, Johnny Ringo."

And here was the Devil's son, visiting with John in the guise of the most beautiful of men. Wheat-gold hair long enough to reach from his high forehead back to the nape of his neck, lifting in the breeze like the mockery of a halo. Striking face, with large features and warm sharp eyes. Unsubtle, divine, powerful. And so damned beautiful.

Surely this creature-spirit knew everything about John; surely he chose to appear in exactly this guise. Nevertheless, John hoped and dared to shock when he announced in casual tones, "Then I want to fuck you."

Amusement at the audacity or perhaps at the triviality requested in exchange for a soul. "All right," the demon replied easily. "I accept the deal."

The scent of danger remained, like the acrid remnants of a lightning strike, but John seemed to have earned some interest from this creature, some room to bargain. They watched each other for a while, John taking in further details of the demon's appearance.

The massive wings were the color of smoke, and some of the large feathers were singed. He was dressed in black, in a simple shirt and long loose pants, almost like a Chinaman's suit. His feet were bare but untouched by the dirt and detritus of this world. *The glory of Satan's son shall be revealed, and Johnny's flesh shall worship it, for the mouth of the Devil has spoken.*

Though he had no idea how this could happen, John took a slow step forward, and then another. The son of the Devil stood before him, within arm's length, awaiting John's pleasure. Beautiful, and willing to be amused by this mortal and his mundane desires. Perhaps the price of this blasphemy was that John's life would be claimed, and he'd be reunited with his soul in hell. But John didn't care.

He reached a careful hand, expecting to find cloth at his fingertips—instead, he touched the fine, blood-hot skin of the creature's torso.

Startled, John saw that the demon was naked now, and almost human. The wings were no more than a shadow in the upper reaches of the trees. Not an ordinary man, though, for he was as perfectly formed as a Greek statue, with that marble long-framed musculature come to life, his flesh warmed and fed by the blood pulsing strong. Deigning to indulge this mortal wretch, just this once, for the sake of entertainment.

A hot wind blew in from a distant desert, bringing the elements with it, seething around this intimate space and opening it up, maddening John as if he needed any more encouragement.

Long fingers working at his shirt buttons… A moment's assistance, and John slid his jacket and shirt back off his shoulders, dropped the clothes to the ground; undid his trousers, and pushed them and his drawers to his knees. That was enough. It was obvious he required no other preliminaries.

The demon turned away, and stood with his arms outstretched to either side, his hands curling around convenient branches. John stepped up behind him, and forced himself home between those generous pale buttocks.

Perfect, to be sheathed in this unnatural heat, this subterranean pressure. John groaned; grabbed at the jut of the creature's hipbones to steady himself; began a relentless rhythm of thrusts. Part of him laughed. To be fucking the son of the Archfiend to the melody of Private Mervyn B. Davis's pitiful whimpers! But the sensation was too powerful for John's humor to remain so observant.

None of this seemed to affect the creature. His head was turned to one side, a cheek pressed against rough bark, his expression curiously impassive. But then the smallest of smiles grew and, no doubt aware of exactly how John liked to do this, the Devil's son hid his face from the mortal behind him. Johnny felt that hot breeze again, felt flames licking at his back and buttocks and thighs. Felt the delicious peril of this encounter, and feared the

result, even as potent completion demanded his surrender. The trees might burn, the conflagration was in his blood now, and who knew where it would end.

Perfection!

Ringo pulled away with a cry, managed to haul up his trousers. Perfection, yes, and the complete absence of pain and need. For a moment he was floating free, drifting unbound through the world. Then the darkness hit him so hard he wasn't even aware of falling to lie in an abandoned sprawl.

A small explosion—not quite a gunshot—and John was starting up from the blankets, chained again, and George beside him likewise. Confusion reeled through his aching head, but he fixed on the urgent sight of Mervyn Davis jumping about trying to snuff out a flame licking at his hip. There was much cursing from him and laughter from the others, a few of whom gathered around. Eventually Davis dropped his trousers and landed on his rear while another Ranger stomped the flame out against the dirt.

"Got too close to the fire," someone remarked. It was still dark, with not even the glimmer of dawn on the horizon, and most of the party were resettling already. If there was one thing they all agreed upon it was wanting to never waste any sleep.

"The fire got too close to me!" Davis retorted, kicking at a stray ember with his boot heel. He scrambled back to his feet, putting his trousers to rights and gingerly feeling around the burnt patch. A moment later he produced an ignited cartridge from his pants pocket. "Let that be a lesson to us all on the necessity of cartridge belts!"

Then he was fussing over the burnt cloth of his overcoat, where it had all started. The Ranger who was due to take the next watch obliged the current one by starting a quarter hour early. Everyone else was returning to their rest—except for John, who remained sitting up staring blankly at Mervyn Davis while trying to account for his own strange adventure.

The encounter had been real, he would swear on his mortal life. John felt enervated… satiated… in ways he'd known far too seldom. He remembered not only the touch and texture of the creature, but his beauty, so wildly beyond anything John could have imagined. And yet here was John, dressed and shackled, and half-covered by the rough gray woolen blankets.

When Davis looked over at him curiously, John turned away and lay back down with his back to George. He didn't want to be quizzed when he couldn't explain the night's happenings even to himself. He closed his eyes, but he did not find rest.

Breakfast was a somber affair after everyone's disturbed sleep. They ate without the usual talk, and then most of them sat around waiting for a second pot of coffee to be brewed while a few men desultorily started packing up camp. Even Corporal Warren didn't seem to mind about a late start to the morning. All was quiet until—

"I had such a nightmare!" Mervyn Davis declared, turning his gaze on the rest of the party. "You were all dead—or dragged down to hell. Didn't anyone else…?"

Most of them were looking askance at Mervyn. One drily remarked, "I was sleeping sound till you woke us up with a bang."

"A nightmare as well as an exploding cartridge," the sheriff mused. "Can't say I'm sorry you had a worse night than me, private."

"The one caused the other, you see," Mervyn explained. "Or the other caused the one…" He searched for a sympathetic response, but they were in short supply—until he fastened on John. "Did you dream last night, Mr. Ringo?" Mervyn pleaded. "Did you suffer bad dreams?"

"No." John shrugged, and lowered his head so that his hat brim shielded him from curiosity. Surreptitious glances discovered not so much as a single melodramatic singed feather lying discarded on the dirt. He couldn't help offering a pinch of reassurance. "I don't know… Maybe."

"What did you dream of?" Mervyn pressed him. "Do you recall?"

John just shrugged again and turned away. He didn't stand yet, though, despite the rest of the party making ready.

The powerful perfect sensations he remembered could have been nothing more than a despairing imagination and an unwise instance of self-abuse. Except that his soul was gone again—or perhaps even that had been part of the fancy, perhaps he'd only dreamed that the lost fraying gray thing had returned to cling to his shoulders that night.

A groan of angry frustration rumbled silently in his gut. If the bartering had been real, surely John would have been smart enough to ask for his freedom. *Surely* he would. Though he supposed it would be natural for the infernal creature to intrigue and gratify his physical lusts, rather than guide him to his best interests.

John dropped his face to his hands for a moment, and roughly tried to rub away the remains of the spell while his chains clanked discordantly.

It seemed that Mervyn was in much the same confused state. He sighed, and brought out his paper of pills, unfolded it to pluck one out. But Corporal Warren paused by his shoulder to remark, "I'm not sure you should be taking those, private."

"Why not, sir?"

"You ain't been the same since we left Llano," Warren said. "You've been… all kinds of excitable." Another Ranger underscored that with a huff, and Warren amended, "Even more excitable than is regular."

Mervyn stared down at the pills held in his cupped hand, and then looked back up at Corporal Warren.

"I'm guessing that maybe you're taking the wrong medicine."

Another moment dragged by, and then Mervyn got up to drop the pills into what remained of their campfire. A flag of flame ran up from the paper, and then sparks prickled as the pills were consumed.

Mervyn's troubled gaze met John's once more, but neither of them said anything, and eventually Mervyn turned away into the belated beginnings of his day.

Chapter Two:

Wildcards

Fort Griffin, Texas;

November-December 1877

"You're Doc Holliday."

Doc slowly drew on his cigarette—if he breathed in the smoke just so, he barely coughed at all—and looked up to see who'd made this announcement. A man stood there, lean but strong, with a heroic jaw and clean-cut features. Dark gold hair brushed back thick from his forehead, and an imposing moustache couldn't quite hide a stern mouth. But what Doc had first noticed, and now returned to, were the thundery blue eyes. "So I understand," Doc replied at last.

"My name's Wyatt Earp. I've been working as an assistant marshal in Dodge City."

"Then you are a long way from home." Doc poured the last of the whiskey into his glass and signaled to the barman that he required another bottle. The afternoon was becoming warm, and the sustenance would be welcome. "What brings you to Fort Griffin? I hope for your sake that your business won't keep you long in this ramshackle dump."

"I'm looking for Dave Rudabaugh. If you have information on his whereabouts, you can shorten my stay, and I'd be obliged."

Doc smiled, entertained by Earp's stolid manner that betrayed—unless Doc was imagining it—a hint of irony. "Why do you suppose I'd divulge such information? In fact, why do you think I won't simply warn Rudabaugh that you're on his trail? The law and I are at odds as often as not, sir."

Earp took a breath as if startled or perhaps even amused. "Rudabaugh's wanted for train robbery, if that inspires your loyalty."

"But you're not here in your capacity as marshal? I noticed you used the past tense, Mr. Earp. Perhaps you've turned to bounty hunting?"

"You have nothing to fear from me. I'm here on behalf of the railroad, and that's all. This is my last task before I head for the Black Hills."

"Seeking gold rather than justice," Doc murmured, considering the fellow while he stubbed out the old cigarette and rolled himself a fresh one. Wyatt Earp was dressed in heavy black, with a white collar-less shirt and a black flat-brimmed hat. Unfortunately, the dramatic effect was obscured by desert dust and the shabbiness of one who has traveled and slept in the same clothes for days. Two pistols graced his hips on a low-slung belt. "I do not fear you, Mr. Earp. However, I would be certifiably mad if I wasn't wary of Rudabaugh. He runs with an overly young and dangerous crowd."

"Yes, he does." Earp let the implication speak on his behalf: that was why he had come from Kansas to Texas to find him.

"I am more than a match for them, of course, but I make it a rule not to choose my enemies lightly." Doc nodded, punctuating his own wisdom. "Do you play poker, sir?"

The change of tack caused no more than a flicker of surprise. In fact, if it wasn't for those visceral eyes, Earp would be harder to read than granite. "Yes, but I don't have enough money on me to lose to you. If I need to bribe you, we are both out of luck."

"What a pity." Doc sat back and looked away, ostensibly calling an end to the conversation. He sipped a nip of whiskey poured from the fresh bottle, while Wyatt Earp stood there, either too stubborn or too stupid to take the hint.

"We needn't play for money," Earp eventually suggested.

"No? What would we play for instead?"

"I used to play poker with my brothers, in front of the fire after supper."

"How domestic." Doc succumbed to a cough, which perhaps undermined his dismissal of the scene Earp was painting.

"We played for matchsticks."

"And I suppose you never even bothered to count up the matches afterwards."

Earp shrugged. "No one really won, but no one really lost, either."

"The problem is, you see, I have a sufficiency of matches," Doc informed him in his laziest Georgian drawl.

The lawman said, "We could play for information. Whoever wins a hand gets to ask the other a question and receive an honest answer."

"Ah." Doc paused for a moment, wondering whether this was incredibly naive or incredibly sophisticated of the man. "How would you know if I was telling you the truth?"

"Maybe I wouldn't. That's not what's important."

Doc raised an eyebrow. "What is important, then?"

"Even a lie tells a truth about the person who chooses to tell it," Earp replied. "And a question can be as revealing as an answer."

Intriguing. "Given that it's inevitable I'd win most hands, what would I want to ask you about? What meets the eye is striking indeed, but is there more to you than that?"

Earp's gaze never faltered. When he spoke now, however, his voice was roughened, perhaps betraying unease. "I don't know. Sometimes I fear there might be."

"Yes," Doc responded approvingly. "But you shouldn't fear it; explore it! Live life to the hilt."

"Is that your philosophy?"

Doc was about to reply, but instead smiled graciously at the lawman. "I apologize. I was so fascinated by your conversation, I neglected to ask you to sit down. Forgive my lapse in manners and join me." And he called to the barman for another glass, as Earp pulled out and settled in a chair on the other side of the little wooden table.

"Thank you," Wyatt said when the barman approached, "but I'll have coffee if you have some hot."

"How very sensible of you," Doc remarked. "I confess the liquor is quite ghastly, at least until you've drunk enough not to care." He began shuffling the deck of cards he'd left on the table as challenge and invitation. His hands were fast and dexterous, his fingers long and fine, and Doc showed off his skills and physical attributes at every opportunity. Meanwhile he mused, "Earp is an Irish name, is it not?"

"Yes. But we've been here so long, we're Americans now."

"My great-granddaddy came here from Ireland." Doc paused to take a mouthful of whiskey—and grimaced again at its raw quality. "The only thing I miss from my father's house is his victuals. He bought the best of everything in great quantities, when they were available. I inherited his appreciation of these things, though I believe his tastes in all things sensual were not as broad nor as adventurous as mine. However, I must admire, from that point of view, his choice of a second wife. She was young and quite splendid, and completely inappropriate to my mother's memory. I hated the old bastard for that…" He mused for a moment and then added "inter alia" for the sake of the truth, the whole truth and all that: *among other things.* Among so many other things.

Doc was watching Earp to see how he took this rambling testimony, but he didn't seem fazed by the story nor the Latin. After a moment's silence, Earp offered, "The relationship between a man and his father is always difficult."

"Yes, I suppose so. Though naturally I resent having my own particular circumstances thrown in with a generalization about half of humanity."

"Anyone else might have assumed I was offering empathy on the basis of personal experience," Earp replied.

Doc laughed. "Then say so, Mr. Earp. I'm a gentleman—far more of a gentleman than these misbegotten dregs of civilization are accustomed to— but I have never let manners interfere with direct speech."

Another pause, while Earp took a mouthful of coffee and considered Doc. "Are you trying to annoy me and drive me away, Mr. Holliday, or are you testing me?"

"Why, I'm testing you, of course." The laughter lingered in his mouth, ready to spill forth again. Unfortunately it became a cough instead.

"Have I passed?"

In response, Doc began dealing a hand of cards. "The game is five card draw, and—to make it easier for the fellow who's only played with his brothers in front of the fire after supper—deuces are wild." He watched Earp examining his cards. The man was a little less stolid now, a little easier to read. Something in Doc's rattled-off words had surprised him, but Doc wasn't sure what exactly. Doc asked, "How many draw cards?"

Earp threw down three and picked up his new cards with a slight frown.

Doc dealt himself three draw cards as well. "How much would you bet on that hand, sir?"

"A whole box of matches," was the reply, a glint of amusement in his eyes betraying the deadpan demeanor.

"I do believe you're bluffing." Doc laid down his hand. He had two pairs, of fours and jacks.

Earp had a deuce, which he'd paired with his highest card, the king of hearts.

"My hand wins," Doc declared. "And my question is… What is your philosophy?"

"I don't know. Not the same as yours."

"You honestly don't know, or you simply haven't put it into words before?"

"I don't know."

Doc frowned. "Surely your choice to be a lawman is as significant as my choice to be an adventurer. It follows that you know who you are."

"I thought I did, once. I was on… a certain path. But that turned out poorly." Earp seemed to pass over the next part of the story—pass over it verbally, at least, if not mentally. "Now I—"

"Now you no longer know which path to tread? Or even where to set your feet?"

A flicker of a smile again, more wry than amused. "My feet are firm on the ground again. But you only get to ask one question each hand."

"Of course." Doc pushed the pack over and watched Earp shuffle. The man had large hands, competent rather than deft, with strong fingers. He let Doc cut the pack, and then dealt. As if making conversation, Doc asked off-handedly, "What's Dodge City like?"

"Quiet, except during cattle season." Earp looked across at Doc. "You'd know how that goes. The cattle drives pass by here."

"Nearby," Doc allowed. "I still want to hear your thoughts on Dodge."

Earp nodded. "It's busiest from May till September or October. The cowhands have spent all spring out on the range here in Texas, keeping the cattle on the rancher's land: that's lonely and boring work. Then they round up the cattle and drive the herd hundreds of miles to Kansas to the nearest railhead: that's months of hard work, terrible conditions, danger, and more boredom. People tend to romanticize the life, but that's a mistake. Once the cowhands get into town and sell the cattle, they're more than ready to celebrate for a few days, before heading back to the ranch and starting all over again. Some spend or lose so much in Dodge that they can't even afford the journey home."

"I see," said Doc. Indeed, none of this was new to him, but it did make Dodge sound like an attractive proposition: bored and lonely cowpunchers taking the first opportunity to have a big time and spend their wages… Plenty of chances for him and Kate to win or earn that money from them.

"Fascinating."

"It can be a whole lot of noise and trouble, but I understand why." Earp dealt the draw cards, and again frowned over his hand.

Doc won, of course, and asked, "What happens after you go to the Black Hills?"

"If I find gold, I'll go into business. There's a woman back in Dodge who might marry me."

"You make it sound as if she'd be doing you a favor."

Earp looked at him. "Of course she would," he said flatly, which might have been a gentleman's prevarication. Earp added, "If I don't find gold, I'll probably work as a marshal again."

After winning the next hand, Doc asked, "Why are you disenchanted with wearing a badge?"

"You're asking questions I don't have answers to."

"Tell me what's on your mind."

A moment's consideration before he started, "I've done all kinds of work. Reckon I'm good at being a lawman. Working for law and order. But I'm tired of supporting someone else's political career and keeping other people in business…" Earp let out a sharp sigh as if impatient with his own doubts or wariness. "It's time I went into business for myself and my family instead, that's all."

To his surprise, Doc found himself hoping Earp wouldn't commit slow suicide by settling down. In fact, Doc had to admit he was interested in Earp. Doc's instinct now was *not* to warn Rudabaugh; though if Doc told each fellow about the other, it would be fascinating to see what happened next. Wyatt Earp may well prove an adequate opponent for Dave Rudabaugh.

Doc Holliday was not used to wishing a good man well.

Adding insult to injury, Doc found himself with a no-pair hand. He was rescued from contemplating his cards and the consequences of losing, by Kate's entrance. Discreet, and respectful of possible scams, she hovered a few feet behind Earp waiting for Doc to beckon.

"Come over here, darling," he said. Doc noticed that Earp stood in the presence of a woman but allowed Kate to draw up her own chair. "My dear, this is Wyatt Earp," Doc said, waving a languid hand in his direction. "Mr. Earp, this is Kate Elder."

"How do you do," Earp said. And he shook Kate's hand, firmly and respectfully, before sitting again.

Doc smiled at Kate's reaction. She never revealed much, but he could tell she was pleased at this polite yet no-nonsense approach. "Kate, I'm afraid you've arrived in time to see me lose a hand to Mr. Earp."

She looked from the table to each of the players, her eyes sharp. "What have you bet, Doc?"

"No money and no favors. Just information."

"What does he want to know?" she asked in that beautiful throaty voice of hers.

"Something dangerous. You love me more the more unwise I am, don't you?" Doc smiled, intimate with her in this public place, and leaned closer for a kiss. And then he laid his cards down. "Mr. Earp, can you beat that?"

"Yes, I can." He had three jacks.

"Then ask your question."

"How can I find Dave Rudabaugh?"

Kate's eyes flashed. "Who are you, Wyatt Earp? Why do you want to know?"

Earp replied impassively, "I was an assistant marshal in Dodge City. The Santa Fe Railroad asked me to bring him in."

"That is dangerous, Doc."

Grinning, Doc quoted, "*Danger, the spur of all great minds.*" He kissed Kate again, savoring it. "I have no fear of Rudabaugh, though it is unwise to entangle myself with his fate. I have no loyalty to him, either."

"You have no loyalty to this lawman, and you're not afraid of him."

"True, my dear, but he is far more interesting than Dave Rudabaugh or any of his young friends, and a promise is a promise. Mr. Earp has answered my questions, and I shall answer his." He met the man's gaze. "But not here or now, I think. It is too public a place for betraying a scoundrel. Why don't you visit me early this evening at our hotel?"

"All right," Wyatt Earp agreed, but with a hint of annoyance, presumably at being given little choice. "I'll be there at seven."

No need to give directions; there was only one hostelry in this poor excuse for a town. Doc stood, took Kate's hand in one of his, and caught up the bottle of whiskey in the other. "Come, my dear, I feel the need for a postprandial nap." He smiled at the woman. Their evenings were for business; afternoons were for their own pleasure. Doc added, "I'm sure Mr.

Earp will excuse us."

The lawman stood as well and nodded a silent farewell to Kate. Doc was amused to note she returned the gesture, with exactly the same inclination of her head.

One thing he and Kate shared was passion. Within minutes they were behind closed doors and kissing as well they could while disrobing.

Kate was beautifully ample in breast and hip, possessing the generous figure which meant, out here in the West, that she was either successful or well taken care of. The fact was, she was far too independent to let anyone take responsibility for her. It followed that, yes, his bewitching Kate was the most successful and popular prostitute Doc had ever known.

Compared to her, Doc was perhaps overly slender. Despite his former love of food, he had always been lean, and this lingering death of his had exaggerated that trait. He liked to think of his figure now as graceful, with its fine muscle providing a little necessary padding between pale skin and long bones. His strength resided in his sinews.

"As spicy as paprika," he murmured, tasting the heat of Kate, watching the lace-patterned sunlight inflame the dark red of her hair.

Doc knew what he was doing, and trusted that the soldiers, travelers and townsfolk from whom Kate earned her money in the evenings would bore her by comparison. The same men bored Doc, after all, while losing to him at poker. Kate had an exotic knowledge that would surely scare most of her customers away if she demonstrated much of it. What she was doing with her fingers right now, for instance… And it wasn't just their existing knowledge, of course; Doc and Kate often whiled away the afternoons exploring fresh ideas.

There was plenty of opportunity for distractions. Doc liked to take his time over his pleasures, liked to let his focus roam in whatever directions it pleased. Today he found himself wondering what Wyatt Earp's reaction would be to some of this. Shocked disbelief, Doc hoped. As for that woman who might do Earp the favor of marrying him… It sounded as if there were little hope for the fellow.

Doc liked afterwards almost as much as anything else. They would laze in bed, skin pungent on skin, and sometimes Kate would listen while he talked and then offer her own sharp observations. Their repose this afternoon was marred, however, by a particularly bad coughing fit.

"You're getting no better," Kate observed.

"I've been dying with a complete lack of dignity for five years now," he informed her, "and I don't intend to stop dying any time soon."

"Five years?"

"They diagnosed me as consumptive when I wasn't yet twenty-one, back in '72. They told me that even if I left Georgia, I would not live much past my next birthday; that was the first thing they were wrong about. They advised me to wear red flannel next to my skin."

Kate glanced at his white undershirt and drawers draped on the foot of the bed and smiled. There was, as always, a not unbecoming hint of mockery to her amusement.

"Red does not suit me, my dear, and flannel is not my style." Doc lit a cigarette and dragged over another pillow on which to prop himself. "They told me to quit drinking and smoking and staying up all night. Suggested I drink milk and seek plenty of fresh air. But I wasn't going to die like that. A temperate life does not make for an interesting death."

"Live life to the hilt," she murmured, and then they said it in unison, as if the words were a prayer or even a talisman capable of working defiant miracles. Kate shifted close, kissed him with those sweet red pepper lips, and they began again. Doc wondered whether, if Wyatt Earp walked in at seven and found them still utterly abandoned like this, he could be tempted to join them for an hour or two...

But it was only a fleeting fancy, and no match for the skills and distractions of Kate Elder.

The weeks wended on, blending one into another. Christmas approached, though nothing in this pathetic town indicated that fact. Back in the South they knew how to celebrate the seasons and the holidays and the festivals. But Doc had left the South and its humidity behind, left his health and his life, left the food and other plunder. Turkey and peach chutney and sweet potato pie crafted by the family's American housekeeper; gumbo and jambalaya and coush-coush created by the Cajun serving maid: that bounty belonged to the time when he'd eaten as much as he drank now.

Instead, here was the dry West, here was his long slow death and his adventuring; here was whiskey and poker and faro and a complete abandonment to sensuality.

Almost Christmas, sometime around midnight, and he was playing yet another hand of poker. He'd always had the right combination of luck and skill and shameless audacity to be successful at the game, and he was making a finer living than ever, now that the country was returning to prosperity after four difficult penny-pinching years.

Doc liked to take his time over these important matters, considering all the subtleties of the game, ruminating about life—and annoying the hell out of the other players.

He had, for instance, just taken a good five minutes to decide to fold. Which meant that Ed Bailey, who sat opposite him, won the hand by default. Bailey had not appreciated the delay, and he was only grudgingly satisfied with this rare victory because the pot was rather small compared to what Doc had been winning.

"Your deal, Holliday," Bailey ground out.

There were two others in the game, both losing steadily, with most of the coins and rumpled dollar bills coming Doc's way. They watched with a mixture of bemusement and irritation as Doc shuffled the cards, fingers deft.

"Get on with it," Bailey added. "We don't have all night."

"Indeed we don't," Doc replied. "We only have the moment."

"What the hell are you on about now?"

While Bailey's impatience indicated he didn't really want an honest answer, Doc provided one. "Too many people live in their memories, or in their plans and dreams of what might be. However, as you are apparently aware, we don't have anything but this moment, and this moment, forever and ever. I live firmly in the here and now. But I must say I didn't expect to find such advanced philosophy in this forsaken place."

"It's you that brought it here, not me, if that's what it is."

"Ah, more philosophy even as you protest! Ed Bailey, you amaze me. You're right: the only qualities you find around you in the world are what you bring to it."

The man growled. "Shut up with this nonsense and deal, Holliday."

Doc nodded politely and dealt. He was aware of the three suspicious gazes fixed on his swift hands, each of the players determined not to be dazzled. But Doc had never had to cheat, and certainly not against the likes of these. Of course, as his familiarity with the game had become intimate, he'd cheated every now and then—to see if he could get away with it, viewing this as another useful challenge to his skills. And he had gotten away with it, every time. But it wasn't necessary, and he far preferred to behave honorably.

He took a long while to examine his cards, which gave him plenty of opportunity to watch the other three examining theirs. This one, Ed Bailey; his eyes betrayed him. Bailey held his face in an unrelenting grimace, but his eyes told Doc whether he was pleased with his hand. In fact, in that regard, he reminded Doc a little of the otherwise deadpan Wyatt Earp.

It had been a month since Earp had come to ask Doc for news of Dave Rudabaugh's whereabouts, and Doc found himself pondering the lawman more and more. There was a mystery in him that Doc hadn't figured out— that was among the many things Ed Bailey didn't share with Earp. It wasn't usual for Doc to think a good man interesting, or to be surprised by such a creature.

Wyatt Earp. Doc was beginning to hear talk of him as a lawman—or perhaps Doc just hadn't paid attention before now. Earp had made a modest name for himself, keeping all those wild cowpunchers in some semblance of order, and earning everyone's respect, no matter how grudging. It must be difficult to find a balance between letting the cowhands spend their money and enjoy their celebrations, while leaving the dull citizens to rest in peace at night.

Imagine a good and honest man being that creative and intelligent. Imagine him being unpredictable, too often underestimated, maybe even having depths. Incredible. Doc wondered for a moment whether he was becoming susceptible at the ripe old age of twenty-six.

But, no, that was how he lived this death, this exquisite haunting state of not-living and not-dying. Having always had a strong sense of himself, he tried to lose that awareness in an abundance of sensation; he opened himself to experiencing all he found, recklessly being all he could be. Susceptible to everyone and everything, he wallowed in crazy self-indulgence. And he should never have survived those first months.

After several years of attempted self-destruction, Doc had begun to pace himself with long lazy periods of moderation. There were so many lovely things he could do while sober. Every now and then, for instance, he drew on his savings, found a comfortably appointed hotel room in an adequate town, and spent days and weeks reading the latest books and poetry, and rediscovering the classics. Sometimes he exerted himself enough to have a quiet liaison with someone inappropriate.

But even his periods of indulgence weren't quite so destructive these days.

"Holliday, you drunken fop, are you making a bet or not?"

"Ah, yes," Doc murmured. For a few glorious months he'd had the heights in life, back in the South; now he sought the depths and breadths out here in the West. Though it was becoming more and more obvious that he'd explored the pitiful shallows that were all Fort Griffin, Texas had to offer.

"Get the hell on with it, then." This Ed Bailey was an angry creature.

Doc had nothing at all in his hand, but he bet fifty dollars, raising the pot by thirty.

That annoyed Bailey even more. "Another winning hand, Holliday?" he asked with bitter sarcasm.

"It becomes quite tedious after a while," Doc commented urbanely. He threw out two cards rather than the limit of three, in order to further fool the man. When he dealt himself the draw cards, Doc found he still had nothing. Catching Bailey's glower, though, Doc tossed in another ten dollars and smiled at him. "Really quite tedious, I assure you."

The player to Doc's left had already folded. Bailey sat there staring at Doc, rubbing a ten-dollar bill between his thumb and fingers, working it from end to end.

Doc asked, "Can you afford to lose an extra ten to me, Ed? Do you want to throw good money after bad?" Letting his smile hint of other pleasures, Doc eased from concerned tones to suggestive. "We could, of course, negotiate other ways of meeting your commitment to me."

"You're filth, Holliday," Bailey declared.

"And you have no trouble recognizing me as such. What does that say about you?"

"Shut your mouth before I shut it for you."

He whispered, "Can you afford to lose to me, Ed?"

The ten-dollar bill was becoming quite worn. It was clear that Bailey couldn't read what Doc was up to, and was having trouble deciding whether to be wise and fold now, or be brave and take his chances. Doc thought that Ed himself must have a decent enough hand. "I'll see you," he finally said, letting the note fall to the table.

The player to Doc's right folded, unnerved.

"It's just you and me now, Ed," Doc murmured, smile lingering.

"Show me your damn cards."

"But it's such a beautiful hand. I think I'm going to have to raise you again." And Doc's fingers strayed toward another fifty-dollar bill.

Ed Bailey growled in frustration and threw his cards down. "Forget it, Holliday. The game's over. You've stolen enough of my money."

"Stolen?" Doc cried out, though his protest was undermined by a fit of laughter, mingled as ever with coughs. He began gathering the pot of money up with the rest of his winnings.

An ominous silence as Bailey stood across the table from him, looming over the scattered cards and money. Definitely ominous, though Doc was having trouble suppressing his mirth. He knew he must take the game and his opponents far more seriously than this, as his life and his livelihood were at stake—but tonight Doc felt far from serious. He and Bailey were drawing attention now, the rest of this rabble sensing excitement.

"I'm in a reckless mood, Ed," Doc announced, looking up at him. "Far too reckless to deal politely with sore losers."

"I wouldn't have it any other way," Bailey informed him, venomous.

Doc stuffed a handful of notes and coins into his coat pocket. Another chuckle escaped him. What Bailey couldn't know was that Doc would have been just as amused if Ed had seen him and won the hand, for the amusement was due to his own audacity. He offered, "Do you want to see these beautiful cards of mine?"

Bailey frowned, full of menace. "Were you bluffing, you arrogant fop?"

By way of reply, Doc turned the cards over one by one. Nothing. Doc smiled at the fellow, charming in victory.

"You bastard," Bailey declared—and the fight began.

It didn't last long. A brief scuffle, and they were falling to the bare dirt floor in an angry embrace, Doc's bowie knife quickly finding its way from the back of his coat to Ed Bailey's stomach. Doc ended up lying beneath Bailey, the breath knocked out of him. For a moment Doc thought the larger man might have unwitting revenge by crushing him.

Bailey was yelling in pain when they hauled him off Doc. The sore loser lay shuddering and yelling in the dirt, and the rabble watched, and no one could do anything except arrest the one who'd killed him. The noise went on for what seemed like hours, until someone poured enough whiskey down Bailey's throat to ease his way.

The futile little town had a marshal but no jail, so Doc was locked up in a hotel room with a citizen hastily deputized. Taking stock, Doc found he'd gained a few bruises, a pocketful of money, and what seemed like a pint of Ed Bailey's blood staining his waistcoat, shirt and trousers.

Meanwhile, the marshal was at the saloon two doors down, talking to the men standing around the dead body. There was a lot of angry shouting going on, though Doc couldn't make out exactly what was being said.

The new deputy hovered by the window, attention torn between the saloon and Doc. "You scared, Holliday?" he eventually asked.

"Should I be?" Doc countered, urbane. He took a turn around the room, which was very similar to the one he shared with Kate on the floor above, and then he sat on the only chair.

"They're wanting to lynch you."

"Ah, vigilantes. One admires them for their initiative. Not to mention their enthusiasm." He lit a cigarette, muffled a cough, and arranged his limbs gracefully. "Even if they have no other qualities, I can always admire someone with enthusiasm."

"They're wanting to come find you, Holliday, and string you up."

"I understood as much before we left the saloon."

"It's not a good way to die," the deputy continued. "Have you never seen it? You might be hanging there kicking for half an hour, if they don't do it right."

"My dear fellow, I have seen plenty. Lynching can be quite an art form— though I'm sure this lot would manage well enough, in their own crude way."

The deputy shook his head in disbelief at this attitude.

Doc observed more to himself than his companion, "And I know more about good ways to die than you can even begin to imagine."

"You think you're getting out of this one? Ed Bailey has friends here. If you don't swing tonight, there's twenty witnesses to tell the judge what happened, and then the law will hang you."

"You know very well it will be ruled a clear case of self-defense."

The deputy remained unimpressed. "One way or another, Holliday."

"Really," Doc murmured, having lost interest. He simply couldn't find it in him to be scared. Surely it was not his fate to die in this nowhere town, at the hands of unformed and ugly men, over a nobody such as Ed Bailey. Death hadn't spared Doc this long for such a trivial end. It wasn't glorious enough. It wasn't even sordid enough.

"They're coming this way," the deputy said, voice betraying excitement. He was peering out of the window.

There was indeed a different quality to the shouting now, and there was the sense of general movement. Doc stayed where he was. "So…" he drawled lazily, "are you going to protect me from this precipitate justice, or are you going to open the door and invite them in? I trust this presents at least some small dilemma to you."

"What in tarnation—?" The deputy fell into a puzzled silence.

"I suppose it must be a terrible decision," Doc remarked with some sympathy.

"Shut up, Holliday. There's a fire, that's where they're all heading. Whole town could burn." He threw up the window, leaned out to get a better view. "Can't see directly, but there's firelight just back of the hotel. It's—"

The silence this time was caused by a sudden case of unconsciousness. The deputy collapsed onto the floor. And Kate climbed through the window. She had a pistol in her hand, grasping it firmly by the barrel; she must have hit the man over the head with it.

"My dear," Doc murmured, standing to greet her. "What a lovely surprise."

"We don't have long," she replied tersely. "The fire won't keep them unless other buildings catch."

"You set that?"

"We needed a diversion." She'd been bending over the deputy. As she rose, Doc saw she'd gagged him with her scarf. "Get moving, Doc."

"Let me help you." Together, they hauled the fellow over to the bed, and tied his hands to the nearest post. "Why are you doing this?" Doc asked her.

The ferocity in her glowing green eyes spoke eloquently of excitement and a shared sense of adventure. Doc smiled, bewitched all over again. In this land of many hues, mingled races and much boldness, Kate's Hungarian blood and her strong manner were nevertheless enticingly different. In fact, he thought, the two of them were both unusual creatures; they could value each other for that. Doc caught her up close and kissed her… Excitement, yes.

But they had to go.

The deputy was beginning to stir. Doc laughed and leaned down to look him in the eye. "It wasn't my fate to die here," he said, "one way or the other." And, in reckless exuberance, Doc kissed him, too.

Silk scarf and horrified lips, the deputy's eyes wide, all of him struggling to get away from this unnatural assault. Doc laughed, took Kate's hand in his, and headed for the window.

She had their horses waiting in the alley across from the hotel, and most of their belongings hastily packed. "Where to?" Kate cried as they cantered out of town.

He didn't pause to consider. "Dodge City!" Doc replied. And they thundered on through the night, heading north; Kate in her pink damask dress that was anything but demure, and Doc in his fine gray suit now ruined by a man's lifeblood. This long slow death of his allowed for a great deal of fun, Doc reflected, and a complete freedom from all strictures.

But then he remembered the beginning of it, over five years and half a country away. That callow creature, the young John Henry Holliday, who had hardly begun learning how to live… That fledgling creature had expected to die within months, the plan had been that he would die at twenty or twenty-one with his beloved cousin Mattie gently mopping his fevered brow. He really should have died.

Sometimes Doc thought the tragedy of his life was that he hadn't.

Chapter Three:

And in Between… He Lived…

New Mexico;

October 1878

John Ringo was walking again. He liked walking, liked the way this lean tireless body of his took him wherever he wanted to be. Liked to visualize his muscles and bones held together by strong sinew, his whole frame fed and heated by blood. Liked the emptiness in his stomach, and the efficient demands of his bladder and bowels. It had been strange to find most people ignored all that, pretending their bodies were solid and completely lacking in functions—perhaps skin through and through just as a statue was nothing but stone. Strange to find that they talked of souls instead, when they couldn't even see the things.

A scuffling sound from over the next rise, which meant something had been caught in this trap; the other two had been empty. It was a rabbit, hind leg secured. A matter of moments to break its neck, slip the animal into the sling he wore around his back, and reset the trap. Then John was walking again, heading back to his camp.

He'd located a bubbling spring up here in the mountains of New Mexico Territory, more than adequate for the needs of a lone man. The water welled over the lip of a tiny pool and tumbled down through some rocks, creating the only music John loved, and then it disappeared underground again. There were no signs that other white men had ever found it but, in the few weeks that John had lived there, small bands of Apache had sometimes visited the spring while out hunting. Ringo had withdrawn tactfully beyond the nearest ridge each time, and the natives had chosen not to notice him or to try stealing his horse. He'd heard the natives referred to as 'savages' often enough, but John knew himself far more savage than any of them.

Working his way along another route made familiar by use, Ringo began collecting dead wood. There wasn't much to be found up here in the sparse forests—or not that he could handle without an axe—but the nights were cold, and anyway he had this rabbit to cook. It would be good to have a full meal of meat, supplemented by the corn he'd taken from a field early that morning. He'd left a couple of cents bound up in a rag and tied to the cornstalk, in the hopes it would be found. He was conscious that it was almost, if not exactly, stealing.

On a barren flat, a distance away from the traps and his camp, Ringo paused to quickly skin and gut the rabbit, working steadily and trying not to think of Jim Chaney's blood-soaked towel and the grey gobbets that had landed beyond, because that led to memories of his own father's death when Johnny was fourteen, the top of the old man's head bursting apart and his hat blown twenty feet in the air…

Ringo grimaced and forced his thoughts back into considering the benefits of settling for a time in this location. Once he'd completed his task, he left the bloody offering for the coyotes, and walked on with the rabbit tucked into the sling again and his arms full of firewood.

There was a town five miles away on the plains, and a poor string of farms and small ranches along the scanty river. It was minerals that had brought people here. Settlements were rare in this part of the territory due to the uncertainty of water, so they were quite isolated. Up here in the mountains there was virtually no one to disturb him despite the weather being kinder; even the Apache lived over twenty miles away and seemed to only hunt here if game was scarce elsewhere. Having spent over a year in prison, John was now reveling in the freedom of all this *space*, all this *air*, unencumbered by walls or roofs, people or shackles.

The town was the right size: large enough to supply the few things John wanted, while considering his unilateral purchases no more than a petty nuisance, and not so large that they had men or women with enough time to organize against him. They must suspect something of who he was… They wouldn't blame the Apache, in any case, because the natives wouldn't be interested in quite the same items nor leave the same coins in return. Over the weeks, Ringo had taken only what he needed, starting with a shirt to replace the tattered one that had lasted him two years. Other than a supply of liquor which never met his thirsts, the costliest item he'd taken had been a decent woolen blanket. There had been small quantities of food, though he lived off the land itself quite comfortably—but what he'd valued most were the books.

There were two houses in town and a farmhouse in which John had found books in English rather than Spanish—books, that is, more rewarding than almanacs or Bibles, or tomes of etiquette such as *The Art Of Good Behavior*. Treating literature with the utmost respect, he'd returned the books to their owners rather than leave them to suffer from the weather. Until he realized his mistake: he'd crept in before dawn to the farmhouse, where an old man lived alone, and had found a new book waiting for him, laid out on the table with half a cake and a jug of milk next to it, as if he were welcome.

John had put down the book he'd brought back, and then he'd turned and left without deigning to even touch the offerings.

Perhaps it was time to think of working again and earning a little money to buy his own books, though he'd have to find and suffer a town to make such purchases. Then he could also pay for enough alcohol to dull his thoughts and his senses. Could he wait for spring next year, when the ranchers would be wanting men to help round up their stock for branding? The cattle ready for sale would need sorting, and then be driven up to Kansas over the following months. At least a cattle drive would keep him out in the wild… Though maybe he shouldn't wait that long to return to civilization.

Because he was good at it, John had no trouble picking up work as a ranch-hand. This was despite people having heard his name mentioned a few times too often in company with Scott Cooley, in the context of the Hoo Doo War. The ranchers and herders liked him well enough in person when he was sober, but he'd been called a mean-tempered drunk, and few appreciated the fact that John inevitably went armed.

He was good at line-riding and at herding cattle, partly due to him welcoming the loneliness of it, and partly because he knew how animals thought. That was what separated the real cattlemen from the hopefuls: an instinct for what an animal might do in any given situation.

John could, of course, rely on being given work at Joe Olney's ranch in the San Simon Ciénega, Arizona Territory. Joe was the reason why John was in this area, after all. The charges against John back in Texas had been dropped finally for lack of evidence, and after that he'd tried settling down in Loyal Valley, Mason County. He'd even been elected as constable. But a debt of honor had sent him west before his term was done, to find Joe—Joe Hill, as he was calling himself—and now John felt untethered. He would always have work at Joe's ranch when he wanted it, he would always be as welcome there as family, but somehow John felt certain that his unexpected chance for putting down his own roots and building on them had dissipated, lost in the ether.

So, he spent weeks and months contentedly enough with Joe and Agnes and their children, and whoever else was helping work the ranch. But every now and then John would make for the wild and empty places, where he felt he belonged.

Not that he sought a wilderness of the intellect. He had a book now, waiting for him wrapped up in his blanket. It was poetry, which he tended to avoid as too difficult for a man lacking much of a formal education. A novel or a history, a travel journal or a memoir, he could read and understand, and that pleased him—but John could never rely on poetry. From the little he'd read, it seemed either boring, or beyond his comprehension, or unsettling in its vividness and intensity. None of which pleased him at all.

Reaching camp as the sun lowered behind the mountains, John set the fire, let the flames die down, and arranged the rabbit to bake over the embers. A full moon tempted him to contemplate reading, though he'd have to wait until he could build up the fire again. He held the volume in his hands, appreciating the fine cloth binding and the gold lettering. John Keats. *Lamia and other poems*. Someone had cared a great deal about Keats' poetry, to present it this well. Someone else had cared enough to buy the book and treasure it. Ringo wondered if this were the kind of poetry that would speak to him.

He sighed, and lifted his head to watch the moon, already well advanced in its orbit. The rabbit would be done soon. He should tend to the meat, cook the ears of corn, and then eat. If he did all that and let the moon set, let the fire die, then there would be no opportunity for John Keats' poetry to either disturb or confound or bore John Ringo that night.

For the hundredth time, he wondered why he was capable of reading and understanding when it made no difference in his life. For the thousandth time, he asked himself what this well-made body and this equally well-made mind had been created for. It sometimes seemed that the sole reason for his intelligence and his sensibility and his sensuality was so that he'd be painfully aware of how miserable he was.

It wasn't quite despair that prompted him to open the book. He turned the pages at random, angled them toward where a flame danced, let his gaze fall on a line: *in pale contented sort of discontent…* And for a moment, John let a wry smile stretch his mouth; a response which felt both unnatural and genuine.

The fire had livened again while his attention drifted, the flames had risen, casting a golden flickering glare against him. The last of the moon's cold blue light was lost over the mountains' edge.

And there, sitting across the fire from John Ringo, was the son of the Devil.

Startled, John scrambled to his feet. The creature-spirit stood as well, though with far more dignity. And then John did nothing more than stare. Incredibly, his memories had not exaggerated the spirit's bold and simple beauty. The blond hair lifted in a breeze John couldn't feel, humor lingered on the sensuous lips, a loose black shirt hid the perfection of the torso. And the echoes of sensation slammed through John as he recalled fucking this creature.

Laughter, and the flames roaring higher. "Is that what you want of me, Johnny Ringo?" the demon asked. "Again?"

"Yes," John replied with no hesitation. *Behold the lion of the Devil who multiplies the sin of the world.* "Not that I've sent you any more souls… How many will it take to earn your indulgence?"

"Tonight, there is something else that I want from you."

This made little sense to the mortal. "What else do I have? I have nothing to give worth anything."

"You have your self."

John frowned. "You already have my soul."

Silence for a while, as if time had no meaning. Satan's son said quietly, "We don't have your soul."

"But neither do I." Though he glanced back at his shoulders, remembering that the demon had granted him a vision of his soul when they'd met among the Texan oaks. Before that, when had he last seen the flimsy colorless thing? Hadn't John lost it when he'd killed James Chaney? Or if not, had he left his soul behind along with his last attempt at a regular life, in order to meet his obligations to Joe Olney? Perhaps this child of the Father of Lies was deliberately confusing him, misleading him. John said,

"You can have my soul, my self, whatever you require of me. I want to fuck you."

Amusement. "Indeed. That was your first thought on seeing me."

"It's been a year, more or less," John said, raw and needy. "Long dry months and too many of them since you last came to me."

"And you have had no one else in all that time."

"No. How could I?" Perhaps there might have been a chance or two, but it took an awful lot of trust to even broach the subject, and nothing ever quite got around to happening. "It's not as if there are many men who want the same things I do, or not that I've met."

"How many men did you have before me?"

John took a breath, though he quickly blurted, "Three."

"Tell me about the first time."

His voice wouldn't cooperate. "Why?" John eventually managed to ask. "You already know everything about me. Don't you?" Silence, until he found the answer himself. "You want my self."

"Yes."

It was difficult but, avoiding any further consideration, he stammered out, "A man, when I was fourteen. Half my life ago. I was alone on the trail west after my father was killed." He didn't go into the details of his father's death nor of that night's encounter. "I drove the wagon out of there as soon as the horizon glimmered the next morning—and I've hardly stopped since, or not for long."

"What did he do?"

"He… fucked me." And maybe it was the demon drawing the memories up out of the dark places: panicked heartbeat, suffocation, invasion; almost as vivid as when it had happened. The death of any vague hopes of companionship that John might once have held dear. And then the brutal truth forced its way out of him: "He did to me what I've done to two others since. And to you."

"But you like fucking."

"Yes." He wanted to explain but was afraid to lose himself in all the complexities and contradictions and urgencies of the matter. "More so if they're willing," John finally added.

The fire, still burning crazily, cast strange shadows on the creature's face. "If you had a choice between me and any man you ever wanted," the son of the Devil said in his slow, melodious voice, "what would you do?"

"How can you ask?" John said, voice roughened by hunger.

The demon elaborated: "If you could fuck me once now, and then never fuck me nor any man for as long as you live, would you choose that? What if I offered you instead the chance to fuck any man or boy you want, whenever you feel the need?"

Shaking his head, John wondered why Satan's son wasn't comprehending him. "I want you. What you describe, it ain't real, it wouldn't happen. Even you couldn't make that happen." And he said again, "I want to fuck you. You know how much I want to do that." Because the creature-spirit's beauty was maddening him, inciting his desperation beyond anything his sanity could bear.

"Yes," the demon said at last. And he began walking widdershins around the fire—taking the contrary direction, just as John had read of demons. His feet bare and treading lightly on the rocks and sand, progressing with steady deliberation to where John Ringo waited. When the creature-spirit stood within hand's reach and John lifted his gaze, he saw that the demon was naked. "Then do what it is that you want," the creature said, and he lay facedown on the blanket that served as John's bed.

John woke slow and dull, as if he'd been unconscious for days. Head pounding as if he'd been drinking heavily, but he hadn't, he'd been quite sober—

The son of the Devil had visited him again, and that meant Johnny Ringo was lost, whether it was real or not. He groaned, vaguely recalling the sensations, the satisfactions, and his body too exhausted and too damned cold to relive any of it for him. When he tried to roll over, having slept too long in one position, his limbs wouldn't cooperate.

An impatient throat was cleared, and John blinked his eyes open, for that hadn't been John himself.

There was a man standing about ten feet away, with gun in hand but demeanor polite. "Good morning," he said.

John was disappointed—though he had to admit his momentary hopes that Satan's son had stayed were ill-founded. He struggled to his feet and fastened his trousers, ignoring the fact that the gun tracked his every move.

This unwelcome companion seemed too slight and well-dressed to pose much threat, and his soul appeared to be an exact clean copy of his body, which only added to John's disorientation.

"I live at the farm north of here," the stranger was explaining. "It's almost two miles away, but I saw your fire last night."

John cast a glance at the fire and was taken aback. The ashes and scorched earth sketched a circle about four feet across, which was many times larger than he usually allowed it. He must have thrown on all the wood—indeed, there were no supplies left. Dangerous, in more ways than one. He crouched to see the blackened, shriveled carcass of his dinner lying amid the cinders.

And there, near the remains of the rabbit, was the book of poetry by John Keats. Ringo reached for it, picked the charred binding up whole, and watched as the pages fluttered away, the fine paper and ink now nothing more than the most delicate sheets of ash. The cool breeze played with the pages, tattering them further as they danced, lightly carrying them away down the slope to the valley below. John wondered if his gray silk soul would be the same after a night in the fires of hell.

"You're the one, aren't you?" the man said. "You're our… midnight visitor. I won't call you a thief, though some do." He didn't let Ringo's stony silence deter him. "There are others who speak of you with understanding, and I admire them for it. The land is harsh and unforgiving out here, and we shouldn't let it teach us to be the same. We must always offer hospitality when it's asked for or needed. But, you see, we only own the things we brought with us; everything becomes more precious the further west we push. We can't let you undermine our trust in each other. Do you understand that?"

He did, of course, but John didn't care for these strangers, and he didn't respond. Instead, he staggered to his feet again, clutching uselessly at what remained of the book.

"Are you not well?" When there was no reply, the stranger continued, "What I'm trying to tell you is that I need to take you into town. We must decide what to do with you. Not that we're in the mood for too severe a punishment—perhaps an honest explanation and apology will suffice—but surely you see this won't do?"

A couple of uncertain steps, throwing the man a pleading look, and John collapsed to the ground.

Stillness for a few moments as the stranger contemplated him sprawled senseless. And then he walked closer, knelt and reached a hand to John's face. Simple matter, then, for John to wrestle him off balance, and hit him behind the ear with his own six-shooter.

He had to work quickly, but Ringo set to without further thought. Going through the man's pockets, he took his money, then his ammunition. The gun had already been slipped into the back of John's waistband. With all this movement, John's sluggish blood was at last beginning to warm him. Moments later, he'd saddled his mare, shrugged on his shirt and jacket, and rolled up his few belongings in the blanket. He walked calmly toward the stranger's horse, murmuring reassuring nonsense, and it soon let him stroke its nose. He led it over to his own and tied its reins to his saddle.

The gun and horse could be identified, and were precious commodities out here, so John would have to sell them to a lone miner or cowpuncher along the way. As for the ammunition and money, they were valuable, too, but he'd keep them for his own use because they were far less likely to be traced.

He walked over to where the stranger lay and saw that he was beginning to stir. John hefted him up by the collar, and before he could wake hit him again in the same spot behind the ear. Maybe, if John weren't so exhausted and so sated, just maybe he'd have considered taking advantage of this situation. But John was still too much the gentleman when all was said and done, and the fellow would be spared that further indignity.

Before he let him go, John looked at the man's hat. It was almost new, made of light gray felt, with a wide, flat brim. He tried it on, and it fit perfectly. A moment's indecision as he regarded his own hat—it was natural to grow attached to such things, to develop loyalties—and then John let the old one fall to shade the stranger's face.

Riding away, leading the other horse, John felt his anger grow. He'd been almost comfortable for those few weeks; he'd found that maybe his discontent wasn't limitless. But that couldn't be the life he was intended to lead, and he was certain it didn't achieve anything. Not that he had any idea of what he should be doing instead. The son of the Devil was silent on such matters, and indeed John hadn't thought to ask him for guidance.

And now, John reflected bitterly, he'd stooped to outright thievery! If he had been able to pretend to himself that his morals were still intact, that any reasonable man would have made the same choices over the past fourteen years, he could no longer do so.

John had such a yearning to turn to the wilderness and live the rest of his life alone with the springs and mountains, the sagebrush and cottonwoods. But there was some reason he couldn't, there was something about civilization that kept him close by.

Civilized values had brought him to this pass. Honor and loyalty were lodged deep within him, and he couldn't leave his fellow men behind—and yet he would never quite fit in. So, John wondered, what the hell was there for him on this earth?

John rode northwest along the edge of the San Simon Ciénega, letting the mare walk at her own slow pace, with cottonwoods and walnuts shading their way. The music of trickling water soon tempted them off the path and through the grass to a broad shallow stream, where the horse lowered her head and drank. John sat there contemplating the strange effect of the bright blue sky reflected over the surface of the water with the black soil as dark as night only inches below.

Once the horse was ready, she set off across country, remembering the way to Joe Olney's ranch better than the human did. John let her have her head, and turned his face to the sun, borne along in rhythmic peace, the horse's hoof-falls silenced by the thick sod.

A timeless while later they passed cattle munching contentedly and, as the twilight began creeping in, there at last was Joe and Agnes's house, and Joe stepping down from the porch to welcome him. "John Ringo! It's good to see you. You've been missed."

"Joe," he acknowledged with as much of a smile as he could summon. John swung down from the saddle, his joints creaking after the long day's ride, and he shook his friend's hand. Joe was curious, he could tell, but Joe had learned not to ask. The curiosity gave way to misgivings, and Ringo could almost read his thoughts: 'One day you won't come back, I know it...'

They were in the stables brushing down John's mare, with John half-listening while Joe caught him up on civilized news—when a whirlwind threw herself at Ringo and wrapped her arms around his waist. "Uncle John!"

He steadied himself by grasping the horse's mane, and stroked the girl's tumble of glossy dark hair with his free hand. In soft tones he responded, "How d'you do, Miss Mary."

"Come into the house! Mama says you can write. I'm learning my letters!"

"Are you now? Good work."

"Mary, leave your Uncle John be," Joe rumbled at her. "Let him rest. Maybe he'll have some time for you after supper."

"It's all right," John said, querying Joe with a lift of his brow. "I have time if your father can spare me."

Joe shrugged his agreement, though he seemed pleased enough on his child's behalf. With no further ado Mary led John by the hand to the cabin—extended by a room or two since he'd been there, from the look of it—and she sat him down at the table next to her books. "See?" she prompted, showing him the sheet of paper on which she'd been copying each letter of the alphabet.

"I do see. That's well done."

"Now *you* write out the letters, too, and I'll copy how you do them. You prob'ly do 'em better 'n anyone!"

He huffed a laugh under his breath, but did as he was told, forming each letter carefully and leaving space in between for her to add her own. Mary was leaning forward on the table, looming close so she could watch him work. It reminded John of his three young sisters—though he was probably more patient now with Mary than he'd been with them. His mother and his brother had been the ones to take charge of the girls' education, while John worked on his uncle's cattle ranch to earn their keep. As long as he could find new books to read, he hadn't missed school so much.

But thoughts of his family inevitably led to memories of his father, and his father's death—and then his baby brother stillborn not long after, bearing the results of witnessing Martin Ringo's stupid, gruesome accident with his own shotgun. 'The babe looks just like Pa,' John had observed, though they all seemed to think he meant his brother's face. And what had he gone and done since then but kill a man in much the same way, with the blood and the grey matter slapping against the porch floorboards, and then the body thumping down lifeless, and a distraught protest inside the house from the new-made widow echoing his own mother's cry...

His heartbeat thudding, his ears echoing, his throat taut—and John realized he'd groaned his agony aloud. He forced his clenched fist to let the pencil drop, and lowered his head in shame at inflicting his torment on a child.

But Mary Olney just called "Mama!" without any great signs of alarm, and she slid the paper from under John's hand and began copying out his letters. He'd got as far as R. It felt like a blessing then, that Mary would continue to sit beside him, steadily working instead of spooking like a calf or a colt might.

When Agnes arrived, though, she shooed Mary away, and took a good long look at John. He sat there, dull, wondering if the reasonable man might weep at such memories. Dry-eyed John Ringo asked, "D'you have any whiskey, Mrs. Hill?"

"Yes," she replied, though this one syllable cracked as if in sorrow. And she leaned in against his back to hold him fast around the shoulders, tucking her head in beside his for a moment, before she went to fetch a bottle and a glass.

Chapter Four:

Courteous Mixologists

Dodge City, Kansas;

May 1878

Wyatt Earp should have gone to visit his sweetheart, Mattie Blaylock. Instead, he walked into the Long Branch saloon and up to the bar and ordered coffee. He took a mouthful at once, and felt the heat in his gut and the clarity in his mind. It was only then that he looked around him, letting his gaze rest with serious intent on each man and woman there. It wasn't difficult to figure which of the cowhands and gamblers and prostitutes were potential trouble. For now, though, in these middling hours of the night, rather than trouble there was simply an alert wariness underlying the noise and general mayhem. The freshly sworn in Assistant Marshal Wyatt Earp was being noticed and measured in turn.

When he was done assessing the temperature of the saloon, Wyatt turned back to the one surprise he'd found there. Doc Holliday was sitting by the far wall, near the door that led out into the alley, a pack of cards on the table before him and Kate Elder at his side. The couple were talking, heads inclined closely, expressions indicating a happy involvement each with the other—but Wyatt knew Holliday had noted the presence of a lawman. Perhaps this situation merited Wyatt's particular attention because, based on his reputation, it was almost inevitable that Doc Holliday would cause a disruption sooner or later. And Wyatt had to admit that Holliday had gotten him curious when they'd met in Texas six months before. For all his unruly nature, Holliday was perceptive, and surprisingly congenial.

"Mr. Holliday," Wyatt said once he was standing across the table from the man, mug of coffee in hand.

"Assistant Marshal Earp. What a pleasure to see you again. When did you reach town?" The tone was urbane but betrayed some unexpected enthusiasm.

"I just returned today." Wyatt turned to Holliday's companion. "Miss Elder." She stood, and he shook her hand, matching her firm grip.

Holliday leaned back in his chair and tilted his head to blow a lungful of smoke toward the ceiling, the elegance of his moves marred by a cough. "It's Mrs. Holliday, marshal, if you please."

"Congratulations," Wyatt offered, meeting her steady gaze, giving her hand one last shake. He suspected there hadn't been a formal ceremony, but a common-law wife was as entitled to respect as any other sort.

Mrs. Holliday smiled at him, amused by these good wishes which should properly have been directed to the masculine half of the couple. "Thank you," she said, eyes glinting. "Call me Kate."

"Wyatt," he responded. She really was a fine-looking woman. Fiery, with her auburn hair cascading over perfect skin and a bronze silk dress. And she was as challenging and self-possessed as her husband. Wyatt decided that, in this case at least, Doc Holliday was a braver man than he.

Bestowing a kiss on Holliday's temple and offering a respectful nod to Wyatt, Kate left in a swirl and rustle of taffeta. Holliday gazed after her, wistful for a moment, before returning his attention to Wyatt. "Why don't you join me, Mr. Earp?"

Wyatt sat in the chair next to Kate's, and downed some more coffee before placing the mug on the table. Indicating the deck of cards left there as invitation, Wyatt said, "I still can't afford to lose to you, Mr. Holliday."

"You didn't strike it rich?"

"No." Wyatt frowned.

"But I hear the Black Hills are almost nothing but gold. Veritable mountains of the lovely stuff."

"That's true. The Lakota don't value the Black Hills for the gold, though."

"Then, what?"

"It's a beautiful place," Wyatt said. He pictured the woods and lakes and wild game in his mind, and tried to put the image and the feeling that accompanied it into words. "It rises out of the Plains, out of nowhere. Anyone would think it's unusual." He struggled on despite knowing that he always sounded stilted when he ventured more than a sentence or two. "The Lakota consider it sacred, and bountiful. But it's full of gold, so they've lost it forever, despite the treaty we had with them. So much treachery, and blood spilled." Wyatt stared across at the gambler. "It was a difficult place to be, Mr. Holliday. Difficult, but very beautiful—and I can't deny there was money to be made."

Holliday nodded, considering his own thoughts and offering in absent tones, "Call me Doc."

"What brings you to Dodge City?" Wyatt asked.

With nary a physical move, all of Doc Holliday's attention was abruptly focused on Wyatt. "Why, you did. Your description of the place appealed to me."

"It's no different from any other cow-town."

"But of course it's different," Holliday declared, as if the reasons were self-evident. "We've been here since January," he continued. "I set up a practice—I am a qualified dentist, you know. But poker earns more and is far more fun. All these troublesome cowpunchers of yours, with their wages and their rotten teeth, are very good for both kinds of business. And they've been lonely, too, so Kate is also doing well for herself. Mind you, I'm sure the poor fellows can barely guess at what hit them. At times, even I have trouble keeping up with my darling Kate."

Wyatt took a swallow of the coffee, and nodded with a hint of sympathy, unsure of how Holliday really viewed this state of affairs. "Yes, you look as if you're doing well," Wyatt murmured, wondering how much of it, if any, was a bluff. He cast a glance over Holliday's elegant gray suit with a discreet diamond pin decorating the lapel, and his blood-red silk waistcoat. The man's hazel-colored hair and moustache were trimmed, and he appeared to have bathed far more recently than anyone else in the Long Branch. His features were neat, and handsome in an understated way—but Wyatt decided Holliday's undeniable appeal was more a result of his character and disconcerting conversation than his physical attributes.

"You're not here for amusement, are you?" Holliday said. "You came in here tonight to announce that Assistant Marshal Wyatt Earp is back in town."

"Something like that," Wyatt agreed. An obvious tactic on his part, but effective. Even necessary.

"Are you intending to make a score of arrests?"

"Only if I have to." Another frown, for he thought Holliday was smarter than that. "I wouldn't make a scene for the sake of it. I'm not here to create trouble.”

“Of course.” Holliday nodded. “Everyone knew they’d sent for you. You’re the answer to many prayers.”

Wyatt very carefully didn’t grimace. He was sorry about the whole situation. Sorry that things were out of hand here, when he’d left the town quiet; sorry that Marshal Ed Masterson had gotten himself killed; sorry that Ed’s brother Bat felt he needed Wyatt’s help to sort out the mess. Being drawn back into law enforcement like this only made it clearer to Wyatt that it wasn’t something to which he wanted to devote the rest of his life. It was a new idea to him, that being skilled at an occupation or having the right disposition for it could be a curse.

“What would you rather be doing?” Doc Holliday asked with all the insight, bluntness and curiosity that Wyatt had already learned to expect from him. “You told me last year that you wanted to hand in your badge. But you found the Black Hills difficult. What would have been next?”

“I don’t know,” Wyatt replied with a shrug. And that was true enough, though he’d begun to have ideas of moving further west, of finding one of the boomtowns newly rich from copper or silver or gold and, if not mining himself, then making a living from those who did. Somewhere that wasn’t as beautiful or as sacred as the Black Hills. ‘Paha Sapa’, that was the name for that bountiful place in the Lakota language. Wyatt had made his money from dealing in lumber, rather than from the gold he’d gone there to find.

“As soon as you figure it out, let me know,” Holliday said, apparently assuming a friendship, or the beginnings of one. “For tonight, however,” he continued, “this place is quite dull. Shall we move on, and announce your return in another of Dodge City’s salutary establishments?”

“All right,” said Wyatt, smiling a little, amused by this fellow despite himself. He stood from the table and left his half-finished coffee behind. There’d be more in the next saloon.

“Do you know,” Holliday said as they strolled down the street together. He paused for a moment to light a cigarette, to suffer through a coughing fit surely exacerbated by the night air and the smoke. “Do you know, Kate is the most independent woman I have ever met, and I love her for it. I truly love the fact that she has no need of me nor of any man for anything. Not for protection, not for money, not for reputation. There is nothing she can learn from me, and I would never want to tame her. And yet I find myself wishing that she did need me, in a small way, even for one tiny thing."

Wyatt couldn't help but smile at this, though his humor was tempered by the notion that Holliday loved to appear shockingly candid—but that didn't guarantee he was telling the truth. Into the silence Wyatt remarked, "It's hardly surprising that a man would like his wife to need him."

"But it's such a complete contradiction!" Holliday declared. "I want the very thing that would lead me to love her less. Human beings," he confided to Wyatt, "are the damnedest, most complicated creatures. At least," Holliday soon amended, "human beings such as you and me and Kate. The rest of the people surrounding us here are distressingly easy to see through."

Another broad hint at a connection between them. While this accorded with Wyatt's instincts and inclinations, Holliday overstated the potential friendship as he did everything else. That Holliday was even discussing such a topic with a virtual stranger… Wyatt's first reaction was to find it disturbing, though he also welcomed the blunt honesty. He said, "Wanting your wife to need you is a very common concern, Dr. Holliday. Perhaps you like to think you're above something that any man would understand."

A pause, and then Holliday laughed out loud. They had just reached Hoover's saloon. Holliday led Wyatt inside to the bar, his laughter quieting to a chuckle. "That's what I like about you, Mr. Earp: you are full of surprises."

Wyatt bought himself a coffee and Holliday a nip of whiskey. Surveying the crowd, he saw a few men he knew to be trouble, and a handful of possibles. "People don't want surprises," Wyatt observed.

"That is one of the many ways in which I am different," Holliday declared. "I'm sure the good citizens of this town and, indeed, the bad ones and all those in between—I'm sure they'd prefer you to be stolid, reliable Marshal Earp, no more and no less. But there are depths to you, aren't there?"

Shrugging noncommittally, Wyatt drank his coffee, watching the crowd. The answer was *yes*, but he'd hardly admitted as much even to himself before now. It would be far easier to go on pretending he was predictable and dull; as dull as he felt when he tried to think these matters through. Pretending that he was ready, willing and able to fit into the narrow place society allotted him. "Yes," he said.

"We can be friends, you and I," Doc Holliday responded. "You know we can, it's happening already."

Another pause, until Wyatt acknowledged this. Though he felt bound to point out, "We've conversed for a few hours altogether, six months ago and tonight."

"Relationships begin with a moment's impressions. Most people aren't even capable of changing their minds after those first few minutes."

"All right." But Wyatt shook his head in bemusement and turned to Holliday. "People don't talk like this."

"I do." It seemed Holliday would never be uncomfortable meeting Wyatt's gaze. "We recognize something of interest in each other. Why, I'm almost as fascinated by you as I am by myself. And neither of us have any use for the formalities." Having thereby dismissed any possible objections, Holliday examined Wyatt as if sizing him up. He must have decided Wyatt could cope with whatever Holliday was thinking, for he said, "You have depths, Mr. Earp. And you are ready to explore them, or you would instinctively avoid me like the plague."

Wyatt let this go by without comment, though it had the ring of a difficult truth to it. Tom Owens, one of the town's well-known troublemakers, had noticed him and was approaching warily. This wariness met Wyatt in each saloon, gambling house and dance hall—perhaps exacerbated that night by the assistant marshal keeping company with Doc Holliday—creating a cautious tension that may shatter rather than dissipate in the days to come. This was the calm before someone made up their mind to challenge Wyatt, test him and his resolve, measure his determination. Wyatt nodded to himself and decided that this time and this place were as good as any for him to declare his intent.

"I heard you were coming back, Earp," Owens said, in a voice intended to carry throughout the saloon.

Wyatt let a beat go by, refusing to be hurried. "Then there's nothing wrong with your hearing, Tom."

"You and Masterson want revenge for his brother being killed?"

"Not revenge," Wyatt said with easy conviction. He spoke clearly so that Tom Owens and the hundred others like him might understand, if they wanted. "I'm just here to do a job that needs doing."

"Hell, I know what's going on. I know what you're up to."

"Yes, it's simple. You break the law, I arrest you. I figured you'd be able to follow that."

Owens looked around him for support. There were a number of people watching this confrontation, though none seemed particularly committed to taking a side. Nevertheless, Owens continued, "No, you're not fooling us."

Another pause, as Wyatt stared at the fellow. "You break the law, I arrest you," he repeated. "Which part couldn't you follow?"

"You reckon you're smarter than Ed Masterson, right? Well, you can be just as dead as him."

The conversation had gone on long enough; Wyatt had stated his position, and there was no point muddying the matter. He turned his back on Owens, leaned on the bar, and remarked to no one in particular, "Not any time soon." Someone was talking to Tom Owens, offering distraction in the form of a drink and a game of cards, offering the opportunity to leave the argument behind. Once Owens had been led away and the general noise had risen again, Wyatt walked toward the door with Doc Holliday at his side.

The pair of them strolled on down the Plaza, past the stores closed for the night, and the gambling houses that were always open. Holliday was silent for once, his expression contemplative as he smoked another cigarette. It was obvious Holliday was a consumptive: his narrow frame and pale skin proclaimed the fact as loudly as the coughs that sounded so often Wyatt was already past noticing them. Surely the tobacco and the whiskey and the late hour didn't help his health—not that it was any business of Wyatt's.

"Not that it's any business of mine," Holliday started, in a strange echo of Wyatt's thoughts, "but you prefer coffee to liquor? I recall you chose the same in Fort Griffin."

Wyatt pondered an answer to this. He should have an acceptable response ready, as his abstinence was sometimes remarked on—though no one ever dared interrogate him as thoroughly as did Doc Holliday. At last Wyatt decided on an honest if not forthcoming reply. "I did my share of drinking already. A lifetime's worth."

Doc was considering him with sympathy. "This was after you lost your way and wandered off the path you'd felt was certain?"

Wyatt shot Doc a glance. He hadn't forgotten how much he'd revealed of himself on the day they'd met, but neither had he expected Doc to remember the details. Wyatt nodded, grateful only that he'd restrained himself from confessing the full truth: he'd become a drunken scoundrel for a few years while mourning all he'd lost. Not that Doc wasn't perfectly capable of guessing most of it.

The two of them were now outside the Comique Theater, so Wyatt took the opportunity to lead the way inside. The place was serving as a dance hall that night; there were two men on the stage playing a piano and a violin with great energy, with a third man keeping time on an old army drum and calling the figures for a square dance. The floor was packed with enthusiastic dancers, making some kind of order out of the general melee. Given that there weren't enough women to go around, many of the men were acting as substitutes for the sake of the dance, which added to the confusion even though those men indicated their role by tying a bandana around one arm.

Wyatt felt there was little chance for trouble here. A handful of fellows loitered at the fringes of the dance, but they seemed content to do nothing more than watch and drink and wait for a partner.

Searching through the crowd, Wyatt saw Kate Holliday in the middle of the dance floor, and caught a flash of bronze taffeta and a wide smile; the encouraging expression was directed at her dancing partner. She moved with as much energy and abandon as the dance allowed, and the young man opposite strove to do her justice. As the pair promenaded toward where Wyatt stood by the bar, he got a better look at her partner: a cowhand, no more than sixteen or seventeen, fresh-faced and rather awed by this woman whose waist fit his arm so snugly.

The dance ended with a flourish, and the band struck up a quieter waltz. While many of the dancers headed for the bar, Kate didn't let go of the boy. They whirled into the new dance, with Kate guiding though her partner was supposedly leading. The boy shook his head as Kate asked him a question. His eyes were wide and his expression astonished, as if he were unable to believe his good luck.

Wondering whether Holliday had seen his wife, and whether to bring his attention to her if not, Wyatt glanced at his companion. Holliday nodded, and said, "She is splendid, isn't she? That young pup won't have the first idea what to do with her. Still, he must learn some time, as we all did."

When Wyatt turned back to the dance floor, he saw Kate and the boy were heading toward the bar, and would pass right by him and Holliday. But it was too late for discretion. The boy had seen Holliday, recognized him as Kate's husband, and had taken off through the front doors at great speed.

Holliday was laughing. "I apologize, my dear," he offered as Kate walked up to them. "I had no intention of frightening away your suitors."

She cast a wry look in the direction the boy had run. "There are many more who won't scare so easy. He was charmingly gullible, though."

"What will you have to drink?" Wyatt asked. And they passed a few minutes in mundane conversation, Wyatt with another coffee, Kate with a glass of beer, and Holliday with his whiskey. The band had also taken a break in order to down a round of beer; they soon resumed another square dance with even greater enthusiasm. Wyatt noticed that Kate's gaze was drawn to the floor. He tentatively observed, "You like to dance, don't you?"

Her eyes flashed as she turned to consider him. "Yes, I do. Was that an invitation?"

"I don't know," Wyatt blurted out, feeling like a fool. He glanced at Holliday, who gave his silent blessing via a quirked smile. "Of course it was," Wyatt amended, turning back to her. "Would you do me the honor?"

With a happy grin Kate took his hand and led him to join the closest set. They were soon caught up in the dance's energy. It felt good to Wyatt to let loose like this, to move in concert with another human being, to work his body so thoroughly and joyfully. He knew he wasn't graceful, that at best he was coordinated, and he guessed that Doc Holliday would put Wyatt to shame if he were in Wyatt's place—but none of that mattered right now.

Wyatt thought his partner the most beautiful woman in the room, even though her smile seemed to taunt him. When they drew near to each other, he asked, "Do I amuse you?"

"Oh, yes," she replied, as if that were the most natural and inoffensive thing in the world. They parted for a moment, and met again. Kate said, "No one else would have asked me to dance, with you and Doc standing up there watching me."

"I won't apologize," Wyatt said, and they parted to follow the steps.

She was intrigued, or at least willing to pretend as much. As soon as they came together again, she asked, "Why not?"

Wyatt had his arm around her lovely waist, where the young cowhand's arm had been, where Holliday and many other men would hold her. For a price. "You know very well how beautiful you are. I wanted to dance with you."

Her eyes flashed at him, conveying both humor and serious intent. She chose to read a double meaning into his words. "You couldn't afford me," she said.

"No," he agreed. "But I almost wish I could." And he did wish it, for her own sake, but also because it had been so damned long since he'd had any woman.

They were parted, required to briefly pair with each of the others in the set, and then Kate was in Wyatt's arms again. "I was worried about Doc liking you," she confided.

"And now?"

"And now I'm worried that I might like you, too. You'd better be careful, Wyatt Earp."

"Why is that?" he asked, envying Holliday the chance to drown every night and every day in her deep green eyes.

"Doc and I, we make dangerous friends." And with that triple-edged warning, the dance ended. Kate escorted Wyatt back to the bar and Holliday. "Take him away with you," she told her husband. "I need paying customers."

"As you wish," Holliday responded. The abrupt words didn't seem to indicate that he and Kate were unhappy with each other. They kissed, far too passionately for a public place, and then Holliday and Wyatt were out on the Plaza again. "Thank you," Holliday said. "She enjoyed dancing with you."

There were a hundred puzzled or irritable or guilty responses that occurred to Wyatt, but he found himself wondering how many of them were nothing more than conventional.

Holliday declared, "I used to love dancing, too, but these days I prefer to save my energies for… other pursuits."

Wyatt was saved from responding when he noticed there were two cowhands sauntering in his and Holliday's direction, wandering vaguely toward them with a great show of nonchalance. Both had guns tucked into their waistbands, and going armed was against the law in this part of town. Wyatt didn't react, other than to quietly tell Holliday, "You may want to stay out of this."

"I may want to back you up," he murmured in reply. "Do you trust me, marshal?"

"For now." Wyatt scanned the street, saw no other trouble; glanced at Holliday and decided he appeared sincere. "If I'm wrong, I'll deal with the three of you."

"Then I'll say goodnight," Holliday offered in clear tones. He shook Wyatt by the hand and walked off toward the nearest gambling house.

Wyatt stood his ground and watched the two cowhands approach. When they were about to pass him, he said, "You can't carry guns here, north of the Dead Line."

"Is that right?" was the response.

"Yes, that's right." From their attitudes, both were aiming to provoke him, but Wyatt decided to treat them as innocent newcomers. "The Dead Line runs along the railroad tracks," he explained. "Anything goes, south of there, but on this side there are rules."

"Who says?"

"The law says, and so do I. I'm Assistant Marshal Wyatt Earp. If you hand those guns over, I'll let you head south of the railroad tracks, and you can do what you like. Otherwise, I'll have to arrest you."

One of the cowhands was itching to draw; his right hand was tensed and ready to wrap around the grip of his gun. The other said, "There's a third choice you didn't say."

"What's that?"

"We could kill you."

"You'd be pretty stupid to try. I'd shoot at least one of you before you got me, and if I didn't get the other, he'd hang for it anyway."

The pair seemed unfazed. "We heard you don't kill, Earp. Before you came here, that was Dodge City justice, killing men. Now you just arrest them."

Wyatt said heavily, "There's always a first time."

"I don't know about you, but I think he means it," said Doc Holliday from the shadows behind and to the left of the cowhands. There was the distinctive click of a pistol's hammer being cocked. "And I'm sure you're aware it wouldn't be *my* first time."

"Doc?" one of the cowhands asked. "Whose side are you on?"

"For now, I'm helping out the marshal. Why don't you hand him those guns? Then we can all get on with enjoying this fine evening." Within moments, the cowhands' guns were tucked into Wyatt's overcoat pockets. Doc walked closer, letting his gun hand fall to his side. "Are you arresting these two, Mr. Earp?"

"They're not worth it," Wyatt replied. He said to the cowpunchers, "You two get out of my sight. Go and do whatever you like on the other side of the Dead Line. You can come pick up these guns from the marshal's office tomorrow afternoon."

"Yes, sir," one of them whispered.

"There'd better not be a next time, because I won't be so lenient." He watched them run off, and turned to his companion, indicating the palm pistol being tucked away in Holliday's blood-red waistcoat. "Do you expect me to make an exception for you? I should arrest you for carrying that."

"Your leniency can't extend to me tonight, marshal?"

"They were just testing the water. That was nothing I couldn't deal with alone." Wyatt sighed. It was getting late, past three o'clock. He said to Holliday, "That was nothing. But I'm thinking something else is going to happen, something big. Not tonight, maybe not anytime soon. But I know it will happen. I'm thinking Ed Masterson was just the start of it."

"Then you need all the compadres you can find. Or as many such as you can rely on."

"Yes." Wyatt met his gaze directly. "It wouldn't be right to take your gun or arrest you, after what you just did for me. But if you want to be my friend, Dr. Holliday, then don't cause too much trouble."

Holliday nodded, though it wasn't really an agreement; more an acknowledgment of the difficulties any friendship might lead them to.

"I'm going to check in with Bat, then call it a night. Thank you for your company and your conversation. Though I'm not sure—"

"Not sure of what?" Holliday prompted after a moment.

"How wise this is." Wyatt huffed a wry laugh. "I end up saying more to you than to anyone. Some of the things I've told you, not even my brother Virgil has heard."

A grin lit up the gambler's face. "Then I thank *you*, Mr. Earp. Perhaps I'll see you tomorrow."

"Perhaps you will," Wyatt replied.

"If you don't think better of it in the meantime," Holliday added with a wink. And they shook hands once more.

It would surprise the many people who didn't see him as romantic, but the truth was that Wyatt Earp sincerely believed in a fierce and true kind of love. He also believed that such a thing happened no more than once in a lifetime, which was grievous for he had buried his one chance with his bride when he was twenty-two.

The story was simple and held meaning only for him; Wyatt was aware that, if he attempted to tell it to anyone, the tale would sound quite banal. Between the ages of sixteen and twenty-one, Wyatt had through sheer hard work accumulated the resources and respect usually accorded men of twice his years. When he'd rejoined his family in Lamar, Missouri, he was appointed as constable—and he fell fast in love with local girl Aurilla Sutherland. The crowning glory of his young life was that she'd married him. The utter despair of it was that she'd died in a typhus epidemic while still his bride, and their unborn child had died with her. The serious, moral young man with thwarted plans proceeded to throw everything else away, too.

That was eight long years ago now, and it almost felt as if it had happened to a different person. Having recently turned thirty, Wyatt figured it was time to settle down once more and build another life for himself. His current plans were coalescing around the money to be made in mining boomtowns. Added to which, he had the idea that his brothers might also have had enough of wandering and doing no better than scraping by. Perhaps they'd join him, and they could be a family again. Which was where Mattie Blaylock fitted in.

Just because a man's chance at true love had passed didn't mean he wasn't lonely, didn't mean he couldn't seek companionship with another woman, didn't rule out the possibility of marrying again and maybe starting a family of his own. Mattie seemed willing to play those roles for Wyatt. She had certain conditions, but that was only fair because so did he.

Even though it was getting on for four in the morning, when Wyatt left the marshal's office he headed for the boarding house where Mattie lived. She'd want to see him now that he was back in Dodge, and she was used to his late hours; sleeping beside her until noon every day was one of Wyatt's fonder memories from his previous seasons here. He had to admit, too, that dancing with Kate Holliday had inflamed a familiar hunger in him. It had been months since he'd last been to this place.

Mattie had left a lamp alight by her window, an extravagance which meant he was expected. One day soon, Wyatt suspected, Mattie might want to live with him, and he would need to rent a house. For now, this boarding house accepted gentlemen callers, especially when they were lawmen and weren't above charming the landlady. Wyatt let out a sigh, climbed the stairs to Mattie's room, and knocked quietly. When she opened the door, it was obvious she'd been dozing, though she was still more or less dressed. "Hello, Mattie," he said in soft tones.

She beckoned him in, closed and locked the door behind him. "Welcome back," she said. Her voice, her whole demeanor was fretful.

Something was wrong. It might be unfathomable to Wyatt, or it might be as simple as him failing to follow or even perceive her unspoken plans. Perhaps he should have come see her before he began work that night. Perhaps he should have done many things in his life differently. "How have you been, Mattie?" he asked, bypassing the two mismatched chairs to sit on the side of her bed. "It feels like such a long time."

"It has *been* a long time," she responded tartly. She had headed aslant across the room toward the window as if they were already at cross-purposes, but now she shook her head as if frustrated by her own impatience with him. "I've been fine, Wyatt. I've been all right."

"You look…" He smiled, appreciating her appearance, though wondering if it would be wise to be honest. The lamplight and the dark wisps of hair that had come loose from her braid formed a halo around her head. "You look beautiful, really beautiful. Like a mussed-up angel. Did you go to sleep waiting for me?"

Her right hand went to her hair, felt its disarray, and then eloquently conveyed her despair. "Yes, I was asleep. I haven't been keeping our old habits, there didn't seem any point."

"No." Wyatt stayed on the bed, and she likewise remained where she stood. "Do you still want me, Mattie?" he asked in the gentle voice he used only with her. "Am I still your man? Because if so, honey, I'm real tired, and I'd like to just cuddle up with you in your bed and love you and then go to sleep, and maybe we can save all the talk for tomorrow when we're both awake. What do you say, Mattie?"

She was nonplussed by him. "Are you still my man?" she repeated. "There hasn't been anyone else, Wyatt, if that's what you're asking."

"I wasn't asking that, Mattie."

"No, you take me for granted."

Maybe the bitter words were intended as a slap in the face, but Wyatt didn't take them as such. "Isn't that what we both want? To get married someday, and take each other for granted?"

"Only if you give up the law, Wyatt, we've talked about this; it doesn't pay. I thought you were going to find gold and make us rich. But instead you come back here and become a marshal again. Ed was killed, Wyatt, and you'll be killed, too, if you're not careful. You can't go on pretending it's not dangerous, not anymore."

"I know it's dangerous, honey, but it's something I have to do right now; I want you to try to understand that. I've been thinking about what else we can do later. What would you say to heading further west, and making our home in one of the boomtowns? Somewhere in Nevada or Arizona, maybe California."

She nodded a little, ran her hands down the crushed linen of her white dress.

"I've had enough of the law, too, if you want the truth. Once I'm done here, we'll get married, and move west. I was thinking I'd ask my brothers to come with us. You like Virgil, don't you? And everyone loves Morg. We'll be a family again, all of us together, and maybe you and I can have children." He watched her as she grew warmer toward him, and less fussed. Perhaps that was enough detail of his half-formed intentions for now. "Come here, honey," Wyatt murmured. "Come here and cuddle up close with me."

It seemed Mattie had made up her mind because, once she'd taken that first step toward him, she was in his arms. So good to hold her, to kiss her, to gentle her into accepting him. So good to make her smile. Yes, her cool face, with its long fine nose, transformed when she was satisfied. So good that brief transcendence, and wrapping her up afterwards and giving himself to blessed sleep.

Chapter Five:

Kind Treatment to All Patrons

Dodge City, Kansas;

July 1878

These days, Doc Holliday shared his afternoons with Kate and Wyatt. For the three of them, the evenings were for work, the mornings for sleeping, and the afternoons for pleasure. This afternoon, Doc was playing a slow game of poker with Wyatt at the assistant marshal's favored saloon, the Beatty & Kelley. Which suited Doc, as the barber was just next door. After being shaved, and having his hair and moustache trimmed, it required little effort in the Kansas heat to wander from one establishment to the next, to find Wyatt in the shadows of the drinking hall.

"Your game is improving," Doc commented as Wyatt won a hand. It had soon become apparent that Wyatt wasn't as inexperienced at cards as he had let Doc believe back in Fort Griffin, though Doc continued to indulge that little ruse. "Perhaps I should be glad you still won't play for money."

Wyatt smiled a little. "If there were money involved instead of matches, Doc, you wouldn't let me win as often."

"I beg your pardon," Doc retorted. The implied insult was tempered, however, by Wyatt using Doc's chosen name. It had been over two months since Wyatt had returned to Dodge City and found Doc there acting on the assumption of a friendship with the lawman. Over two months, and Wyatt still called him Dr. Holliday as often as not. Doc continued, "That was a vicious thing to say, Wyatt, and I'll thank you not to repeat it. 'Let you win', indeed."

"I certainly can't afford to lose to you," Wyatt said, glancing up at Doc while shuffling the cards in those deliberate, competent hands. "It's very quiet this year."

"Not as many arrests, and therefore you receive fewer fees."

"That's right. And a lower salary this year, too."

Doc raised an eyebrow. "They were so keen to have you back here after Ed Masterson discovered himself to be *desperately mortal…*" Shakespeare's words returned to Doc, and he recited in a murmur: "*A man that apprehends death no more dreadfully but as a drunken sleep; careless, reckless and fearless of what's past, present or to come; insensible of mortality, and desperately mortal.*" He looked over at Wyatt, and continued, "They wanted you to return so badly; I assumed they'd offer you worthwhile recompense."

Wyatt shrugged, not reacting to Doc's brief dramatic distraction. "The money's fair, given the work involved. Things have really settled down since I was first here in '76, and we haven't had much trouble since Ed was killed." He let Doc cut the deck, then dealt.

"And yet," Doc murmured while he pondered his cards, "you still feel that something big is going to happen. Is that a lawman's instinct, or did you have a premonition?"

No answer for a while, as Wyatt thought about this and about his cards. "I don't believe in premonitions," he eventually replied. "Not for me, anyway." He threw in a card, not bothering to wait for Doc to discard. "I guess an experienced lawman picks up on all sorts of things. Events, or people behaving oddly, or the way they look at you. Though if I think too hard about it, I end up figuring I'm imagining it all."

Doc also discarded a card and contemplated its replacement. A long easy silence stretched between them; Doc valued Wyatt for the unusual trait of being that comfortable with him. "I have two pieces of advice for you," Doc said. "The first is to trust your instincts. If you feel something is going to happen, then act accordingly, and don't confuse yourself by trying to think it through."

The marshal was looking at Doc, expression stolid. He nodded once, perhaps accepting this.

"The second is to take poker as seriously as you do your work. But even when you're working, Wyatt, you are in danger of being betrayed by your eyes—though I assure you that the rest of you is as unreadable as uncarved stone." Doc frowned and continued, "For instance, I can tell that you have another good hand."

Those intense blue eyes were fixed on him. "That's strange, isn't it?" Wyatt remarked. "You giving me advice that might help me win at poker."

"I am your friend, Wyatt," Doc declared, not liking to be on the defensive, "and we don't play for money." Finally he added, "Your instincts seem to be saying that you may soon be playing for your life."

"Maybe. I don't know."

"Is that why you're thinking of quitting the law? It's a dangerous profession, and I know how tiring it is to be forever watching your back."

"That's why Mattie wants me to quit."

"And you?" Doc pressed, hoping Earp had a better reason than that. A breath later, he congratulated himself for no longer flinching nor even smiling wryly when Wyatt mentioned his Mattie. At first Doc had been unable to muster the necessary control, but now the name slid past him with nary a flicker.

Wyatt was explaining, overly serious as was his wont, "I believe it's a job that needs doing; I believe in the law when it's used to prevent or punish unnecessary violence."

"But you're not the best man to enforce the law?"

The assistant marshal was having difficulties with this. Perhaps he had never put these ideas into words before. "I'm the best kind of man for it, in a way. I think the law uses every part of me. But some of those parts, I'd rather I didn't need."

Doc nodded, thought again of the Shakespeare, and skipped ahead a scene. "*They say best men are moulded out of faults and, for the most, become much more the better for being a little bad.*" He added with a tiny mocking smile, "*So may my husband.*" Answering more directly, Doc said, "To prevent violence, you need violence. Which can seem a contradiction."

Apparently Wyatt agreed. "A lot of marshals and sheriffs used to be outlaws and gunmen, for that very reason. Their reputations create fear, which helps keep the peace."

"But there's more to your disenchantment than that?"

A frown, and Wyatt dropped his cards facedown onto the table, as if he'd forgotten the game. "The law can be very simple—though you can't always apply a simple law, because every situation is different. But when the law becomes complex, then people who should be convicted end up slipping through it." Wyatt shook his head. "I know one thing for sure, and that is I'd never want to be a judge. I could do a better job than a lot of them, but I wouldn't want to be in that position, making those kinds of decisions. It's bad enough being here with you," Wyatt added with a sly smile.

"Whatever do you mean?"

"If I applied a simple law then I'd arrest you for carrying that gun of yours. You know you shouldn't, north of the Dead Line. But I decided not to arrest you, for a whole lot of reasons, and I don't even know whether that decision was right or wrong. I'm tired of it all. Tired of arresting people for things I don't care about, and tired of making exceptions for things I do care for. Tired of not seeing justice done."

"Justice is a fine concept," Doc commented.

"Yes, but we have trouble putting it into practice." Wyatt glanced about him for a moment as if casting for an example. "One night last year, this dance hall girl, Frankie Bell, was swearing and cursing me. She had the foulest mouth, and she wouldn't quit. I don't even know what started it, maybe I'd arrested a friend of hers, maybe she just didn't like me. I ended up slapping her. Some of the things she said—if she were a man, I would have hit her, and I figured she shouldn't get away with the same thing just because she's a woman. Anyway, Frankie gets a night in jail and a fine of twenty dollars for disturbing the peace. I get fined one dollar on the same charge— the minimum allowed—and no time in jail. You tell me where the justice is in that. Even when the law itself is fair, it doesn't get applied that way."

"And I thought you would just tell me it's a thankless job."

Wyatt sketched a grin. "It's that, too. You're always doing it for the sake of someone else, not for yourself or your family. And if there isn't enough work around, or you're between cattle seasons, then they get you to do things like clean up trash and shoot stray dogs. It's time to think about me and my brothers, and Mattie, too."

"I see," said Doc. He wanted time to consider what this told him about Wyatt Earp. For now, Doc felt inundated with impressions and information.

"I just want to go into business and start making some real money," Wyatt concluded. "I figured you'd understand that well enough, Doc."

He was saved from providing an immediate response when Wyatt's attention was caught by a figure waiting at the doorway. Wyatt beckoned him in.

The bartender called, "We don't serve Indians here."

Wyatt Earp didn't so much as turn his head but simply declared, "He's with me, Harry."

Doc nodded in greeting as the fellow approached the table, and smiled in private amusement. Surely only Wyatt Earp, of all men, could join the Black Hills gold rush and return with a Lakota man for a friend.

"How are you, Storm Cloud?" Wyatt asked.

"Hello, Wyatt." He politely returned Doc's nod, and Doc's smile grew. They both knew that Oliver Storm Cloud was far too wise to trust Doc an inch. "Wyatt, I met up with Miss Blaylock at McCarty's drugstore, and she asked me to give you a message."

"Yes?" Wyatt prompted. Doc was fascinated to note a flicker of reaction around Wyatt's eyes; something of annoyance.

"She'd like you to have an early supper with her before you start work tonight."

"All right. Thank you." Wyatt looked up at him. "Would you like a drink? Hot weather today."

"If you want to buy me a beer, Wyatt, I'd appreciate it, but you know you'll be buying yourself trouble as well."

The lawman shrugged this off and headed over to the bar. Doc watched as Harry sullenly poured a beer, a coffee, and a nip of whiskey, perhaps unwilling to force the issue with a marshal. When Wyatt returned to the table, Doc said, "I wonder why Mattie didn't deliver her message in person." Privately he congratulated himself on saying the name without his voice breaking. His heart was another matter.

Doc's sortie was met with silence. Wyatt was too much the gentleman to comment.

Storm Cloud said, "It's hot today. No doubt she wanted to save herself the walk."

"But the drugstore is only a few doors down the street."

Storm Cloud turned his broad and friendly face to Doc, shrewd enough to know that Doc was trying to provoke Wyatt. "Then perhaps she is too much a lady to visit a saloon."

"No doubt," Doc replied urbanely.

Wyatt muttered, "I first met her in a saloon just the same as this one."

More silence. "Ah, who cares?" Storm Cloud declared with a laugh, lifting his glass. "Not only did I get to pass the time of day with Wyatt's lovely lady, but I got a beer, too. I'm a happy man."

Wyatt's brief annoyance passed, and he saluted Storm Cloud with his mug of coffee. "Your health," he offered, and then he picked up the deck of cards and began shuffling. "Storm Cloud, do you have a box of matches?"

The vaudevillian Eddie Foy had become particularly popular in Dodge City after one of his shows the previous year. Some of the ranch-hands in the audience had been so offended at being the subject of his disparaging jokes, that when they saw him the next morning, they threatened to hang him. A lasso around his neck, Foy was asked whether he had any last words. He was cool enough to reply that he could say them better at the bar in the Long Branch saloon. The cowhands appreciated Foy's spirit so much that he became quite the hero.

One of Eddie Foy's best routines was when someone pretending to be his tour manager, alarmed by the affronts Foy was offering his audience, would come out on stage and sack him. Foy would then sing his very saddest song, overflowing with the most poignant pathos, and win everyone's hearts. But he hadn't performed that routine in Dodge City since his loyal cowhands almost shot the man playing the manager for daring to sack their idol.

Doc knew that Wyatt Earp never missed a show. Tonight, because he was on duty, Wyatt was loitering in front of the Comique Theater, where he could hear the music and the jokes, and keep watch on the Plaza at the same time. Doc himself was sitting inside, playing Spanish monte with Assistant Marshal Bat Masterson and idly admiring his dapper attire, topped with a derby hat and finished off with an elegant walking cane.

This was where the night's action was, but Doc wasn't working for now as the crowds were too distracted by the show. Afterwards, he would take advantage of their elated mood, and invite them to risk their luck with him.

Eddie Foy came to the end of a patter about a tenderfoot ranch-hand—the person that everyone laughed at, the naive youngster many of them used to be. Fresh from the trail, and unused to the amenities available in town, the tenderfoot was the reason hotels posted signs saying *Gentlemen are requested to remove their spurs before retiring*. Or, Foy added with a lift of the eyebrows, perhaps that sign was intended for the more… experienced and adventurous cowpuncher. The tenderfoot was the one who, warned that his room contained a folding bed, slept the night cramped up in the bottom drawer of the bureau.

Amidst the laughter, the band launched into a rambunctious tune, and

Foy began calling a square dance, which was another popular pastime in Dodge. No doubt Kate was there dancing with some fellow; her color high, demeanor bright, her promise paprika-hot.

Under the mayhem, Doc heard hoof-beats from maybe four or five horses, galloping fast down the Plaza—and then a gunshot, the bullet tearing through the front wall of the saloon, heading across the stage and out through the back. Doc was already flat on the floor out of harm's way, Bat likewise, and then the rest of the crowd piecemeal. The less experienced were inclined in their panic to stand first, and then they cowered, not knowing what would provide shelter if the walls didn't.

More gunfire, as if at least a handful of rowdies were out there. Women and not a few men were caterwauling, and glass was crashing. The plank facade of the Comique was as useless as the windows when it came to stopping bullets from Colt 45s.

And Wyatt—Wyatt was out there, with not even the benefit of a plank wall to shelter him.

Answering gunfire, and horses galloping down the street and away across the toll bridge.

But at least two men were left in the game. Another couple of shots were exchanged, and then Doc heard hoof-beats easing to a halt on the bridge. The soft thud of someone falling. Again, Doc led the way. He was on his feet, grabbing his money from the table, and heading for the Plaza and Wyatt before anyone else dared stir.

Wyatt was at the far end of the bridge, crouched over a figure sprawled on the wooden decking, apparently trying to discover whether the man was dead or alive. A rider-less horse stood waiting by them even though spooked; the horse was obviously loyal and well-trained.

"Are you all right?" Doc asked as he neared them. Bat arrived a moment later.

"I wasn't hit." Wyatt's voice was deliberate and heavy. "But this boy. I've shot him." People were crowding around, a hundred or more of them drawn from the saloons and gambling halls, wanting to know what had happened. "Someone get the doctor," Wyatt said, a little louder. "Get McCarty. We'll meet him at the marshal's office."

"Wyatt—" Doc began.

"Help me with him," the lawman said. "I think I've stopped the bleeding.

I might be doing more harm than good. The rest of you," he called out, "the drama is over. Go on back to what you were doing."

Between them, Wyatt and Bat carried the unconscious cowhand down the street. People stood solemnly watching, and a few followed in impromptu anticipation of a funeral procession.

Once at the marshal's office, Wyatt was careful in arranging the boy on the cot. Bat lit all the lamps, gathering them on shelves and a table around the narrow bed. Seeing Wyatt in the light, Doc was fascinated. Earp's face was the familiar granite mask, but those blue eyes were as bleak and distant and cold as a northern winter. Every move he made was as stiff and deliberate as his words had been, as if he had to think about what to do and what to do after that or else he'd simply stop. *He fears this boy is dead, or as good as*, Doc figured.

Dr. Thomas McCarty arrived and examined the cowhand. The bullet had mangled an arm, and the boy was ghastly pale, no doubt having lost a lot of blood. "I'm not sure which way this is going to go," the Doctor said after a quick examination, "or whether he'll lose the arm. He's too weak right now to cope with surgery. If he starts regaining strength or at least is no worse by this time tomorrow, we can begin to hope. You fellows go on about your business, and leave him with me until then."

Bat Masterson looked at Wyatt, as if expecting him to speak. When he didn't, Bat said, "Doctor, the hard fact is, we need to know what this was about. When the kid wakes, we need to ask him some questions."

McCarty sighed, accepting this. "Then it's a matter of waiting and making the boy as comfortable as we can."

"What happened, Wyatt?" Bat asked.

"I don't know. This one rode by a couple of times earlier in the evening. Maybe he was making sure it was me. They made it look as if they were just hurrahing the town, but it felt more deliberate than that."

"And?" prompted Bat.

"The third time he rode by, he tried to kill me. I tried to stop him, I fired warning shots. I tried to slow his horse down—"

Silence for a moment. Bat commented, "Wyatt, I've said it before, and I'll say it again: you've got the softest heart of any gunfighter I ever knew... Did you shoot to kill?"

Wyatt said, "Yes." His stoic tone barely betrayed his unhappiness. "Yes, once he was getting away. He'd already fired at me at least three times. Took my hat off with the last one." A brief pause in which no one even breathed, before Wyatt continued, "My last chance to take him, I crouched down so I could see him against the sky."

"That's the first time you've shot to kill, and no one here would even think about blaming you."

They settled in to wait, then, except for Bat who went to keep the peace elsewhere. Doc stood by the office's open door, smoking cigarette after cigarette. McCarty sat by his patient, feeling his pulse at intervals, ensuring he was warmed by a blanket, cooling his forehead with a damp cloth. When Doc began coughing, McCarty glanced at him, but Doc made it clear he wouldn't welcome the medical man's interest; he already knew more than he'd ever wanted to about consumption, and had no need to rely on others.

Wyatt sat at the marshal's desk, staring at nothing in particular. Every now and then McCarty would ask him for something—to brew some coffee, or to trim a lamp that was smoking—and Wyatt would silently obey.

Though he remained unconscious, the young ranch-hand became restless after a time. And finally, as dawn began turning the darkness gray, he began waking, though at first he was too delirious to make any sense.

Bat returned, and listened for a moment to the babbling. "His name's George Hoy," Bat told them. "He's up from Texas. I found a couple of men who'd gone back to the Comique who recognized him. But they don't know any more than that, they don't know why he shot at you. There were other men firing as well, weren't there?"

"Yes," Wyatt replied. "A few of them. But they didn't do any harm; they were just providing him with cover, confusing the situation."

"The others did seem to be firing over people's heads," Doc observed. "No one was hurt, though the Comique was bursting at the seams."

Bat said, "We're out there looking for them. I have men searching south of the Dead Line, but they must have ridden off right away."

"Forget about them. They're long gone, and they didn't hurt anyone."

"All right." Bat glanced at Doc and McCarty. "I'll leave you to it. But if Hoy comes around, we need answers. Doc, you make sure we get some answers, all right?"

Doc nodded assent, amused that he was acknowledged as the one who recognized the distasteful necessities.

Once Bat had gone, Wyatt sat by the boy, held the hand of his uninjured arm in both his own, and began talking to him in a gentle voice Doc had never heard from him before. "George, can you hear me? Do you know me? This is Wyatt Earp. Don't be afraid of me, we can be friends, George. Can you understand me?"

Not wanting to watch the pathetic little scene, Doc stood outside on the veranda, leaning back against the wall, smoking, turning his silver cigarette case from end to end in one restless hand, listening to that infinitely patient voice ramble on.

"Do you know what's happened, George? Do you understand where you are? We have you safe, we're taking care of you. Do you know who I am? I'm Wyatt Earp. Talk to me, George, you have nothing to fear from me. There's nothing to fear anymore."

And at last, after the cowhand's babbling had quieted for a time, he said quite lucidly, "You're Wyatt Earp?"

"Yes, George."

"Hell of a thing," the boy groaned. "Won't get my thousand dollars now."

Wyatt didn't even pause. "The doctor's here to help you. This is Dr. McCarty. You've probably heard of him. His friends call him T.L., though I never did learn what the L stands for. Is there anything you want right now?"

"No… Hurts, it hurts. Hell of a thing. Didn't get you once, did I?"

"You got my hat," Wyatt offered.

Doc smiled at this unexpected reassurance that anyone else might disapprove of—and the boy painfully gurgled amusement.

"You came damned close to hitting me," the assistant marshal continued. "Tell me why, George."

"Thousand dollars on your head. I was broke."

"No other reason?"

There was no reaction that Doc could hear. People passing by on the street stared at the marshal's office, curious. Otherwise, the noise and mayhem of Dodge City continued, oblivious to this banal tragedy being played out.

"Those other men backing you up. Are they coming for me, too?"

But the boy reverted to babbling nonsense, and soon McCarty was saying, "That's enough for now, Wyatt."

"George," Wyatt said with gentle obstinacy, "I'm going to need to know who put up the money."

"He needs to rest," the doctor insisted. "I'm going to give him something to help him sleep."

"I'll come back this afternoon, George." There was the scrape of a chair, and a pause, and then Wyatt quietly confessed, "You might not believe me, George, but I'm sorry for all this."

Which appeased McCarty, at least. "You go on home, Wyatt, and get some rest yourself. I'll take good care of this one."

A whisper drifted into the new day. "*Hell of a thing...*"

"All right, then, T.L.," Wyatt agreed.

Dodge City was changing shifts when Wyatt joined Doc outside on the veranda. Some people were making their way to bed, as the music and laughter became muted and then still, while others emerged to open their stores and other places of business. Daylight had flooded through the town between one blink and another.

Doc asked, "Is this the something big you saw coming?"

"Guess it might be," Wyatt replied wearily. He listened for a moment to George Hoy's incoherent fretting and McCarty's comforting murmur. "Hell of a thing," Wyatt repeated. "Maybe that's the end of it, though. Ed Masterson getting killed, and now this. That will be enough for Dodge, this place is going to get real peaceful. I doubt anyone else will be trying for that thousand dollars. I've seen this before, towns growing up. The law's come to Dodge."

"I believe your instincts are correct. It's time for people like us to move on."

"Not just yet, Doc," Wyatt murmured. "Not yet for me." And then there was silence for a while. Wyatt accepted the last of Doc's cigarettes, and smoked it, frowning over his thoughts. Doc snapped his empty silver case shut and slid it away in a breast pocket. Finally, as if Wyatt's thoughts were bursting out of him, the lawman said, "This young kid, he didn't know any better. There was no harm in him." Wyatt confessed, "I've never shot a man before, Doc. I always found another way. Damned if I ever want to do it again."

"I hear it gets easier," Doc offered, and then he suffered through those thundery eyes protesting the idea.

"I don't want anything to hurt like this ever again. But I don't want it not to hurt, either." Wyatt shook his head. "Listen to me, feeling sorry for myself. *He's* the one I should be sorry for. I should have just let him go. I should have just kept firing over his head."

"It's all right, Wyatt, you're perfectly entitled to some self-pity."

"If I needed another reason to quit the law, here's one of the best."

"But you'll never quite get away from the challenges, will you? You'll always be Wyatt Earp. Though I suppose it's up to you to decide how you answer those challenges." Doc let the remnant of his cigarette fall, and stepped on the tiny ember. "Come back to my room with me. I think we could both do with a whiskey."

Wyatt seemed to feel this wouldn't be proper.

"There's nothing more you can do for him right now, Wyatt. Leave him with the Doctor, and come with me." No reply. Doc said, "The boy isn't important, Wyatt. You are."

That won a reaction: the dark blue eyes stabbed right through into Doc's heart. "And you?" Wyatt asked.

Doc sighed. Wyatt would expect the truth, and if Doc's callous arrogance turned him away, then Doc would simply have to live with a Wyatt-sized hole in his vitals. "Ah…" he drawled, "I'm the most important one of all."

After a moment, Wyatt nodded—which meant that he accepted this, as he surely wouldn't agree with it. Accepting Doc for who he was and liking him regardless. *No wonder*, Doc thought. *No wonder I want this man to be a friend.*

Wyatt went inside to talk to the doctor. The cowhand was unconscious again, and would no doubt remain that way for a while yet. Then Doc Holliday and Wyatt Earp were walking side by side, wordless, to Doc's hotel.

Dim memories afterwards, of downing a bottle of whiskey between them, and Wyatt either silent or talking as if he'd never before found another human being who could understand him. Genuinely hurting one moment, and then full of surprising humor the next. Doc providing brutal truths to comfort him. Wyatt telling Doc about his interminable family, and his half-formed plans for their shared future. Mourning for the worthless ranch-hand and for himself. Explaining that his Mattie was someone you comforted, not someone to go to for comfort. Wyatt quite beautiful, with his stony mask left abandoned in the drink.

Companionably climbing into Doc's bed with him, still clothed, and falling fast asleep halfway through a grin. "Friend," Doc whispered. Abruptly, he wanted more than this, wanted it badly though of course it was impossible. The whiskey for a start, let alone Wyatt's lack of adventurousness in this area; not to mention running the risk of Doc's greed spoiling the riches already lying beside him. "Friend," he said again, with gratitude and determination.

Even dimmer but infinitely amusing memories of late the next morning. Wyatt confused and bleary waking in Kate's arms, the length of him comfortable and warm against Doc. Wyatt, unsure on his feet, making polite fragmented excuses, grabbing his boots and gun, his coat and hat, and stumbling as fast as he could out through the door. And Kate smiling, lewd and wise, taking Doc into her embrace. "Friend," he said to her before he gave himself to sleep again. And his dreams were threaded through with the word... *Friends*.

CHAPTER SIX:

DEMON LOVERS

Arizona;

October 1879

"Howdy, stranger."

John Ringo frowned at the bottle of whiskey set on the bar before him. The greeting had to be real, because his imagination wasn't that banal. He glanced over his shoulder, turned when he saw two men there, badges on their waistcoats. Town marshals.

"Haven't seen you in town before," the nearer one continued. "You just get in?"

Assuming this was the welcoming committee, John swallowed some more whiskey, left an insolent silence. There were a dozen other men in the saloon, all pretending they weren't paying attention to this little confrontation. "Yeah," John finally said.

"What's your business here, friend?"

"What business is that of yours?"

The lawman held out a pacifying hand. "Now, don't take this wrong, stranger. We've had some trouble here, and we're a bit cautious. You're welcome here, if you're as straight with us as we'll be with you."

"All I want is whiskey and a bed for the night. Leave me alone, and maybe there won't be any trouble."

"'Maybe' ain't good enough." The marshal's gaze wandered as he considered the matter, and then returned to meet John's. "What's your name, sir?"

Another mouthful of whiskey. "John Ringo."

That gained a heightened interest. "Ringo? I've heard of you. They say you're fast on the draw. They say you're a killer."

"Yeah, and they say I'm trouble, too, so why don't you leave me be?"

"You just want a drink and a bed?"

John stared at the man, gave him the answer he wanted. "Yeah. Leave me the hell alone, and I'll be out of here tomorrow."

More consideration, a glance exchanged with the other marshal. "All right, Ringo, if you're playing true with us. Have your drink on me." And the marshal left a few coins on the bar.

"I don't want your money." He turned his back on them, on the rest of the place, on everything but the whiskey.

"You don't have the most helpful manner, Ringo."

"The deal was that you'd leave me be," he reminded them, pouring himself another drink.

"All right," the marshal repeated. "But we'll be watching, seeing you keep your side of it. Goodnight, Mr. Ringo. I hope you enjoy your stay here."

He didn't bother replying. The marshal spoke briefly with the bartender, then with another man, and left with his silent partner trailing behind. John drank some more. He hadn't wanted much from this town, and he was used to being asked to move on the few times he didn't move on of his own volition. In fact, he hadn't been at all settled since those couple of months he'd spent by the spring in the New Mexico mountains. Since then, he'd spent time helping Joe Olney work his San Simon ranch, but John was restless, forever wandering off into New Mexico, or down into Mexico, and back up through Arizona again. Always moving on, occasionally coming back, and he'd forgotten, if he'd ever known, whether he was searching for something or running from it.

What had he wanted in this pitiful scrap of a town? To make a few purchases: a new bridle for his horse, some new clothes, essentials such as food and whiskey. To sleep in a bed with sheets and a mattress—he wasn't hardened to such pleasures though he rarely indulged. Perhaps to pay for the cooperation of a young man, if there was one to be had, for it was so damned long since the son of the Devil had visited him, and John was growing impatient with waiting. Sacrilegious for this mortal to expect the creature-spirit's attention on demand, and likewise it would be foolish to rely on him, but the notion of it always being a long dry year or more between visits made John despair.

He swallowed another nip of the whiskey, let it burn his throat. "Where's the hotel?" John asked the bartender.

"There's Mrs. Dickinson's just down the street. You can't miss it."

John threw some coins on the bar, and headed out, ignoring the curiosity and speculation, regretting losing the anonymity he'd known in years past.

As John walked down the empty street, something caught his eye down an alley between two tall buildings. It was dark in there, but there was the faintest glimmer of movement, a gust of wind disturbing the stillness for a moment, the hint of music, something golden. John backed up, turned to see the moon, which was full-bright, leaving the alley in shadows, lowering toward the horizon distant down the street. He took a few steps into the darkness. "Is that you?" he whispered.

Silence again, stillness.

John took another step. "Let me see you."

"Here I am."

He whirled. A youngster stood just inside the alley, silhouetted by the street's moonlight, face barely discernible. But John didn't need to see his face, it was enough to see the left hand tensed by his gun.

"I've heard you're fast on the draw," the kid said. With a provoking grin evident in his voice he added, "They called you handsome, too, and at least that much is true."

John huffed wryly, part of him already responding to the flirtatious attitude, so starved as he'd been.

"But I don't believe you're faster than me."

"You don't?" John asked real smooth.

"Not with that much liquor in you."

It was almost laughable. "You think you're faster, boy? You want to say you beat John Ringo at gunplay, you want to steal my money? Or d'you have something else in mind?"

"Actually, I want your guns. It would be a fine thing to have John Ringo's guns, don't you think? You rode with Scott Cooley! But I'll take your money as well, if you have any."

John's right hand flew, drew one of the guns in question, aimed it at arm's length between the kid's eyes, all faster than thought. The kid had barely grasped the handle of his own gun before he froze in fear, focusing on the muzzle of John's pistol. "You want my guns, boy?" John asked. "Take them."

The kid couldn't speak.

A step closer, another slow step. The gun deadly unswerving, maybe two feet from the kid's face now. "You been drinking, too, boy? Or are you just plain stupid? I don't reckon you're exactly dazzled by my good looks."

Perhaps he would drop to the ground, faint from the fear.

Another step, and stillness for a moment. Then John tossed his gun spinning up into the air... The pistol caught a hint of silver starlight, the kid's eyes following it dazed—John caught it by the barrel, brought it down hard behind the kid's ear. The boy staggered, dropped—and John gathered his opponent's shirt and coat by the collar and dragged him further into the darkness.

A groan as John bent over him, disarmed him, began working at the buttons on the kid's trousers. "I reckon you're just plain stupid, boy, but what do I care about that? See, it's been over a year since I last had the pleasure, and your ass will do me just fine. All right? That's the welcome I was looking for in this one-story town. You waking up yet?"

Something wordless and confused.

"You keep it quiet, boy, or I'll hit you again—and you've figured out that I mean what I say, haven't you? You make this difficult and I'll kill you. Do you understand?"

It seemed he didn't, for the boy asked on a breath, "What you doing?"

"I'm going to fuck your ass," John said flatly. "All right? Don't make a noise about it and bring the whole town down on us."

There was a protest, so half-hearted it might have been a mere token.

Oh God, John thought. *What am I doing? "Do unto others what's been done unto you*," he muttered.

"Mr. Ringo," the kid began in clearer tones—but that wasn't what made Johnny pause.

The world dimmed as the moon set; the alley grew darker. A breeze unseasonably warm swirled around him, danced away, and there was that hint of music again, chiming. A glance of gold, but John couldn't focus on it, couldn't make out whether it was a few feet away or a hundred yards. "Is that you?" he asked again, hoarse. He thought of that beautiful bold face, lit by the fires of hell, and how in the darkness it would appear to float above the black clothes. He searched for a glimpse of the large, elegant hands, the bare feet. "Please... You know I'll do anything you want."

The boy began struggling, and John took firmer hold of his loosened trousers and shirt, grabbed one of the flailing hands in his. "Let me go!" the kid said, though not loud. He was still too scared to yell.

"Are you there? Let me see you." An idea occurred to John. "Do you want this boy? Do you want his soul? Will you visit with me if I send his soul to your father?"

Another hint of the weird wind, a lick of heat. John let the boy stand, intending to drag him further away from the town's lights—but the kid managed to squirm free, and he ran off toward the street. Johnny sent a bullet after him, high over his head, wanting to encourage him on his way.

John turned and headed down the alley, searching. It seemed to continue forever into the darkness. There was already a stirring of curiosity behind him, footsteps and voices, as people tried to find the source of the gunshot.

"Where are you?" John asked. "I almost raped that kid, and I will be damned for it—and you could say I did it for you. Ain't that enough? Don't you approve?" He saw the beautiful face then, saw the wry warm smile. There was a house tucked away behind the long buildings, facing into the alley. Perhaps John would be safe there, perhaps Lucifer's son would hide him and indulge him.

But the face blurred as he drew near, though there was movement still. "Please," John said, broken. The blur became brass wind chimes hanging from the eaves, tinkling faint in the random breeze. "No!" he yelled in frustration, and it roared out of him, *"No!"* He fell to his knees in the dirt. Had the son of the Ultimate Trickster been teasing him, or had it been his own despairing imagination? "No..."

The marshal found him, of course. The yelling had become muttering by the time they put him in the damnably tiny jail cell, but the raving didn't quit, and they told him he'd been disturbing the peace. He tried to explain he hadn't known peace for so long that he couldn't even remember it. "No, no, no..." The good people of the town thought he was expressing remorse.

By morning they'd added assault to the charges, though the kid apparently complained only of violent rather than sexual intent. Spinning a sad story that had the benefit of being true enough, John told of the boy challenging him and forcing the confrontation, of John taking him out with as little harm done as he might. He had fired, yes, but even in the darkness of the alley he could have shot the kid if he'd wanted to. "He's just a stupid boy who's maybe learned something now," John finished, hating himself for the sanctimony.

And the marshal let him go, because it would have been a fair fight provoked by the boy, even if the kid had ended up dead.

So John Ringo left town without the benefit of purchasing a bridle or clothes, without having slept in a decent bed or found brief satisfaction with a young man cooperative or not. All he had gained was a bottle of whiskey which the silent assistant marshal let John buy as he was being escorted out of town.

Maybe, John thought as he rode deeper into the wilderness—maybe he was a fool to try to end this frustration. Watching him over the crazy fire in the New Mexico mountains, the demon had after all offered him a deal: *If you could fuck me once now, and then never me nor any man again, would you choose that?* And naturally John had accepted what he could have then and there. He didn't regret making the deal, but that didn't stop him wanting satisfaction again here and now.

Perhaps the demon had appeared in that alley the previous night to prevent John fucking that boy. Perhaps the creature-spirit would never indulge John again—though of course the son of the Devil knew what kind of man Johnny Ringo was, knew his lusts and his hungers, could expect that John would try to attract his attention again.

How to do that? John had already lost his poor disheveled soul, even though the son of the Evil One denied possession of it, and if that had earned him favors, they were done now. The last time, the spirit had said he wanted John's self, whatever that meant, and had drawn the truth from the mortal, rekindled fearful dark memories.

This time… how to capture the demon's attention?

Emptiness, wilderness, wildness. The incredible moonlight rivaling a fire built high. Conflagration in his blood from the flames and the whiskey. Alone in the barren expanse of the world, abandoning all he was to this plea: "Come to me!"

He danced, taking occasional swigs from the bottle, and danced some more. Around the fire he went, swaying and rocking with his arms outstretched, stepping and leaping on his tireless legs, thrusting and humping with his hips, miming the act he desired. Around the fire, dancing widdershins as if he were a demon himself, his energy and his need building to heights no spirit could miss noticing. "Come to me!" he cried.

Another swallow of the whiskey burning his throat, glowing in his narrow hungry belly. Dancing around and around. There was music in the world's silence, music primitive in his ears, tune throbbing low with his blood's pulse, and some creature singing deeply, wordlessly, throatily of sensual pleasures. John lifted his arms high, spilled whiskey raining down his face finding his thirsty lips, dancing hips rutting, phallus hard against the heavy cloth of his trousers.

"Come to me!" Good to hear his own voice loud and sure, echoing across the emptiness to the stars and beyond. Good to—yes, good to put the need into words. "Come to me, hellion," John cried. "Bring me your fire, heat my blood. Bring me your beauty, your wickedness, all your glory. Come to me!"

He envisioned the creature-spirit, called on him with all the strength of his imagination. Remembered the golden bold perfections of the physique, the infinite power and danger behind the amusement, the indulgence of John's mortal hungers. The moon slowly sank behind the line of jagged mountains on the distant horizon.

"Make the Word flesh again! Let me burn in you, let me burn in hell. Come to me!"

The music was pleasure incarnate: his hips responded to the tune of the driving blood-pulse; his arms stretched and lifted and snaked to the deep wordless singing. Another swig of liquid flame.

A man standing across the fire from him. John's imagination tried to see him as the Devil's son—but his rationality had already drawn his pistol and aimed it at the man's heart.

"*A savage place!*" the stranger intoned; demeanor cool but words reverent. "*As holy and enchanted as e'er beneath a waning moon was haunted by man wailing for his demon lover!* That's Coleridge, you know, with a slight modification."

"Who the hell are you?" John demanded. Instinctive fear fueled his anger at being found so vulnerable.

The stranger seemed thoroughly at ease, as if unaware of the gun trained on him—or as if he were indeed a demon and need have no care. "Who the hell am I? A fellow creature of darkness. So rare to find such an interesting vision, such a captivating vision in the countryside. Even less likely to look for it in civilization, however." A drawling Southern accent, the tones of a gentleman.

"What do you want here?"

"Why…" The elegant gent reached into his breast pocket. When John thumbed the pistol's hammer, he paused to ask, "May I smoke?"—then without waiting for an answer he drew out a silver cigarette case. "Why," he continued once he'd lit up, once he'd coughed out his first lungful of smoke, "I was curious. When I understood you, I thought I might offer myself as a substitute. If your demon doesn't appear, would you care to cavort with me?"

Anger became fury at the fellow's daring.

"I'm presuming too much?" he asked, still cool. "Your taste encompasses only demons, I suppose. What a pity, when so many here on earth have called me evil."

An idea occurred to John, cutting through the fear and fury and resentment. "Did *he* send you?" John whispered. Difficult to see the man's soul in the flickering firelight, if indeed he had a soul. "Did he send you to me?"

Consideration in the stranger's expression as he took a long draw on his cigarette. He coughed again, but he was so focused on John that he seemed barely to notice. "Could it be chance that allowed my path to cross yours, out here, so late at night? Chance would appear unlikely, would it not?"

"If you're humoring me, mortal, when I discover it, I'll kill you."

"But in the meantime, why don't we amuse each other? Come here, pilgrim, and burn in me."

Lucifer's son must have sent this man to Johnny, for his boldness and wickedness could come from no other. John said, "Take off your gun belt, and leave it on the ground."

The stranger flicked the cigarette butt into the fire. "Indeed. But an equivalent show of faith is called for."

"All right." After a moment John slid his gun into its holster and then, warily watching the other do the same, he unbuckled his belt one-handed, let it fall to lie harmless. And then they each walked around the fire—John widdershins and the stranger clockwise—to meet where John had spread his blanket on the earth, ready for the demon to lie on.

Stillness, as if neither knew quite how to proceed. "May I have some whiskey?" the stranger asked. John found the bottle was still in his left hand and gave it to him; he took a generous mouthful, and then another. "Now, where's all that commendable enthusiasm?" the stranger continued. "Your dance was so desperate. Why come to a halt when I'm within reach?"

Indeed. Why should this self-possessed fellow be any more daunting than the son of the Devil? John said, "Lie down."

Again, they watched each other carefully as they knelt. The stranger took off his hat and stretched out to lie on his back; he seemed not to care that John kneeling beside him then had the advantage. John ran impatient hands over his expensive clothes, feeling the smooth weave of the coat's fabric, the textured pattern in the silken waistcoat. He and John were similar in height and slim build, perhaps John taller and his shoulders wider—but the stranger was neat and civilized where John was dirty and wild. He was obviously a gentleman; not that he betrayed any aversion to rough rather than refined.

John worked at the gent's trousers and said, "Turn over."

"Ah. Your enthusiasm has returned." Despite the dry comment, he obeyed, even assisted in a further rearrangement of his clothes.

Slim pale buttocks, subtle curves, willing to be plundered. John did so. Hunger far too insistent to be denied or even delayed; he found relief within a few thrusts, relief too intense to really be pleasure. Not as devastating as fucking Lucifer's son, but how could it be? This fellow served his purpose. John withdrew, sprawled back on the blanket, panting heavily.

"Well," the man drawled after a time, "I'm impressed by your urgency. I think."

John looked over at him. He was leaning up on his elbows, considering.

"You are too hungry, perhaps, to bother with finesse?"

Remaining silent, John felt his resentment of this intrusion returning. The stranger's neat, handsome features were nothing compared to the son of the Devil's bold beauty.

"Tell me," he was insisting. "You haven't had a fuck for a while, is that right?"

"Long while," John muttered, though it was no one's business but his own. Avoiding the man's gaze, John nevertheless kept wary watch on him.

"All right." He sounded pleased. "Spend your hunger, pilgrim, and then perhaps we can indulge each other with a little more complexity, a little mutuality. How often will it take, do you think, to regain your finesse? Six or seven times?"

John glared at him, feeling murderous. He had no idea what the stranger expected from sex, but he sure knew when he was being ridiculed. Getting up to his knees, John began fastening his trousers.

"Now, slow down for a moment, pilgrim. Don't take offence and ride away. Stay for a while, be my demon lover this night, what do you say? If you run off now, you won't get to fuck me again, will you?"

Anger at being reasoned with like a fool—but the stranger had a point. If he was willing to repeat the experience, it would be self-defeating for John to leave. The fellow was sitting up, reaching for the bottle of whiskey, still cool and self-possessed despite his state of undress. His gentleman's soul towered behind him, fine and upstanding and completely unexpected for one who was capable of meeting a stranger in the wilderness and letting the man fuck him.

"What's your name, pilgrim? Just your first name, if you like."

"John."

"Of course. My name is also John—John Henry. Though no one calls me that, not anymore."

"What do they call you?"

A slight smile grew, indicating secrets withheld. "If you're still here in the morning, Johnny, I'll tell you then. Do you have a middle name?"

He did, though it was rusty through lack of use. Ringo replied, his voice thick with old memories, "Peters. My mother's name."

"John Peters," the other John repeated, sounding satisfied to have received an answer. "You know what I like about you, John Peters, even though I tease you for it? Your enthusiasm. I like that you gave yourself to the dance so wholeheartedly. I like your hunger, and your directness. Now… you're still here. Does that mean you want to fuck me again?"

John nodded once, abruptly.

"And ready so soon," the gent commented with dry amusement. He smiled to balance the sting of it, murmured, *"And the Word became flesh and dwelt among us…* What was the Word, John?"

"Beauty," he declared before he could stop himself. "Lust," he said instead. "Beauty."

"Come to me," the man whispered.

The third time, the stranger wanted something different. With blunt instructions he arranged for them to lie on their sides rather than John lying on top of him. "Now," he said, "the deal is that you fuck me slow and sweet, you keep it going for as long as you possibly can. All right? I'm going to take care of my own hunger, which I assure you is almost as urgent as yours, and you may help me if the notion isn't too abhorrent. I promise that if you manage to let me finish first, you will have a pleasant surprise."

"Don't talk to me like that," John said. "I'm not an idiot." But the annoyance couldn't prevent him from pushing himself between those welcoming buttocks. They were both still mostly dressed; John's free hand fumbled to find the other's phallus amid his shirttails. It should prove easier to keep his thrusting at a slow rhythm he'd never tried before if he made the effort to help the other fellow.

"Here," the man murmured, guiding John's hand to cup his balls. "Gently, pilgrim, but with feeling."

They managed to find a balance between the movements of their hands. John Henry moaned and moved back further into John's embrace, apparently enjoying himself.

Difficult to hold back, but interesting to watch this stranger, to discover how he found his pleasure. And the deal soon proved worth it—as John Henry approached his climax his hold on John tightened, and then as he finished with an appreciative cry the man's whole body shook and clutched—and took John into pleasure with him.

They lay like that for a while, both breathless, the stranger laughing every now and then. Eventually he declared, "*I have sinned exceedingly in thought, word and deed, through my most grievous fault.*"

"Desire," Johnny amended; "*through my most grievous desire.*"

John Henry turned enough to consider John over his shoulder. "Yes, I like that a lot better. Perhaps you should rewrite the entire Missal, pilgrim." More consideration—John shifted uncomfortably under the knowing gaze. The stranger said, "Shall we share our blankets for what's left of the night?"

"All right," John agreed, figuring it was safer to have the fellow within arm's reach rather than out there in the darkness. He watched, with his back to the firelight and with the guns in easy distance, as the gent brought his horse closer and returned to John with two rolled-up blankets.

The fire had burned down. John gathered it all into a smaller circle and fed it a couple of the thicker branches to help it last through the night.

Despite the strangeness of having someone beside him who seemed to like maintaining physical contact—and despite the fellow's irregular coughs—John slept well until dawn, no doubt due to the lack of sleep the previous night and to his recent exertions. The morning dew woke him, though, and he pulled the blanket higher to cover his head. His companion shifted still closer into his arms, and John tried to accommodate him. Even that kid who'd stayed with him for a couple of months, years ago now—even he hadn't been this keen on John's embraces.

"You're still here, pilgrim," was the first thing John Henry said after waking slowly.

"Yes."

"Does that mean your hunger remains unsated?" he asked, managing to convey both hope and ironic suffering.

"Yes."

"*O for a life of sensations rather than of thoughts!*"

John cast him a sour look. "Coleridge again?"

"Keats, actually, from a letter. Do you live a life of sensations, pilgrim?"

"I have thoughts as well," John said with some resentment. "But mostly I don't know what to do with them."

"Ah, what a fascinating predicament." Despite the overstatement, it seemed John was being taken seriously. "Would you be so kind as to allow me a moment?" And the man wandered a few feet away and relieved his bladder, unashamed.

John couldn't make this fellow out. He presented as a gentleman and he possessed such a righteous soul, yet he was as forthright and earthy as John had ever wished for.

The stranger walked over to his horse, which was a fine animal, and returned with a water bottle; they shared a drink. "Call me old-fashioned," the fellow said, "but is it too much to ask for a kiss? For the sake of encouragement. Not that I really need any; it simply seems the thing with which to kick off proceedings."

Something else that was new. John dealt with the request as best he could, confused by the intimate tastes and strange sensations, suspecting that on further development this might prove quite pleasurable. It felt like a devouring. And then they fucked, the slow sweet way John Henry had shown him in the darkness. They even managed to work another kiss in as well.

"That's good, pilgrim," the stranger said afterwards. "You're learning fast."

"Don't talk down to me," John muttered, not bothering to really make an issue of it. He sat up, crossing his long legs.

"All right," John Henry replied, though it still sounded condescending. "Tell me your full name. John Peters…?"

"Ringo. John Ringo."

Recognition, and the other sat up as well, interested rather than threatening. "Your reputation precedes you. Fast on the draw, they say, and deadly in the attitude."

"The fastest and deadliest."

"You rode with Scott Cooley in Texas," the stranger remarked thoughtfully.

John couldn't help wincing, for ten reasons and none, but he turned his thoughts away from the old loathly path. "Scott Cooley's dead."

"You're not."

"Not yet!" He barked out a laugh. "But it's never far distant, is it?"

"Oh my…" The other John was intrigued now. "And there I was thinking I was the only one waltzing with Death."

John prompted, "Your name?"

"My full name is John Henry Holliday, but they call me Doc."

They watched each other, both sitting on that blanket on the ground with their trousers unfastened, infinitely wary. It occurred to John not to believe the man, for anyone could claim as much—though who else but Doc Holliday would be so infuriating and contrary, so self-possessed and so incredible? Who else would have such an arrogant soul? A few careful moments passed, neither of them provoking any action.

"I should kill you," Ringo informed him at last. He saw in his mind the two of them in a sudden mad scramble for the guns, both with serious intent; John winning, though only just, and calling on the son of the Devil, calling for his favors in return for Doc Holliday's righteous soul. "I should kill you right now."

"Why, pilgrim?"

"Why should I let you live if you can get the drop on me?"

"I'm not competing with you."

"A kid challenged me just the other day because—"

Holliday waved a dismissive hand. "You and I are above such petty competition."

"Maybe." John frowned, yet again not understanding this strange creature. "I'm finding… some like to force the issue."

"Those who do are nonsensical!"

"It's not how I was raised; I came to it late, so maybe I'm not seeing clearly. But in Texas, it was one retaliation after another, and once my name was in the newspapers, it was one challenge after another as well. Not that anything's really come of it yet."

Holliday leaned toward him to underscore his intent: "What is the difference between best and second best?"

"I guess second best is likely to be dead."

"No, John," was the impatient reply, "there *is* no difference. What does it matter? You and I, we're among the best few gunslingers in all the states and territories. That's enough."

"Maybe for you. But anyone hearing that would conclude *you're* not the best."

"That's it, exactly—if you want to be the fastest draw, then be it. You don't need to prove it by beating me. No, I'm not competing with you, Johnny Ringo, whether you're the best or not." Holliday considered him, apparently still having something to convey. He said, "There's no point challenging and meeting challenges. One day you won't be the best anymore, or Luck will turn her back on you for a moment; you'll have exhausted yourself drinking and fucking all night, or someone will sneak up behind you because they're too scared to face you. Some young kid will gain a moment's fame and glory, and for nothing."

John shook his head, amused. "You come at this from an odd direction, Holliday."

"Why, thank you." Holliday tilted his head in acknowledgment. "Now, with that out of the way, let's address the important issues. Do you have any food? I had to leave town without any, and I'm in need of nourishment."

"I'll find us some. There'll be enough roots and leaves around here that we can eat; maybe nuts, too. Bugs, if you're not fussy."

Holliday raised a skeptical brow. "Isn't there a town nearby?"

"Yeah, but I can't go back there. Not for a while, anyway."

That earned an ironic laugh. "The kid who challenged you…?"

A nod was John's only response. He wasn't keen to find out whether the kid remembered that John was halfway to assaulting him in a rather different manner before being distracted.

"All right, go find your roots and leaves and the rest if you must. Just don't expect me to partake of the repast."

It was only as he was digging through the sand with his hands that John realized how quickly Holliday had talked him around, from challenging the fellow to a gunfight, to searching for their breakfast. Arrogant, manipulative bastard. When John returned to camp, he found that Holliday had done nothing: the man was lying back on the blankets again, more than half-asleep. And, having taken care to find a variety of edibles, John wasn't surprised when Holliday ate his share of it.

"You know," Holliday said, as he lazily watched John gather together the few items he'd unpacked, "you'll regret it if you let me ride on without you."

"Why?"

"You won't have anyone to fuck tonight."

John looked down at this unexpected companion, and despite himself let his gaze rove over the slender willing body, attractive in the fine, now slightly rumpled clothes. Sure, he'd like to fuck him again, to better Doc Holliday in sex if not in gunplay; he'd even like to listen some more to his strange infuriating ideas. "This is ridiculous," John said. "We can't be friends."

"Maybe not, but we can fuck, can't we?"

"Is that the only thing you think of?"

Holliday laughed. "We have a great deal in common."

"You're crazy. Would you do this with *any* man you met? It's a wonder you're not dead yet."

"Don't try it, Ringo." Abruptly Holliday was more serious than anyone John had ever faced. With eyes that fierce, and an expression that didn't have to prove anything, Holliday didn't need a six-shooter to make his point. His soul loomed dark behind him. "Don't get ideas of crossing me, don't think I'm vulnerable having you around. You just keep wondering why I'm not dead despite all the risks I take."

Refusing to be daunted, John flatly predicted, "We'll kill each other."

"I don't look for safety in my relationships." The serious tone became distant. "I have somewhere to be, a friend I'm meeting up with, but not for a couple of months."

"Got some trouble planned?" John asked.

Another laugh, though quiet this time. "No, not with him."

A long silence, as John saddled his horse. Finally he said, "Guess I don't have anywhere to be for a while either."

"All right," Holliday said with great satisfaction. "Then let's head for the nearest town of adequate size that won't refuse you entry. I could do with some civilized food and a bed tonight."

John sighed, wondering what else the fellow wanted. "All right."

"And baths," Doc Holliday was saying, standing tall in the center of their hotel room. "We are in desperate need of baths, and I apologize if you are already aware of that fact. Can you arrange that for us, my dear?"

"Of course, sir," the girl replied, apparently awed by all this to-do. Holliday was behaving as if he were royalty. "The bathing room's down the hall on the right, sir. There's some water heating already, but if you can wait half an hour, sir, there'll be plenty for both of you, and I'll build the fire up. I can bring the pot of coffee you wanted right away."

"Half an hour it is, then," he declared, handing her a generous gratuity and ushering her out of the door. Holliday turned to John. "What do you think, pilgrim? A pleasant room indeed, considering its surroundings. Though I do believe this town will prove quite a rich lode. I can smell money in the air, and fools waiting to part with it."

John let his saddlebags drop to the floor, looked around him at the lace curtains, at the porcelain jug and bowl standing before the mirror. At the wide bed with green padded silken spread. It wasn't that his family had been poor, but the fineries in this room were beyond anything he'd known. Everything seemed fragile and ridiculously expensive and dangerously seductive. "And you reckon they won't care about us both in the same bed?"

"Of course not, people do it all the time. There is a distinct shortage of beds out here in the West, especially in new towns such as this. We were lucky this room was available."

"I guess I always figured if they said I'd have to share a room they were politely telling me to get lost." It felt foolish now, having taken umbrage at something that was apparently quite accepted.

Holliday, in the midst of unpacking, cast a glance at John. "Are you really one of those half-wild people who rarely visit a town?"

"No, but… maybe I'm more myself out there," John said, indicating the world stretching beyond the outcropping of humanity. "This is… small—"

"I don't find it so."

"—and my earnings have been pretty irregular lately."

"Don't fret about that," the other murmured.

"Who the hell are you, Holliday?" John demanded. "Is this your world? Because you sure seemed comfortable out in the wilderness last night."

"You like that about me, that I belong in both?" He waited until John shrugged, then continued, "Well, if you do, why don't you learn to belong here as well, and then you can like yourself for it, too. Share the luxury with me, Johnny. As you said, I shared the darkness with you last night." Holliday smiled, walked over to stand before John, reached up to run a hand back through John's hair. "There's a handsome face hiding behind that long hair and trail-dirt, I've already worked that out. You will come and bathe with me, pilgrim—won't you? I want to see what's under those rags." He leaned close and whispered, "I'm sure you're quite superb naked." There was a knock at the door—and Holliday stole a kiss from John's mouth.

John pushed the man away, glaring fury. Holliday let the girl in, and John suffered through an impatient wait as she arranged a tray of coffee and cups and a whole lot of unnecessary fixings, as Holliday chattered inanely with her. "You're crazy," John said once they were alone again. Holliday just laughed, at ease. In fact, it seemed he was enjoying himself immensely. "Are you always like this?" John asked, wondering how long he could suffer it.

"Oh yes," Holliday replied in airy tones. "Well, I suppose I'm in unusually high spirits. I promised myself, for these couple of months, complete abandonment. And you do seem to be the kind of fellow I can completely abandon myself to…"

"Don't talk like that, maybe people can hear us. And—what you did before she came in—if she caught us, we'd get run out of town, if they didn't hang us first."

"Now there's an ambition: to be so absolutely debauched we get thrown out of every town we visit. What's the matter, pilgrim? With your reputation, you must be used to finding yourself unwelcome."

"Yes, but for gunfights, not for something like that."

"You don't care about them, do you? Surely it doesn't matter to you what they think."

"No, but it's personal, it's private." Under Holliday's interested gaze John shrugged again, uncomfortable.

Smart enough to change the subject at last, Holliday headed for the coffee and began pouring two cups. "How do you want it, pilgrim? Let me guess… you like it just as it is. Now, I like coffee with cream and sugar—though they only have milk here, I'm afraid—but that's too civilized for you, isn't it?"

"Yes," he said. Holliday brought one of the cups over, and John eyed it dubiously. The thing was so delicate it might shatter in his hands, though of course it seemed quite safe in Holliday's fine fingers.

"Take it, pilgrim. It's either this lovely little cup, or drink straight from the pot." Holliday laughed. "But you would, wouldn't you? Don't let me give you ideas."

John quickly swallowed the coffee, felt the heat of it spread through his chest and the strength of it clear his head. He poured himself another cup, then sat cross-legged on the floor, pointedly ignoring the chair opposite the one Holliday sat in—avoiding even the rugs. The wooden floorboards, though polished, were the most natural part of the room.

They sat in silence for a while, finishing the pot of coffee between them. Then Holliday asked, "Where were you from before Texas? You don't speak like a Texan."

"California before that. We traveled west from Missouri. Before that, Indiana."

"And before that?"

"My family?" John shrugged—but such things had mattered in Mason County, when it was the newer German immigrants versus the longer-settled Americans. "The Dutch part of Belgium, if you go back far enough, but that never made no difference to me."

"I see…" was the response. However, Holliday didn't ponder on it long. Instead, he sat up as if about to stand, saying, "Let's inspect the bathing room. I haven't felt clean for a couple of weeks now, and tonight I want to make the best possible impression." Perhaps he saw John's reluctance, for he said, "I suppose from the look of you, my dear, that your ablutions involve jumping in a river once a year whether you need it or not. But would you indulge me? I like that you're so vivid to all five of my senses, that you assault me so thoroughly, but I'm looking forward to seeing your handsomeness as well as your wildness."

"Don't call me 'dear'," John said sullenly. "I'm not made for words like that. I don't know what you want from me, Holliday, but I'm not your dear."

"We just fuck, yes, and keep each other company between our amorous bouts. But don't mind me if I treat you affectionately." He confided, "Most of the time, I promise you I don't mean a word of it."

John was familiar with the cheaper options available in a bathhouse, and he'd sometimes had a barber shave him and trim his hair. Otherwise, he dealt with the latter two operations on an irregular basis with his knife, content that he never seemed likely to grow a beard beyond rough stubble. He wasn't sure what to expect here. With some misgivings he followed Holliday down the corridor and into a room with tiles on the floor. The heat of a roaring fire and the steam of the hot water enveloped them.

Holliday locked the door and began undressing. John watched the pale slim body emerging into the light provided by the fire and one lamp. While shorter than the Devil's son, and a great deal leaner, Doc Holliday was still beautiful in his own way and—for now at least—a satisfactory answer to John's lusts. "Take off your clothes, pilgrim," Holliday murmured, before he turned away and climbed into one of the two bathing tubs.

As he began to draw off his jacket, John tried to quiet his hunger. Embarrassing to be in this constant state of arousal. Foolish to let Holliday know how much he was wanted, even if only for that one thing.

"It's all right, my dear. I know you're hungry." Soothing tones, though John found it difficult to take offence this time. Holliday promised, "You can fuck me any time you want. Just so long as, every now and then, you take care of my hunger as well as your own."

The man wasn't even looking at him; Holliday was lying back in the tub with his eyes peacefully closed. John sighed, and eased out of his shirt. The thing was nigh in pieces, the sleeves almost free of the body. He examined it, and then slid off his undershirt, the smell of which offended even him. "You have spare clothes?" he asked, made gruff by this further embarrassment.

"Of course, pilgrim."

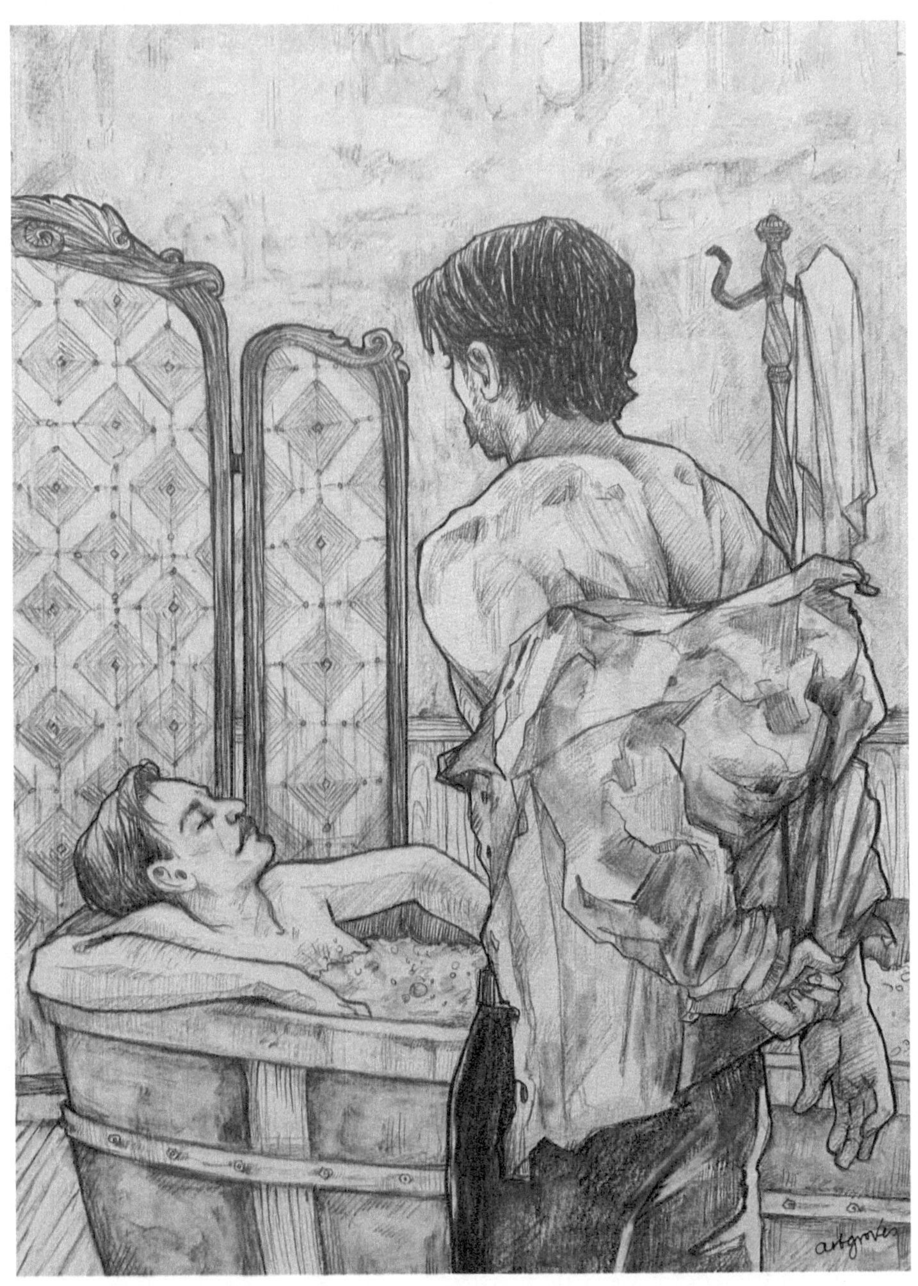

Once he was naked, John walked to the fire and tossed the two shirts and his drawers into the flames. He watched for a moment as they caught, then he headed for the other tub and stepped in, matching Holliday's lazy posture. Strange, the hot water making him its own. Something had been added to it that made it soft, scented, intimate. He couldn't relax, but watching Holliday's surrender to the bath's sensuality provided further fuel for his hunger.

Perhaps quarter of an hour later, Holliday stirred, reached for a cake of soap and began cleaning himself. John echoed him, lathering up the soap, washing himself down. Much of his skin remained nut-brown, having absorbed so much sun and dirt it would never be white again. Even his groin and hips were a toasted color compared to Holliday's rich cream. The dirt from the wilderness was ingrained in his very being.

Still sitting in his bath, Holliday was shaving now with quick efficiency, having dragged over a chair on which to prop a mirror. When he was done, he turned toward John, speculating. "Let me shave you," he asked, his tone unexpectedly seductive.

"Not a chance," John replied, indicating the cut-throat razor. "I'm not letting you near me with that thing."

The fellow laughed, and John wondered if it was possible to ever offend Doc Holliday. "All right, maybe some other time." He stood in the tub and used a jug of water to rinse off the last of the soap, then he brought the chair, mirror and razor over to John. "You can at least let me watch, pilgrim."

"However you get your thrills, Holliday," he said flatly, which earned him another laugh. Holliday stood by the fire, taking his time drying himself, while John began shaving. Again imitating Holliday, he lathered up the soap and covered his stubble, which certainly made the task easier. He was as skilled with the razor as Holliday had been, and reminded himself to be wary of the other man with a knife as well as with a gun. When he was done, he rinsed off, grabbed a towel and joined Holliday by the fire.

"I was right," the fellow said in soft reverential tones, "you are lovely naked." He ran palm and fingers down John's chest and belly.

"Don't," John said, shifting away, terribly aware of his body's eagerness.

"I locked the door, we're quite safe."

"No. Our room, at least. You *can't* want people to know!" John exclaimed in disbelief. He shifted away again, else he would have just pushed the man to the rug and done what he wanted, what they both wanted, despite himself.

"But you care as little for people's opinion as I do. Perhaps even less, though I'd never thought to find anyone who cared less than me." Holliday was looking at him, puzzled. "Ah, perhaps I understand," he eventually said. "It's personal, you said, this is something from your very heart, and you don't share *yourself* with anyone. Is that right, pilgrim? Except you'll share with me, for this brief time. I've earned the privilege."

John said, "I'm not made for being with people. Maybe I was once, but not anymore. Took me a while to figure that out, but it's true."

Holliday nodded, and let the topic go. They each pulled on their trousers, gathered up the rest of their clothes, and wrapped a towel around their shoulders for the short walk back to their room.

Once there, John locked the door and for good measure propped one of the chairs under the door handle. Then, ignoring the bed, he pushed Holliday to the wooden floor and fucked him. He could barely silence a cry of surprise: the act was always intense, but this time his hunger was fiercer than ever, and his skin against Holliday's added unbelievable sensation to the muscle and sinew working below it. An agonized full-throated groan muffled on Holliday's shoulder as completion slammed through him, and then he rolled away to lie on his back alone, breath harsh.

"Ah, pilgrim," the man said softly, perhaps regretfully. When John had quieted, Holliday caressed his face with one hand, leaned over to kiss his mouth.

And then Holliday stood, cleaned himself, and began sorting through his bag and through what he'd unpacked. He started dressing in some of the most impressive clothes John had ever seen. The suit of dark gray and the white shirt were fine and good and expensive; the waistcoat was also dark but made of woven leaves and flowers which as Holliday moved seemed to reflect all the colors of nature. The last item was a diamond pin placed in the lapel of his coat.

"Now, my dear," Holliday said, standing in all this finery over John who still lay on the floor with his trousers around his thighs. "I know you're not a social creature like myself, but would you care to join me tonight? I have work to do."

"What sort of work?"

"I make my living playing faro or poker, or whatever other card games are available. Tonight, though, I simply want to visit the saloons and gambling halls of this promising town, announce my presence, and calculate the best strategies for separating as many fools from as much of their money as quickly as possible."

"All right," John said, curious to watch the man in action. He stood, liberated Holliday's plainest shirt and drawers from his suitcase, and began dressing.

"What sort of work do you do, pilgrim?" Holliday asked with no great curiosity, lighting a cigarette.

"I take work on the ranches as a cattleman, mostly for a friend, but not real often now. I don't need much money."

"Oh, I do," Holliday replied. "I like to live extravagantly, so I'm in exactly the right trade. Poker befits a gentleman of style, and is exceedingly lucrative for someone of my talents."

"I thought professional gamblers dressed in black," John observed, hauling on his boots. "Like preachers do."

"Indeed, but I like to demonstrate my own style, and I wouldn't look quite so elegant in a frilled shirt. Wearing black has its uses, but I like to save it for fighting rather than gambling. There's no need to be that somber when the idea is to entertain."

"That's what the finery's for, to entertain?"

"It's all about looking the part, playing a role to the hilt. A cowpuncher or miner or farmer doesn't mind losing money to a well-dressed gentleman, that's simply part of the game. But he doesn't want to lose to a crude rough-looking fellow who is obviously no better than himself or his friends; that would be unfair and demeaning."

"You mean they'd take offence at losing to someone who dressed like me? They'd expect the game to be more equal? But if they didn't know who you were, they'd take me more seriously in gunplay."

Holliday smiled, perhaps in agreement. They were both at the door now, ready to leave. Holliday put his hand to John's as John reached for the chair. "Kiss me," Holliday murmured. "Make it hot enough to last me the evening."

"All right," Johnny said, looking him over. "But don't go thinking I like you, Holliday."

"Oh, I know you don't," came the reassuring response, before John captured his mouth with his own. He was getting the hang of this, or perhaps was inspired. Holliday moaned surrender through the kiss, body drawn to John's, showing his appreciation. When they broke apart, Holliday whispered, "One last favor."

"What?"

"Don't shoot any of my potential customers, Johnny Ringo. Let me win their money first."

He felt his mouth stretch into an unfamiliar smile, amused by this acknowledgment of who he was—or what he could be. "All right," Johnny said, and for once he meant it.

CHAPTER SEVEN:

DARKLING MY HEART

Arizona;

November–December 1879

"You'd fuck anyone, wouldn't you, Holliday?"

Ringo's tone was one of disgust, but Doc smiled and said, "Of course, my dear. Wouldn't you?" He glanced over, and his smile grew at the sight of Johnny Ringo naked and thoroughly beautifully natural; his skin was as brown as Doc had expected on a wild creature, his form as wiry and strong; added to which, his eyes were the purest of blues, and flashed as sharply as Kate's. "But I forgot," Doc continued with a show of sympathy, "you're remarkably particular about whom you fuck. In fact, you won't even consider fucking a whole half of humanity. You do limit yourself, don't you?"

Grimacing, Ringo turned back to the novel in his hands. Doc watched him, still fascinated by how much this misanthrope loved reading. This discovery had been made on their first full day together in town. Doc had wanted to laze in bed for the afternoon, as was his habit, but Ringo had been too impatient to indulge him. Despairing, Doc had thrown a book at him to drive him away, and was amazed when Ringo simply sat down and began absorbing it as if his eyes were starved for words.

Their afternoons were for pleasure. Ringo would wedge a chair under the door handle, and they would fuck, though this activity was of course far less sophisticated than Doc was accustomed to. And then they would talk and read, Ringo sitting up against the bedhead, and Doc often lying propped on pillows at the foot of the bed so he could watch this handsome, unusual man. Maybe they would fuck some more, between conversations, though Ringo was becoming somewhat less desperate as the days passed.

"If you weren't so particular," Doc remarked in a lazy drawl, "you'd get lucky far more frequently."

Ringo's gaze didn't shift from the book. "If I were choosy, I sure wouldn't fuck you, Holliday. As for frequent, I've lost count of how many times we've done it today."

"No need to boast, my dear. I assure you I am inordinately impressed."

A pause, and then Ringo looked over at Doc and said again, "You really would fuck anyone, right?"

Difficult to tell if Ringo was jealous of this propensity, or simply sought understanding—or was indeed disgusted. Doc said, "If a fuck is all I require then, yes, anyone will do fine. Sometimes my mood demands a woman, sometimes a man, or someone who isn't a neat fit for either; most of the time I don't mind which. But for it to mean something—" He frowned at the fellow sharing his bed, and hesitated a moment, because oddly enough this brief abandonment was getting dangerously close to meaning something. "They must have some kind of beauty, some kind of intensity. Though I suppose my notions of both are idiosyncratic. For it to mean anything, I need some kind of truth."

"Whose truth?" Ringo asked. "Yours or theirs?"

"Theirs, I suppose. Or both, but then I am always prepared to be—" Doc sat up, suddenly realizing that had been a rather intelligent question. "Do you know, pilgrim, I also like to be surprised. It happens so infrequently that I often risk missing it entirely."

John Ringo was watching him, careful and vulnerable and damnably handsome.

"You are right, of course; we each have our own truths. Perhaps I look for a person who is as true to themselves as I am true to me. Now, Kate, for instance—she is my wife, pilgrim—Kate is as independent as any man, and doesn't—"

"You're married? To a woman?"

It was definitely disgust this time, mixed with disbelief. Doc laughed. "That tends to be the way it works, my dear. Much as I'd like the alternative to be available, though please don't take that as a proposal, society is unlikely to ever agree with me."

John was sitting there with his head clutched in his hands now as if he were about to tear out his hair. "Your vows mean so little to you, Holliday? I surely wouldn't be accepting any proposal of yours!"

And Doc was surprised all over again. He considered the man coolly, searching through his memories and reminding himself that John Ringo was always the chivalrous gentleman with women. It wasn't misogyny Ringo suffered from, but simply a desire for nothing more than friendship from the so-called gentler sex.

Which made the retort about Doc's vows sting even more. Still, he wasn't going to explain to Ringo the definitions of personal faith shared by Doc and Kate. Instead Doc continued, "I hope to be rendezvousing with her—"

"She's the one you're meeting?"

"No, I'm meeting up with a friend in a few months; actually, it's less than two months now. But Kate is intending to join us. At least, that's what she said." Doc shrugged, though he would mind it dreadfully if he lost her. "She is such a mystery, so bold and so bewitching. So open and passionate, yet so unknowable." He asked Ringo, "Why don't you care for women?"

The man shifted as if uneasy. "I don't dislike 'em. I just don't want one!" After a moment, he said, "I don't know them the same way I know men. I trust them but… it doesn't go as deep, I guess."

"You trust men?"

Ringo sketched a grin. "I sure don't trust you, Holliday."

"But you've mentioned friends. Joe, wasn't it? And his family, too, in the San Simon Valley."

A pause stretched. Ringo was not used to being interrogated about such matters. "I've had a few good friends," he said, "and I get along well enough with women." Then he shrugged and declared, "I like fucking men."

"So you do, pilgrim," Doc agreed in light tones.

"The friends and the fucking don't combine."

"I'm sorry to hear that." Doc continued, "You know, men haven't given women any power or status, so how can we be surprised when they conspire and plot against us? We give them no trust, so how can we expect them to be trustworthy? But I give Kate the same freedoms I want from her, and she honors that as fiercely as any gentleman."

Ringo expressed his complete lack of interest in this topic by a renewed involvement in the book he was reading. Doc smiled, lying back again, considering Ringo while he was oblivious to all but the printed word. There was something interesting about the fellow, which made a grand total of four people in Doc's life who meant something to him because of their beauty and intensity and truth, and their ability to surprise. Despite Johnny Ringo being crude and unformed, despite his attitude of *fuck and be damned*, there was something fascinating at the heart of him and Doc couldn't figure what it was…

Doc began rambling in an effort to discover more. "I was wholly unformed until I was thirteen, when my cousins fled Savannah during the war and came to live with us in Valdosta. I was nothing but raw material. But then I fell in love—"

"With a cousin?" Ringo asked, having let the novel fall to his lap.

"Martha Anne, but we called her Mattie. She was sixteen, already a young woman, and as sweet and true as anything you can imagine. More so! No one approved. She was… nigh on a saint, and they'd already picked me as a sinner."

"At thirteen?" John echoed with a wry grin.

"Do you accuse me of misremembering?"

"No… I was made a man with responsibilities at fourteen. Go on."

Doc nodded, and resisted the urge to follow up on John's story instead. "I took myself off to Philadelphia at nineteen, to study dentistry. I came of age, I graduated—then I found out I was dying—slowly, yes, but a little faster than most."

John didn't even blink at this. But Doc could hardly keep his illness a secret, when anyone could link his persistent cough to his slender frame and arrive at the truth. But most people were flustered when the matter came up in conversation.

"I came west with no intention of surviving, though the doctors recommended the climate, and I've discovered they were right. But I've been dying ever since, and having a fine time of it. It's been seven years now." Doc let out a sigh. "Meanwhile, my cousin retired to a religious order and became Sister Melanie." He shifted further down in the bed and curled up a little, murmuring wistfully, *"The day is gone, and all its sweets are gone…"*

An unexpected nod from Ringo, though Doc didn't suppose that conveyed either understanding or sympathy. Ringo lifted the book again, flipped through to locate a particular page and said, "Listen to this: *I am a lone lorn creetur… and everythink goes contrairy with me.*"

Perhaps that was an offering of Johnny's truth, in exchange for Doc's. "What are you reading, my dear?" Doc asked, stirring from his grief.

"*David Copperfield* by Charles Dickens."

"Of course." In a matter of days Ringo had read the three novels Doc carried with him, so Doc had gone out and bought him some more. He knew Ringo had been grateful, despite his refusal to show any appreciation. Doc said, "You're still here, pilgrim. It's been a few weeks, you know, and I'm beginning to suspect you're not here just for the fucking. Not even for the new and interesting ways in which we fuck…"

"Why the hell else would I be here, Holliday? The pleasure of your company? I don't think so." Irritable tones, and then defensiveness: "There's nothing wrong with just fucking."

"Of course not, my dear."

"So why are you still here, Holliday?"

"I do admit… you interest me." Doc sat up cross-legged, the better to watch his companion. "I've never met anyone with a demon lover before." Aiming to seduce, Doc said, "Tell me about him. He's beautiful, isn't he?"

Ringo's impatience with Doc was forgotten now as if it had never been. He said with voice raw, "The most beautiful thing I've ever seen. *He is fairer than the sons of men; beauty is poured upon his lips; therefore he has claimed me forever.*"

Fascinating, this odd habit of Ringo's, reworking the Bible and other religious texts to his own impious purpose. "What does he look like? How does he appear to you?"

Ringo frowned as if unsure how to begin. "Golden," he eventually said. "Illuminated by his own golden beauty. His skin is blood-hot. Bold and tall, like a man, though he had wings the first time, big dark wings all singed around the edges. He wears black, just a shirt and long pants, and his feet are bare." Ringo glanced away, puzzled. "I love that his feet are bare."

"Why?" Doc asked.

"I don't know."

"What an interesting notion. Perhaps you like it because it's a sensual thing," Doc offered in speculation; "he's as sensual as you are. Or because he's one with the earth, he's connected to your wilderness. Maybe he's as uncivilized as you, and you love him for that. Or perhaps because it proves he isn't mortal, he has no need of boots. Perhaps his feet never quite touch the ground!" This was indeed interesting, and proved at the very least that Johnny Ringo had an imagination.

The fellow was staring at him, seeming taken aback by actually discussing his demon. Or perhaps his lusts had been re-kindled by this talk of his other lover.

Doc let his anticipation show, breath stolen from him, falling back a little in willing passivity, exposing his throat. The mime worked. Ringo stalked down the bed on hands and knees, and pounced to maul Doc mouth-to-mouth.

A few glorious moments of rough embrace, hands and teeth demanding, and then Ringo pulled back with the familiar intention of pushing Doc to lie facedown.

"No," Doc whispered urgently, "do it like this. I want to see you."

Ringo was angered by this delay, this complication. "Don't want to see you. Doesn't matter who you are, except you're not *him*. I don't like you, Holliday."

"I know. But do it this way, pilgrim."

A pause, which Doc interpreted as grudging agreement. He grabbed the nearest pillow and pushed it under his hips, encircled Ringo's waist with his legs, and guided the man within him.

Maybe this was why Ringo liked to press Doc's face into the pillow. He was overcome by sensation, by delirium, his expression left completely vulnerable. He faltered a little, perhaps realizing all that Doc could see. "Fuck me, brother," Doc murmured, and he arched back to take Ringo further inside, encouraged the man to move by digging his heels into Ringo's buttocks. Took his own phallus in both hands and quickly provoked an answering pleasure.

John Ringo began thrusting despite his reluctance, despite what he might consider to be his better judgment. Perhaps his lingering discomfort helped prolong the act enough for Doc to find completion first; in any case, the cry Ringo choked out as he climaxed indicated potent satisfaction.

They lay bound up with each other, until Ringo regained his breath and pulled out of Doc's embrace. This lover was not one for cuddling, Doc noted with regret. Time passed; the afternoon stretched on. Ringo hadn't picked up his novel again, but lay beside Doc as if his passion had cast him back sprawling, and abandoned him there.

"I believe I know why we understand each other," Doc said into the silence. "You see, I've had a long lingering affair with Death for all these years. He is my constant companion; we tease and amuse each other inordinately. One day, maybe tomorrow or maybe next year, one day he'll decide to take me. I wonder if I'll try to defy him one last time, or if I'll surrender. I wonder what blaze of glory he'll consider to be a suitable end, and how many souls I'll take with me."

Ringo was looking at him from where he lay, head turned toward Doc. Those blue eyes belonged to a strange, wistful, desperate kind of fellow who might say or do anything. A heartbeat, and then Ringo asked hoarsely, "Do you believe in the Devil?"

Doc frowned, considering all his opinions on the topic. However, realizing that Ringo might be about to blurt out something interesting, Doc settled for an answer both true and brief: "I don't know. Do you?"

"Yes. He has a son."

"I see. How did he manage that? The Devil can't create or procreate, can he?"

"I don't know." The fellow was obviously telling the raw truth, at least according to his own lights. He sat up to continue in rushed tones, "The way I figure it is, maybe that story's true, that the Devil rebelled because he resented God's love for his son. Maybe the Devil did a deal, and said he'd stop fighting the archangels and he'd leave heaven, but only if God gave him a son, too."

"A beautiful son," Doc murmured. "Your demon lover."

"Yes. I've sent him a soul. I gave him mine." Ringo's expression grew more and more desperate. "It's not enough, though, he doesn't allow me any favors in return. I don't know how to call him back. I don't know—"

Doc clasped the fellow's hand in his, impressed by all this madness. If one was going to imagine such things and torture oneself unbearably, one might as well be extravagant about the matter. Still, perhaps it would be wise to talk Ringo back down to the here and now. "During my love affair with Death, I haven't had your creativity. I have relied on the words of others." Doc reached for the volume he kept in a small bag of essentials by the bed. "Have you read Keats?"

"Poetry? No." Ringo turned his back to Doc, bored and dismissive, no doubt annoyed at the topic being changed.

"Listen to this, brother." Doc had already found the worn page, the book falling open to a few particularly beloved verses.

"Darkling I listen; and, for many a time
I have been half in love with easeful Death,
*   "Called him soft names in many a mused rhyme,*
To take into the air my quiet breath."

Doc fell under the rhythmic spell of it yet again, reciting the words in gentle rapture.

"Now more than ever seems it rich to die,
To cease upon the midnight with no pain,
While thou art pouring forth thy soul abroad
In such an ecstasy!"

Doc looked up to find that Ringo had fallen under the same spell: he was staring at the book, eyes bright and mouth agape. Despite the possibility of appearing ridiculous, he was instead handsomer than ever.

"Read it to me, pilgrim," Doc murmured. He gave the book to Ringo, indicated the stanza. "Let me hear you say the words." Long moments passed, as Ringo read the poem through silently. Doc was patience itself, for which he anticipated a great reward.

John Ringo had a clear, almost mellifluous voice—and he sounded educated despite an amusing way of mispronouncing words in ways that indicated he had read far more than he'd talked. Not that he seemed to mind Doc's infrequent corrections. Once Ringo had pronounced 'awry' as 'awe-ree', which Doc had found too amusing and oddly appropriate to want to change. But beyond such pernickety details, John's voice betrayed him far more often than he realized, for any emotions Ringo managed to keep from his face would color his speech just as a musical accompaniment could convey more feeling than the lyrics.

At last John began reciting—except that he was adapting the words to his own purpose. And, where Doc had been all seduced romantic submission, Ringo was tormented.

"Darkling I wait; and, for too long a while
I have been lost in need of your true beauty,

"Called you hot names and cursed you many times,
To take into yourself my angry lust;
"Now more than ever seems it rich to fuck,
To know completion in the dark night so intense.
While thou art prowling round to deal in souls
I am in ecstasy!
"Again I would deal with you, but plead in vain—
My fiery dance brought me a mere mortal."

"'A mere mortal'," Doc repeated with some resentment. He was impressed by Ringo's quick adaptation, though he wouldn't admit as much, and of course it wasn't Keats. That voice, though, was as beautiful and heart-rending as Doc had hoped; it fell into the cadences with a natural instinct, reminding Doc of how Ringo rode a horse. "Very clever," Doc said tartly, "though it doesn't rhyme."

That earned him a full-blooded glare. Another few moments, and Ringo began again:

"Darkling my heart; throughout my wretched life
I have been half in want of your peace, Death,
"Many times dared you, courted dangers rife,
To take from out my lungs my mortal breath;
"So clearly now it seems I need to die,
To cease from this frustration and this pain.
While thou art gathering souls this day, take mine,
Where here I lie:
"To burn in Hell tonight—ah, let me gain
Pleasures above words, beyond what I can say."

Doc sighed, and gave in. "That was very good, brother, and probably better than I could do, even though it was a plea to my lover and not yours. The words went directly from your poor heart to mine." He reached to run his fingers through the long brown hair that hid Ringo's face, but he pulled away. "Come here and let me hold you," Doc said quietly. "I think we both need some reassurance right now."

Ringo stood from the bed, letting the book fall unheeded to the floor, and began dressing. Within moments he was unlocking the door, and then he was gone. Doc had a strong suspicion that the fellow felt inclined to kill something.

Another hand of poker drew to its inevitable close. Doc laid down his full house with a flourish, and waited with pleasant patience for the two opponents remaining to show their hands. Both threw down their cards in disgust—in his time Doc had seen that same disgust on faces across so many counties he'd lost track. Doc began gathering up the pot. He'd won almost a thousand dollars that night, which wasn't bad at all, though of course he'd had better. "I do believe it's my deal," he said. "Why don't we play one more hand, and then call it a night? Though, if your luck returns, I'd be happy to see you another evening. Maybe you could win some of this back."

There was a resentful muttering around the table, each of the three other players restless in their seats. Yes, it was time to finish the game before they decided to try taking the money back by force. Doc smiled, maintaining his unruffled demeanor, and began shuffling the cards in his long fine fingers.

Doc took the opportunity to glance around as he shuffled, and saw Johnny Ringo walk into the saloon, and stand by the bar where he could keep an eye on Doc; he ordered a nip of whiskey and sipped it. Doc's smile grew, for he'd wondered if he might not see Ringo again after he'd left their hotel room that afternoon. Imagine being driven apart by Keats; what a pointless and terrible fate. When Ringo looked over at him, Doc silently said, 'Hello, pilgrim.'

The silent response was, 'I don't like you, Holliday.'

Doc nodded, amused by the persistence with which this statement was made. He had expected that, if Ringo returned, he would at least be drunk—which seemed to be Ringo's only defense against anything that bothered him—but while the fellow seemed a little the worse for whiskey, he appeared clear-headed. And, perhaps because of that lingering sobriety, Ringo was obviously still angry. Maybe he hadn't yet found anyone to kill.

"Are you going to deal those cards, Holliday?"

A cough shook through him, but Doc's focus remained on Ringo. One of the players followed his gaze, and then another one turned around as well.

The third player muttered, "Deal those cards, and get this over with."

"I beg your pardon?" Doc asked, voice pitched to carry. He stood, as if shocked. "What did you say?" He gave the fellow the barest chance to reply—the idiot was too confused to take advantage of it—before Doc beckoned Ringo over. "Say it again," Doc advised. "I want Johnny to hear what you just said about his mother."

The victim of the hour spluttered a little.

Ringo said very dryly, "You have got to be joking, Holliday."

"Forget it, mister," one of the other players said. "No one's mother has got a mention here yet." He glanced around the table and suggested, "I reckon this gent is just trying to distract us from the fact he's been cheating."

"I beg your pardon?" Doc repeated. He could feel they had the attention of everybody in the saloon by now. "I don't need to cheat to win money from fools like you—but if I did, you would not have the wits to know about it. There," he added, pleased with himself: "I've managed to insult you in words of one syllable, except for *money* and *about*. I assume you understood?"

"Why, you slick son of a bitch, you're no better than any of us."

"Do you feel like busting some heads open?" Doc invited Ringo. He added in a louder voice, "If you're not going to defend your mother's honor, Johnny, surely you'll defend mine."

Ringo grinned at last. "Honor has nothing to do with it." And he landed a good hard punch on one man's jaw before anyone saw it coming, swung his left forearm into another's stomach, kicked out at one who got too close behind him. By that time most of those nearest had joined in the fun, arms and legs flailing; the rest settled for providing loud encouragement and shouted advice. Chairs were smashed, tables were overturned, broken glass glittered across the floor and crunched under Ringo's boots. The bartender looked on in horror. Having gathered up his money, Doc stood safely out of the way, content to watch Ringo abandon himself to the fight. The man was supremely physical, coordinated and lean, graceful in his economical strength. His eyes still held that grin, though his face had become full of serious intent.

The player who'd been smart enough to answer back to Doc came within range. Doc picked up a heavy pottery jug of water from a nearby table and hit the fellow over the head with it, trusting that his memory wouldn't survive the impact. And then, when he could capture John's attention, Doc beckoned him away. "Let's go before the law arrives, brother."

They ran off through the back of the room, down a corridor, and out into the dark night. Doc was laughing and coughing too much to run far, but he grabbed Ringo's hand and drew him past the last buildings and tents, led him out to the edges of the surrounding wilderness.

The stars were distant and cold, but Doc's amusement and excitement kept him warm. "Did you enjoy that, pilgrim? Did you burn off some anger?"

"Yeah." Ringo hadn't freed his hand yet, Doc was pleased to note. They wandered on at a comfortable pace, alone out there though the town's lights weren't far behind them. Ringo said, "You're crazy, Holliday."

"And so are you," Doc replied fondly, as if they were exchanging compliments.

"My mother was so far above reproach," Ringo confided, "that no slander could survive the thin air up there."

Doc's mouth quirked in an amusement to match Johnny's. "Mine, too, brother. The epitome of piety. How did they end up with such reprobates for sons?"

"You know what I reckon? I reckon I'm a changeling, I'm the son of the elf-king. He stole a baby and left me in its place. It's no wonder I don't belong anywhere, I don't belong with anyone, nobody knows who I am. I'm a half-wild elf-child, a savage made of the earth and leaves and sky, born of the river, strengthened by the sun's fire, raptured by the spell of the moon… I'm an elf-child, and I'm capable of *anything*."

They eased to a halt, and Doc took Johnny's other hand in his as well, met those maddened blue eyes. With the lightest sincerity, Doc said, "Do you know, my dear, I more than half believe you."

Ringo laughed, and replied easily, "No, you don't, you arrogant bastard."

"I can think of explanations for who you are that make far less sense," Doc assured the fellow. He stepped closer. "But we're in danger of losing the mood. I ran off with you into your precious wilderness with one thought in mind: to burn off some of this excitement. Do you feel like indulging me, pilgrim?"

"Of course I do," Ringo replied, hoarse with his constant need, still amused. Indeed, Doc had never seen him in such a good humor.

"Then kiss me."

Though Ringo was still new to kissing, and refused to imbue it with any affection, his wildness and hunger made up for any lack. Doc surrendered to

the embrace for long heady moments, then began working at opening
Ringo's trousers and his own.

Ringo broke away, and Doc knew what the man expected next. Instead,
Doc crept his hand in through Ringo's loosened clothes to grasp his phallus,
and guided Ringo's hand to hold Doc's. "Show me what you like," Doc
murmured. "Do to me what you do to yourself, so that I know what you
like."

"You want to stand out here and—" Ringo's body was obviously
enthusiastic despite his reluctance.

"Yes, pilgrim." Doc suggested, "Let me show you what I like, then, and
you match me." Any objection was overcome the moment Doc began to
work his hand in as subtle and devastating a rhythm as he knew how.

Ringo followed suit, though his lack of experience and the distraction of
pleasure meant that he reached his goal before Doc had even caught sight of
his own. Groaning, Ringo clutched at Doc almost painfully, and then
stepped back, letting him go. Sad how Ringo always pulled away, barely ever
let the wariness slip, never let Doc hold him or comfort him.

Doc folded his legs and sat on the ground, with his back to the wilderness
so he could keep an eye on the town and any movement. Johnny settled
beside him, close but not touching, and facing the other way. At least the
ruction at the saloon seemed to have died down again. No one seemed to be
looking for them.

Ringo propped himself back on his elbows, relaxed and yet strong and
ready. Doc was tempted to just reach into Ringo's trousers without asking
first, and bring the man's hand to meet his own need. Whether it was
intentional on Ringo's part or not, they were perfectly positioned.

A time passed; the stars moved a fraction in their eternal dance. "Why
don't we do that again?" Doc suggested at last. "Because my hunger remains
unabated."

"All right, Holliday. It's not like fucking, though."

"No, it isn't." Doc turned to look at him. "How's this for an idea?
Whoever climaxes first loses—and remember you're one ahead of me now."

"Loses what?"

"The winner gets to fuck the loser."

If Ringo had ever glared at Doc before, it was nothing compared to this
most malignant of expressions. Eventually he ground out, "No chance,

Holliday, you bastard. No chance you'll ever get to do that."

"Why not? Why shouldn't I do to you what you do to me?"

"No chance," Ringo muttered. He had sat up now, turned away from Doc, shifting restlessly.

"Do you think less of me because I let you fuck me?"

"I couldn't think less of you if I tried, Holliday."

"Do you think there's no pleasure in it for me?" No reply. "Why is it such a problem, brother?" Doc asked carefully. "Is it that vivid imagination of yours? You don't like to think of someone fucking you like you used to fuck me not so long ago? Or has something bad happened to you in the past?"

To Doc's surprise, Ringo turned to face him, and was watching him with some confused kind of wonder. "He *did* send you, didn't he?"

"He…?" As if Doc really had to ask who he meant.

Ringo was rushing on regardless. "He told you about the first time, he was asking me about it, making me remember. He sent you to me, and… What the hell does he want of you?"

"I don't know. But if we had more time together, you and I, then I'd work my way toward fucking you, Johnny, and I'd make damned sure you enjoyed it. Might take me a couple of years—though I probably won't even live that long—but you'd enjoy it once we reached our goal, brother."

Johnny Ringo, this strange and handsome fellow, was staring fiercely at Doc and looking something akin to stunned. And Doc discovered he felt much the same way; yes, fierce and stunned. But this rush of emotion made little sense to him; this unlooked-for connection, these words that felt as if they were a kind of commitment, surely they did not belong to him or to Ringo. This was the last place Doc had expected to find himself during the few months before he met up again with Wyatt.

At last Ringo spoke, and he was bitter now rather than fierce, full of finality rather than stunned and open. "Yeah, you could devote the rest of your life to it, Holliday, and I still wouldn't let you."

"Then it is just as well," Doc responded lightly, "that I have many worthier things to occupy my efforts during these days and months and seasons." He stood, suspecting this must mark the end of their companionship. "It has been fascinating," he offered urbanely, brushing the sand from his trousers, "and I thank you for it."

"For what?" Ringo muttered, looking anywhere but at Doc.

"Why, for accompanying me during this portion of my complete abandonment."

"Are you moving on?"

"Perhaps not immediately, unless there's no other method for us to arrange this parting of ways. There are so many more fools in this place with plenty of cash and gold and silver."

Silence for a moment. "I'm staying out here tonight." Another pause, as if the words rankled. "Don't use the chair to lock the door."

Doc found himself smiling, and decided that he would have to ask himself some very serious questions. "You're sleeping in the wilderness without any essentials, such as a blanket or a bottle of whiskey?"

"If I need anything, I can get it."

"I'm sure you can. But does this mean I might see you tomorrow? Am I to infer that you'll return to share the luxury with me for a while longer?"

"Yeah. Now leave me alone, Holliday."

"All right, pilgrim," he said, and Doc nodded a polite farewell to his oblivious companion before turning away and heading for town.

Doc spent the night with a great deal of whiskey and those serious questions. The plan had been to have some fun, some wild times for these months, this season. He'd had no intention of confronting anything that wasn't frivolous and meaningless, and it certainly didn't suit him to care what happened to a crude and unformed cowpuncher. A cowpuncher who, when one considered the notions he blurted out, was quite mad.

However, it occurred to Doc late the following afternoon that this proved yet again that Doc Holliday himself was a wonderful creature, always surprising, forever unusual. This familiar revelation re-cast everything in a bright perspective, banished the confusion, and returned the smile to Doc's face. "Well, that's all right, then. Of course I care about the idiot," he declared to his empty hotel room, waving the whiskey bottle expansively. "It's inevitable that I do the things no one else is prepared to."

Ringo returned before supper that evening. It seemed he felt the need to explain his absence, for he stood just inside the door, shrugged at Doc and said, "Seemed like a long day yesterday dealing with you. But it's always like that, isn't it? A day for you is like a year for anyone else."

Doc murmured an inarticulate agreement, before observing, "Dying does that to a man." He beckoned Ringo closer. "Don't worry about it, don't worry about being true to yourself. You're perfectly entitled to go wild, and eat roots and berries, and sleep in the dirt, and kill things whenever you want—and just you remember it."

That didn't even earn him a smile, which disappointed Doc. Ringo sat on the bed beside him, and confided uneasily, "I'm not made for this. I don't mean the fucking—I want that. But I'm meant to be on my own, I'm not made for people."

Doc sat up a little. "Your world, when you see it in your mind's eye: are there any people in it?"

"No."

"That seems so odd to me. My world is fully peopled, and yours is nothing but wilderness."

"I've had friends, a few true friends, and I still do—but I'm meant for thinking on my own, being solitary. I don't know why."

"Tell me anyway. Simply blurt the truth out no matter how silly you fear it sounds."

"No, I don't *know*, Holliday. Far as I can figure, everything to do with thinking is part of being with people. Out in the wilderness, there's just *being*, that's different. I'm meant to think as well as be, but I'm not made for being with people."

"All right," Doc said. "We can figure it out."

Refusing to be comforted, Ringo caught up the bottle and began thoroughly drowning his despondency. It was a wonder he'd remained sober that long. As for Doc, he was left with another serious question or two.

Over the next few days, they moved on to another Arizonan town, heading more or less toward Prescott, and spending two nights in the wilderness on the way. They fucked, and they drank whiskey; they read novels and talked of many things that did not relate to what Doc was considering; they fucked some more. In town they settled in another hotel room, though less fancy this time, and Ringo again loitered ominously around the saloons and gambling halls while Doc plied his trade each night. Doc wasn't sure if Ringo's silent presence helped by unnerving Doc's opponents, or hindered by scaring away the timid. In any case, Doc found he had less need to defend himself than usual.

Meanwhile, Doc forced himself to face a few facts. The problem was that the other three people who most interested him each had some quality that Doc didn't possess himself. It was therefore an uncomfortable idea, that this half-mad creature should be better than him in some way. Doc was not used to resenting such a person for anything.

He hadn't been plagued by resentment with Wyatt—Doc wasn't jealous of Wyatt's innate decency, though Doc did admire his thorough coolness. Wyatt's older brother Virgil had a temper, but Wyatt himself remained stoic. Doc didn't want that for himself, however—he liked that Wyatt was a rock against which Doc could crash. So perhaps Doc's resentment of Johnny meant that whatever Johnny had that was different, Doc wanted.

Another week passed, comfortable in some ways and unsettling in others. Strange how easy it was to keep company with a man well-read but of scant education, and unused to conversing at length. A man with unsophisticated notions of sex. A fellow who, while he was prepared to share a bed with Doc, would not indulge in the luxury of cuddling. Despite all of which, Doc had to admit he continued to be fascinated. Ringo would blurt out the damnedest things, change in a moment from taciturn to sharing ideas both surprising and vivid. Doc had never expected to be interested in learning from someone who knew the wilderness as thoroughly as Doc knew civilization. And, ignoble though it was, Doc couldn't help but be seduced by that lean brown body, the handsome changeable face, the pure sharp blue eyes. As a wise man once said, *Beauty is truth, truth beauty—that is all you know on earth, and all you need to know.*

"I like skin," Ringo said as they lazed in bed one afternoon. Doc was sprawled on his front, and Ringo had begun to run a tentative hand down Doc's back while Doc wondered whether to move or not. His instinct was to stretch and purr, arch into the caress, though he felt sure Ringo would withdraw from such a hedonistic reaction, confused and maybe even repulsed. "I like my skin against yours when we fuck."

"You haven't taken the time to get naked before?"

"Not really. Not even with *him.*"

Doc watched his companion. It was unusual for Ringo to volunteer information, and he could too easily be scared silent. "You said his skin was blood-hot," Doc prompted.

Ringo shivered, as if caught unaware by a potent image of his demon lover. "Yes. I like blood. Muscles, too, and bones and sinew. I like the framework of a body, I like how efficient it is, how it all works together. And I like blood; blood feeds a man and warms him. But I never really appreciated skin until now."

"Well, that's good," Doc said, stretching a little under the slow exploration. "Maybe you'll see what I like about holding you close, then; my skin against yours just for the sake of it."

But Ringo wasn't paying attention. His hand stilled, and his focus became internal. Eventually he said, "I have this well-made body. But I also have this well-made mind, and I don't know what to do with it."

"I know," Doc whispered.

"I can think, but most of the time now all I can think about is how thoroughly miserable I am, and what's the use of that?"

Doc sighed. Johnny Ringo needed a great deal of guidance, which would involve time that Doc simply didn't have left to him, and an effort Doc wasn't prepared to make. Which was frustrating, for who else but Doc Holliday was capable of even seeing what Ringo's problems were, let alone working with him to help solve them? There was something tragic about the whole damned situation.

"John, come here and fuck me," Doc murmured, heart raw. He really hadn't thought to care for this man. "Make it slow and sweet, brother, can you do that? And kiss me, and feel as much of your skin against mine as you possibly can."

In the midst of it, Ringo said, "There's nothing to be sad about, Holliday."

"Of course there isn't," Doc murmured. But inside he felt as if something vital were breaking apart.

A shabby boarding house room in yet another barren little town in Arizona. The quietest hours before dawn, after a long tiresome night working for scant reward. He and John had built up the fire, and fucked, and fucked again, so both were still warm enough to lie naked on the sheets. Doc was watching Ringo, examining him in the moonlight from the window that etched lace-patterns across his skin. Ringo's eyes looked eerie, pools of perfect blue in the bright colorless light. He lay there, beautiful and apparently untroubled, all that lean hungry anger lying dormant, though surely he would not prove compliant if provoked. Doc wondered whether it was the night, or his own responses, or this creature beside him that he found so bewitching.

Sadness stretched on, infinite under the cool moonlight.

Doc surrendered to a yawn which became a cough. He felt so damned tired, worn by these unwanted complexities. He knew himself well enough to admit he was only playing at melodrama; he indulged himself in this excess of emotion, drowned in the depths of reaction, and usually he enjoyed every moment of it. But even as he watched this fascinating man, Doc knew he would leave John behind, knew he would meet up with Kate and with Wyatt, knew nothing would change that, even though it meant abandoning John to his miserable ignorance. Once free of this, once reunited with the people he wanted to be with, Doc's heart would harden and the memory of this would seem like a theatrical he'd seen performed.

But even though this was self-indulgence for Doc, that could not change the fact that for Johnny Ringo it was tragedy.

The fellow had seemed oblivious to Doc's resentment over the past weeks, and then to his growing frustration. Even when Doc had become angry about being part of the whole damned mess, and angry at his own inevitable callousness, John hadn't noticed. No, he wasn't oblivious—Ringo was aware of Doc's anger, but seemed to consider it had nothing to do with him.

Doc knew that he and John were reaching the end of their unlikely partnership. It had been a fascinating and challenging encounter, but Doc would have to leave soon if he was to meet up with Kate in Prescott. And Ringo was beginning to get restless, chafing at the constant company, even while he still obviously enjoyed all the things he wouldn't find anywhere else.

The moonlight caught at Doc's wandering attention, caught at his eyelids and closed them. But he couldn't surrender to the tiredness yet; he had to live through the last of this terrible sadness. Doc spread a pale hand on the darker skin of John's narrow belly, and examined how the lace-patterns stretched and flowed over his fingers. He said very quietly, "I need to talk to you, Johnny."

Those unsettling blue eyes shifted slow in the moonlight, as if John were under a spell as well. Even once his gaze met Doc's, it slid right past him.

"I've been thinking about you, pilgrim, and I need to talk to you now, I need to try to help you."

The fellow seemed to be looking for something beyond Doc's shoulder. He said, voice raw, "How can you still have your soul?"

"What?" Doc asked, frowning in confusion.

"Your soul. I lost mine years ago; I don't know, mislaid it, or gave it to *him* in return for a fuck. How can Doc Holliday still have his soul?"

"John, that is a fascinating question, but I want to help you figure out what you can do with that well-formed mind of yours."

"Haven't you ever made a deal with his father?"

Sighing, Doc said, "Let me talk, brother, and then you can tell me about the state of my soul." Doc sat up, because he feared he'd fall asleep if he remained lying down.

Johnny had turned those eerie blue eyes away, and was gazing out through the window. "He's the most beautiful thing I've ever seen. Part creature and part spirit, part of this world and part of his father's. Worth a soul to fuck him, Holliday, worth my soul. Never had anything so intense."

"I want you to listen to me, all right?" Though Doc really didn't know how best to proceed, or even whether he should say anything at all. He didn't have the time or the need to help Ringo, and he suspected that Johnny's familiar ignorance might be preferable to the torment of a knowledge John couldn't do anything about. Doc began rambling, hoping to capture the fellow's attention and to make up his mind as he went. "My cousin I told you about, Mattie, who I loved, whose love— No, it was my love for her that formed me as a man. That's not my point. My point is that she was independent, thoroughly independent. Different from me, because I'm the most selfish person on this earth, and she was the most selfless. Except that when it came to loving her, I became selfless for once, and if she could ever have been selfish it might have been for love of me. She had absolute independence, Johnny. She had the bravery to be exactly who she was, never any less than that, the strength to follow her own principles. She taught me that independence, even as she was learning it herself, even as everything I'd hoped for from life was blighted."

"But my soul," Ringo said, as if he hadn't heard a word of Doc's, "it wasn't much. Just this gray tattered thing, like an old rag hanging forgotten for years on a washing line, all forlorn and weathered." He was speaking lightly, as if this were of no consequence when the truth was that it was fundamental. "My poor soul, I thought I'd left it behind somewhere. I thought he already had it."

"Listen to me, John," Doc insisted with some vehemence. The sad blue eyes turned toward him, though Doc then suffered through an ill-timed yawn and cough, fighting off the deepening exhaustion. "Listen to me," he continued when he could. "You have something I don't, brother. If I had the time, I'd help you learn about it, and maybe I'd learn as well just as I learned true independence from Mattie. I want what you have, there's no denying that, and I resent you to hell and back. But I don't have the time to help, I only have a short while left on this earth, and I am abysmally selfish. I want to be with this friend of mine, and with Kate, and that means I can't be with you. It means I can't learn from you."

Ringo said, "I miss having it around."

"What?"

"My soul. It wasn't anything much, but I miss it."

Doc indulged a groan of frustration. "If you're not going to pay attention to me, you could at least not contradict yourself. Why should you miss your soul, if your demon lover was worth losing the poor tattered thing to?"

Ringo's expression was sharper now. "Holliday, you never hold back from feeling and being everything possible, even if that means contradicting yourself."

"All right," Doc grudgingly allowed.

"In fact, you love being contradictory and unexpected. You'd love being caught believing three completely inconsistent things at once."

The fellow was too smart sometimes. "Listen to me, damn it," Doc said, "because this is important, and I need to say it and then I need to get some sleep."

"Do you think I care what you have to say?"

"I don't care whether you care. I don't even know if telling you will do more harm than good at this stage, but I'm telling you anyway." Doc paused to draw breath. This really shouldn't be done in anger, but he was far too tired now for a proper approach. "John, I'm clever and I'm perceptive, I can appreciate books and art and music and such things, I can converse in style. But you're more than that."

"My soul was just this old silk rag, worn and fraying, clinging to my shoulders by a thread or two. But yours is so damned righteous, Holliday. It towers there behind you…"

Determined to ignore Johnny's mad ramble, Doc leaned close over him, and finally said it: "You have a creativity in you, John. Yes, you have thoughts; yes, you have a well-formed if uneducated mind; you have an ability with language. Use all that to create, John. That's what you're here on earth for."

"It's a gentleman's soul, Holliday, all fine and righteous. It looks dark, but in a rich way, like the waistcoat of yours that's all leaves and vines and flowers, all the colors under the sun woven in, but pitch black below. And how can you still have your soul, Holliday, let alone such an upstanding one? I resent you to hell and back for it."

"You *are* listening, aren't you?" Doc broke in. "Now this is the sort of thing I mean. You have such an imagination; you talk in incredible images. What are you saying about souls?"

"How can Doc Holliday have a soul that's so complete, so unassailable? How can he be the fastest gunman in the West, how can he fuck so often, how can he win all the riches he desires, how can he be so educated, if he hasn't bargained away his soul for any of it?"

Doc couldn't stifle another yawn. He needed to sleep, soon and deeply. "Why do you need to bargain away your soul, Johnny?" he asked. "Why do you think that's necessary?" But his heart wasn't in the question. Doc lay down again, made himself comfortable beside this strange, beautiful man. Pity the fellow was quite mad. This idea about souls was interesting, yes, but crazed. "I'm sorry, Johnny," Doc said, with quiet genuine regret. "I'm sorry, my brother." But the blue eyes were directed toward the window again.

The moon was lowering, and the lace-patterned light was sliding off the bed. As it crept up the wall behind them, sleep cast its net over Doc, and he finally surrendered to the spell.

Chapter Eight:

Faith Rewarded

Arizona;

December 1879

At last Doc Holliday had quit talking nonsense and fallen asleep, and his soul—which during all that palaver had drawn close in concern—had now retreated to the darkest corner of the room. Johnny cast the man a sour glare and turned away. Why the hell had Holliday thought John wanted to hear about some woman Holliday once loved? Surely he was smarter than that.

Restless, John climbed out of the bed, careful not to disturb Holliday's sleep for fear of him insisting on talking some more. John headed for the window once he was free, watched through the lace curtain as the moon set behind a distant mountain range. Tonight, the world seemed full of mystery; even Holliday had felt it, though he'd seemed determined to fight it off and prattle on about prosaic matters.

The night darkened, and the horizon lost the moon's glow, while the stars shone more vigorously. This beleaguered outpost of mankind was quiet. Except... there was a figure standing just down the street, leaning nonchalantly back against a railing. John dragged the curtain aside, ripping it in his haste, though he knew who it was even before he saw the details of the fall of golden hair, the simple black clothes, the strong and perfect figure. He threw up the window, wanting to catch the creature-spirit's attention— but realizing he didn't know his lover's name. "Darkling!" he cried.

That beautiful face turned toward him, and a self-satisfied smile graced those lips.

If the room hadn't been on the second floor, Johnny might have climbed out into the cold night, naked though he was. Instead, he reached out an imploring hand. "Wait for me, just a moment or two."

Not expecting an acknowledgment, Johnny turned away, began hauling on his clothes, grabbing his saddlebags and gun belt in the process, and headed out of the door. It was time to leave this place behind. Down the stairs at a fast trot, still buttoning his trousers, then buckling the guns around his hips. Out through the hall and into the street, searching for the Devil's son, frantic for a moment when John couldn't see him—but there he was, still waiting, having wandered a little closer. Johnny ran up to him, skidded to a halt maybe a foot away, grinning with rare joy.

A time passed as Johnny took in every detail of the creature-spirit's face. "You're always far more beautiful than I can remember," he said at last. "Even the idea of you… it's too much for one mind to hold."

"Thank you," Lucifer's son responded politely.

"Only thing ever scares me is thinking I might not see you again."

"Oh, I'm never far away."

"But that's worse," John said. "I mean, if you're close, but not close enough."

The creature nodded.

John had never felt so well understood. He confided, "I feared we had a deal."

The diabolical smile, never far from those generous lips, grew wry. "Would we require chastity from you?"

"I guess not." John reached a tentative hand to touch this beauty made flesh. When he saw the caress was permitted, John lifted his other hand as well, framed the bold face. The creature was tall, an inch or so taller than any man, but he was so perfectly formed that his height didn't seem unnatural. Johnny had always wanted to shock this spirit, right from the first night when he'd said, *I want to fuck you.* This time Johnny murmured, "I want to kiss you."

A flicker of something—John couldn't tell if it was surprise or amusement—and the creature obligingly bent closer. John stretched up and met that blood-hot mouth with his own. So intense this intimate devouring; beyond pleasure, beyond recognizable sensation. John's head falling back, body drawn to the creature's as those strong arms circled his waist, as the mouth followed and answered his hungers… For the first time Johnny felt the sensual tug of surrender.

But, no. He would not submit, not even to the son of the Devil; he would not suffer that terrible invasion. Johnny pulled away, regained his breath and his sense of balance. The demon was smiling widely, mockingly.

"Let's leave this place," Johnny whispered, hands still worshipping his lover's beauty. "Let's return to the wilderness, and fuck in the starlight."

The son of the Devil seemed perfectly amenable.

"I need to get my horse. Will you ride with me? Or will you meet me out there?"

"I will be there."

"All right," Johnny said, stepping back and letting him go.

A vast amusement widened the demon's smile. "You trust me?"

"No, I don't trust you at all." He said it simply, for it was true. "How could I? But that doesn't stop me adoring you."

"You are pleasing to me."

"I don't trust you," Johnny added, "but I have faith in you."

The creature's golden illumination, and his darkness, and his stature, all seemed to grow a little larger, along with his smile.

John returned the smile, delighted that his belief could so increase his lover, could have such a direct influence. "I have faith in you," Johnny said again, and he drew close and kissed the creature, not caring that he was being remarkably daring. There was danger here, of course, with his soul already forfeit, and his life given over to the care of the son of the Devil. But Johnny felt nothing but excitement. He whispered, "I want to feel your skin blood-hot against mine."

And Lucifer's son smiled with wickedness rather than amusement, and said, "Then go fetch your horse, and I will meet you in the wilderness."

Johnny grinned, and headed for the stables at a run.

Those few hours that night—or did it even last an hour? John could never bother keeping track of time when there were such pleasures to be had. Those few hours were astonishing, of course, and then John plunged into sleep and a maze of dreams. But he woke dazed and alone, naked and bootless. So dry-mouthed that his head ached with it, and while it only took a short while for him to track his horse, he was nigh in agony by the time he'd recovered mount and water-flask, clothes and boots and guns.

Every time, after every precious visitation, John woke to find the world drabber than before, and he had to suffer through wondering if he was ever likely to see his lover again. Not that it wasn't worth it… but now the waiting and the wanting started.

He wasn't going back to keep company with Holliday, who was heading northwest to Prescott, so John rode southeast until he ended up in some burg named Safford. Not that he cared what it was called; he only cared that there were saloons.

The first such establishment he chanced upon served whiskey, and that was good enough for Johnny Ringo. He sat at the bar and applied himself to transferring as much of the liquor as he could from the bottle to his gut.

"Drowning your sorrows, friend?"

A man sitting on the stool to his right. No knowing how long he'd been there. John turned a slow glare upon him, and was relieved to discover that at least it wasn't Holliday. There was still too much whiskey in the bottle for John's peace of mind. He nudged it toward the stranger. "Drown some yourself, if you want," he said, "but I ain't your friend."

"No matter," was the prickly reply. "I'd sooner have beer, anyways."

Rage roiled through Johnny Ringo, in proportion not to the response but to his frustrations. "Y' interrupt my only solace, and *then you don't deign to drink with me?!*"

"Now, see here, friend—" the fellow retorted in quavering tones. *Devil take him!* If a man didn't have the courage to say what he meant and then stick to it—

Johnny's hand came up—Johnny's right hand had already curled around his six-shooter, and it came up to deal the fellow a heavy blow across his head—he staggered back off the stool and was crumpling down into just the wrong location—when the gun went off, and he was hit in the throat—

If Johnny had intended to shoot the wretch he'd be dying now, his blood pulsing a pool on the saloon floor. As it was, John could see the wound wasn't serious. Men were tending to him already.

John let others prize the gun from his hand. He'd already swooped up the whiskey bottle with his left, and was busy pouring as much down his gullet as he could manage. There was no other answer to what ailed him.

Then the law came, and the next John knew he was confined to a jail cell once more—a lone lorn contrary creature indeed.

CHAPTER NINE:

UNEASY PROSPERITY

Tombstone, Arizona;

January 1880

Ed Schieffelin had spent years searching for gold and silver. He would go out alone into the land around the Dragoon Mountains of Arizona Territory, occasionally returning to Fort Huachuca for supplies. Being wary of the Chiricahua Apache, as was only sensible, the soldiers wondered at Schieffelin's luck in remaining alive. He was excited by working the earth and coaxing away her riches. He was certain he would find something.

"You'll find your tombstone," was one dry retort.

In 1877 Schieffelin discovered silver, named the area as appropriate, and helped a boomtown spring up in the desert. A couple of years later he left to tour the nation, a wealthy and happy man. But he never stopped prospecting.

Wyatt Earp strolled through the early morning streets of that boomtown, overcoat buttoned against the cold. It was January 1880 and Tombstone, Arizona was still a new and exciting place to be, growing apace as mine after mine struck rich lodes of silver.

He had at last left Dodge City in September the previous year, and had taken work as a Wells Fargo guard while he traveled, arriving here with Mattie almost two months before on the first day of winter. His brothers Virgil and Morgan, along with their wives Allie and Louisa, were gathering in Tombstone as well. It seemed that Wyatt had made a good choice of location—with a prompt or two from Virgil, who had moved some months before to Prescott, Arizona, where it was impossible to avoid the buzz about Tombstone's silver strikes.

Wyatt had planned on starting up a stagecoach service, but discovered the business was already being well met by local operator Charles 'Sandy Bob' Crouch. That had been Wyatt's only disappointment. He continued riding shotgun for Wells Fargo, while the Earps began buying property, investing in mines and businesses, working as gamblers and as guards in the saloons. Opportunities abounded for men who weren't afraid of working hard and risking capital, especially when they had brothers who could pool resources, back each other up, and make progress together. It was early days of course, but the Earps were on their way to being wealthy.

The brothers had bought three blocks of land next together on Fremont Street—the cheaper ones to be found on the other side of Fremont's junction with First Street—and they had built a cabin for each couple.

Meanwhile, the womenfolk were enjoying their own success. Virgil's wife Allie had insisted on bringing her sturdy little sewing machine with her to Tombstone, and Wyatt was now glad he'd been the one to find space for it in their overloaded wagons. As with all boomtowns, there were never enough wooden or adobe buildings available no matter how quickly they were constructed—and so Allie and Mattie soon had a fine business running from Virgil's cabin, making and repairing canvas tents. In fact, Wyatt had to acknowledge that the women were the first of the family to make a steady income in Tombstone.

The town was still raw and rough, with few families as yet. There were children, though, and the promise of more arriving, so when an unemployed schoolteacher was discovered to be visiting, he had been persuaded to stay.

At present, civilization was taking the form of a quilting bee held at Wyatt and Mattie's cabin. Wyatt was usually in bed at this hour, having returned to the habit of sleeping until noon, but there had been a knock at the door and several women had invaded. Poor Mattie had been fast asleep, too, and had needed a liberal dose of laudanum to deal with a panic-induced headache. Luckily, Allie had been ready and able to act as hostess until Mattie could cope. Unluckily for Wyatt, the two Earp women had chased him from the house without even the benefit of a cup of coffee.

Reaching the offices of the *Tombstone Epitaph* in town, a few blocks along Fremont Street, Wyatt strode up onto the wooden sidewalk. John Clum, who edited the paper and was also the town's mayor, came out to greet him, wiping his ink-stained hands on a rag. "Wyatt. It's a bit early for you."

"My house is full of women," he explained flatly.

"Oh, I remember: the quilting bee." He paused before asking with a slight edge to his tone, "My wife was among them?"

"Yes. They caught us unawares, but I remember seeing her."

"Before you were summarily dismissed," Clum finished the story for him. "They must be planning a full day's sewing. I'm told," he added with a lift of a brow, "that it will be a traditional wedding quilt."

Wyatt didn't react to this. Perhaps he was supposed to be pleasantly surprised by this attempt to make the Earps' common-law marriages appear respectable. It was out of Wyatt's or Clum's hands of course; the women would sort it out as they thought best. But even in frontier towns far removed from the social stratifications of the East, Wyatt suspected that Mattie, Allie and Louisa would remain… on the wrong side of First Street.

Clum continued, "At least my house will be quiet. We've just finished printing this week's edition and as soon as I get cleaned up, I'm heading home to sleep."

Nodding, Wyatt turned away a little. Clum laughed, no doubt assuming aright that Wyatt was envious of these intentions. The paper's new assistant editor came out to join them on the boardwalk. "How are you, Storm Cloud?" Wyatt asked.

Storm Cloud nodded a greeting and handed over a copy of the newspaper. "Want some light reading over breakfast? It's always good to start the day with a laugh."

"Thank you." Wyatt hid a smile, as Clum obviously didn't appreciate the humor. He tucked the paper under his arm, careful not to smudge the ink. "You're enjoying the work here?"

"Oliver is the paper's most valuable asset," Clum declared. "I hardly know how I managed without him."

Storm Cloud agreed. "I tidy up his grammar and spelling, and make him look as if he knows what he's writing about."

"That's good."

"You must have been busy last night, Wyatt," Storm Cloud commented. "People usually complain about us running the press, but they wouldn't have heard us over all the merriment."

"Yes. There were a couple of groups who were out having a big time, and they all came through the Oriental."

"And they all played and lost at your faro table?"

Wyatt did smile then. "It was a good night."

Clum broke in. "One of the groups was Curly Bill Brocius and his compadres?"

"Yes."

"You know most of that lot are cattle rustlers, don't you? They were already thieves and outlaws, or they've become it since. Who knows what they'll be tempted to do as Tombstone grows richer and richer."

Wyatt nodded, uninterested in getting into all this. "You're not wrong to be concerned."

"I've been talking to your brother," Clum continued, terribly serious. "I want to appoint him as town marshal."

"Which one?" Wyatt asked, watching people pass by in the street. A fair number were men who were apparently heading off to work the mines despite the fact they hadn't slept a full night.

Exasperated, Clum said, "Virgil, of course. Not Morgan, he's too young yet."

"He's twenty-eight," Wyatt remarked—though he knew what Clum meant. Morgan was competent and hardworking, but still boyish in his enthusiasms; perhaps still a mite too reckless to lead rather than follow.

"Virgil already carries a deputy U.S. marshal badge," Clum continued. "You can't tell me he's not interested—but there won't be much to do for the territory. I need him working for the town."

A silence stretched, which the mayor seemed to expect Wyatt to fill. Eventually Wyatt asked, "What did Virgil say?"

"What do you think? He's going to talk to you, but he thinks you all have other priorities right now. Wyatt, you know as well as I do that we need to concentrate on law enforcement here. You're doing well, and so am I, from business and from mining directly or indirectly, but it isn't worth a damn if we don't have any law."

Wyatt nodded, but apparently that wasn't enough.

"Read today's paper, Wyatt. We have confirmation that the Southern Pacific railroad will reach Tucson by March—and they'll be bringing a line down to Tombstone after that. We mustn't lose the battle before it's even begun."

"I understand, John, I promise you. But right now, what I need is coffee and breakfast." Wyatt looked over at Storm Cloud. "If you've finished your work, you might join me?"

John Clum sighed, and quit the argument for the present. "Go on, Oliver. I'll see to distribution. I'll talk to you later, Wyatt."

"Thank you, John," Storm Cloud said. Wyatt lifted his chin in farewell, and the two of them headed down the street. Storm Cloud commented, "He's a good man."

"Yes, he is," Wyatt agreed.

"You know John ran the San Carlos reservation for three years? The Apache respected him. He's arrogant, sure, and a lot of people think he's greedy, but everyone agrees that John Clum is brave and honest."

"That's true."

"The Apache are sorry he's gone, for certain sure. He let them live their own lives, by their own practices, as far as he could. I've never heard that before—from any of our peoples—about an Indian agent."

"Yes, all right, Oliver. He's a good man." They walked on in silence for a minute or two, past stores that were opening, and saloons still busy from the night before. Wyatt finally said, "In my experience, John forms his opinions too quickly, and there are some he might do better re-examining."

"You mean like blaming every crime in the county on Curly Bill and the Clantons and that lot?"

Wyatt nodded. "And believing the Earps should always enforce the law."

Storm Cloud laughed. "John is persistent, yes, but you can't blame him for trying. You and Virgil have solid reputations."

"I was planning to build a new reputation," Wyatt muttered, "as a solid businessman."

They reached the Cosmopolitan Hotel on Allen Street, and walked into the restaurant. Oliver Storm Cloud drew some resentful stares, but no one bothered to try refusing him service anymore, given his friendship with Mayor Clum. Storm Cloud and Wyatt sat at an empty table, and ordered a generous breakfast each and a pot of coffee.

Wyatt sat back, content to be silent for a time, trusting Storm Cloud not to take offence. Everything seemed to be going well for Wyatt, everything seemed to be working out according to plan. He had found a town with opportunities, and he was already benefiting from taking advantage of them. His brothers and their wives were here, and some of Wyatt's closest friends had also come to Tombstone: Storm Cloud had already been here to greet Wyatt, and Doc Holliday had finally arrived a week ago. The Earps were a tight-knit family with connections and resources, settling down in a genuine boomtown. So why was Wyatt feeling uneasy?

The local deputy sheriff of Pima County walked into the restaurant, talking to the new schoolteacher. Seeing Wyatt, the sheriff made a point of coming over to shake his hand. "Good morning, Mr. Earp. How are you?"

Wyatt stood. "Sheriff Behan."

"I don't believe you've met? This is Gregory Vaughan, who'll be running our school. Vaughan, this is Wyatt Earp. You've probably heard of him; everyone else has."

"Mr. Vaughan," Wyatt greeted the fellow, shaking his hand. He introduced Storm Cloud, and was pleased to note that Vaughan's manner remained polite. "Are we building a schoolhouse for you?" Wyatt asked. "What are you using in the meantime?"

"The manager of the Grand Hotel has agreed to me using their dining room for two hours between breakfast and noon each day," Vaughan explained. "I hope to begin taking classes there from next week. We're inquiring further about raising funds for our own school building."

"How about it, Wyatt?" Behan asked in jovial tones. "You're one of our more shrewd and successful businessmen, though you're still new to Tombstone. I'm sure you consider a school to be a wise investment in the community."

"Of course," Wyatt said to Vaughan rather than Behan. "Come and find me once your plans are more settled. I'm sure my brothers and I can help."

Vaughan smiled at him, appreciative but perhaps also a little unnerved. "Thank you, Mr. Earp." And then John Behan dragged young Gregory Vaughan off to meet someone else.

"That one tries too hard," said Storm Cloud.

"Behan? Yes, he does." Wyatt watched the sheriff do his back-slapping best for the schoolteacher—which would be useful to Vaughan in many ways, for Behan also had his connections and resources. He was a political animal and a popular man, whose dress and behavior were influenced more by the cultured East than the pioneering West.

Vaughan himself, who Wyatt understood came from New York State, also presented as neater and more civilized than most of the parents whose children he'd be teaching. He was tall but slight in stature, and seemed both overly earnest and lacking in confidence, but at least there was something more genuine about him than Behan.

Wyatt and Storm Cloud had just begun eating when the relative peace of the restaurant was broken. Six inebriated men wandered in, calling loudly to their friend John Behan, and suggesting they join him for breakfast—or, from their point of view, a late supper. Three tables were soon rearranged to cater for Behan, Vaughan, Curly Bill Brocius, Frank Leslie, Phin and Ike Clanton, and Frank and Tom McLaury. To Wyatt's eye, it appeared that a few of the restaurant staff were as unimpressed to be serving these people as they had been about waiting on Storm Cloud. Not that the hotel owner would mind. Money was money, and it wouldn't afford him to be too nice about its source.

Curly Bill seemed particularly rambunctious. "Hey, Wyatt!" he called across the room after looking around. "This is on you, right?"

"Why is that?" Wyatt asked in quieter tones that still carried.

"What we lost to you a few hours ago at faro. You're rich now, damn you!" The fellow seemed quite cheerful about it, however. "You can afford to buy us breakfast. Some might say you owe us!"

Wyatt suggested, "I'll buy you a round of coffee, and we can negotiate from there."

Curly Bill laughed, and then his attention was distracted by one of the others at his table.

"All I wanted was some peace and quiet."

It might have been Wyatt muttering, but it was his older brother Virgil who was now standing by their table. Wyatt said, "At least you have your house to yourself. Mine is full of women."

"Yeah, I figured when Allie left, I'd get some more sleep. But you saw the people on the next lot have started building? Axes and saws and hammers going, and yelling advice to each other, most of which was wrong…" Virgil shook his head in despair. "And now this rabble still rowdy from last night."

"Sit down, Virgil," Wyatt suggested.

"Morning, Storm Cloud," Virgil offered, taking a seat. "Wyatt, you know what Curly Bill Brocius is wanted for in Texas? I've been checking into these people."

"Don't you start, Virge. John Clum was already at me this morning."

"I have to wonder what they're celebrating…"

"They're just having a good time. It's not as if they come into town very often. Leave them be."

"And look at them, all cozy with the deputy sheriff. Something about

Behan and his friends don't sit right, Wyatt."

"This isn't our problem."

Virgil was still staring at the noisy group on the other side of the room. "Is that the new schoolteacher? That's the wrong crowd to get in with. Poor fellow probably doesn't know any better yet."

Wyatt put down his knife and fork, rapidly losing his appetite. "We don't have to take sides anymore, Virgil. There don't even have to be any sides for us to take."

"Don't be naive, Wyatt." Virgil at last swung around and faced his younger brother. "You know as well as I do there are sides already, and we're with John Clum and his friends. We are *not* with Behan, and he knows it; you've seen how wary he is with us. We aren't with the rustlers or the outlaws, or the ranchers who turn a blind eye to where they came from when the rustlers are looking for somewhere to rest and fatten up a herd of cattle."

"Virgil, you're short on sleep, and you're in a bad mood. Under those circumstances you shouldn't think too hard about what Mayor Clum says. He told me he's asked you to be town marshal."

"Yeah, and I'm considering it."

Wyatt groaned. "I knew you would. I thought we agreed we're giving up the law. It's time we led our own lives, Virgil. It's time for *us* now, and our families." He was met with obstinate silence. "Being town marshal doesn't give you jurisdiction over the rustlers and ranchers in any case. If you're after those men, all you'll get them for is disturbing the peace when they come to town."

"Then I'll get them for that. They didn't exactly make any new friends last night, the way they were behaving. I had to help throw them out of the Capitol Saloon; Curly Bill decided the place needed a vaudeville act, and he was prepared to star in it himself."

Storm Cloud couldn't repress a snort of laughter, which Virgil didn't take very kindly.

At last a second pot of coffee arrived, and Wyatt gulped down a mouthful though it was too hot. "Virgil, these men are small ranchers and cowhands, in town to spend their money and have a good time. We're familiar with the sort." He asked, "Where is this vindictiveness coming from?"

"They're the kind of small rancher who rustles horses and cattle from the big spreads, and rebrands them before selling them on."

"You don't have any evidence of that beyond hearsay. This is ridiculous."

"Well, next time Clum talks to you, *listen*, Wyatt. He knows what he's saying. You've got to support the right people, make the right friends." A pause, and then Virgil asked, "How long is Doc Holliday going to be in town?"

"A long time, I hope," Wyatt said firmly. "Doc is a good friend, the best kind of friend a man can have, and I don't care whether you think that's right or wrong." He stared at his brother, wondering if he even really knew him anymore. "All I can tell you, Virgil, is this: September '78 in Dodge City, Doc Holliday saved my life. There was no particular reason he should have. He'd backed me up before, but this time he took one hell of a risk doing it. I owe him for that, and I figure my brothers owe him as well."

Virgil said nothing to this, though in previous iterations of this conversation he had pointed out that owing gratitude was one thing, and offering staunch friendship was entirely another. He must have finally decided this no longer needed saying. Virgil ordered his own breakfast, and the three men sat in silence for a time, sullen on the part of the Earp brothers. Then Virgil muttered, "Speak of the Devil."

Looking up, Wyatt saw that Doc Holliday had arrived. No doubt he hadn't been to bed yet, for he was still in his gambling finery. Curly Bill called him over, and Doc politely passed the time of day with the group. "No chance," Curly Bill was declaring loud enough for the whole room to hear. "You've won it already. Wyatt's buying us breakfast with his faro winnings. I reckon you should buy us dinner and supper all damned week with your poker winnings."

"Why don't you win it back from me tonight?" Doc invited.

Curly Bill shook his head; no doubt he'd been burned once too often. Phin Clanton, who was perhaps the oldest of the group, said, "Not on your life, Holliday. You just want to win some more."

"We're heading home," Tom McLaury added. "Buy some cattle and supplies off Higgins before he leaves the county. That's if this lot haven't lost all our cash."

"Very wise," Doc commented. As usual his appearance and manner were that of a well-bred gentleman of means. In fact, he made Behan look foolish and second-rate without even trying. As for the other men—the ranchers and the cowhands—they were comfortable in scruffy, torn work clothes, and perhaps owned no better. Though, Wyatt reflected, he had seen Doc dressed casually often enough, and his manner remained that of a gentleman. Curly Bill's bold friendly air, with his handsome features and generous head of dark hair, couldn't compete with Doc's urbanity. Tom McLaury's fresh-faced vigor was nothing to Doc's self-possession.

An argument had broken out over whether all the group's money had been lost. Various members were throwing crumpled dollar bills and worn old coins on the table, of all denominations, and Tom was trying to gather it up and count it, hindered by Curly Bill's own enthusiasm for the task. Gregory Vaughan was watching all this with wide eyes, seeming somewhat overwhelmed.

Doc nodded a farewell to the oblivious group. "All that money is like a red rag to a bull," he remarked to no one in particular as he wandered over to the Earp table. "Wyatt, whatever are you doing up at this hour? Didn't you recently retire for the night?"

Wyatt groaned. Storm Cloud said it for him: "His house is full of women."

"Quilting bee," Virgil explained.

"Ah. How domestic." Doc lit a cigarette and drew on it, suppressed a cough. "What a pity Kate isn't in town at present; I'm sure she would have loved to participate. Well, perhaps next time. Virgil, you might mention it to the lovely Allie."

Silence. Storm Cloud slid his gaze away. Virgil looked mildly affronted. And though he tried, Wyatt couldn't help himself: he laughed at this impossible notion. "Let's get out of here," he suggested. "Doc, come for a walk, I feel like stretching my legs."

"Of course."

Storm Cloud said, "I'll head back to the paper, see if John's confused the distribution arrangements yet." Virgil must have decided to go with him, for he nodded to his brother, and followed Storm Cloud out of the door.

After Wyatt settled his account, he and Doc wandered off through the streets, instinctively matching each other's relaxed pace. Doc offered Wyatt a cigarette from his silver case, and they both smoked in thoughtful silence. At last Wyatt said, "Virgil's going off half-cocked. Clum wants to appoint him as town marshal. Everyone's taking sides, and we only just got here." He let out a sigh. "Why can't the Earps get away from the law, Doc? Why is that so difficult?"

"You tell me, Wyatt."

They leaned back against a hitching rail and turned their faces to the sun that was only now beginning to warm the day. "Maybe it's this place, maybe it's Tombstone. I thought I'd chosen well. It's certainly the place to make money; there's wealth for the taking if you're smart about it."

"Yes, there is."

"But it isn't the place to be a family. Not yet. Remember Dodge a few years ago? It was all rough and raw and eager, just like Tombstone is now— and then it grew up. The law came to Dodge City, and it finally became peaceful. Tombstone isn't ready for that yet. I guess I didn't choose so well after all."

"You chose well enough, Wyatt. Maybe you can't have the opportunities and the family at the same time, but there's a progression from one to the other. We've both seen it a score of times."

"And you've always moved on, chasing the opportunities."

"Until now, so have you, Wyatt."

"I wanted something different this time. Is that so strange?" He sighed. "The hard thing is that if I've made a mistake, I'm not the only one who'll face the consequences. You all came with me. That's one hell of a responsibility."

Doc said lightly, "You can leave us to take responsibility for our own lives."

There was activity all around them. The saloons and gambling halls were doing a roaring trade, the stores were flourishing, men of all kinds were everywhere with their horses and possessions. Women of the frontier kind wandered alone or in pairs, bold and strong whether respectable or not, knowing they were few in number and therefore in great demand.

"No, though I thank you for the kind offer," Doc was saying to a woman dressed daringly in black satin. "Perhaps on another occasion."

Wyatt said quietly, "I never actually got around to marrying Mattie, you know." A pause, which Doc didn't fill. "Nothing's actually how I planned it, nothing's quite what I thought it would be. Clum tells me the women are making us a wedding quilt, but there hasn't been a wedding, and there probably never will be."

Doc said, "Surely she's your common-law wife by now. That carries the same obligations."

"Yes, but I thought we should do this right. And now here we are in Tombstone, and it's not going to happen."

"You have a handful of priests and ministers to choose from," Doc remarked. "Are none the correct flavor?"

"That hardly matters out here," Wyatt said dismissively. "No, something's wrong, and not just with me and Mattie."

Long moments of reflection, before the pair began wandering again. "Would it help or not," Doc asked after a time, "if I told you that Kate and I aren't actually married either?"

"I don't know, Doc." Wyatt considered this. "I don't think it matters. You and Kate, there's something— There's something true about you, a real partnership, even with her living in Globe now. She'll still visit you regularly, won't she? And you her?"

"Absolutely, yes. Though I suspect Kate's the one who calls our visits short when she suspects she's in danger of inadvertently becoming a wife."

Wyatt huffed a quiet laugh, but didn't remark on this.

"So…" Doc continued. "A real partnership, you say."

"I don't know how to describe it."

"But please endeavor to do so."

"It's not romantic between you. It's—" Wyatt felt himself perilously close to discomfort, and quickly checked that no one could overhear them. "It's a sensual thing. But it seems truer and surer than any young kid moaning on about being in love. And it's always there—reliable, strong—even when you're apart."

"Thank you, Wyatt. One does like to be reassured one's not imagining things."

Though he acknowledged this, Wyatt didn't want to admit he was envious of the pair. Still, he'd had his chance at true love, and she had died, and he couldn't really expect anything more now. He and Mattie would do well enough, cabin and quilt and all.

Putting this behind him, Wyatt asked, "How are you, Doc? You seem to have recovered your health. You're none the worse for wear after a long night."

"Yes, it was only a chill. Overall, the climate here has helped, as advertised."

"It affected you badly, whatever it was. Morg was telling me you were quite ill when he saw you in Prescott."

Doc dropped his cigarette butt to the dirt and stepped on the ember. "It was nothing. Some idiot, some thoughtless ingrate I was sharing a room with at a boarding house—he left the window open one night, and I caught cold." He paused for a moment before adding in reluctant yet forceful tones, "I don't deal easily with these things."

Wyatt watched his friend, surprised at the vehemence. Doc rarely made much of being consumptive, and he never let a mere human being disturb his equanimity. "You'll be glad when spring arrives," Wyatt offered.

"Indeed."

As Wyatt and Doc were heading back into Allen Street, they met up with John Behan again. Wyatt stopped him, and asked, "What *are* you doing about the cattle rustling in this county, sheriff?"

The fellow was naturally resentful of this direct question. "It's difficult, Wyatt. People are just as happy to eat Mexican beef as American, and once the herds are branded there's no evidence to be had."

"You know the rumors," Wyatt said bluntly. "People are saying that Curly Bill's lot are behind it, and ranchers such as the Clantons turn a blind eye at best, for the sake of not losing their own cattle in retribution. At worst, they're complicit."

Behan drew himself up tall, and still seemed second rate. "You're talking about men who are friends of mine, and I don't give any credence to the rumors. People are spiteful."

"The law applies to all, Behan."

"Can you throw the first stone?" Behan gestured angrily in Doc Holliday's direction. "You have friends with reputations, too. Were those reputations earned, or were they unfairly acquired?"

Doc smiled with no humor, but no rancor either.

Wyatt continued, "Why don't you investigate further? If you exonerate your friends, you'll be doing everyone a good turn. Tombstone doesn't need to be divided in two like this."

"You tell that to your lot. It's not *my* side who are rumormongering."

Wyatt sighed. "It comes down to this, Behan: the sheriff and his deputies need to have investigative skills, and no conflicting loyalties to hamper them."

"Someone like you, is that what you're saying?"

"Maybe." Wyatt nodded, though he already knew he would regret this. Not that he wanted to move to the Pima County seat of Tucson, which he would have to do as sheriff, but being a deputy based in Tombstone seemed a fine thing—useful, and lucrative, too. "Maybe, at the next elections I'll get involved. It's nothing personal, Behan, but it doesn't look as if the job is getting done. And a change in the roles we're all playing might help break up these sides that are forming."

"It's too late for that," Behan said, venomous. "I knew when you came here, Wyatt Earp, you'd want everything running your way, but the world won't always turn according to your view of it." And Behan stalked off with barely a nod of farewell.

"That's the truth," Wyatt remarked with some despondency.

"Wyatt—"

"I know, Doc. I know."

"Do you?" Doc asked. And he sounded sad. "Come on, then, Wyatt. I'm calling it a night. Walk me home."

CHAPTER TEN:

HALF IN LOVE

Tombstone, Arizona;

January 1881

Doc Holliday had been a year in Tombstone. A year of everyone prospering and Doc behaving like a civilized man. There were tensions in the town, with occasional minor skirmishes between the two loosely formed groups of locals. Doc delighted in the ragged edges of this otherwise peaceful existence, but his personal loyalties meant he was committed to Wyatt Earp—and of course Wyatt was committed to his brother Virgil, who had successfully run for town marshal representing the law-and-order crowd. Doc wasn't quite a neat fit with the Earps and their wives and followers— but then again, the other side, who'd become known as the Cowboys, presented a crew just as motley.

They all managed to jostle along together most days. There were times and places in which the two groups interacted readily enough; there were even a few friendships formed across party lines. The Montagues and Capulets it was not.

A few people remained aloof or refused to declare an allegiance—Kate Elder, for example. She had taken a dislike to Wyatt and his brothers since leaving Dodge City, and would never have cared for their side of the difficulty. Perhaps it was lucky that there was no one on the Cowboys' side that she liked any better. Or at least not enough to prompt her to disoblige Doc.

He was astonished that Kate was still with him, more or less, despite her increasing discomfort over Doc's friendship with Wyatt. When Kate was visiting from Globe, however—as she was at present—she was still loving Doc as fiercely as ever. She was also still as fiercely independent. The only reason she was working less these days was because she'd already amassed a small fortune; it wasn't due to sentimentality. Kate would do business with anyone, so long as they'd bathed recently and they treated her right.

Doc cleared his throat as a cough threatened, but it would not be suppressed. He dug out a handkerchief and let the cough have its way with him. When it was done, he saw it had left a small spot of blood on the linen—but that didn't necessarily mean anything, Doc reminded himself. An effect of the cough's roughness rather than a worsening of the disease's symptoms... He folded the handkerchief with the bloodstain inmost, slipped it away into his coat pocket, and sighed softly enough not to disturb his throat.

There were times when even that much would enervate him for much of the day, but he was determined not to let his health ruin his current plans.

He wanted a few hours to himself. This wasn't always possible, so ensconced as he'd become in the happenings of this town in which everyone knew everyone else's business and didn't mind surmising more. Doc had developed an escape, which involved him discreetly wending his way to the Grand Hotel, known to be the haunt of Curly Bill Brocius and the Cowboys. Doc would take a seat at the corner of the bar nearest the door, work his way through a few whiskies, and ignore the other patrons.

During the day it was quiet enough, as most of the regular patrons in Tombstone and nearby worked the sunlit hours. Curly Bill and his friends worked the ranches out to the west, just beyond the San Pedro River, so they usually sought entertainment in the town of Contention. They came to Tombstone less frequently, on business or when they had a few days free. But if they happened to be there at the Grand Hotel, they would let Doc be, or do no more than exchange a few genial words with him. No doubt Curly Bill was astute enough to realize that ordinarily Doc Holliday would not have been on the conservative side of the argument.

The town's schoolteacher—another man with misaligned loyalties—walked through from the back rooms of the hotel, and spoke with the bartender. When he turned to leave, he caught sight of Doc and hesitated, which seemed to inadvertently become a pause—and their gazes locked. After a moment, Doc deigned to greet him. "Mr. Vaughan."

"Dr. Holliday," the teacher acknowledged, shifting his stash of books to sit in the crook of his elbow. "I trust I find you well."

"Oh, still dying," Doc replied, "but very slowly."

A smile quirked Gregory Vaughan's mobile mouth, and he murmured,

"As are we all." He glanced toward the hotel dining room as if remembering the discretion owed to his young charges—not that they were to be found at the Grand anymore, as Tombstone had at last built a schoolhouse. When Vaughan turned back to Doc, his expression had grown serious. Respectful. "May I ask…?"

Doc considered him narrowly for a long moment—usually enough to dissuade the inquisitive. When Vaughan didn't retreat, however, Doc invited his question with a lift of his chin.

Perhaps Vaughan took that as more of an invitation than Doc intended, for he placed his books on the bar and sat on the barstool beside Doc's. Vaughan was tall enough that he could slide onto the seat without hefting himself up. "Is it true," Vaughan asked sotto voce once he was settled, "that the dry climate here is beneficial to your condition?"

He tried not to recoil. It wasn't as if it weren't obvious that Doc was seriously ill, and God knew this tawdry disease was common enough among the populace—but a gentleman wouldn't have pursued such a personal matter in conversation.

"Forgive me," Vaughan was saying now, his voice smooth though Doc noticed his nearest hand trembled; Vaughan pressed it flat against the topmost book as if trying to still it. "I am incorrigibly curious…"

Doc attempted a response, partly for the sake of politeness, true, but mostly because there were too few people in Tombstone who could use the word 'incorrigible' in a sentence. "Do you inquire on behalf of someone who…?"

"No. No, I don't have even that as an excuse." Vaughan cast a glance over Doc from head to toe, but uneasily, almost as if he couldn't help himself. "I was just curious." He patted the books, and offered, "Perhaps an inevitable trait of teachers. Forgive me, if you will, and forget I mentioned it."

Doc had found himself glancing over Vaughan as well—and he noticed, not for the first time, that while Vaughan was tall and apparently healthy, he was also slender as a reed. The comparison between his frame and Doc's was not so mortifying as many such were, even if Vaughan's leanness was natural and his own was not.

Their gazes met and locked again, and for a moment the vulnerability relating to Vaughan's apology became vulnerability of another kind. It seemed that Vaughan was also imagining his body and Doc's in close conjunction though in a different context… An answer, or perhaps more precisely a confirmation, softened his expression still further, and—

A ruction from the front door broke this momentary understanding as Curly Bill and the Cowboys strode into the bar, calling out in high spirits. "Line up those whiskies!" – "We're back and we're thirsty!" – "Good Lord, what's going on? It is *far* too quiet in here."

In the very first moment of this interruption, Vaughan had blushed—as if Doc needed any further clues to the tendency of his thoughts—and though Vaughan was hailed by his friends, he stood and made his exit as quickly as he could.

Which left Doc sitting alone at his corner of the bar again, while the tumultuous Cowboys milled around down the other end or claimed their preferred chairs and tables, and the bartender began pouring shots. Doc took a sip of his own whiskey and—

He started as his glance slid across the mirror behind the bar, and he realized that one of the Cowboys was standing close behind his right shoulder, shadowy in the dimness of the room.

A moment later, the figure tilted his head up just far enough that his eyes gleamed in a stray beam of light—Doc mentally ran through the disreputable cowpunchers he knew, quickly placed that provoking stance, and found himself grinning in welcome. "Pilgrim!"

They stared at each other via the mirror's reflection. John Ringo appeared to be amused. "You're not leading the schoolteacher into temptation, are you, Holliday?"

"No, no. Quite the opposite, I assure you."

"What, he's leading you…?" A smile glinted on Ringo's handsome face, and without waiting for an invitation he settled himself on the stool that Vaughan had vacated. Ringo looked… self-assured. Almost civilized. And Doc had been assuming Johnny Ringo must have run mad and been lost to life this past year.

"Made friends, have you?" Doc asked in skeptical tones, tipping his head to indicate Curly Bill's crew.

Ringo's smile grew into something oddly wholesome, and he replied, "I've been working on Old Man Clanton's ranch when I'm not in the San Simon. I usually stay behind when this lot come into town."

"Working and…?" Everyone knew most of the ranchers were as involved in rustling and related crimes as their outlaw allies, even if such involvement was no more than a carelessness about the provenance of the cattle they pastured.

"Never you mind about that," Ringo countered. "I heard you've made friends here, too."

"You left the window open!" Doc blurted, unable to retrace the path of his thoughts, but suddenly remembering he had cause for resentment. "In the room at the boarding house. It may well have slipped your mind, but you left the window open when you absconded—and for once I slept through till morning, and suffered a full dose of the night air."

Ringo was watching him impassively, appearing neither guilty nor concerned.

"Inconsiderate of you," Doc muttered, turning away with a sniff, "to say the least."

"The night air's no good for you," Ringo murmured as if pondering his memories.

An ill-timed cough provided a more explicit response than Doc cared for. He didn't deign to add any words to it, even once he was able.

"Well, you know they say whiskey cures all ills," John said—and he gestured to the bartender for a bottle.

"What miracle is this?" Curly Bill asked in hearty tones, obviously playing to the room. He stood by them watching while John filled Doc's glass and one for himself. "What's your secret, Doc? We rarely get three words out of Johnny in a month, and here y'all are, having a proper conversation."

John laughed under his breath, and produced a battered old volume from a coat pocket. "We're talking books, Bill. Join us if you want."

"Oh, no, not me!" He took a step back, his hands warding off the very idea.

Doc took the book from John's grasp and turned his back to Curly Bill while he looked at the spine. "Keats again," Doc remarked. "You've really taken to the man."

"His words, anyway," John replied.

Curly Bill had found someone more interested to go bother among the cluster of Cowboys at the other end of the room.

"You know… he died young, of a consumption."

After a moment, John prompted, "And you?"

"Not so young as he was, anyway. I'll be thirty this year, if I make it through to August."

John laughed again, and picked up his glass and the bottle of whiskey. "Let's get comfortable, Doc."

"Oh, my…" he murmured, feeling far too easily persuaded—and then he laughed when he realized that John only meant retiring to the leather couch placed against the wall behind them. Doc picked up his own glass, and brought it and the book of poetry with him. They settled, both sliding low on the seat so their heads were supported by the sturdy back of the couch, sharing an illicit hot glance as they each remembered sharing a bed—though this time, at least, they remained a careful yard apart. They silently toasted each other, before Doc murmured, "How civilized you've become, Johnny Ringo. How refined."

"Not so much as all that," John replied easily.

"Scratch the surface, and—?"

"You'll find the same savage."

"Glad to hear it. Myself, likewise."

And yet they spent the hours of the afternoon reading poetry and conversing as if they were both gentlemen and glad to be so.

Doc didn't drink too much, for he was expected at the Oriental Saloon's poker tables that evening, as usual. "You'll have to excuse me," he said to John as the clock neared six. "I have a living to make."

"Cards?" John queried. "I'll come with you."

Doc took a breath and paused for a moment's consideration. Eventually he said, "I'm a regular at the Oriental."

"All right." John was already standing and shrugging on his coat. He seemed unconcerned about visiting an establishment strongly associated with the Earp brothers… Which Doc supposed was reasonable, given that Doc himself had spent his afternoon at the Grand.

With a shrug, Doc turned and headed for the door. "All right, then. If anyone gives you grief, tell 'em you're with me."

John grinned. "My reputation's tarnished enough already, thanks."

Doc caught his eye and they shared a laugh, before walking a block along Allen Street shoulder to shoulder.

Once Doc was settled in his usual place, John claimed a seat at the bar opposite him, and he sat there watching Doc for all the hours that Doc played, those pure blue eyes of his becoming more and more heated. Which luckily for both of them only sharpened Doc's wits rather than distracting or befuddling him.

"Reminds me of old times," Doc murmured in Johnny's ear, when he took a break from the game around midnight. "Me cutting loose, and you loitering in the background unwilling to participate."

"Flamboyance don't appeal to everyone, Holliday."

Doc winked at him, and they grinned just about as wide as each other.

It seemed already understood between them that they would fuck that night, so as they walked out of the Oriental together at two in the morning, Doc simply asked, "Do you have a room?"

"Not yet," John replied.

"Come to mine, then. I'm at Fly's, on Fremont Street."

John turned to keep pace with Doc readily enough, though he asked, "Don't you share with your woman?"

"Yes, but she'll be out working. We agreed a signal to indicate that one of us already has company."

"We could just ride out of town, Holliday."

Doc drew his coat collar closer around his throat. It was true that they'd fucked in the wild before now, but it was mid-winter, and Doc was more reliant on human comforts these days. "Come to my room," he murmured again—and moments later they were at the lodging house, and climbing the stairs to Doc's room.

Kate, as predicted, was absent, so Doc flung one end of her red scarf over the top of the door before closing and locking it. "If she returns and sees the scarf, she'll go stay with one of her woman friends instead—and, yes, you can infer as much as you wish from that."

John laughed and shook his head, seeming at least mildly impressed. But then he turned serious in the blink of an eye—and he strode toward Doc, grabbed his shoulders, and pressed a hungry kiss to his mouth.

They fucked with Johnny's old urgency, and then again slowly with an attempt at the finesse Doc had taught him. Afterwards they lay sprawled on the bed together, enjoying the mutual contact though Doc couldn't have classified it as an embrace. They dozed, and woke, and settled in closer, seeking each other's warmth before dozing again.

Soon enough the approaching dawn lightened the window, making the room seem drab by comparison. John tightened his hold on Doc for a moment, pressed his mouth fiercely to Doc's temple, and then pulled away to sit up and start gathering his clothes.

Doc felt an alarming poignancy at this parting—and no doubt it put him in mind of their last farewell, for he found himself observing, "Did you find your soul again, brother? Does that explain the change in you?"

"What?" John said, frowning in puzzlement as if his mind were already elsewhere. "No."

"It's as if you're at least halfway sane now." Doc considered the matter for a moment. "Maybe it's the poetry. Is it the poetry, pilgrim? Because I can't attribute this to keeping company with Curly Bill and his boys!"

John was almost dressed, but he paused now, and reached for his book of Keats which had been placed on the nightstand beside the bed. He began slowly leafing through the pages, as if looking for something.

"Have you read 'Lamia'?" Doc asked into a silence that was beginning to feel somewhat eerie. "I rather liked 'Lamia'. It teaches one not to inquire too deeply into the things one most cherishes."

Eventually John reached the last page, which must have been his goal all along, for he slipped a few folded pieces of paper out from where the book's endpaper had come loose from the back cover. He shuffled through them, and then glared a challenge at Doc before dropping his gaze again. "It's called 'Death'." And he began to read.

> *"The man falls dead to the sun-hot sand; blood weeping beautifully for a moment and then drying.*
>
> *"I've sent another soul to the fires of Hell. For a moment those fires warm me;*
>
> *"I know success for a moment, I know peace; blessed reward from He who reigns beneath,*
>
> *"From the Father, the Son and the Evil Flame.*
>
> *"But then the cold returns, the need, the pain.*
>
> *"Another soul I'll have to find to send Him, since He is so dissatisfied with mine."*

Doc just stared at the fellow. After a quiet breath, John folded the papers again and tucked them away safely in the back of his book. And then he waited a little longer, turned half away from Doc as if wanting to present the smallest possible target. When the silence continued, John stood and resumed dressing.

"Brother!" Doc exclaimed at last. "Don't leave *now*, for the sake of all that's…"

John cast him a wry glance, which conveyed a sense of Doc's failure more forcefully than anything else could have.

Doc scrambled up to kneel on the bed, naked in all possible ways. "That was… unexpected. And astonishing! I was too astonished to speak." He made a successful grab for the book and managed to retrieve the poem.

John was watching him warily, one hand hovering as if ready to reclaim the book or reach for his gun at any moment.

It was cold out from under the bedclothes without another body to warm him. Doc tried to suppress a cough, and then surrendered to it for the sake of getting it over with so he could talk again. John waited patiently enough through all that. At last Doc continued, "That was very… modern. Forgive me if I hardly know what to say in response. It was as… vivid and as true as anything more traditional."

The silence stretched further.

Doc coughed again, still staring at the poem—and then for lack of anything more intelligent to say, he blurted, "You haven't signed it!"

A sardonic grin, and at last Ringo stepped forward to retrieve the paper from Doc's hands and rest it on the nightstand. He produced a pencil, and wrote *John R.* at the bottom of the page, as naturally as if that were how he signed everything.

Doc stared at the signature for a moment while John gathered the book and the other papers, and then folded 'Death' into the collection and slid it away.

"John Rex!" Doc declared in jubilation. "King… King of the Cowboys!"

Ringo laughed under his breath, picked up his hat—but paused partway to the door.

The rising sun cast a glow through the natural ripples in the window glass, creating a weird effect in the corner of the room, almost as if a ghost made of daylight was endeavoring to appear. Johnny seemed to notice it, too, and he turned toward it with great curiosity—but when Doc was overtaken by another, harsher cough, John's attention returned to him.

This time there was more than a spot or two of blood, and Doc had no handkerchief to hand. He grasped the corner of a sheet—but before he could use it to wipe away the evidence, Johnny was kneeling on the bed before him, pressed against him from knees to hips, and he was holding Doc's head in both hands while he leaned in and… almost reverentially lapped up the blood with his tongue.

"Don't!" Doc protested—but Johnny held firm and finished his task. Most people kept their distance from such things, and with good reason, but when had Doc ever known Johnny Ringo to be sensible? He sighed, and murmured, "Brother, you may well be half in love with easeful Death, but there are kinder ways to go than this."

Johnny pressed a kiss to Doc's mouth, and then clambered back off the bed. He turned again to the corner of the room where the light was now nothing more than mundane sunlight—and with a last enigmatic glance at Doc he strode to the door and was gone.

Doc sighed, wrapped the blankets snugly around himself, and burrowed back into the bed.

CHAPTER ELEVEN:

LAMBENT

Tombstone, Arizona;

January 1881

It had been a fine night, so fine, and John didn't want to sully the intensity with the everyday. So, he slipped into the stables and collected his bedroll and blanket, before walking right out of town. He strode through the crisp air of early morning, enjoying the length of his legs, the roll of his hips, the ease of his breath. After an hour or two the lack of sleep caught up with him; before it could overtake him, Johnny found a dry old watercourse tucked away in the larger landscape, and a dilapidated old tree under which to shelter. He spread out the bedroll, wrapped himself up, and within moments was deep in the sleep of the damned.

Even once he'd returned to town, John still wasn't in the mood for other people, so when he wandered into the Grand Hotel, he didn't greet anyone but simply settled on the barstool that yesterday had been claimed by Doc Holliday. Maybe people would take that as enough of a hint to leave him be.

Not that Curly Bill was ever ready, willing or able to take a hint. "Had fun last night, did ya?" he asked in insinuating tones, leaning on the bar beside John and visibly waiting for an answer.

John considered him, but soon decided that nothing had changed. Curly Bill didn't have the imagination to even suspect all the sins that Johnny had committed. "Yeah," he eventually agreed.

"Yeah, a *powerful* amount of fun!" Curly Bill hooted in laughter—but then he added in quieter tones, "Careful of that Doc Holliday, though. I wouldn't trust him… not with a grain of sand, though I owned a whole desert."

"I don't."

"Good! Good. *He's* all right, I guess, but I don't like his friends—they can't mind their own damned business." Curly Bill looked as if he were about to walk away muttering to himself discontentedly, but then he apparently decided to stay and say it out loud. "What's that Wyatt Earp got over him to make him so loyal? Ain't they the strangest partners you ever saw?"

John laughed under his breath as he belatedly gained an insight into the nature of Doc Holliday's attachment to Wyatt Earp. Not that Curly Bill or the Earps, or maybe anyone other than John and perhaps that Kate Elder, would be aware of it. But now it seemed plain as day. Doc's deepest affections were engaged, no doubt a rare happenstance, and John had heard and well believed that there was no reasoning with such things. He laughed again at this proof that Doc's instinct for self-defeat was as strong as his own, or maybe even stronger.

"What's amusing you?" Curly Bill demanded.

Time to deflect this curiosity—though only the most obvious change of topic occurred to John. "I don't like them much, either," he said, "but I reckon Wyatt Earp saved your life back when Fred White died."

Curly Bill huffed and turned away again uneasily, before saying in low, sincere tones, "I was as sorry about that as anyone. I can't say it about most marshals, but Fred White was a fair-minded man."

"Yeah, and folks here wanted to lynch you for a killing—I heard them calling for it—and it was Earp who got you safe to the court in Tucson and told them it was an accident."

"It *was* an accident!"

"And it was Earp who made sure the judge heard that."

"I know, I know! If he hadn't buffaloed me without cause…" Curly Bill lifted a hand to the back of his skull, as if it were still tender all these months later.

John just shook his head. He could try reminding Bill that Wyatt had—understandably enough—assumed the Cowboy was still armed, but Curly Bill wasn't amenable to reason on this matter. A grudge was a grudge.

"Anyhow…" Curly Bill huffed some more. "Never will like him, nor what he stands for—and they sure as hell don't like us." He elbowed John in the ribs, and repeated, "You be careful of Holliday. If the time comes when he has to choose between you and his mate Wyatt, I know which way it'll go."

And John figured he did, too. But that was all right. The town was a mess of conflicting interests, and this made no real difference—not when Curly Bill wasn't aware of the interests that John and Doc had in common as well.

He was deep into the whiskey early that evening, as the dusk loitered for a while in the far reaches of the room and then stealthily arched up to the ceiling and drifted down over the queerly hushed gatherings of men.

Johnny sighed as a lamp was lit on the far wall behind him. He could see the glow reflected in the mirror, blooming warm over his shoulder… and then there was something more, something taking form, and the blur of light resolved into… a man, taking a considered step toward him.

Could it be the son of the Devil making an appearance? Johnny glanced around at the other people in the room, but no one seemed to notice anything amiss. Maybe they were under an enchantment so they couldn't see, or Johnny was bewitched so that he alone could. The figure was both like and unlike Johnny's lover; he had the same golden beauty of face and form, but he was dressed in a full set of regular clothes, and they were blues and tans rather than his lover's eternal choice of black. He'd advanced to stand behind Johnny, just as he himself had waited on Doc Holliday the previous day, misaligned so they could watch each other in the mirror. Such a gorgeous vision to conjure…

"Damned fine whiskey," John muttered to himself, taking another vitalizing mouthful.

Then a hand settled on Johnny's shoulder, and he started, his heart suddenly clamoring.

A soft smile quirked the other's mouth. "My apologies. I thought you had seen me." He dropped his hand and stepped up to the bar at Johnny's side. "I understand you're a man it would be useful to know."

"You—" Johnny felt lost, and fearful… and excited. The stranger stood there—and he *was* human, he was regular flesh and blood. He didn't glow; that must have been a trick of the lamplight. He wore boots, well-worn but well cared for—and it was this detail that grounded him in the everyday world for Johnny. "I don't know you," he said.

"No, but if I may introduce myself." He offered his right hand. "My name's Lucian."

"Lucifer?" Johnny echoed in surprise.

"Lucian," he repeated. "It means 'of light'."

Johnny stared hard at the fellow for a long moment, and when he didn't flinch, when he in fact remained perfectly at ease, Johnny took the offered hand and shook. "John Ringo."

"Pleased to meet you, Mr. Ringo."

"Likewise," John found himself saying. He was usually far warier of strangers, especially when they were as unnerving as this one—but if the son of the Devil had ever appeared to Johnny in the form of a man, then surely he would be very much like this.

"I have a business proposition for you," Lucian announced after a moment in which John might have been supposed to inquire his purpose. "A couple who are returning to California, having made a small fortune here in silver. They require protection."

John considered this, but had to ask, "Why me? Why someone who's found on the wrong side of the law, often as not?"

"You have a reputation for… fierceness." Lucian was holding his gaze as if he'd never known fear. "They trust me—and if you give me your word, I'll trust you."

Lord, though, did he really want the hassle of a trip to California, sober and behaving civilized? Not to mention feeling obliged to visit his sisters in San José and risking their strait-laced disapproval of what he'd become. And then to travel all the way back again, as he guessed he would. Pima County had proved far more welcoming to John than he'd come to expect. Though maybe the couple would pay enough to make the journey worthwhile…

He'd meant to say, 'I don't know,' but the words that left his mouth were, "Maybe, then. Yeah."

A smile rewarded him, bright now rather than soft; bright and intriguing. "Let's talk some more. Come back to my lodgings. I've whiskey there, too."

John glanced around the barroom, but no one seemed to be paying them any mind. "All right," he agreed with a shrug. He left a few coins on the bar by his glass—probably more than he needed to, but it wouldn't do to be tight-fisted under the gaze of a potential business partner—and then John stood and followed the stranger out of the saloon.

No one took any notice of them as they slipped into the lodging house and headed upstairs. Not that anyone would care about them sharing, out here at the edge of civilization; Doc had taught him that. In the East, John had heard, people were in a position to demand privacy—and while that was attractive enough in many ways, John wouldn't have been able to mask his real intent so well in circumstances such as these.

Lucian opened the door to his room, apparently having left it unlocked, and ushered John inside. There wasn't much in there other than the regular furnishings. Nothing personal of Lucian's other than saddlebags propped by a bedpost, and the bags hardly seemed full.

The door was locked now, though Lucian left the key in the lock which John was grateful for; he felt secure but not confined. Lucian was pouring two nips of whiskey, and he brought one over to John with the most bewitching smile… John took the proffered glass and was about to raise it to take a drink—but Lucian didn't stop, he pressed forward at the same measured yet determined pace, and he leant in to urge his mouth against John's.

They were still for a moment, but then John's surprise thawed a little, and he opened his lips to voice a query, maybe a protest, maybe not—and the other took advantage of him, and transformed the slight movement into the boldest of kisses. Johnny voiced an inarticulate objection but then that changed, too, into a needy groan.

A moment later they broke apart. Lucian grinned, taking the glass from John's hand and putting it down out of the way. "Do you want to fuck?" he asked, without even a shade of shame in the clear blunt words.

And the Devil only knew Johnny *did* want to, but could this be the very *least* wise in all these years of unwise impulses? John backed away a pace, cast a serious look across Lucian and around him—but the man didn't appear to have a soul. Perhaps he had lost it in a bargain of some kind, just as Johnny had, so that was either reassuring or not depending on one's perspective.

"Mr. Ringo…?" Lucian asked.

He had an accent that was English, or something like, and somehow both warm and cool. The Devil's son had had no accent at all, Johnny reflected, or none that he could identify, though the demon had the most beautiful voice, modulated as if it were music. If Lucian's voice reminded him of anyone, it might be Doc Holliday, though without the drawl—and that name prompted the reflection that Johnny had felt superbly satisfied only hours before as dawn broke, he'd felt the lust had been burned out of him—but here he was, hungry once more. Ravenous.

Lucian's gaze fixed on Johnny's mouth with intent, and John took another step away—and he found he'd been backing toward the bed, not the door, which seemed to indicate the decision was made. A moment later they'd fallen entangled across the bed, and were mouthing kisses like crazed things.

John woke from a doze, and returned to contemplating Lucian's beauty. He hadn't been able to tear his gaze away while they fucked and neither had he wanted to. Lucian was nothing more nor less than human, that was clear enough, but he was so perfect, so unblemished that Johnny suspected he was the Word made flesh, new-formed. Could it possibly be that Lucian was the mortal incarnation of his lover?

"*Lucian appears…*" John whispered to himself. "*For the Devil was so pleased with Johnny Ringo that He gave His only Son, that Johnny who had nothing but pain and craving may not die but have someone to fuck.*"

"What was that?" Blue-green eyes blinked awake and considered him calmly.

John shifted away a little and propped himself up on an elbow the better to watch this man. "You inspire me," he said.

"To what? Hunger?" A hand found the hardest part of Johnny and wrapped around it, and a smile broadened that delicious mouth. "Good. Come back down here."

"To poetry," he confessed, even as he moved to follow their mutual wishes.

Lucian laughed, a full-throated and happy sound—though he also said in scornful tones, "Forget that. We don't need that."

Johnny gathered Lucian close again, for in that moment he also had a rather more earthy priority.

Dawn found Johnny sitting cross-legged on the floor—under the window for the growing light, but turned toward the bed so he could still feast his gaze. He dug the Keats volume from his coat pocket, along with the only stub of pencil he had left, and then leafed through his small collection of loose paper for a blank page.

Having found one, he settled in with it placed flat on his book, and the book held firm on one knee. The words themselves didn't take long to write, as they'd been welling in his mind through all the hours he'd spent in bed, asleep or awake. He took care, though, to form the letters clearly.

> *'Fucking L–'*
> *I lie behind him, fucking him, holding him close to me;*
> *An arm locked around his neck so he can't move, so I'm safe from him,*
> *For there is violence between us.*
> *His surrender to me lacks emotion, as if he does not care;*
> *No trace of resentment, no spice of defiance,*
> *But surely he cares, surely he bides his time, revenge burning hot and slow in his head and his heart.*
> *For now I trust him*
> *Not an inch.*
> *I tighten my hold, and he turns his face slightly toward me; no more reaction than that.*
> *I am devastated anew by his beauty.*

He considered it as a whole, liking the shape his marks made on the paper, and then he read it through carefully. It occurred to him that the words were as much about the son of the Devil as about the mortal Lucian, probably more so… but maybe that was inevitable. And maybe Lucian should know—or Johnny needed him to know—that Johnny Ringo wasn't fooled.

John lay the poem on the dresser to await a reader. And then he slipped back into the bed, his cool flesh seeking Lucian's warmth.

He woke later that morning to a cold room and empty bed. Blurrily he looked around for any clue as to Lucian's whereabouts, but there was nothing. When Johnny hauled himself out of the bed, he saw that the saddlebags were gone—and his poem was nothing more than ashes on top of the dresser. A few fragments of paper had burned edges but contained no words, and the rest was gone. Johnny touched gentle fingertips to the ashes, and pondered them.

It wasn't that the poem itself had been destroyed, for that was held safe in his own mind. But he wondered why Lucian had felt the need to do this. The obvious reason, Johnny supposed, was that it contained a secret Lucian didn't want betrayed. But could he really think Johnny so reckless as to share the true nature of their desires with anyone who wouldn't understand…?

John strode over to pick up his coat, but found that the Keats volume and the poems hidden within it were safe. So that was something. His stub of a pencil was missing, though. It was small, so John hunted about for it, kneeling to examine the cracks between the floorboards—with no luck.

After the third time around the same space he sighed, and instead clambered clumsily into his clothes. Alone, he slipped out of the lodging house with no one noticing, and then returned to the Grand Hotel. He sat again on the same barstool—Doc's barstool—so that Lucian would know where to find him. And he waited.

The Cowboys also knew where to find him, of course. Two of the Clanton brothers, Ike and Billy, swung by on their way out of town, heading home to their father's ranch. "Ready, Johnny?" Ike asked, more of a prompt than a question.

"Not yet," he replied.

Billy, the big dumb boy, immediately looked worried. "We were expected yesterday. The old man won't be happy as it is."

"You don't take this job for granted!" Ike warned Johnny. "There's a dozen men like you looking for work."

John sighed and shook his head. "It's usually me out there tending to things and covering for you staying too long in town. Don't seem right you can't return the favor."

The two of them exchanged glances, full of misgivings. Eventually Ike said, "We'll go saddle up. You finish your drink and come join us."

"Not yet, I said. I'll meet you out there, and if the old man wants to fire me, that's his privilege." John met each of their gazes in turn, and then deliberately poured himself another shot.

"Blazes!" Ike swore, earning himself a reproving stare from the bartender.

"Come on, Billy," he muttered, before striding to the door as if all wrath was about to break loose.

The Clantons were met by Curly Bill coming in with the harsh light of midday behind him; the three of them conferred for a long moment. Curly Bill glanced at John more than once as Ike angrily shrugged his shoulders. After a time, the Clantons stepped out, and Curly Bill came in and stood close by John's shoulder in order to speak confidentially. "Trouble you want help with?"

"Nothing like that," Johnny replied.

"I'll stay if you need me."

Johnny grinned at him, meeting Curly Bill's gaze for a rare moment of sincerity. "No need," he said, "but I thank you for the offer."

Curly Bill considered him for one moment more—and then nodded, and he headed for the door. "Don't take too long!" he called over his shoulder.

When Bill looked back for a response, Johnny lifted his chin in acknowledgment. Then Curly Bill disappeared into the severity of the day, and the doors swung closed behind him. Johnny took a mouth of whiskey and resumed waiting, warmed by memories and fancies.

Several whiskies later, and the world was dark outside. Was it that same night, or had several days drifted by? Johnny hardly knew. But he saw a reflection in the mirror of a man spun from gold, and at last a flesh-and-blood hand settled on his shoulder, and Lucian was there at his side. "I knew I'd find you here," the other said.

"And I knew you'd know," Johnny replied, which was far more of an admission than he'd wanted to give. "You said you had work for me."

Lucian nodded, though his focus turned internal as if pondering. A moment later he was looking directly at Johnny and announcing, "That fell through. But there's another opportunity I'm following up…"

"Yeah?"

"A prospector looking for silver in the foothills of the Dragoons, wanting protection from the Apache. He's willing to share a portion of any proceeds."

It sounded plausible enough, but Johnny had to wonder if this scheme would come to nothing as well. Still, what did he care, really? There were other things he wanted from this man who was both like Johnny and nothing like him, like the son of the Devil and nothing like. Maybe it was his own whiskey-blurred gaze, but Johnny was aware of something large and dark that hovered restlessly behind Lucian now, as if it were the smoke to his fire. Was this the mortal's soul, or the presence of another being, or a presentiment of the threat Lucian brought with him? Did it even matter?

"Still got your room?" Johnny asked.

A quiet moment passed between them, while Lucian's smile grew. "Yes."

"Let's go make use of it, then."

When he stood, Johnny wasn't quite sure on his feet, but that gave Lucian an excuse to offer his arm to lean on, and they walked down the street together feeling shameless.

They fucked, and slept, and when Johnny woke in the darkest hours of the night, he was ready to fuck some more. There wasn't much light in the room, but there was enough to see scratch marks down Lucian's shoulder-blade— his left one, just where his wings would be. John paused, and asked, "What happened?" He traced the slight wounds with gentle fingertips; most were grazes, but three were deep enough to show darkly. "What happened?" he asked again. "Did I do that?" Not that he could remember any such thing, but the marks felt fresh.

Lucian cast him an odd look over his shoulder. "No. It wasn't you."

He didn't seem inclined to talk, and Johnny was likewise disinclined to wait any longer. Johnny pushed himself home, locked his hold on Lucian, and found his face pressed to the scratch marks. He lapped at them with his tongue, and one of the wounds responded with a welling of blood. It tasted hot—sharp—potent. He swallowed and it went right to his heart. His orgasm was… a conflagration. Divine.

They slept; their two bodies welded into one.

But when Johnny woke late the next morning, he was alone.

Chapter Twelve:

Twisting the Tail of the Tiger

Tombstone, Arizona;

March 1881

Doc showed up at the Oriental Saloon just as Wyatt was shuffling the deck of cards for a new round of faro. Wyatt found himself smiling despite a decided preference for maintaining a serious demeanor while working. But a smile was a natural reaction to Doc's presence. Even Virgil, who would roll his eyes at the very *thought* of Doc, could never prevent his pressed-together lips also quirking in wry amusement.

"Evening, Wyatt," Doc greeted him, ignoring the waiting players and taking the chair beside Wyatt as if it were his natural right. "I trust I find you gainfully employed."

"I'm doing all right," Wyatt allowed.

"'All right'?" one of the players protested under his breath. When Wyatt chose to meet his gaze rather than ignore him, the punter continued in regular tones, "Don't mean no disrespect. Other bankers might cheat, but I reckon a smart banker has the same edge—or better."

Wyatt nodded once, and said, "I'll take that as a compliment, then."

The player visibly relaxed, and presumably that was that—but Doc was ferreting around under the table, and when he sat up again he was brandishing the case keep. "I'll prove him honest, if you like," Doc offered. "Though no doubt you'd prefer the excitement of bucking the tiger rather than the triviality of counting cards."

The punter was trying to suppress a grin, and Wyatt found himself smiling again. There were a lot of people who were sensibly wary of Doc, but for those who dared to enjoy him there were riches to be had. A glance from one to the other of them, and the player obviously decided he could be brave enough to banter. "Thanks all the same, but no. If *he's* cheating, I reckon *you'd* cheat worse!"

Silence for a moment as the breath of everyone within hearing distance snagged in their throats. Then Doc barked out a laugh that became a cough, and Wyatt guffawed, and the others all chuckled in relief. Talk rose around them again, and Wyatt took the opportunity to break the momentary connection between himself and the player. He turned to Doc and quietly asked, "Where's Kate?"

"Oh, off on another adventure, I imagine," Doc replied easily.

"You weren't in mind of an adventure?"

"Sure I am, Wyatt. I'm here with you, aren't I?" Doc smiled at him, all warmth and a comparative lack of complications. Though Wyatt figured that he was in no way clever enough to unpack all of Doc's meanings from even his simplest statements.

The cards were well shuffled by now, so Wyatt loaded them into the dealer's box. "Place your bets for a new round," he announced in his working voice. One of the punters wanted to buy an extra hundred dollars' worth of checks, so Wyatt took the man's cash and slid over the required chips. He drew the first card once all the players were paying attention again. "Queen of Hearts is the soda," he said, discarding it as was the custom. "All checks down? All right, then." And he drew the next two cards for play.

A few hours later, Wyatt was ready for a break, so he handed the faro bank over to one of the Oriental's other dealers and accompanied Doc to stand at the bar. He must be getting old, Wyatt mused, when a short evening of sitting would have him stretching out the kinks in his back like a day's riding used to do.

Doc was watching the process, with an amused glint in his eye. "Wyatt?" he prompted.

"Back's all knotted up," Wyatt grumbled under his breath.

"Ah, you look supple as a snake to me."

Wyatt cast his friend a look. He was never quite sure whether to be flattered or offended when Doc directed that suggestive tone his way. Although he didn't suppose Doc might mean it. The truth was more likely that Doc was being outrageous for the fun of it.

Either way, a change of topic seemed in order. "You off to a poker game?" Wyatt asked.

Doc sighed, and turned away to lean back against the bar. "No… I don't think so…" Another sigh, and then Doc asked, "Can I interest you in supper, Wyatt? Care to join me at China Mary's, perhaps?"

"Maybe," he replied. Wyatt wasn't feeling very hungry yet; not enough to tempt him away from the faro table, anyway. "You don't want to be earning tonight?"

A moment stretched, before Doc turned back to slowly consider him. "Money's not the be-all and end-all, Wyatt. Besides, I already have plenty. I'd rather stay with you, if I may presume I'm welcome."

"'Plenty'?" Wyatt mused. He wondered how much that might be—not for Doc, but for himself. When would enough be enough? The Earp brothers' mining claims were starting to draw a good income, and Wyatt was doing all right with his interest in the Oriental's faro banks. Which wasn't so bad, though the truth was he'd be doing a whole hell of a lot better if Behan hadn't talked him out of running for sheriff of the newly formed Cochise County… It had seemed like a good deal at the time, with the county seat right here in Tombstone, and Behan promising Wyatt the undersheriff position and a fair share of the abundant income—but Wyatt was coming to regret the matter.

How much was plenty…? Well, one thing for sure was that Wyatt didn't have close to enough yet.

"Plenty for now," Doc was clarifying about his own situation, for once apparently oblivious to Wyatt's distracted thoughts—and then Doc broke off when Virgil suddenly loomed at Wyatt's shoulder, his face fractured in consternation.

"Sandy Bob stagecoach to Benson's been held up," Virgil said in a low, urgent tone, obviously trying to keep this between the three of them. "Not that they scored anything, but Bud Philpot's been killed—"

"The hell you say," Wyatt blurted in shock. Everyone liked Bud—even the Cowboys.

"—and a passenger shot, too. Happened just north of Contention. Bob Paul drove up to Benson before sending a telegram." Virgil was gazing at Wyatt, and then flicked a glance at Doc. "Ride out with me, Wyatt. You, too, Doc."

Wyatt nodded, and Doc straightened up and said, "Of course."

"Pack for a few days. God only knows where this will lead us, but a few days should see the job done."

Doc tapped a knuckle against the polished wood of the bar for luck, and then the three of them strode out of there, amidst a growing buzz of conversation. No matter how discreet Virgil tried to be, news like this traveled faster than anything natural.

Deputy U.S. Marshal Virgil Earp formed a posse including his brothers Wyatt and Morgan, and Doc Holliday. The stagecoach had been carrying a Wells Fargo strongbox containing twenty-six thousand dollars in silver bullion, which was obviously the target of the robbery, so Virgil also sought the company of Wells Fargo agent Marshall Williams—'Marshall' being his first name and not a title. County Sheriff Johnny Behan joined them, along with his deputy Billy Breakenridge. The seven of them rode out of Tombstone around midnight.

It was the small hours of a dark night when they arrived at Drew's Station, which was only a few hundred yards from where the attempted hold-up had taken place. The men at Drew's Station had taken up Bud Philpot's body from the road, and laid him out on a table. Virgil, Wyatt and Behan gathered around to examine him, while the locals—who'd been expecting the stagecoach to halt as usual at their station—told overlapping tales about how they'd instead heard shots, and shouts from the various people involved, anxious whinnying from the horses. They'd run out to see the coach thunder past with the horses in a panicked bolt, and one man grappling with the reins.

Wyatt carefully parted Bud's coat, waistcoat and shirt to find the bullet wound. The flesh was torn but there was very little blood. "Through the heart, or as close as makes no difference. Bud wouldn't have known much."

"It's a damned shame," Virgil intoned. "He was a good man." Then he mused, "Why would they shoot the driver? If the horses bolt, as happened here, the ruffians end up with naught but trail dust."

Behan suggested, "They were aiming at Bob Paul riding shotgun, and missed."

"Guess so," Virgil said in tones that indicated he wasn't agreeing so much as being agreeable.

Wyatt stared down at the body with a sense of foreboding. He'd ridden shotgun for Wells Fargo for a few months when he first came to Tombstone—and Morgan still did so on a regular basis. Perhaps that was one reason why Morgan was keeping a nervous distance.

There was nothing more to learn here. Wyatt turned away, and asked the station men, "Can you show us where you found him?"

It was too dark to pick up the trail of the fleeing highwaymen, so Wyatt and his party prepared to camp where they were for what remained of the night. Behan and Breakenridge headed back to the station, to lay their bedrolls on the floor if they had to, and keep company with Bud. "At least we'll be under a roof," Behan remarked.

"A fine night like this," Virgil opined, "I'm just as happy to be under the stars."

"Goodnight and good luck to you, then," Behan said.

"Sleep well!"

Doc was already stretched out at full length on his back. He lit a cigarette and took a long drag while contemplating the night sky. Once he'd exhaled with only the mildest of coughs, he remarked, "I never knew you were such a romantic, Virgil."

"Well, if I'd known you'd like me for it, Doc, I'd have confessed long ago."

"Ah, a sense of humor, too… I'm impressed! All these depths you've been hiding…"

"All right, all right," Wyatt grumbled as he settled, wrapping himself up as snug as he could in his blanket. "There's barely a few hours till dawn. Let's get some sleep while we can."

"Rest easy, Wyatt." Doc assured him, "Of all the multitude of Earp brothers, you're still my favorite… It seems I underestimated your competition, is all."

"Enough, Doc! Go to sleep." Wyatt glanced at Williams, but while he was watching them, he didn't seem unduly concerned by the repartee. When Williams nodded a goodnight and closed his eyes, Wyatt put his head down—and he knew nothing more until the night was almost done.

Being a town-dweller now, and a gambler, it had been a long time since Wyatt had seen a sunrise. The saloons and hotels on Allen Street in Tombstone were in business all day every day, and Wyatt worked at the faro tables most of the night, then headed home to sleep through the morning. The rhythm of his days was not tied to the natural world, as it must be for the local ranchers and cattlemen, and Wyatt had no regrets about that.

The land was wide open here, with low scrub sparse across the dirt. Standing, Wyatt could see the jagged shapes of mountain ranges on the horizon, distance turning those mammoths into miniatures, showing dark purple against the increasing golden glow to the east. There was a hush, as no one and nothing stirred, not even a breath of air disturbing the silence.

Then the glow broke bright across the edge of the earth and rose like a god emerging from vast waters. The sight became painful, and Wyatt turned his gaze away. For a moment night lingered behind him, but then the light swept across the country from east to west, and everything he could see was now day.

His companions stirred, and Virgil tended to their campfire which had reduced to embers. Soon there was water heating, and Morgan passing around portions of bread and cheese, and Williams grumbling under his breath about a night too short and too cold for comfort.

Doc was sitting quietly on his bedroll, cross-legged and smoking, and contemplating Wyatt. A nod of greeting, and Wyatt turned away, uncertain as always about what Doc found of such interest in him.

Instead of bothering about that, though, Wyatt walked the few yards back to the road, and started searching for the trails left by the robbers. It didn't take him long to find the running footprints of a couple of men, joined by a third. After a hundred yards or so, there was a confusion of hoof-prints, and then a trail formed by perhaps three but probably four horses leading away in a northeasterly direction.

Wyatt looked back toward their makeshift camp to get his bearings. He tied his neckerchief to the highest branch of the nearby scrub—and then lifted his hand to acknowledge Virgil, who was watching him with a keen eye. As Wyatt began walking back toward camp, Virgil signaled his understanding with a nod and a wave, and Wyatt could see him likewise taking his bearings on the direction of the trail.

By the time Wyatt got back to camp, there was a mug of hot coffee waiting for him, and Billy Breakenridge had brought two buckets of water for the Earp party's horses.

Just as they were about to set off, Bob Paul came riding in at a canter, having returned from Benson. "It should have been me," he tersely announced as the posse, already mounted, gathered in front of Drew's Station to greet him. "Bud took ill near Contention, so we stopped and swapped places. It should have been me that was shot."

"You weren't hurt, though, Bob?" Virgil asked.

"No. Not that I've had any sleep this night." Bob left a pause, and then asked, though he obviously knew the answer, "I don't suppose Bud…?"

Virgil shook his head. "No. He's laid out inside."

Bob's posture drooped for a moment, and then lifted against the weight of these consequences. "The passenger didn't survive, either. We got him to a doctor in Benson as fast as we could, but it was already too late. I didn't know him—a Mr. Roerig. Peter Roerig."

No one seemed to recognize the name.

Bob dismounted, and announced, "I'll come with you, if you'll give me a moment to pay my respects."

"You'll be welcome, of course," said Behan. That would make eight of them: the three Earp brothers, Doc, and Marshall Williams; Behan and Breakenridge; and Bob Paul.

"Glad to have you," Virgil agreed. "Wyatt cut the trail just down the road. We'll head off soon as you're ready."

The trail led them in a long arc northeast toward the Dragoon Mountains— avoiding Drew's Station and Ranch to begin with, and then the town of Benson—before curving back toward the San Pedro River.

Along the way the posse found a dilapidated wooden shack which had apparently provided shelter within the past few days. There was a recent campfire out front, and fresh refuse from men and horses, but also signs that the shack had been used regularly in the past. No doubt a useful place to hide out for those wanting to avoid attention.

Inside there was little more than a litter of books. "Huh," said Wyatt, and the other posse members who stepped inside echoed him. Wyatt searched around, picking up the volumes—to discover they were all dime novels. *The Blue Clipper; or The Smuggler Spy* was one, and *The Gray Scalp; or The Blackfoot Brave* another.

The others lost interest, but Wyatt diligently sorted through them all until he found what he wanted. One of the books had been torn down the spine, with the back half missing. *The Buffalo-Trapper*, announced the cover, with the title page adding, *A Tale of Strange Adventure in the North-West*. Wyatt kept looking until he was sure the rest of the volume wasn't in the cabin. Then he headed outside and slid the book into his saddlebag.

"A little light reading?" Behan asked.

"You could say that," Wyatt responded. Doc caught his eye and nodded his understanding, and Virgil was pondering the matter, but no one else seemed to pay it any mind.

The rest of the party was mounted and ready to go, so Wyatt swung up onto his horse, and they headed off with Virgil in the lead keeping an eye on the trail of hoof-prints.

Once they reached the San Pedro River again the hoof-prints turned north and at last, after three long days of careful riding from Drew's Station, the posse found the trail had led them to a ranch belonging to Len Redfield and his brother Hank.

It was immediately apparent they were in the right place. Two hard-ridden horses were hitched to a railing before the house, and someone peered nervously at the newcomers from around the corner of an outbuilding for a long moment—before promptly making a run for the thicker scrub and trees down by the river.

Morgan murmured, "Come on, girl," to his mare, pressed his knees into her sides, and the pair took off after him. Moments later the fellow had been rounded up. Wyatt joined Morgan in case the man tried to break away, but they herded him successfully back toward the open area between the buildings where the posse members were milling about and dismounting.

The Redfield brothers had come out of the front door of the main house, and Virgil went to them to explain something of the group's business. What with the eight members of the posse and their horses, and the three locals and their two mounts, all was chaos.

Wyatt dismounted while Morgan kept an eye on their captive. "What's your name?" Wyatt asked.

The man stared at him hard for a long moment, and then glanced at the deputy's badge Wyatt was wearing. "Luther K-King," he eventually stuttered.

"I'm Wyatt Earp, my brother's a deputy U.S. marshal for Arizona." Wyatt looked about him, and found Behan nearby with nothing occupying him. He handed his reins to Morgan, then took a firm hold on King's upper arm and escorted him over. "This here is John Behan, the county sheriff. Behan, take care of this one for me, would you? The name's Luther King. And *don't* let him talk to the Redfields or anyone else here. I don't want them getting their stories straight."

"All right, Wyatt," Behan replied, considering the anxious King and apparently finding him as unimpressive as did Wyatt.

Wyatt headed for Bob Paul, wanting to consult about how they approached this. "Says he's Luther King. Do you know him?"

"Not by name," Paul replied, "and he doesn't look familiar." Which might not mean much. Tombstone was booming, and it was nigh on impossible now to keep track of everyone.

"He's scared, and he knows why we're here. I don't doubt he's involved." Wyatt paused for a moment's thought, and then said, "I have an idea about how to frighten a confession out of him."

"Go right ahead, Wyatt. Do what you can."

But when Wyatt turned around, he saw exactly what he didn't want to. King was in urgent discussion with the Redfields, and Behan had been distracted by something to do with Breakenridge's reins and bridle. Wyatt muttered a curse under his breath and glanced back at Paul. It didn't need saying that Behan had just disqualified himself from being trusted with anything relating to justice in this case.

A moment later, Hank Redfield unhitched one of the local horses, sprang onto it, and galloped off—heading southeast once he was past the ranch's fence, Wyatt noted. He stood with his hands on his hips, watching Redfield go. Someone in their party should have been able to ride off after him, but everyone had dismounted by now, and they'd been caught short. Anyway, there was still Luther King to question, and it seemed clear that King or Len

Redfield or both would know Hank's destination.

"Right," said Wyatt, meaning business. He went to grab Luther King by the collar, and started walking him toward the house. "I'll talk to this one inside, if you don't mind, Mr. Redfield."

Wyatt and King were already on the steps leading up to the door. Redfield seemed to realize he was being given little choice in the matter; he muttered an ironic, "You're welcome." Then he made to follow them.

"No, you wait there," Wyatt told their reluctant host. "Bob, you were just as much a part of this as Mr. King; you come in. And, Doc, I want you, too."

Bob Paul had already been close on their heels. Doc was no doubt surprised at being invited, but he simply followed them, saying, "As you wish, Wyatt."

Soon, King was sitting on a hardback chair in the middle of the only clear space in the front room, and Wyatt and Bob were looming over him. Doc leant back against the door, now closed, and lit up a smoke, making for a nonchalant threat. There'd be no escaping past him.

"You know why we're here," Wyatt finally said to King after a long, imposing silence. "The Sandy Bob stagecoach was robbed just before Drew's Station on its way to Benson. Bud Philpot was shot and killed—and you were part of it."

None of that would have been news to Luther King, but he paled at this mention of murder—and the murder of a popular man, at that.

"That's not all," Wyatt continued. He paused, letting King's fear intensify. "You know better than me how many shots were fired; how many went wild. You're lucky Mr. Paul here wasn't hit. He had the reins that night."

King glanced from Wyatt to Wyatt's grim colleague, and back again.

"One of those wild shots hit a passenger." Wyatt leaned in a little closer. "A woman," he announced. If Paul was surprised into a reaction by this untruth, he turned it readily enough into an echo of Wyatt's threatening posture.

King had gone paler still, and his mouth worked as he tried to find his voice. "A-a woman?" he asked.

"Not just any woman, either," Wyatt continued. For a moment he leaned in closer still, but then he shifted up again. "Do you know Miss Elder, Mr. King? Kate Elder." Wyatt gestured behind him with one hand. "Companion to my friend here, Doc Holliday."

An inarticulate squeak of terror greeted these words.

Wyatt was aware of Doc shifting his weight back onto his feet and standing tall again. With his reputation, he need hardly do more.

"I didn't—" King began babbling. "I wasn't—I mean, I never shot anyone. I was just holding the horses for them."

"Is that so?" Wyatt mused.

"My gun was in my pocket the whole night, I swear."

Wyatt considered him for a long moment, then asked, "Who were you holding the horses for?"

Luther King swallowed hard, and looked at Paul again and at Doc, before apparently deciding he'd better confess as much as he could. "Billy Leonard," King said.

Wyatt barely suppressed a reaction himself then. The name itself wasn't surprising in the context, but he knew that Leonard had been one of Doc's friends from his time in Las Vegas, New Mexico, and maybe still was. He took a breath and prompted, "Who else…?"

"Harry Head."

"And…?"

"Jim Crane. That's all. The three of them did the hold-up. I was just waiting with the horses."

"So you said." Wyatt took another breath, and drew away.

"I wasn't even near enough to see anything." King turned to gaze up at Bob Paul, who still loomed over him. "I was mighty sorry to hear about Mr. Philpot. Everybody liked Bud."

"We did indeed," Paul intoned.

"And M-Miss Elder… I'm…"

Wyatt could feel Doc's glower, by watching the effect of it on Luther King.

"So, where are they now?" Paul continued. "Where are Leonard, Head and Crane now?"

King swallowed again, before answering, "They're camping a couple of miles away. Do you know this country? I'll sketch the path for you, if you want."

"I take it that Hank Redfield went to warn them."

"I-I guess so."

Wyatt rolled his eyes at the prevarication, and stepped close again. "Are we going to be met by gunfire when we get there, or are they going to ride off and try to escape?"

King had to think about it—perhaps he hadn't expected the question—but he seemed certain when he answered, "The last. They'll be escaping. No point making a bad situation worse."

So they knew it was a bad situation already, Wyatt thought. That would make them desperate, but there was no help for that. "Where are they heading, then? They must have somewhere in mind." No one rode aimless through this country; it was too unforgiving.

After some pushing, King at last said, "Cloverdale. A ranch near Cloverdale."

"In New Mexico?" Bob Paul responded in surprise. "That's a lot of riding. And isn't Leonard—" He half-glanced in Doc's direction, obviously thinking twice about mentioning the fact that Billy Leonard was consumptive.

"Yeah, but they don't want to be close by, do they?"

Paul turned to Wyatt. "We'd better plan on catching up with them *long* before then."

"You're right about that." Wyatt nodded at King. "You stay here for the moment. We're heading outside—but I'll have Doc waiting on the other side of that door, just in case you're thinking of going anywhere."

"Y-yes, sir," said King.

And Doc winked in amusement at Wyatt as he and Paul walked on past.

County Sheriff Johnny Behan formally arrested Luther King, and was the most appropriate person to take King back to Tombstone. Breakenridge would go with him. The two of them promised to rejoin the posse with fresh supplies once things were settled in town.

After a silent exchange of glances between the Earps and their friends, Williams also volunteered to accompany Behan.

"You know you can't trust Behan," Doc quietly remarked as he and Wyatt stood shoulder to shoulder, watching the group of four men riding south. "If you didn't before, he's made it plain enough now."

"Yeah," Wyatt agreed with a sigh, "but I've still got to work with him, Doc."

"Do you?" Doc seemed skeptical.

Wyatt turned to consider his friend. "Didn't I tell you? He promised to make me undersheriff, if I withdrew from the election for sheriff."

"Ah."

"I can't say I don't regret it," Wyatt continued, voicing his doubts for the first time, "but a deal is a deal. Maybe it would have worked out better all-around if I'd run for sheriff anyway."

"Maybe," Doc replied in light tones. Wyatt knew he wouldn't deign to have any strong opinions on such matters.

"But it's not like we don't all have to work together anyway, or cooperate at least, with Virgil wearing a badge, too. And the bigger Tombstone gets, the less we can avoid each other."

The two of them fell silent. Soon they were joined by the remaining posse members: Virgil, Morgan and Bob Paul. "It's getting late in the day," Virgil announced. "We might as well stay here for the night."

"But *they* left," Morgan protested, indicating the direction in which Behan and his companions had gone.

"They have a road to ride, and they'll reach Benson tomorrow. We have to follow the tracks of men who don't want to be found. *Armed* men, and desperate. It's best we wait for the morning."

Morgan was still young and unseasoned enough to be impatient, but the older men were ready to settle in for the night. "Come on, Morg," Wyatt said, grasping his brother's shoulder reassuringly. "Let's go brush down the horses."

They found the first campsite easily enough the next day—and would have been able to thanks to Hank Redfield's trail, let alone that of the three highwaymen. King's sketch had proved to be skewed out of true proportion, but after puzzling over it Wyatt figured that could well have been due to King's poor skills as a cartographer rather than any deliberate intent to deceive.

The camp itself, as expected, seemed to have been hastily abandoned. The others sifted through the various signs of life, while Wyatt picked up a couple of discarded papers. Sure enough, the heading at the top of each page announced the title *The Buffalo-Trapper*, and when he compared them to the torn dime novel in his saddlebag, the page numbers picked up only a few pages after where the novel left off. "It's them, all right," he said, knowing he was stating the obvious.

Bob Paul returned to the camp from a hundred yards off. "Reckon Hank headed off that way," he said, jutting a thumb back over his shoulder to indicate the direction. "Probably take a while circling back to the ranch; give us time to get clear."

"I won't forget his part in this," Virgil said. His face was long and his tone grave. "But our trail is clear. The other three are heading a shade south of east. That's gonna take us into rustler country, and beyond that are the Apache. If any of you want to head back to Tombstone instead, there's no shame in it. There's a job to be done there as my deputy."

Wyatt wasn't about to step down, and he knew that Virgil would know that. They were probably both hoping that Morgan might make the safer choice, but there was little chance of it.

After a moment's intense silence, Bob Paul said, "Count me in. I owe it to Bud, and to Mr. Roerig, who were in my care." He nodded firmly. "I'm in."

"Me, too," said Morgan.

"I'm with you," Doc declared in his lazy drawl—and he was looking at Wyatt as he said it rather than Virgil, but Wyatt didn't suppose any of them expected anything else from him.

"Let's go, then," said Virgil, and he swung up onto his horse.

The highwaymen had fresh horses from the Redfields' ranch, and made better progress than the posse whose horses had already been ridden for three long days. Their trail was easy enough to follow, but the posse had to push harder than they'd have liked in order to reach the robbers' campfires each night. Added to which, the posse's supplies were greatly reduced.

"We should have brought more with us," Morgan complained one morning when they had little with which to break their fast. "Why didn't we think to bring more?"

"Didn't know we'd be out this long," Virgil rumbled in response.

Wyatt was blunter about the matter. "If Behan hadn't let Luther King talk to the Redfields, chances are Hank wouldn't have ridden off to warn his friends, and we'd have had them locked up safe in Tombstone before now."

"And Louisa would be frying me bacon," Morgan murmured wistfully, "and there'd be bread fresh from the baker."

The others were all in danger of drifting off into their own reveries, but Virgil said sharply, "Enough of that! You're making the hunger worse, and the thought of bacon makes me thirsty, too. Let's get packed and be off."

Fresh water was scarce, and ranches were few and far between in this country. The trail they were following had eventually circled back toward Tombstone, and a peace officer less diligent than Virgil might have been tempted to quit and head home—so it was a relief to instead find a ranch in the evening of the sixth day out from the Redfields'. Hospitality was always offered in this harsh place, no matter what differences might otherwise exist between the host and the visitor.

Virgil's polite but honest questions earned him an acknowledgment that Leonard, Head and Crane had been there the day before, though they hadn't stayed overnight. But the posse members were exhausted, and their horses were worse. "We're in no position to continue on today," Virgil was forced to conclude after he discussed the situation with Wyatt and Bob Paul, "even if that means they gain more of a lead. We'll stay the night."

"Thank God for that!" Morgan was heard to mutter—and Doc laughed at him.

The posse woke the next morning to find that Bob's horse had dropped dead overnight. Wyatt and Doc's horses were in little better shape, and Doc himself—already ill—seemed weakened by their exertions, and not much revived by a night spent in relative comfort.

"I'll leave my horse here, and walk back to Tombstone," Wyatt said to Virgil. "If Behan hasn't left yet, I'll tell him to bring fresh horses with him, along with food and water."

"If he ever meant to come back in the first place," Morgan muttered. Wyatt hid a wry smile. His younger brother was growing up enough to have become a bit cynical.

"I'll come with you, Wyatt," said Doc.

"Are you sure? It's probably near twenty miles back to Tombstone, and that's if we don't go astray."

"I'm sure. Bob can have my horse."

Bob Paul, who was the heaviest of the party, had a better idea. "We'll leave your two horses here, if they'll lend me a fresh one in return. No point in me wearing out another one."

And so it was settled. Virgil, Morgan and Bob would continue on the trail of the highwaymen, while Wyatt and Doc walked back to town.

Wyatt set a steady pace, though slower for Doc's sake than Wyatt would have liked for his own, and Doc diligently kept up with him and voiced no complaint. When they reached Tombstone late that afternoon, however, Doc excused himself and headed for his room at Fly's boarding house. Wyatt shook his hand before they parted company, and thanked him for his service.

Doc looked at him levelly in return, with a glimmer in his tired eyes. "You never have to thank me, Wyatt."

A firmer grasp of their hands and a respectful nod was all Wyatt had in reply to such a sentiment. Wyatt didn't have Doc's agility with words, though his friend usually had a way of drawing more words out of Wyatt than anyone else could. As Wyatt turned away, he reflected that Doc no doubt understood him regardless.

Wyatt would have given much for a drink and a meal, a bath and a change of clothes—but his first priority must be finding Behan, and sending relief to Virgil and the remaining posse. Wyatt headed for the sheriff's office.

All was quiet. There was one man there, sitting at the sheriff's desk reading a newspaper—the *Nugget*, of course. And when he stood, Wyatt saw that he was wearing the Cochise County undersheriff badge.

"Can I help you?"

Wyatt forced himself to speak. "Looking for Behan."

"Sheriff Behan rode out on the trail of some wanted men. Undersheriff Harry Woods at your service, sir."

He was still flabbergasted, and this unwelcome news only set him back further. "Did he take supplies? Fresh horses?" Wyatt demanded. Then he shook his head, dismayed at himself, and belatedly offered his hand. "Wyatt Earp. I just left my brother Virgil, who's deputy U.S. marshal, and our friends this morning. They've been on the trail of those men since the night the stage was held up, and Behan said he'd rejoin them when he could." *Still,* Wyatt thought to himself, *Behan has said—and promised—many things that never came to pass.*

"The sheriff was only here one night before riding out again, Mr. Earp."

"When was that?"

"He and Mr. Breakenridge left on… Tuesday. The twenty-second. They took Frank Leslie with them."

Wyatt let out a sigh. "And they took supplies? We were running short, and our horses were suffering. I just walked twenty miles back to town for the sake of saving my horse."

Woods was unbecomingly apologetic. "I'm sure they took plenty of food and water, but I can't say that they took extra horses, Mr. Earp. Maybe I'm mistaken about that, but—"

"Never mind, it's too late to worry about it now." Wyatt was about to turn away in frustration, but then remembered the other urgent business he was here for. "What about Luther King? You have him in custody?"

"Yes, sir. He's under guard in a room at a lodging house on Fremont Street."

"Would that be Fly's place?" Wyatt asked, figuring that if so he could deputize Doc to help keep an eye on the prisoner.

"No, sir, he's at the house my wife runs."

Wyatt considered Harry Woods for a long moment. Woods might well be loyal to Behan and the *Nugget* and that crowd, but Wyatt figured he himself didn't have any real reason not to trust him. Yet. "How many guards?"

"Just the one: Deputy Sheriff Perkins. He and King are in the same room, night and day."

He almost groaned—but then stepped forward and looked Woods directly in the eye. "I don't deny you mean well, but I think you're underestimating the danger, Mr. Woods. There are always fifty or more Cowboys in town or hereabouts, and any one of them might try to bust King out of our hands. You should at least have a second guard to switch shifts with Perkins."

Woods seemed unconvinced, or maybe just unwilling to take advice from anyone but Behan.

Wyatt pondered for a moment, muttering to himself, "Better have someone take him to Tucson." The nearest proper jail was in Tucson, seventy miles away; it would mean riding to Benson, and then escorting King on the train. Meanwhile Virgil and the others were still out there, and could be gone for a while yet. Luther King was a key witness to a serious crime, but such informal jailing arrangements had served well enough before now…

Another moment passed, before Wyatt came to a decision. "There are no good choices here. I'd take King to Tucson myself, but I think I'm needed more here. I'm deputy to my brother, so you'll let me know if you need anything from us."

"I will," said Woods, plainly enough.

"And for God's sake keep King safe!"

Wyatt was furious, but not greatly surprised, to hear that Luther King escaped soon after Wyatt's return to Tombstone. Taking advantage of various distractions, King had simply walked out of the back door of the sheriff's office and then rode off on a horse that had been held there waiting for him.

Undersheriff Harry Woods was at a loss to explain the matter—and at least it hadn't happened at his wife's lodging house—but Wyatt was almost as reluctant to forgive such egregious incompetence as he was outright corruption. He blamed Sheriff Behan, when all was said and done, for colluding with the Cowboys and thereby creating the conditions in which outlaws knew they could get away with such outrages.

Taken in all, after Behan's performance in relation to Luther King, Wyatt couldn't see the Earps ever trusting him again. Added to which, the injustice of the undersheriff position being awarded elsewhere was starting to bite at and bother Wyatt as if it were an untamed horse.

Well, at least Wyatt could continue as deputy town marshal under Virgil, though there was little money in it. During Virgil's continuing absence, there was work to be done, despite Tombstone resting quiet for now. Wyatt made a few inquiries into King's escape, but met with resistance or ignorance.

The priority for now was finding and arresting Billy Leonard, Harry Head and Jim Crane—to which end, Wyatt was glad to receive telegrams from Wells Fargo offering a reward for the capture of the three would-be robbers, totaling thirty-six hundred dollars. Even with this enticement being offered, however, Wyatt learned no further worthwhile information. There was talk of a possible fourth highwayman being involved in the hold-up, but nothing King said had even hinted at such a possibility, and the trail followed by the posse hadn't suggested more than four riders as far as the Redfield ranch and three after that, so Wyatt was inclined to disregard such speculation.

Eventually the remains of the posse returned, in poor shape after covering four hundred miles in seventeen days, with little food or water. Virgil and Morgan arrived in Tombstone on April 3rd, on foot—Virgil's mount had died, so they'd loaded what was left of their gear onto Morgan's, though it had lost two of its shoes and its hooves were torn, and then driven it before them.

After Wyatt and Doc had left them, the posse had continued east to Galeyville and the San Simon Valley, and then southeast to the Animas Mountains in New Mexico. All to no avail, for Leonard, Head and Crane remained always out of their reach. It made for a disheartened reunion for the brothers, but no one could say the Earps hadn't tried their utmost to serve justice.

There was no reward, of course—but it seemed that even their expenses wouldn't be met.

Virgil and Morgan walked into the Oriental Saloon one afternoon, and sat beside Doc at Wyatt's faro table. It was quiet and there were no punters currently looking for a game, but still they sat in a half-circle at one end of the table so as not to deter any interest. Both the newcomers bore disgruntled expressions.

"What's bothering you two?" Doc asked. "Did you get up on the wrong side of the bed today—or from the wrong bed entirely?"

Virgil, forever loyal to his darling Allie, manfully ignored this sally, but Morgan's cheeks pinked and his mouth quirked. "Just spoke to Johnny Behan," Virgil said in heavy tones.

Wyatt sighed and sat back in his chair, feeling almost as if he had to brace himself for bad news now whenever that name came up.

"He put in a claim on the county for expenses incurred by his posse. Almost eight hundred dollars' worth. D'you know how much we'll be seeing of that?"

Wyatt grunted an inarticulate inquiry.

"None of it," Morgan announced.

"Don't know why I'm surprised," Wyatt responded with a sigh.

"Guess he thought we were doing it out of the goodness of our hearts."

"Speak for yourself," Doc protested, which at least made Morgan smile.

"He explained he didn't deputize us," Virgil said, "and I can't deny that. You were riding as my deputies. But we worked together with Behan's men, and it seems… well, parsimonious to consider us as two separate posses."

Wyatt pondered on possible alternatives. "Maybe Wells Fargo can contribute. They should at least cover Marshall Williams' expenses, and Bob Paul's, too."

Virgil tipped his head doubtfully. "Not sure I want to ask on behalf of us four, but I'll back up claims from Marshall and Bob." It must have been obvious that Wyatt remained dissatisfied, for Virgil said, "It's not like we don't have the funds ourselves, Wyatt." He laid a hand flat on the faro table. "You're making a good income here, and with your mining interests. Which wouldn't be possible if we didn't put the work into supporting law and order, too."

"I know that," Wyatt replied mildly, and he nodded to indicate that was enough said, they could drop the matter. Not that it didn't rankle, but Wyatt figured anything to do with Behan was going to rankle from now on.

"Speak of the Devil," Doc muttered, putting them all on their guard.

Behan himself stood in the Oriental Hotel's doorway, faltering at the sight of the four of them sitting there together. After a moment, though, he put a good face on it and walked over to them with a purposeful stride. "Good afternoon, gentlemen."

"Sheriff," said Virgil. "Afternoon," said Morgan. Wyatt and Doc acknowledged him with a nod.

"There's something I need to discuss with you all," Behan said—and then he didn't risk a pause, as if aware there was already another issue on their minds which he didn't want to talk about. "There have been rumors of a fourth highwayman being involved in the hold-up of the Sandy Bob stagecoach. I don't mean King, but another man doing the shooting along with Crane, Head and Leonard."

"I heard that, too, once or twice," said Wyatt, "but I didn't think much of it." He turned to Virgil, who shook his head to indicate he hadn't learned anything more reliable. "Do they have a name?"

Virgil said, "We were only ever on the trail of three men apart from King. Or do they suspect one of the Redfield brothers?"

"That's the thing, you see," said Behan, glancing nervously from Virgil to Doc to Wyatt and back again. "They're suggesting the fourth man was following the other three."

Wyatt took a breath, knowing what would come next. Doc got in before him: "You mean me, I suppose."

Behan had grace enough to sound apologetic. "I'm afraid so, yes." After a pause, he asked, "What can you tell me about that evening, Doc?"

Wyatt replied firmly, "Doc was right here with me at the Oriental."

"You'll understand, Wyatt," said Behan, "that people will question the notion of Doc setting up an alibi for himself with his closest friend."

Doc was sitting back in his chair, taking a relaxed draw on a cigarette, as if none of this could possibly concern him.

Wyatt explained in steady tones that nonetheless betrayed his frustration, "He didn't have to manufacture an alibi. He was with me. He can't have been out at Contention as well."

"Playing the Devil's advocate here—"

"You flatter me," Doc drawled. "The Devil rarely argues *against* me."

"He's friends with Billy Leonard," Behan continued to Wyatt, ignoring Doc. "Everyone knows that. The question arises: How did they know the coach was worth robbing…?"

"You're suggesting that Doc tipped Leonard?" Virgil asked.

"They knew each other back in New Mexico, didn't they?" This was a rhetorical question from Behan. "And there was a whole heck of a lot of stagecoach robberies there. Las Vegas was notorious for it."

Wyatt shook his head. "You're spinning a yarn out of nothing at all. Doc was here with me from early that evening, and he was as surprised as I was when Virgil came in and told us the news."

Behan tilted his head and grimaced as if unconvinced.

"What if I were to start asking where John Ringo is," Wyatt said, "and seeing where that notion took me?"

"You can't do that!" Behan protested. "He wasn't part of it."

"Well, neither was Doc."

"It's an insult to even consider me!" Doc declared.

Behan and Virgil rolled their eyes in unison, and Virgil murmured, "Reckon you're used to accusations, Doc, whether false or true."

"Oh, I don't mind the accusation, Virgil," Doc easily replied. "My point is that if I'd taken part in the hold-up, it would have succeeded, and I'd have got the money."

Morgan let out a bark of laughter. "That's true. All twenty-six thousand dollars of it!"

"Which is another thing," said Doc. "Where did that figure come from? Wells Fargo itself?"

None of the others had an answer. They all looked at each other, as if never having thought to question it before.

"They generally carry silver bullion in their boxes, don't they, when hauling from Tombstone? But that amount of bullion would be one hell of a load for a regular team of horses to pull. Wouldn't it be more usual to carry about a tenth of that?"

A pause for further thought, before Wyatt offered, "Maybe it was gold specie, then. That's worth about ten times more than silver, so the equivalent weight would be reasonable."

"Ah," said Doc. "No doubt you're right, and I'm just reading too much into it."

"What were you reading into it?" Wyatt asked.

"I wondered if the rumor was deliberately inflated to provoke interest from Billy Leonard and his like."

Behan shook his head in disbelief. "Why would someone want to provoke a hold-up *knowing* that such a rumor was false?"

"No idea," Doc said with an amiable shrug. "It gave me pause, is all."

None of them seemed interested in pursuing the matter further, so after a moment Behan nodded politely at the Earps and Holliday. "Good day to you, gentlemen."

"Good day, sheriff," Virgil responded.

Silence for a while, and still there were no punters wanting a game of faro. Morgan went to buy a round of drinks for the four of them.

As Wyatt pondered the robbery and the subsequent ride, he remembered the pages he'd recovered of *The Buffalo-Trapper* and a query he'd thought of for Doc. "Didn't you once tell me, Doc, that Billy Leonard likes to read novels?"

"I did, yes. You're thinking those dime novels were his?"

"Seems a fair assumption."

Doc nodded. "Leonard idolizes Wild Bill Hickok. They haven't started writing stories about him yet, have they?" After a moment, he added, "Then again, there is not a picayune of a chance that Leonard would destroy or discard a story about his hero."

"I don't know," Wyatt said, "but this one wasn't about Wild Bill." He accepted a coffee from Morgan, and they all settled in for the rest of a quiet afternoon.

Though Doc was heard to remark, "Johnny Ringo also likes to read…"

CHAPTER THIRTEEN:

LOYALTIES

Tombstone, Arizona;

June-July 1881

The Earp women did not like Doc Holliday. Virgil's Allie disapproved of him, Wyatt's Mattie resented him, and only Morgan's beautiful Lou would occasionally let herself be amused by him. So the tea was poured with a longsuffering air—and poured by Allie rather than Mattie, despite this being Wyatt's house.

Doc sat back in an armchair, crossed one leg over the other, and let the scented steam from the tea rise over his face. The women were all busy, sewing either for their own households or having taken in work for pay—an income more modest than his own from gambling, but probably far steadier. None of the Mrs. Earps seemed inclined to start a conversation, but it would seem an odd thing to sit there in silence.

"How are you ladies coping with the heat?" Doc asked—though the weather was a risky topic for once, as the women were dressed somewhat more loosely than usual, here in the privacy of home. A gentleman shouldn't be suspected of noticing the lack of corsets and such. "I don't remember June last year being quite so uncomfortable."

"At least the nights are cool," Lou contributed. "Sleeping well helps make most things bearable."

"That's true, Mrs. Earp, and it seems Wyatt would agree with you. When the clock struck one without him appearing, I thought I'd come hunt him down."

The women's heads were all bent over their sewing tasks, but after a rather long pause Mattie shot a glance at Doc and said, "He didn't come home until almost dawn. I would have thought you'd know that. Weren't you with him?"

"Ah, yes, of course. He was doing well on the faro table when I retired somewhat earlier. I'm not surprised he found it fruitful to continue taming the tiger."

Another sharp glance from Mattie. Maybe she was wondering why Doc would bother walking this far down Fremont Street when he could have just waited for Wyatt at the Oriental. It wasn't as if Doc had suspected Wyatt was in any trouble… But, he mused, he didn't want to admit even to himself how bereft he felt these days when Wyatt wasn't in the immediate vicinity.

As if at last conjured by this thought, Wyatt himself walked through from the other room, still in his shirtsleeves and nimbly adjusting a cufflink. "Doc! Didn't expect to see you here. Something going on?"

"No, no. Just wondered where you'd got to."

"Didn't get in till late."

"Or early," Doc suggested. "So I've been told."

That was probably an injudicious remark. Wyatt's restless gaze settled on Mattie, and after a moment he walked closer to stand over her shoulder. "Thought you were making me a new shirt," he remarked in deliberate, steady tones.

"It's finished, Wyatt," she retorted—and then with a slight softening she added, "I'll iron it this evening, once it's cooler. Then it's done."

"All right," he said, not sounding placated.

Doc leaned forward, his curiosity snared by Mattie's current occupation. "What's that you're working on?" he asked. It was a square of white fabric, with a design being picked out on it in red thread. "Will those be flowers?"

"Yes." Mattie's lips pursed for a moment, but then she offered Doc at least half a smile, as if grateful despite herself for the kind attention.

There was no pattern drawn on the fabric, nor any image sitting before her that she was following. "And you're creating them by yourself, with nothing to guide you?"

"Yes." She'd warmed a little now.

"I'm impressed," he told her in frank tones.

Mattie shrugged, but then stilled her hands, and turned to him to say, "The women here welcomed Wyatt and me with a quilt we all stitched together. It was… interesting. I've already made another quilt by myself, and this is for a third."

"Excellent. And you're blessing the squares with your own designs." Doc's mother, aunts and cousins had sewn for the household, of course, but none had been so creative—and few so ambitious.

Allie said rather pointedly, "Mattie has a good imagination, and she's practical, too. People pay up plenty for such things."

A pause—and then everyone's focus turned to Wyatt even if they didn't look at him, as if awaiting his verdict.

Slightly too long a moment later, he laid a reassuring hand to Mattie's shoulder and said, "Good work, Mattie." He took a breath and added, "Well done." Then he strode to the door, saying to Doc, "Come on, then. We're just in the way here. Let's get breakfast in town."

Doc swallowed the rest of his tea and stood, then offered a half-bow to the women. "Au revoir, my dears."

Three smiles rather fonder than before saw him out of the door.

Doc walked back toward the business end of town with Wyatt close beside him. The heavy afternoon heat felt so burdensome that Doc was glad of his new walking cane, though he was endeavoring to make the thing appear more of an affectation than a practical necessity.

After a block or two, Wyatt finally broke the silence—not even glancing at his companion but still staring forward. "I should arrest you, Doc."

Ah, yes… It seemed likely that at last Virgil Earp would be permanently appointed as the town marshal, after a long stint of acting in the post on a temporary basis. "Did Virgil deputize you again?"

"A citizen's arrest."

"What for this time?" Doc asked in mock longsuffering tones.

"You know you can't carry a weapon in town."

Doc huffed a laugh, and muffled the ensuing cough. "You have keen eyesight, Wyatt." The pistol was just a small piece, tucked into his waistcoat pocket. "I plan to stow it at the Alhambra. If trouble breaks out over the faro table, it won't do me any good to have left all my weapons back in my room."

"But the men causing trouble in this scenario—they won't be carrying either. Or shouldn't be," Wyatt conceded.

Doc promptly followed up on that. "If they're from out of town," which they both knew meant the Cowboys, "and they've handed over their weapons at the saloon, then their guns are within easy reach. I only want the same chance."

After a moment Wyatt nodded once, and then announced, "I've got to head to court. You check in your weapon at the Alhambra, and then we'll meet up for breakfast."

"All right," Doc agreed. Out of nothing more than idle curiosity, he asked, "What's happening at court?"

"Virgil arrested me last night," Wyatt replied in even tones.

Doc stopped and stared—and then laughed in disbelief. "What…?"

Wyatt started walking again, and Doc followed. "A punter had a… disagreement with me over a faro game, and we got to arguing."

There had to be more to the story than that. Well, more than that and the unbearable hot weather which put everyone out of temper. "So…?"

"He wouldn't back down, and I was in the right."

"Of course you were."

Wyatt shot a bright glance at Doc which almost amounted to a wink. "Even Virgil couldn't talk him into backing off. So he ends up charging us both for disturbing the peace and fighting."

"I guess that explains your late return home."

"Virge didn't insist on locking me up for the rest of the night. He knew I'd turn up at court."

"You're planning to challenge the matter?"

"No," Wyatt replied, though again he looked askance at Doc, this time more in puzzlement than appreciation. "You've got to back your brother's play. I'll plead guilty and pay the fine."

Doc was staring at him again. Perhaps he would never be done gazing at Wyatt and trying to learn him. For a man who appeared so very straightforward, Wyatt could throw down the most extraordinary surprises. "I'll come with you," Doc said, wanting to witness the scene in court, or perhaps just not wanting to part from Wyatt.

"No, you go and stow that gun," Wyatt said, "and I'll meet you at the Cosmopolitan afterwards for breakfast."

He reluctantly agreed—and hurried himself along despite the heat.

Doc strolled back to the Alhambra in the middle of the afternoon, but it was far too quiet to offer any sort of entertainment. So then he headed for the Oriental, and sat with Wyatt at his faro table. The saloon was likewise quiet, of course, but at least offered the solace of Wyatt's company.

"I guess it's too hot to play," Wyatt reflected.

"They'll come out at night, then, ready for action after a boring day." For now, no one seemed to want to buck the tiger… though Doc was aware that a few of the potential punters seemed warier of the banker's companion than of the banker himself or the game.

Apparently Wyatt noticed that, too. "Something happened I should know about?" he asked sotto voce.

"Probably," Doc replied. "But I'm not familiar with the details. You'd better ask someone else what I'm supposed to have done now."

Wyatt sighed, and perhaps began reflecting—just as Doc was—that ever since Doc's name had been linked to the Benson stagecoach hold-up, Tombstone's citizens felt freer than ever to assign him responsibility for any untoward event.

They sat in a comfortable silence together, as others came and went in a desultory manner. And then, when Ike Clanton of all people came in and went to the bar to order a drink, Wyatt excused himself. "Would you mind the table for a short while?"

"Of course," Doc murmured—though he didn't scruple to watch his friend, indirectly at least.

Wyatt went to stand by Ike and proffered money to the barkeeper, paying for Ike's whiskey and a mug of coffee for himself. Ike seemed wary and confused by Wyatt's approach, as well he might be, but he wasn't one to refuse a free drink. He downed the shot in a moment, and let Wyatt buy him another—and then with a tilt of his head, Wyatt invited Ike toward the rear of the saloon for a confidential conversation.

Luckily for Doc, the unlikely pair headed outside and stood in the shade thrown by the building across the yard where deliveries were made. Doc had already abandoned the faro bank and followed them, and the chosen location for this tête-à-tête enabled him to listen in while ensconced in the shadows by the rear doors.

"You and your family are ranchers," Wyatt was saying to Ike Clanton, referring to Clanton's father and brothers. "You have no reason to consider these stage robbers and rustlers as friends."

Ike grunted in a wary but interested way, as if he couldn't quite agree with the statement but nevertheless wanted Wyatt to continue.

"I'm running for sheriff in the next election, and if I could arrest Billy Leonard, Harry Head and Jim Crane, that will help me against Behan. No one wants the men who murdered Bud Philpot to go free."

"Well," Ike allowed, "Billy Leonard is no friend o' mine. I've a ranch in New Mexico he says is his." A breath later, he added in a rush, "And maybe it *was* his, but nobody was expecting him to turn up, knowing he was wanted by the law."

Wyatt nodded—not reacting to Ike looking a bit shamefaced about the situation—and then he leaned closer to speak more confidentially still. "Leonard has been a friend of Doc Holliday's, though, and people are making too much of their connection. *I* know Doc wasn't part of the Sandy Bob hold-up—he was with me all that night. But that's two solid reasons I have for bringing those men to justice."

Ike stared up at Wyatt for a long moment as if considering. Wyatt, of course, didn't twitch or falter. His face was usually impassive, and in moments like these Doc knew that came across as resolute.

"There's a reward from Wells Fargo," Wyatt eventually added, in a more direct appeal to Ike's self-interest. "They're offering twelve hundred dollars per man. I'll make that up with my own money to two thousand dollars. That's six thousand for the three of them, Ike. Money like that makes a real difference to an honest rancher."

Ike was still chewing something over, and at last he burst out with it. "You'll have to kill 'em, you know. They won't never surrender."

"I need them alive—or at least one of them for long enough to exonerate Doc, with witnesses that can't be gainsaid. You understand that, Ike?"

"Yeah," Ike responded with a shake in his voice. "Yeah, I do. But I don't want to get in a fight with them. They'll end me."

"I don't want you to do any fighting," Wyatt explained patiently. "I was thinking you could find a reason to bring them to a place we agree on, and my friends and I will be there waiting for them."

This gave Ike a whole lot more to chew over. "Guess I could do that." He gave a gusty sigh and suggested, "I could get them to come to Willow Springs, near the McLaury ranch. We all know the place. They wouldn't think twice about it, if I said there was a job on."

"That's good," said Wyatt.

Doc knew the place, too. There'd be plenty of cover for the waiting posse, and if they were led by Deputy U.S. Marshal Virgil Earp, no one would question their legitimacy.

"I'll get Frank in on it," said Ike. "Frank McLaury. We'll be right near his place. He'll have to know."

The McLaurys had much in common with the Clantons—and were likewise a lot friendlier with the Cowboys than the Earps. Wyatt said, "All right."

"But you have to promise me you won't say a word about this to anyone," Ike blundered on. "Frank will understand—we're ranchers, like you said—but I wouldn't last longer than a snowball in hell if anyone else knew about this."

"I promise this is between you and me, Ike. I've no good reason for letting anybody know—except when the time comes, I'll explain it to Virgil."

Ike seemed to accept this—Virgil was one of the few men in the county whom everyone trusted. But then, just as it seemed settled, Ike protested once more, "I told you they'll put up a fight! Chances are you'll kill 'em all. Then what's in it for me and Frank?"

Wyatt nodded. "I'll pay you my share regardless, but if you want, I'll confirm with Wells Fargo whether the reward is for capture 'dead or alive'."

"All right," Ike agreed at last. "All right. You let me know. Then we can talk about when."

"I'll have a telegram sent today," Wyatt promised. And the conversation seemed to be drawing to a close—with no sign of the two conspirators shaking hands, Doc noted. Not that he waited around to see. Instead, he turned and made his way back to the bar, where he bought himself a drink and was innocently resettling himself at the faro table when Wyatt reappeared.

Doc sat there for another hour or two beside this steadfast, honorable man, warmed through to the core. Wyatt had a number of reasons for catching the three murderers, the would-be robbers, and all those reasons were in Wyatt's own interests. But one of the reasons was concern for Doc and for Doc's freedom. Doc's reputation. Even that was in Wyatt's interests, too, of course, but it had been a long time since anyone had felt at all concerned about Doc Holliday's welfare. Such a thought warmed his heart and his vitals so that the very core of him felt expansive.

If ever there had been a time when he'd been unaware of the impossibilities he wanted from Wyatt, that time was gone. Maybe Doc had tried to fool himself, and maybe that had worked for a few years. He couldn't deny it any longer.

Not that he had the slightest hope… Doc sighed. Well, if he wanted to spend his last years in a sweet state of poignant yearning, that was perfectly fine. Yes, it was *fine*, in various senses of the word—it was satisfactory, it was superb, it was pleasant, it was bright, it was delicate, subtle, translucent… And more than that, it was robust. His heart was blood-rich with it in these moments—but Doc felt this love in a deeper, more fundamental place within him, as if Wyatt was his center of gravity and would continue to be so until Doc was once more dust and ashes…

It was hopeless, indeed. There would be no return of this love, but it was sufficient unto itself—and Doc knew all too well that there were far far worse ways to feel.

As the sun began lowering and the punters emerged to seek a drink and a game of cards, Doc at last dragged himself away from Wyatt and the Oriental. He should have gone to work at the Alhambra, but instead he found himself strolling into the Grand Hotel and taking his accustomed stool at the bar.

The usual crowd were there—Curly Bill Brocius, two of the Clanton brothers, Johnny Behan, Frank Leslie, a couple of others Doc neither knew nor cared for—congregated on the chairs and tables in the rear corner of the room. They ignored him, as they usually did, although Ike Clanton was stupid enough to be staring at Doc with a suspicious look on his face. Doc ignored him, as was only reasonable given that he wasn't supposed to know why Ike was worried.

The bartender served Doc, and then Doc pondered the mirror behind the bar, remembering Johnny Ringo materializing in it, and wishing the same might happen again. There was nothing of love between them, of course, but Doc wistfully remembered that long-ago night when Ringo had bedded him, read him poetry… licked the blood from his mouth…

Doc sighed. There was no sign of Ringo in the barroom, and Doc hadn't even heard his name mentioned for a puzzlingly long time. Perhaps the fellow had left the county, the territory.

When Curly Bill came up to the bar to order more spirits, Doc took the opportunity to ask, "Where's Johnny Ringo these days? Do you know?"

Curly Bill contemplated Doc for a long moment. "Depends why you're asking," he responded.

"It's been far too long since I had an intelligent conversation, that's all. I had poetry on my mind—lyric poetry, not drama or tragedy, I assure you."

The Cowboy seemed relieved, as if always ready to be reassured. Not so Ike Clanton, who came bustling up close to Doc, attempting to loom threateningly over his shoulder. "Concerning yourself with things that are none of your business?" Ike demanded. "Who are you asking about? Or— what. What are you asking about?"

Doc turned a little to consider him coolly, while Curly Bill said, "Take it easy, Ike. Doc's just asking about Ringo. You know they like talking about books and stuff."

"Books?" Ike echoed, his eyes narrowing. Doc wondered if Ike's mind had linked the subject to Billy Leonard, known to be another reader, or if he was skeptical about Doc's stated interest.

"Yeah," Curly Bill continued. "You haven't seen Johnny, have you, Ike? I remember you saying he hadn't been working at the ranch in a while."

"No, I ain't seen him." Ike was not at all reassured, but luckily someone else entered the bar and managed to derail him.

"Here we are!" cried Curly Bill. "Welcome, Mr. Vaughan. Doc, you've met Gregory Vaughan, our schoolteacher, haven't you? He's someone you can have an intelligent conversation with, surely."

"Mr. Vaughan," Doc greeted him. "How d'you do?"

"How d'you do, Dr. Holliday." Vaughan hovered for a moment, his gaze falling a little too warmly on Doc.

"Come on, Ike," Curly Bill said. "Lend me a hand with this tray and leave them to it."

Ike threw one last resentful, conflicted look at Doc, and then withdrew to accompany Curly Bill and their tray of drinks back to the gathering of Cowboys.

Vaughan slid onto the barstool beside Doc's, and ordered a bottle of red wine. "Two glasses," he said to the bartender, before turning to Doc and asking, "If you'll join me?"

Doc thought twice about it, but ended up warily nodding his agreement. He didn't say anything, though; once it was poured, he just raised his glass to Vaughan and then sipped the wine, which was dark, rough and bracing.

"I'd welcome an intelligent conversation myself," Vaughan remarked after a while. "My days are spent with children, or their parents who care only about telling me what to teach them, and how."

"Sounds tiresome," said Doc.

"I heard you're one of our readers. I wonder how many of us there has to be before this town builds a library."

Doc murmured something unintelligible even to himself and took a mouthful of the wine.

Vaughan persisted. "Perhaps we might lend each other our own books in the meantime."

"I have so few with me," Doc demurred. "They tend to get left behind in the rush."

"The rush to leave town…?"

"As you say."

A weighty pause before Vaughan ventured, "I have had occasion to leave a town promptly myself, once or twice. Maybe thrice."

Doc slid a sardonic glance toward Vaughan, acknowledging the matter and—he hoped—heading off any more heavy-handed hints.

"I have a room here," Vaughan continued boldly, indicating the upper floors with a lift of his brow. "I have books… You might come up with me and choose one to borrow."

Doc sighed, and allowed himself a wry smile—or perhaps gifted the smile to Gregory Vaughan. "That's a kind offer, but I'm afraid I'm not at liberty to take you up on it."

"Tonight?"

"Or any night," Doc found himself saying. Not so long ago he would have gladly taken advantage of such a straightforward proposition, but things had changed. True, if Johnny Ringo were there and had made a similar suggestion, Doc would have been happy to oblige and be obliged. But Ringo was an established fact, and while he was full of surprises, Doc felt he could rely on Ringo to remain peripheral to the rest of Doc's life in Tombstone. Striking up a new connection with someone—well-meaning, no doubt, but still a stranger—who lived and worked in town was another matter entirely.

Some while before, Doc had realized he was aligning all his doings to follow one new rule. And that was 'Don't embarrass Wyatt'. He had become more aware of why it was so that very day, but—regardless—fucking the local schoolteacher was no longer an option, and that was that.

He briefly pondered giving Vaughan a push subtle or otherwise in Billy Breakenridge's direction, but soon enough he remembered that Doc Holliday was no matchmaker. Let the two men figure that one out for themselves, if they hadn't already!

Doc finished the wine in his glass, and then stood, offering a slight but respectful bow to Vaughan. "Thank you again for the kind thoughts, and for the wine, but I will bid you goodnight."

Vaughan was looking regretful, as well he might. Not that Doc's rejection would pain him long, but such men rarely found a companion to talk with so openly as they had. "Goodnight, Dr. Holliday," Vaughan said, raising his glass in farewell.

Doc turned and stepped out of the hotel—and headed off to see if he could find Kate instead.

"Live life to the hilt," Doc murmured as he drew Kate into a close embrace in the middle of their bed. The words had been their worldly prayer, but instead of saying it in response Kate smiled one of her enigmatic smiles.

For a while they didn't voice anything coherent, but loved each other with a sweet wickedness, a passionate familiarity. Doc liked to think he could pleasure Kate in ways she didn't find anywhere else, and she was kind enough not to disillusion him, though he suspected—a suspicion so certain that it had become fact—that she would never have given up her woman friends for him. Not that he would ever ask her to.

Once they were done, they lay there together for a while, comfortably close. A rare indulgence for these late hours, as they usually spent the afternoons together, and their separate nights were for business. Doc nestled in nearer, cheek against the plump swell of her breasts.

"I'll return to Globe soon," she said, her throaty voice direct yet gentle in tone. "In a few days, perhaps."

Doc pressed a kiss to the warmth of her flesh, and shifted back a little so that they could see each other as they talked, their heads resting on the same pillow. "I'll grieve your absence," he said, "as is only natural with such a boon companion."

She laughed under her breath. "You involve yourself deeper and deeper with the Earps. Are you aware of that? Or has it been such a slow process that you haven't even noticed?"

He didn't reply, and she knew him well enough to expect an argument if he really disagreed with her.

Kate sighed. "So long as you know, Doc. It's not a choice you would have made when I first met you."

"Isn't it?" he asked lightly, though he knew it was true enough. These solemn Northerners wouldn't have been a good fit with John Henry the Southern gentleman, nor with Doc at his most reckless. Perhaps the serious young Dr. Holliday was a better match for the Earps as businessmen, though he'd been abandoned once Doc's consumption made the dentistry trade impractical. Now, of course, Doc and Wyatt both relied on gambling income, so they had plenty in common—though were they each in the game for the same reasons…? Probably not, now that Doc pondered on the matter.

"A few days," Kate repeated, "maybe a week, and I shall leave you to your friends."

"I'll miss you," he repeated likewise, but he didn't insist on the point.

She said, however, "Come with me. Come with me, then, and leave them behind."

Doc watched her for a moment, and realized to his surprise that she was sincere. He couldn't answer her in the affirmative, though, so he pressed a warm kiss to her mouth that ended firmly as if in farewell. Instead of loving each other again, they disentangled and settled next to one another, and eventually fell asleep.

"Did you hear?" said Wyatt when Doc found him standing at the Oriental bar the next day.

"Probably not," Doc replied. "I'm barely awake yet. Yes, please," he added when Wyatt gestured toward his own freshly poured coffee.

Moments later Wyatt joined him at the faro table and placed the two mugs of coffee between them. Even the fragrant steam rising helped to clear

Doc's sleep-befuddled mind. Doc took a mouthful, though it was still too hot, and asked, "What haven't I heard?"

Wyatt was considering him carefully, as if taking his measure.

"Out with it, Wyatt."

A nod, and then Wyatt said, "It's about Billy Leonard. I know he was a friend of yours—"

"Was?"

"—back in New Mexico."

Had Billy finally succumbed to the consumption? He'd always been more poorly than Doc—not that Doc had liked to compare, and such things could be deceptive. Perhaps all this business with the stage hold-up and then outlasting the posse had taken a severe toll. "Do you mean—?"

"He was shot, Doc. Billy Leonard and Harry Head were shot and killed."

A powerful angry resentment surged within Doc. "By whom? And where?"

"Near Hachita in New Mexico. By two brothers named Haslett. I don't have the details—they haven't tried to claim the Wells Fargo reward, though of course they still might, or maybe it was about something unrelated." Wyatt took a moment, and added, "I'm sorry about your friend, at least."

Doc nodded. The anger had already dwindled to grief, and even that was already fading. "I'm sorry, too," he said evenly, "but it's not as if I excused myself from Virgil's posse once we knew it was Billy Leonard we were chasing, and that might well have ended the same way."

Wyatt took up his coffee and drank down half of it. He was still frowning with worry.

"What about Jim Crane?" Doc asked.

"He wasn't involved, far as I know. Seems he's still out there, whether in Hachita or further afield."

"All right." Doc followed Wyatt's suit and swallowed a goodly portion of coffee. He felt sharper for it, and took a moment to regret that it didn't make for such useful medicine as did alcohol.

Wyatt was troubling over something, so Doc let him be for a while—until at last Wyatt leaned toward him and quietly burst out, "You know people are saying you had something to do with the stage robbery."

"Yes," Doc acknowledged, looking elsewhere. He didn't want to see any doubt in Wyatt's eyes.

"With your friend and Harry Head dead—and Luther King gone,

probably to meet the same fate—we're down to Crane alone to clear your name."

Doc huffed a skeptical breath. "People will believe what they want to believe, Wyatt."

"Yes, and if the Citizens' Vigilance Committee wants to see justice done…?"

The skeptical breath became a laugh. "Wyatt, in all these months they have done nothing but hold meetings in order to gossip and complain to each other."

Wyatt returned his gaze levelly, unconvinced. "If it were just a botched hold-up, then I might shrug it off, too—but it was the murder of Bud Philpot and a passenger, and the possible killing of Bob Paul or of anyone sitting in the coach with no way of defending themselves. Committees have been known to become lynch mobs, faced with such a crime."

Doc sat there watching his friend. There was no denying he felt a thrill of fear up his spine at the thought of being dragged out onto the streets and hanged from the nearest convenient structure. But still—the prospect of it hardly seemed real, and there was little to be done about it even if it were. Instead, Doc pondered Wyatt and wondered what Doc himself had done to earn this earnest man's loyalty.

When Wyatt had been questioned about their unlikely friendship—as he often was—he simply answered that Doc had watched his back and once, in Dodge City, saved his life. This was accepted as explanation enough by most people, though Doc felt it lacked a certain something. Doc might well have earned Wyatt's thanks by such means, but there was more to the matter than gratitude. A great deal more.

Doc couldn't explain it, and maybe never would—and he wasn't going to prompt Wyatt to doubt himself. One thing was clear: the connection from Wyatt's perspective certainly had nothing to do with the desires that had grown within Doc. So, what could it be about…?

Perhaps some attractions must remain mysterious. Doc smiled at his friend, his dearest friend, and said, "Never mind, Wyatt. We'll do what we can, or what we must, and otherwise all will unfold as it will."

Wyatt seemed not to take much comfort from this thought.

Perhaps Wyatt's friends had had cause before now to consider Doc Holliday as Wyatt's shadow, figuratively at least. They might now apply the notion literally. Whenever Wyatt was in town, Doc was often to be found trailing behind him like a loyal hound with no will of his own. No one seemed to notice anything very different, mind, except that every now and then Virgil would glance pointedly at Doc and, with deliberate effort, choose to make no remark.

That afternoon, Doc had accompanied Wyatt to the town marshal's office, and was sitting there at his ease while the three Earp brothers discussed matters of business.

They looked so alike, these three—Virgil, Wyatt and Morgan. All tall, well-made and handsome, with their light brown hair worn in the same style, neatly combed from a side parting, and all sporting long moustaches. Virgil was blessed with a little silver at his temples, and Wyatt's moustache tended toward gold, but that was about it. Doc had witnessed people mistaking the three for each other—most often muddling up Virgil and Wyatt—and the brothers hadn't always troubled themselves to correct the misapprehension.

Doc had never muddled them, even in the early days of his acquaintance, and was so familiar with them by now that he had to make an effort to see them as a stranger would. Virgil was solid, proper and upright, always respectable, though he did let his temper get the better of him on occasion. Morgan was obviously younger than the other two, and not only in years. He had a slighter build, and his demeanor was less serious and more relaxed; there was something of the scamp betrayed by the light in his eyes, and Doc loved him for it.

They were all fine men, it was true—but Wyatt was the pick of them. Something about his features was a little more than handsome, and his figure presented a strong yet lean ideal. Doc was not alone in finding Wyatt charismatic. Men on the right side of the law wanted to be his friend, for he was respectable but had enough of the rascal in him to appeal. Those on the wrong side couldn't help but pay him close attention, especially if they knew him as an enemy. As for his family, Wyatt was the middle brother in terms of age, but the others would follow him anywhere. Which was obvious right now, for it had been Wyatt's idea to come to Tombstone though he'd first heard the town's name from Virgil.

The Earps had done well here, with business interests in mining, property, gambling and the rest. But they had invested more than money on the side of law and order, and that set them in opposition to a great many in the county. As was also becoming obvious just now.

"That's the third time Ike Clanton has walked past the window," Virgil rumbled.

"So?" said Morgan.

"He's been staring in here as if he has an itch only one of us can scratch."

Morgan was all disgust. "Sure hope it ain't me!"

"Likewise," Doc murmured.

"It's probably me," Wyatt said with an irritable sigh. He headed toward the open door, and next time Ike drew near, invited him in. "Something I can help you with?"

As Clanton strode inside, Morgan retreated, leaving the office with a "See you this evening, Virge!" thrown back over his shoulder.

Wyatt closed the door behind Morgan, despite the heat of the afternoon. "Ike," he said calmly. "What's bothering you?"

Clanton glared at Wyatt, and then looked hard at Virgil and Doc before staring some more at Wyatt—all the while walking back and forth across the limited space and shaking with nerves.

"You can talk in front of Virge and Doc," Wyatt reassured him. "I'd trust them with my life and with everything else that's dear to me."

Which Doc knew already, but it still warmed the cockles of his heart to hear it stated so plain.

Clanton declared, "*That's* what's bothering me! How many men have you told about our… agreement?"

"None. Not even these two. Like I always said, Ike, when the time comes, I'll have to explain it to Virgil, but I haven't said anything yet."

Clanton stared at Virgil and Doc, but perhaps wasn't prepared to trust them. After all, everyone in the room except for Ike had a damned fine poker face.

"Ask them, if you want!" Wyatt prompted.

Virgil shrugged, his face remaining impassive. "I don't know what you're referring to, Ike, but now it's raised, Wyatt better explain it sooner rather than later."

Clanton turned to Doc—who echoed Virgil's shrug. "You know I saw you and Wyatt go off for a confidential confab the other day at the Oriental, but he never told me what it was about." After a moment, he thought to add, "If that has anything to do with your current distress. I'm not aware of anything else between the two of you."

"Distress!" Ike cried out, with a long glare at Doc. "You're damn right I'm distressed!" Then he turned back to Wyatt. "What about Williams? Marshall Williams."

Wyatt paused for a moment's cogitation, but then said readily enough, "You know he's the Wells Fargo agent. I asked him to send the telegram about the reward—confirming the terms. You've seen their response."

"You told him *why*…?" Ike demanded.

"No." Wyatt was frowning now, as if carefully reviewing what had passed between him and Williams, but soon enough his brow cleared. "No, I didn't. If he's added up a few clues and reached a conclusion—right or wrong—that's not down to me."

Clanton stood in the middle of the room, apparently accepting their reassurances, but still baffled and afraid.

After a moment, Virgil said, "Ike. What's this about? What happened with Williams?"

"He just— He just stopped me in the street. Talked low, but you never know what people are gonna hear, or how they're gonna take it."

"Yes…?"

"He said… if I did business with Wyatt, he'd be my friend."

"Williams promised to be your friend?"

"Yes, sir," Ike replied to Virgil. "I guess he meant… if I needed protection." Fear lit up his gaze again. "No one can know! You know what they'll do, if they think I betrayed them. You know what Jim Crane's just done to the Haslett brothers."

"What's that?" Doc asked, having not been paying much attention to anything other than Wyatt lately.

"Justice for Billy Leonard," Wyatt replied, "and for Harry Head—if you want to call it that. Crane gathered up a group of his rustler friends and went to shoot the Haslett brothers dead."

Doc lifted his chin in acknowledgment, not sure himself anymore whether he'd call it justice or not. He was sorry about Billy's death, that was for sure, but Doc himself had had no scruples about riding in the posse that was chasing him. A lawful posse, with the intent of capturing him, though, rather than a group of rustlers out to gun someone down…

"You see what kind of men I'm dealing with here!" Ike pleaded.

"I see," Wyatt quietly confirmed. He paused for a breath before saying, "You were going to get Frank McLaury into it. Can you trust him?"

"O' course! He sent a man after Leonard and all, to bring them to Willow Springs, but—"

"He sent the *Hasletts?*" Virgil demanded—while Wyatt protested at the same time, "A *third* man?"

"No! I mean, yes." Ike looked in fright from one to the other of them. "Not the Haslett brothers. That was naught to do with us. But a friend we trust. Another rancher." Ike threw his hands up in frustration. "Chances are he didn't reach them before the Hasletts did."

Wyatt gusted a sigh, already returning to his usual stoic demeanor. "You've told more men than I have, Ike."

"Yeah," he acknowledged, a bit shamefaced. "Yeah, guess I have."

"And it's gotten complicated. But Crane's still out there," Wyatt said firmly, "and he needs to be brought in. Ike, let me talk it over with Virgil, and we'll work out what's best to do from here. Come and find me tomorrow, and I'll have an answer for you."

Clanton shook his head, more in disbelief than in negation. "No one more must know. They'll come gunning for me if they do."

"You work with us," Virgil promised him, "and we'll protect you." As evidence of this, he let Ike Clanton make a discreet exit out of the back door.

The heat of June climaxed with a fire that began in the Arcade Saloon on Allen Street one afternoon, and spread like the wild creature it was. Buildings were destroyed—not only by the flames themselves but by men demolishing the awnings and porches and the smaller wooden constructions in the fire's path in an effort to starve it into submission. The men couldn't do much, however, and by the time the fire was out half the business district was little more than charred ruins.

The Oriental Saloon was gone, and with it Wyatt's faro table, at least until they could rebuild—but the Alhambra was untouched, and Doc immediately conceived the plan of inviting Wyatt to join him in a partnership there. The Grand Hotel was also still standing, so that Doc's preferred place for a quiet retreat was secure. It didn't seem a bad outcome for him personally.

Perhaps he should have been paying closer attention to the portents. July entered in with heavy rains and a particularly drenching storm on the Fourth of July.

On the fifth day of July, Doc was arrested by Sheriff John Behan.

Lawyer and justice of the peace Wells Spicer had lost his offices in the fire, so could be found working out of his courtroom in the Gird Block building on the corner of Fremont and Fourth. Spicer didn't need prompting; he shifted up to the bench when Behan paraded in with Doc strolling easily at his side. "Your Honor," Doc greeted him in genial tones.

"Dr. Holliday," Spicer responded.

Behan cleared his throat and announced the two charges, both relating to the Sandy Bob stagecoach hold-up in March: an attempt to rob the U.S. mail, and the murder of Bud Philpot.

"How do you plead, Doc?"

"Not guilty, Your Honor," he said, "and I'd be obliged to know what makes the sheriff so certain I was involved at all."

"I have a signed affidavit," Behan said, gleefully brandishing a legal document, "from someone who knows in detail *everything* that you're involved in."

Doc's heart stopped for a moment as he thought, *Wyatt,* followed by, *No, he'd never handle it this way, even if—*

The answer was both better and a whole lot worse.

"Miss Katherine Elder."

His heart snapped shut like a clam. Doc was saved from making any kind of verbal response by Wyatt striding into the courtroom, slightly out of breath, followed after a moment by John Meagher, co-owner of the Alhambra Saloon. "Your Honor," Wyatt said, with no more than a glance at Doc, "has bail been set?"

Behan grimaced and turned away, obviously annoyed by the informal— even familiar—way in which Doc and now Wyatt were conducting themselves.

"Not yet." But Spicer went right ahead and did that without hearing anything more from Behan. "Bail is set at five thousand dollars," he announced, "and the matter will be referred to the District Attorney forthwith," punctuating that with a bang of his gavel, thus ending the hearing.

A bond for the bail was soon organized, with Wyatt and Meagher along with the other Alhambra owner, Joseph Mellgren, acting as sureties. Doc was a free man—for now, at least—and the lone Johnny Behan was left to stalk off toward his offices, his feelings apparently caught between victorious and furious.

"There'll be nothing to it," Wyatt said to Doc as the two of them stood close together in the middle of Fremont Street, a quiet pair amidst the bustle of Tombstone. "We'll clear your name of this once and for all."

"Thank you," Doc responded in a mere whisper. He felt hollowed out by sorrow and gratitude, an empty husk. If the wind picked up, he'd be blown away across the barren plains.

Wyatt nodded once to acknowledge his gratitude, but wouldn't meet Doc's gaze. There was still something on his mind.

When it seemed clear that Wyatt wouldn't speak, Doc offered, "Once this is over, I'll leave town if you want me to."

Wyatt at once shook his head—and Doc was weighted again, his feet were firmly on the ground, even while his heart soared.

"No," Wyatt said after a long moment. "No, it's not *you* causing trouble."

There wasn't even a 'this time' appended to that.

"Doc, Kate had been drinking hard when she signed that affidavit, and she hasn't quit yet. Virgil's going to arrest her for being drunk and disorderly if she continues. Probably in an hour or so." This last statement ended with an upward inflection and a pause, as if Wyatt was suggesting Doc could head this off if he took charge of the situation himself.

"I see," said Doc. He pondered for a while on whether he could do anything to stop her when he'd never been able to before. Kate liked to have her own way just as much as he did. Doc wondered whether he even *wanted* to help her at this point… No matter what she'd done in the past, it had never felt like a betrayal. But this affidavit did. This most certainly did.

When Wyatt realized he wasn't being argued out of such a course of action, and Doc wasn't offering to go deal with her instead, he sighed heavily and said, "Once this is over, it's time for Kate to go back to Globe, Doc."

He nodded, with his head bent before Wyatt's judgment. "I know."

"It's not like she doesn't have a business of her own to run there."

"I know," he murmured. And with that Doc made his choice. Wyatt had a surfeit of loyal brothers and did not need a friend who would stick closer still. But Doc would do so regardless.

Kate was fined twelve dollars and fifty cents for being drunk and disorderly, and then released. Sober now, but suffering and still furious, she launched such a tirade against Virgil that he arrested her again for making threats against his life. Judge Felter found her guilty, but she appealed the verdict and was eventually discharged.

When she finally caught up with Doc in his room at Fly's boarding house, he was just as furious, though he was cold with it while she was hot.

"They won't want you," she declared as she banged the door to the room closed behind her. "They won't want such a friend now!"

"The Earps?" he asked urbanely. "On the contrary, my dear. Such friends are loyal through thick and thin."

"Thick as thieves, that's you and them together! I should have named Wyatt in that statement, too—" Kate halted, and frowned in puzzlement. "Did I…?"

Doc scoffed. "You can't even remember, can you?"

"As if you haven't been drunk before!"

"Never so drunk as to be taken advantage of by an enemy or to betray a lover."

She was still at last, and quiet, though her eyes were a sharp, tumultuous glitter.

"Go back to Globe, Kate. You're not welcome here anymore."

After a moment, she said raggedly, "Come with me, Doc."

"No." He already had his wallet out and was counting the bills. "I have just over a hundred dollars. I'll give you seventy-five of it, if you'll leave Tombstone today."

"Doc—you won't be welcome here either, when they hear the case. No one's going to forgive anyone involved in killing Philpot."

"There's no case against me other than the word of a woman drunk and scorned. Kate, you played your hand, and you lost. Go back to Globe."

She took a breath, as if about to argue further—but then she glanced around the room in a more rational way, as if considering the possessions she had here.

Doc dropped the money onto the bed, and walked toward the door. "I'll leave you to pack." And, with his hand on the doorknob, not even turning his head in her direction, he said, "Goodbye, Kate."

As Doc had predicted with a confidence marginally crumpled, and that only in private, the District Attorney declared in court that there was not the slightest evidence to show the guilt of the defendant. With a more public sense of relief, Doc heard the District Attorney add that the witness statements didn't even prompt a *suspicion* of his guilt. He was free of legal entanglements, and the embarrassment for Wyatt was over and done with.

Nevertheless, Doc apologized as the two of them walked down Fourth Street together, heading for a celebratory drink at the Alhambra. He finished by promising, "Such a thing won't happen again."

"Of course not," Wyatt surprised him by declaring. "And I wasn't worried about the outcome."

"You weren't?"

"Anyone who had any idea of your character would realize you're not the sort to hold up a coach." Wyatt huffed a laugh. "Not that you're law-abiding in *all* ways, but—"

"—that's not my style," Doc concluded.

"—you're no thief," said the ever-practical Wyatt.

Doc's heart was singing in response to Wyatt, who was rarely as lighthearted as he was right now. There was something deliciously uninhibited about how Wyatt was strolling along at Doc's side. Doc said, "Well, I'm delighted that *you* know me, at least."

It was to be inferred that Kate Elder did not. As Doc and Wyatt turned onto Allen Street, Doc saw a raggedy crowd of Cowboys entering the Grand Hotel, and looked in vain for a familiar figure. It had been months... Not that Doc was worried about the fellow, but he could admit to having missed him a little.

"Wyatt," Doc asked, "have you seen or heard of Johnny Ringo lately?"

"Ringo?" Wyatt responded in surprise. "No. No, I haven't, thank God."

Chapter Fourteen:

Into the Rain

Galeyville and Tombstone, Arizona;

August 1881

They knew Johnny Ringo in Galeyville, and he wasn't above making use of that—though only one of them seemed to like him, and that was Abe Franklin, who owned and ran the general store. Franklin was polite and genial with all his customers, of course, but whenever his eyes met Johnny's, he would smile as if he just couldn't help himself. "Good afternoon, Mr. Ringo. How may I help you?"

"Afternoon," Johnny replied, for all the world as if he were still a civilized man. "I'll have flour, bacon and sugar, to start."

"You're staying locally, then?" asked Franklin, in easy tones as if simply making conversation. He appeared to be a good few years younger than John, no doubt still in his early twenties—contrarily, though, Franklin's competent business manner made him seem rather older while his open goodwill gave him a boyish air. Few people in this part of the world remained innocent for long, but it seemed a natural part of Franklin.

"Cabin further up in the hills," Johnny answered him with a sigh. He'd been getting quite domestic with Lucian, the two of them settled in a hut abandoned by—they assumed—a prospector or unlucky miner. Anyhow, the regular deluges made it impossible to live out in the open. Until he could have the stars for his roof again, then a wooden one would have to do, even with all its leaks.

"Anything else?" Franklin prompted.

Johnny asked for some other food and household goods, despite the fact that Lucian had disappeared again a few days before, and John wasn't sure whether or when he'd return.

Once John was done, Franklin said, "I've a packet of Beadle's Dime Novels, Mr. Ringo, delivered just before the weather turned." He brought over a selection, and John picked out six of them at random.

"Thanks." John paid up, met Franklin's gaze, and was the recipient of another uncomplicated smile. He was sure Franklin didn't mean anything by it, but what would he know? It wasn't as if Johnny Ringo was used to people smiling at him. He returned it in kind, as best he could, and took his leave.

Johnny had no more business in town, and his saddlebags were full and overloaded and included two bottles of whiskey—so he really should have headed back to the cabin. But the town's saloon was calling his name. Soon he was standing at the bar, with a shot of liquor warming his narrow belly and another one on the way.

The noise rose around him, everyone keeping their distance and ignoring him as best they could. Johnny had heard, care of Curly Bill Brocius, that he was reputed to be a mean drunk, and Johnny saw no reason to sway anyone from that view. Times like this he wanted nothing more than to be left in peace.

Evening came early under overcast skies. Johnny felt well-fortified by half a bottle of whiskey by then, and was slowly, heavily pondering whether Lucian might show up, if he was in the area. Visiting town might prove to be a way of tracking him down, and Johnny wondered why he hadn't thought of it before, rather than waiting and waiting alone up at the cabin.

Meanwhile, a ruction was rising down the far end of the bar, and Johnny turned to watch in the hopes that it involved Lucian—though even as he shifted he knew it was hopeless. Lucian had the knack of slipping in or out of places with no one even noticing. It wasn't his style to draw attention to himself.

Instead, Johnny found Abe Franklin in the midst of the noise. Not that Franklin was creating it, but it seemed a roughened old-timer—with pistols jammed in his waistband and cartridge belt—had taken exception to the presence of an apparent greenhorn. Franklin—who was unarmed—looked as though he'd been trying to weather what might have started out as teasing but was now becoming nasty. He was a good man, a decent man; not weak, but not a fighter, either.

John cleared his throat, and called, "Barkeep!"

The barman's posture sagged a little as if he dreaded the notion of Johnny Ringo entering the affray. However, he stepped toward John with a prompt

"Yes, sir?"

Johnny had taken the folded bills out of his pocket, and now slapped a goodly portion of them down on the bar. "Drinks for all of Franklin's and my friends!"

"Yes, sir!"

A general cheer erupted. Through the surge to the bar, Johnny glimpsed Franklin's gratitude as the old-timer backed away and perhaps tried to blend into the crowd for the sake of a drink. No doubt everyone there—except perhaps Franklin—had heard the stupid story of Johnny shooting that fellow in a Safford saloon for refusing to drink whiskey with him.

Despite the good mood, the bar's patrons still kept their distance from Johnny, and he had no problem with that. The barkeep had left a whiskey bottle with him before attending to the new orders, so Johnny was content.

Another shot or two of liquor—and he wasn't surprised when Lucian appeared beside him, resting a hand on Johnny's shoulder and murmuring, "Where else would you be?"

"I was waiting at the cabin," Johnny replied, utterly failing to sound resentful. "I got bored. Where have you been?"

Lucian smiled one of his big, glowing smiles, and in its light all other considerations fell away. "I've found us some work."

Johnny hadn't lost his memories, but they had no force. "You always say that, and then it always falls through."

"This one won't."

And it wasn't as if Johnny didn't appreciate the chance to keep company with Lucian. Still, he felt that a show of resistance was in order. "I should be heading back to Old Man Clanton's ranch…" After a moment's thought, he added, "If I still have a job there, he'll have work for you, too. Come with me."

Lucian's smile had softened, but he shook his head and murmured, "No…"

Johnny sighed. "Where are we riding to? I bought food and stuff for the cabin."

"Then we'll go back there," Lucian replied.

"What happened to the work…?"

"At present, I have urgent business to conduct with you," was the response. "In private."

An unexpected pinprick of regret for the Clanton ranch and the usefulness to be found there—but there were undeniable benefits offered by Lucian that Johnny had trouble finding elsewhere. "All right, then," Johnny said, straightening up from the bar. "Let's go."

So they walked out of the saloon together, and if this was even noticed, Johnny figured there were no regrets from anyone at seeing their backs—except perhaps for Abe Franklin.

The hut still had a working fireplace, which provided warmth, light and the possibility of rudimentary cooking. The chimney wasn't in great shape, and if any of the sky-bound sparks were snared in the wooden walls then the whole thing could flare up in an instant, with Johnny and Lucian caught inside. Lucian just shrugged off the risk, and Johnny liked daring fate—which Lucian promptly undermined by pointing out that the rains had probably soaked the outer planks enough to avert any real danger.

Hence that night they lay close to the fire on their makeshift bed, warmed and bathed in golden light. They'd already fucked, and now were sprawled naked together waiting for their energies to replenish enough to fuck again.

Johnny felt full of a wild spirit that stirred him to press close to his lover once more and murmur against his skin, "*My soul faints for your damnation...*"

Lucian stared at him for a long moment, and then turned away. "Don't do that."

"Why not?" Johnny laughed under his breath. "*Be thou envious of evil men, and desire to be with them, for their hearts study destruction, and their lips talk of mischief...*"

"I said don't."

"Why? You're not religious. Are you?" Johnny pulled away and sat up with his elbow leaning on one bent knee. "How can you be? If *your body is a temple of the Holy Spirit*, you let me desecrate it every day we're together."

Lucian didn't say anything, but appeared pained.

Johnny let out a sigh, and reached for his volume of Keats. "I got words in me," he muttered, scrabbling in his coat pocket for his stub of pencil—why hadn't he bought a new pencil at Franklin's store while he was in town?—and then leafing through the loose papers at the back of the volume, looking for a blank piece.

Finally he settled cross-legged, near the fire for light, with the paper flat against the book and the book resting on one knee. Then he let the words out, turning them into careful pencil-marks, maybe murmuring aloud as he did so.

> *'Friendship'*
> *A genial man*
> *meets your eyes with his own, with no hesitation,*
> *smiles at you, as if it's only natural,*
> *thinks the best of you,*
> *disregards the worst.*
> *The world shifts*
> *when you see yourself through another man's gaze.*

Once he was done, he silently read it through again, and nodded to himself, feeling satisfied that he had caught something of the truth of life and set it down in words.

When Johnny looked up, however, he found that Lucian was lying there with his head propped up, his expression disenchanted. "What nonsense," Lucian remarked.

"What?" he protested, alarmed at how weak he sounded. "No…"

"So very modern!" Which Doc Holliday had also said, though not mockingly. Lucian gestured at the book Johnny clutched in one hand. "Do you think Mr. Keats would be impressed?"

"I-I don't know. I guess not." Did Johnny even care? Sure enough, he'd liked that Doc declared himself astonished by Johnny's poetry. And Johnny cared deeply about impressing the son of the Devil… and hadn't he been working on the assumption that Lucian was somehow the son made flesh? When he stared at Lucian now, he saw darkness looming restless behind him as if it were the wings of Johnny's demon lover, or maybe Lucian did have a soul after all and it was doomed, or perhaps the darkness was something more prosaic such as smoke gathering lethally in the confines of the small room.

Johnny forced himself to consider that it was nothing more than a trick of the flickering firelight. He swallowed hard, and grasped his papers together with the book in both hands. "The poetry… it's all I have," Johnny found himself confessing. "Perhaps Mr. Keats might understand that."

Lucian just stared at him for a few horribly long moments—but then at last he relented, his posture eased, and he beckoned Johnny close again. "Leave that and come here," he said.

Johnny left the poetry on the margin of floor between their bed and the fireplace, and crawled into Lucian's embrace. The fucking was… bright and hard and overwhelming, and afterwards Johnny fell deep into sleep.

But when he woke the cabin was cold and gray, and the roof was leaking again as the heavens beat down. Johnny shivered in the gloom, and hauled on his trousers for warmth, looking about him for any signs of—

His book had been burnt, so that only the cover remained. He must have left it too close to the fire. Worse still, all his loose papers—both full and blank—were nothing more than ashes and a few charred fragments in the fireplace.

And he was alone.

The supplies were gone, the dollar bills were gone, the horses were gone. Thankfully he still had his hat, which protected him from the worst of the torrents falling from the sky. He set out to walk back to Galeyville, but the land had shifted and blurred under the downpour, and the few markers he'd left on bushes to show the path had been washed away. He staggered on, chilled to his marrow.

Eventually, as mid-afternoon became early evening and darkened enough for him to glimpse a faint flush of light from town, the way became clearer— and at last Johnny was stumbling into the saloon and up to the bar, where he proceeded to warm his innards with whiskey.

Half a bottle later, he discovered his old pal Joe Olney sitting at the bar beside him troubling over his thoughts. "Joe! What are you doing here?" Or had that already been asked and answered? "It's good to see a friendly face," John added, feeling somewhat feeble.

Joe cast him a quizzical look before glancing around to see if they'd be overheard, and leaning close to mutter, "How far d'you think I can trust Ike Clanton?"

An unexpected question, to say the least of it. "Oh, Ike's all right," Johnny blurted out. He thought a moment, and added, "Doesn't always make the smartest decisions. Is this… Are we talking life-and-death or just buying the next round?"

"Life and death."

Johnny opened his mouth to quip that Ike was comparatively more reliable in those matters, but the words caught in his throat. Instead, he gulped a breath and eventually asked, "What's on your mind exactly?"

Another glance around and Joe shifted close again. "Ike had a scheme to claim the reward money for Billy Leonard and that lot, for killing Bud Philpot. I was to bring them to Willow Springs."

"And—?" John demanded.

Joe shrugged. "They're dead already. An eye for an eye for an eye, and so on I guess until there's no eyes left."

"No," John gritted out. "No, I mean—what was gonna happen at Willow Springs?"

"Law was gonna be waiting." Another shift of his shoulders that should have been a shrug, but ended with Joe's hackles raised.

Something—some little thing within Johnny Ringo that had remained hale despite every other thing—something within John withered and died then. "Joe… Joe…" he ground out. "I killed a man—the only one I ever killed—it was for just exactly that. Luring friends into an ambush, and being paid to do it, too."

"Billy Leonard was no friend of mine," Joe declared, sitting upright again, apparently determined that his conscience was clear. "And it was the law meeting him, not a pack of murdering bastards such as met Moses Baird."

"The difference being…?" John rasped, not out of cynicism so much as knowing that Billy Leonard would have forced a fight.

But Joe had set his jaw mulishly—and Johnny doubled up with the pain of it, both arms wrapped around the sharpness in his gut, and his forehead resting on the cold wood of the counter. He felt adrift, as if the bar and the stool and the floor beneath him were as wayward as water.

When he lifted his head again, Joe was gone—if he'd ever been there. No, of course he must have been there. Johnny could never have dreamt up such a thing as Joe had told him. He reached for the only solace available.

Another half a bottle later he found himself playing poker at a round table down the back of the saloon with four other men and a vague memory of someone lending him fifty dollars to get started. For a while he'd been winning, not every hand but enough to slowly build up his stake—but then a few shots of whiskey later, doubt had crept in and he began losing, and of course he could not afford to lose when he had already lost everything.

Johnny snarled at the thought, and the other players flinched in fear. Lucian had gone and left him with nothing, nothing, which might have been a death sentence for a tenderfoot, but not for Johnny Ringo. Still, he had gotten himself into a situation here that was not viable, and he really should quit this and get himself back to Tombstone and the few men who… who weren't friends but were at least comrades. Johnny would go back to work at Old Man Clanton's ranch, and take a deep breath, and maybe Doc Holliday would condescend to be a comrade, too, whenever Johnny visited town.

Before he knew it, Johnny was on his feet and pointing his pistol at the other players, aiming at each one in turn, and forcefully—yet quietly so that few others in the long room even realized what was going on—forcefully telling them, "On your feet. Back away." They did so without arguing, and Johnny scooped up what money was on the table—about five hundred dollars, he figured, which was plenty for a fresh start—stuffed it into his pockets, and then he headed for the front doors, keeping an eye on the players who were wary enough to still have their hands held out.

In a moment or two he was amongst men who had no idea what had just happened, so Johnny holstered his gun and walked out of the place. There were a couple of horses hitched outside, so he picked the best one, took the reins and swung up into the saddle. Her ears twitched once or twice when she didn't recognize him, but Johnny knew how to treat a horse right, so soon she was trotting along the road heading west out of town, and Johnny was patting her warm, strong neck and murmuring approval.

They didn't reach Tombstone until the following afternoon, for even nature was behaving lawlessly. All the roads and trails had been washed away, and the ground itself was broken apart by arroyos gushing water. The glowering skies hid the few landmarks, or misrepresented them. Johnny had probably been a fool to set out, and in the darkest hours of the night, too, but what other choice had he been left with? He and the mare picked out their way, and at last arrived in town wretched and waterlogged.

Handing over the mare at the Dexter stables, Johnny announced barefaced that she wasn't his and they could do what they liked with her—and then he walked out on legs that were tired through and trembling. The Grand Hotel was half a block away, which was plenty far enough. Johnny hadn't quite reached the front door before hearing the news, the disastrous news.

There'd been a serious shootout in Guadalupe Canyon, in the Peloncillo Mountains down where the Arizona, New Mexico and Mexico borders met—and Old Man Clanton had been killed.

In his utter exhaustion of mind and body, Johnny's legs would no longer support him, and he promptly sat on the edge of the boardwalk outside the Grand with his boots in the mud of Allen Street. "The hell you say," he muttered. Others had been killed, too—Charley Snow, Jim Crane, John Gray's kid brother, maybe more—but it was Clanton's death that grieved him. Not that Phin and Ike Clanton wouldn't give Johnny work on the family ranch, but it had always been the stern old father who people relied on.

"Mexican soldiers did it," Curly Bill Brocius was saying, looming over Johnny, with his voice bold but his hands fidgety. "They're saying it's revenge for what happened in Skeleton Canyon."

He shot a pointed look down at Johnny, but the meaning of it escaped him. "What happened in Skeleton Canyon…" Johnny echoed, not quite asking.

"*You remember*." This was muttered, with a nervous glance around the street. The rain had relented enough to encourage people outside again, and no one wanted to be overheard discussing matters only the guilty would recall.

Johnny pondered for moments lengthened by confusion. Mexican smugglers carrying silver bullion through Skeleton Canyon into Arizona, ambushed by the Cowboys, and four of the Mexicans killed… He could see it in his mind's eye, but was that memory or imagination? And had Lucian been there, too, or had he just goaded Johnny into taking part?

"I… don't know," said Johnny.

Curly Bill rolled his eyes in exasperation. "It was barely even a month ago. How much drinking have you done since then?"

"Plenty," he replied with a shrug—before being distracted by Doc Holliday emerging from the Alhambra Saloon down the other side of the street, and then Wyatt Earp strolling out, too, to stand by Doc's shoulder, conferring confidentially. The two of them looked as if they belonged together, entirely at ease in standing so close.

Despite the fog of his thoughts, Johnny had already noticed that there must have been a serious fire to the east of Fifth Street, and the Oriental Saloon was now little more than blackened wreckage. Not that Johnny cared, but it had always been Wyatt's haunt, and why wouldn't he set up business with his friend in the Alhambra now that the Oriental was gone?

As Johnny watched, it seemed Wyatt caught sight of him, and after a slight pause Wyatt leaned closer still to murmur something in Doc's ear, indicating Johnny with a subtle gesture of his hand. Doc's gaze followed the prompt and alighted on Johnny. They stared at each other for a moment or two, until at last Doc nodded a politely cool greeting, and Johnny lifted his chin in response.

And then Doc turned back to Wyatt, and the two of them continued along the planks of the opposite sidewalk, heading in Johnny's direction but ignoring him entirely, caught up only in conversing with each other. Two doors down from the Alhambra they entered into the Maison Doree, perhaps intending to share a meal.

John sighed, feeling that something significant had shifted, that it hadn't just been the fire and the floods changing the landscape. "I need a drink," he announced.

"Well, come on, then," Curly Bill replied in hearty tones. And he reached down a hand to help Johnny to his feet.

Even Johnny Ringo knew that this was neither the wisest of moves nor the best of allies. But what else did he have?

CHAPTER FIFTEEN:

COURAGE, COOLNESS AND FIDELITY

Tombstone, Arizona;

September–October 1881

Late on the night of September 8th, the Sandy Bob stagecoach to Bisbee was held up just outside the Hereford settlement. Word reached Tombstone the next morning, along with a vital clue: while one of the robbers was grubbing through the driver's pockets, he explained, "Maybe you have got some sugar."

Wyatt turned away when he heard that, not wanting to roll his eyes or groan too obviously. Frank Stilwell was known to use the term 'sugar' for money—and Frank Stilwell was also one of Sheriff Behan's deputies. It was the starkest proof yet that Behan was in too deep with the Cowboys and their friends.

The town marshal and his men were still required to work in cooperation with the county sheriff and his, however, so Wyatt and Morgan were soon riding out to Hereford along with Deputy Sheriff Breakenridge—who seemed a decent enough if unimaginative man.

Once they'd examined the site of the hold-up, the posse rode on toward Bisbee, eventually tracking one of the horses to a chicken ranch belonging to a colored gent who introduced himself as Bob Henderson.

"Is this your horse, sir?" Wyatt asked, indicating a bay mare corralled near the house.

Henderson sighed and his posture deflated. "No, sir. I should have known…"

"Known what?"

"That someone with a badge would come looking for her." Henderson paused for a moment, but it seemed he already realized that he'd better tell the tale. "She belongs to Spence—Pete Spencer—a friend o' mine." By then he and Wyatt had walked over to the corral to consider the horse. "She's gone lame, d'you see? He asked me to care for her."

"All right," said Wyatt, unsurprised by the familiar name; Pete Spencer had a house on Fremont Street in Tombstone. "And where will we find Spence?"

They were directed to Frank Stilwell's livery in the town of Bisbee, where they found both Stilwell and Spencer. Wyatt arrested the pair. By then, Deputy Sheriff Dave Neagle, and Wells Fargo agent Marshall Williams and his friend Fred Dodge had joined them, so the Earps and Breakenridge had plenty of company while escorting the prisoners back to Tombstone.

Which didn't prevent the furious Stilwell and Spence muttering threats against the Earps along the way, and speculating between themselves about how they'd get their revenge. Wyatt just ignored it as best he could, and let Breakenridge try—with little effect—to reason them into peace. Morgan must be growing up, as he studiously followed Wyatt's example in not letting it rile him. Wyatt rewarded him with a wry smile and a nod, and didn't care who saw him.

Once the posse reached town, Stilwell and Spencer appeared in court before Judge Wells Spicer and were released on bail of seven thousand dollars each—paid in part by Ike Clanton. But matters didn't rest there. The Citizens' Vigilance Committee was grumbling back into life, and the tension in Tombstone seemed to brood like a hot afternoon threatening a thunderstorm.

The Cowboys' affiliations were proved to be wider still when a likewise furious Frank McLaury confronted Morgan on the sidewalk outside the Alhambra Saloon. Seeing this from where he was sitting inside with Doc, Wyatt got up and stepped close enough to overhear without intruding.

"I'll never speak to Spence again, for getting arrested by you boys!" McLaury was declaring. "Why d'you go after them?"

"They held up a stagecoach," Morgan calmly replied.

"So *you* say!" McLaury spat out.

"It's out of my hands now, anyway," Morgan continued. "There's a federal warrant for them robbing the passengers and robbing the mail. If you're so concerned, you'd better make sure they have a good lawyer."

None of this seemed to make a dent in McLaury's rage. "If you ever come after me, you'll never take me."

Wyatt was proud to see that Morgan remained reasonable. "If I ever have cause to come after you, Mr. McLaury, I'll arrest you."

"Arrest me? Hang me, more likely!"

This accusation at last provoked an irritable scowl. "Why in hell should you think that?"

"If that Vigilante Committee put you up to it."

"We're no part of them, and we don't stand for that brand of justice."

Now there was a change, but it was only to sharpen McLaury's anger into something meaner and more focused. "Maybe you never heard it, but I threatened the lives of you boys before," he declared, "and I took it back. But after what you've done, it now goes."

Morgan stared at him for a long, hard moment—and then he just shook his head once, turned away, and walked into the Alhambra. Wyatt watched as Frank McLaury seethed in impotent silence and then stalked off down Allen Street.

Once the immediate threat was gone, Wyatt went to join Morgan at the bar, where Doc was buying the two of them whiskies. "Coffee, Wyatt?" he asked.

"Thanks, Doc." Wyatt grasped Morgan's shoulder. "That was well done, Morg," he said quietly but firmly.

Morgan turned to him, and it was only then that Wyatt saw the turbulent fury and fear on his brother's face. "Was it?" Morgan asked in broken tones.

"Yes," said Wyatt.

"Yes," Doc echoed—and he slid an arm around Morgan's waist and squeezed in reassurance.

When Wyatt and Virgil encountered Billy Breakenridge the following day, Virgil warned him that Frank McLaury was making threats against the posse who brought in Stilwell and Spencer. "If you see the McLaury brothers in town, you'd better be prepared to defend yourself."

Breakenridge took this in with a thoughtful nod. "I heard Frank was talking large. When I saw Tom McLaury, though, he said he was sorry for Stilwell and Spence but it was none of his fight."

Virgil exchanged a glance with Wyatt, before turning back to Breakenridge. "That so?"

"Yes. He said he'd have nothing to do with it, as he had troubles enough of his own."

Wyatt could see Virgil's shoulders relax a little, though Virgil grimaced in confusion and reflected, "It's not like brothers not to stand by each other."

Billy Breakenridge seemed to be suppressing a smile at this, as he looked from one Earp brother to the other.

Wyatt decided to ask a difficult question while he could. "Virgil's maybe too discreet to mention it, Mr. Breakenridge, but did you have any thoughts on Frank Stilwell remaining a deputy sheriff while awaiting trial?"

A long moment passed before Breakenridge finally replied, "Maybe I'm too discreet to respond, Mr. Earp, but I note your concern."

"I guess even Behan can see how that looks…" Wyatt muttered under his breath.

"And Spence and his wife are living across the street from you both," Breakenridge observed. "It can seem a very small town, can't it?"

"You're right," said Virgil—and, with a polite tip of his hat, he farewelled Breakenridge, and he and Wyatt continued on down the sidewalk.

A small town, and a small county.

The Chiricahua Apache, abandoning a reservation commonly referred to as 'Hell's Forty Acres', headed through a pass in the Dragoon Mountains to the northeast of Tombstone. In early October, Billy Breakenridge found the body of a wood hauler in the pass, left in the Apache's wake—and soon a posse was riding out after them, through the Dragoons and into Sulphur Spring Valley.

An unseasonably heavy rainstorm set in, and a few of the party turned for home, but that still left almost twenty men in the posse, including Breakenridge and the three Earp brothers. Stopping for a short night's rest at Major Frink's ranch, the posse learned that the Apache had stolen a total of twenty-seven horses from Frink and his neighbors, the McLaurys.

The posse, along with Frink, followed the trail by moonlight, until it petered out in Leslie Canyon as if the Apache had cunningly dispersed. Frink and Breakenridge volunteered to scout on ahead, but the rest of the posse decided to retire for breakfast—at the ranch owned and run by Frank and Tom McLaury.

There was no question that hospitality would be offered, as always in this barren country, but Wyatt was glad for the posse being much larger than usual and including a fair number of regular citizens. If it had consisted only of the sheriff's and marshal's men, the meal would have been impossibly awkward. Wyatt and Morgan, figuring that the better part of valor was discretion, remained in the background.

Virgil, though, was more amicable, and could strike up a conversation with anyone. As he proved soon enough, seeing that Curly Bill Brocius was already there at the ranch along with a couple of Cowboys who Wyatt didn't recognize. Virgil and a citizen headed over to shake Curly Bill's hand and exchange views on the weather or whatever in a pleasant manner, while Wyatt and Morgan watched quietly from the far side of the room. Wyatt had done little more than offer a polite nod to the McLaurys and to Curly Bill, and they had done nothing more than acknowledge the courtesy.

"Do you reckon," Morgan asked after a while, "that Curly Bill remembers you saved his life from the vigilantes that time, and testified on his behalf?"

Wyatt huffed under his breath. "Memories can be awful short around here…" After a moment he added, "If he remembers anything, it's that I'm interested in law and order, and he knows he's usually on the other side of that argument."

Morgan sighed and muttered an agreement. The tense gathering wound on.

In the event, Frink recovered the horses by himself; suddenly riding out from cover as the group passed through a narrow canyon, and stampeding the horses back into Sulphur Spring Valley. The Apache, perhaps admiring his grit, let him and the animals be, and they faded away into the mountains to try making a new life for themselves.

October continued tiresome. Wyatt sat at home one morning with a pot of strong coffee, brooding over the consequences of Jim Crane's death. Leonard, Head and Crane had all been killed in other incidents—and it was generally agreed now that the Cowboys must have organized Luther King's escape from custody with a view to silencing him. Which meant that Wyatt's plan to clear Doc's name of participation in the Benson stagecoach hold-up was likewise ended. So, too, this particular chance for Wyatt to enhance his reputation as a successful lawman. He was determined to run against Johnny

Behan in the next elections for county sheriff, and win—and for that Wyatt needed the credit for an important arrest and conviction. The sort of arrest that Behan didn't seem ready, willing or able to make.

It had therefore become more vital than ever to see justice done in the Bisbee stagecoach hold-up. To that end Wyatt and Virgil had rearrested Frank Stilwell and Pete Spencer on the federal charges, and taken them to Tucson to stand trial. Both Virgil and Behan were there now, in order to testify.

Meanwhile, Ike Clanton was in town, and making loud remarks to Wyatt about broken promises and ill-kept secrets. Their agreement was null and void now, of course, but no one wanted the matter made public. Ike didn't want to be known as someone who would betray his friends—and neither did Wyatt want people to know he'd been prepared to pay someone to do so. He wondered which the Cowboys would think the larger sin, and suspected that maybe his own sin was the worse. Not that it made any difference. They would both be facing retribution.

"Wyatt?"

He started, and his right hand wandered by instinct toward the pistol he wasn't even wearing—but it was only Mattie and Allie coming in the front door. "What?" he replied, gruff in the aftermath of the spike of fear.

The two women came and stood by the table, Mattie looming over him, and Allie—well, she was too short to loom over anyone, but she was about the feistiest person he'd ever met. They were both tensed up with their fists clenched, and patently anxious.

"What's wrong?" he asked again.

"Marietta Spencer just visited," Allie announced.

Wyatt scowled up at them both, and addressed Mattie: "I told you to have nothing to do with them."

"*Listen*, Wyatt," Allie insisted.

All right, then. He didn't quit scowling, but he didn't say anything more, either.

Mattie burst out, "Marietta said the rustlers are plotting to get you—all three of you brothers."

Wyatt considered them carefully. "Have you got something specific? Because otherwise it ain't exactly news."

"They're planning to send Ike Clanton and Frank McLaury after you,

Wyatt," Allie explained. "Is that specific enough for you?"

"Maybe."

"They're telling Ike and Frank they'll be backed up by the rest of them—but they won't be."

"Just the two of them, then?" Wyatt nodded, feeling somewhat cooler about the odds, though Frank McLaury was reputed to be a deadly gunman.

Mattie said, "The rumor is that those two have been dealing with you, so their friends don't care if you get them in a fight—but, Wyatt, that'll just make them more desperate when they realize they're standing alone!"

Wyatt pondered this. It wasn't surprising that Ike's ill-kept secret was now known—through no fault of Wyatt's—and it seemed that Frank McLaury was known to be involved as well. Wyatt wondered who the third man had been, and if he would also be sent after the Earps.

"Wyatt—"

"It's all right, Mattie," he said, as soothingly as he could with most of his mind elsewhere.

"They might not get you all, with two against three," she retorted, "but chances are they'll get one or two of you."

"And that's one or two too many," Allie bluntly concluded. "I'm not losing Virge over trouble that you and Doc Holliday stirred up."

"It's all right," Wyatt repeated. "Leave it with me. I'll make sure Virge and Morg know, and our friends." He found a smile tugging at his mouth as he offered the thought, "Mattie, you know Doc wouldn't let anything bad happen to me."

"Oh, that *Doc*..." Mattie rolled her eyes in exasperation, just exactly as Virgil and Allie did. But at least that distracted her somewhat from the worry.

"You two and Louisa stay home—"

"Don't we always?" Allie muttered. Then she fired up again: "You buy land and build houses down the wrong end of town, with the Mexicans on this block and the Chinese on the next—and then you blame us for being friendly with Marietta. What do you *expect*, Wyatt, when the society women decided to have nothing to do with us?"

Wyatt didn't respond.

And apparently Allie decided she wasn't done yet. "I guess you don't mind Annie Kee doing the laundry for us, seeing as she does such a fine job of it for hardly no pay—so you'd better not mind that she takes a cup of tea with us when she makes a delivery!"

He held Allie's fierce gaze until she grimaced and gave up, and then finally Wyatt replied in heavy but level tones, "I've got no problems with your laundress. It's not her married to an outlaw who's threatened the lives of me and my brothers. Is it?"

Allie took a breath and began a retort—but then nodded instead, acknowledging his point. "All right. But Marietta doesn't owe Spence her loyalty, Wyatt. It's unconscionable the way he treats her, and her mother, too. She took a horrible risk, telling us about the rustlers, and I won't have you just dismissing it."

"I'm not," Wyatt concluded. "You two and Lou will be safe here. And I'll telegraph Virge in Tucson, all right, Allie? It'll be fine."

Allie lifted her chin in acknowledgment, and the two of them headed back to Virgil and Allie's house next door. Wyatt swallowed the rest of his coffee, and went to finish dressing.

Virgil returned to Tombstone on October 21st, having testified in the case against Frank Stilwell and Pete Spencer, and now declaring that he trusted in the court for a conviction. Wyatt was pleased and—he had to confess—relieved to see him. Not that the threatened trouble had erupted, but surely the ongoing tensions were less likely to come to anything with the more reasonable and most respected Earp back in town.

Wyatt was rather less pleased by another return. He was taking a break from faro late on the night of the 25th and eating a beef stew at the Alhambra Saloon's lunchroom, when he saw Doc Holliday enter in with Kate Elder on his arm. Wyatt suppressed a groan, and the food sank heavily in his gut. He knew all too well that Doc and Kate would argue heatedly and part ways on a regular basis, and then reconcile just as heatedly. But Wyatt had assumed Kate's sworn affidavit against Doc must have been the very last nail in the coffin of their relationship. Apparently not!

Doc spied Wyatt sitting at the lunchroom counter and began weaving between the tables toward him. On his way, unfortunately for all concerned, Doc brushed by Ike Clanton who was sitting alone over a meal. Neither Doc nor Ike was the sort to let a minor irritation fade away. Ike was on his feet in a moment and the two were loudly cursing each other as sons of bitches.

Wyatt was about to go over and tell them both to quit being idiots, but when he heard Doc start accusing Ike of calling his best friend a liar, Wyatt figured he'd only exacerbate the situation. Or maybe even join in the yelling himself.

Instead, Wyatt looked around to find Morgan watching from the Alhambra bar, and beckoned him over. "Go get Doc out of here, would you? Let Ike be, but get Doc out of the way. He won't mind it, coming from you."

"All right," Morgan agreed. Virgil had deputized him a month before, so Morgan took a moment to make sure his badge was clear to see on his coat's lapel—and waited for Wyatt's nod of approval—before gamely wading in.

When Morgan took Doc's arm in his, Doc went readily enough, with Kate following. Doc was still exclaiming against Ike despite Morgan talking low in his ear, perhaps cautioning him or counseling peace.

Ike, still fuming, mustn't have seen that Wyatt was also there in the lunchroom, as he soon stalked outside so he'd have someone to keep yelling at.

By the time Wyatt made it outside as well, Virgil had emerged from the Occidental Saloon next door, and stood there on the sidewalk glaring at Doc and Ike facing each other in the street. "If you two don't break this up," he cried out in a voice that cut through all manner of noise, "I'll arrest you both as drunk and disorderly. You want to spend the rest of the night in a cell and be fined in the morning, that's all right by me."

Doc and Ike at last shut up and now stood there glaring at each other. It seemed that Doc wasn't going to be the first to back down, and Wyatt muttered a fond curse at him for that, but after a long tense moment, Ike took a step back. "I ain't heeled!" he said, loudly enough to carry to witnesses. "I told you that. So don't go shooting me in the back."

Ike turned and walked away—which was just as well, for Doc did not take kindly to the notion that he would do such a thing. After directing a fierce scowl Ike's way, Doc turned and tipped his hat to Virgil, and then he and Kate headed back into the Alhambra. Morgan headed for the Oriental—rebuilt on a modest scale since the fire in June—and disappeared inside.

After watching everyone part ways, Virgil went back into the Occidental, and that left Wyatt to make his own way toward the Oriental and his faro game. He'd lost the taste for stew.

And he was reminded why soon enough. While Wyatt was still in the street, Ike caught up to him and started in again about Doc. "I won't take this fighting talk any longer. He comes at me when I ain't heeled… Well, I'll be heeled in the morning, and we can fetch this to a close."

"He didn't mean anything by it," Wyatt wearily tried to explain. "Doc was just defending a friend."

"I will be ready for all of you in the morning!"

"All of us?" Was Ike Clanton really fool enough to be threatening not only Doc Holliday, but also Marshal Virgil Earp and his brothers…? Wyatt shook his head. "I don't fight anyone if I can avoid it," he declared. "There's no money in it." And he turned and walked away toward the Oriental.

Ike wouldn't quit, though, tagging along after Wyatt as if he couldn't comprehend discouragement. "Don't go thinking I won't be after you all in the morning!"

"Ike, I didn't tell anyone about that deal we made. Doc doesn't like a friend being called indiscreet. That's all there was to it tonight. Leave it be."

And Wyatt strode into the saloon, shaking off Clanton at last.

Wyatt wasn't in the mood for a full night in town, so he headed for home not long after. Doc emerged alone from the Alhambra as if he'd been watching for him, and walked with Wyatt as far as Fly's boarding house. They didn't have much to say to each other, and Wyatt was comfortable enough with that. Although he did have one thing on his mind. "Kate's back in town, then," Wyatt remarked.

"For now," Doc replied, in easy tones but promptly as if he'd been expecting to be quizzed. "Her boarding house burned down."

"She couldn't find anywhere else to stay in Globe?"

Doc snorted. "No, I mean *her* boarding house that she manages. She thought she'd come visit while they're rebuilding."

Wyatt acknowledged this with a neutral huff of breath. It wasn't his place to get between a man and a woman who'd partnered up, though he didn't think he'd ever forgive Kate for signing that damnable affidavit…

"Don't worry," Doc murmured, as if he knew exactly what Wyatt was thinking. "It won't happen again."

It would be presumptuous to even respond to that reassurance, and in any case they had reached Fly's. Wyatt and Doc nodded a goodnight to each other, and Wyatt continued down Fremont Street to his own home.

Mattie was already asleep, and Wyatt was fine with that. He stripped off as far as necessary, rolled into bed beside her, and fled into a deep sleep.

He was shaken awake too early on the cold morning of October 26th, and cracked open an eye to see Ned Boyle, bartender at the Oriental, leaning over him. "Sorry, Wyatt. Thought you should know."

"What?" he croaked. Mattie pulled a shawl around her shoulders, got out of bed in a dignified silence, and headed through to the front room, hopefully to see to the fire. Wyatt stayed right where he was, huddled under the blankets. "What time is it?"

"Bit after eight," Ned replied. Wyatt blearily figured Ned must be heading home after a long night's work. "I just spoke with Ike Clanton, in the street down near the Grand."

"He's up already?"

Ned grimaced. "Hasn't been to bed at all, from what I could make out."

Wyatt let out a groan. If Ike was at last heading into the Grand Hotel to sleep it off, that was all well and good, but knowing Ike…

"He's looking for a fight, Wyatt, with you boys and Doc. He's telling everyone—and he's carrying a pistol, too."

"He's all talk," Wyatt said. "He'll get tired of it and go to bed, and that'll be that for today."

Ned looked skeptical. "Well, I hope so, but I thought you ought to know…"

"Appreciate it, Ned. But I need my sleep, and I'm sure you do, too."

"I'll head home, then," Ned replied, standing and putting on his hat. "Morning, Wyatt. Ma'am," he added as he stepped through into the front room.

"Morning," Wyatt mumbled, probably too late for his visitor to hear, before turning over, resettling and drifting off heedlessly.

It was past twelve when Wyatt ventured forth. The air had a bite to it which threatened snow in this year of extremes. As he headed up Fremont Street, Wyatt was approached by Harry Jones, one of Behan's deputies, who also passed on the news that Ike Clanton was roaming the town, hunting the Earps with a pistol and, Jones added, a Winchester rifle.

Wyatt sighed. It seemed that Ike had taken no rest that night, nor would he until a conclusion of some sort was reached. "I'll go find him," said Wyatt, "and see what he wants."

Virgil and Morgan had heard the same news, of course, from other sources. The three Earps spoke together briefly, and then broke up to go searching for Ike. Wyatt headed alone along Allen Street, having no luck.

It was Virgil and Morgan who found Ike emerging from the Capitol Saloon on Fremont—they buffaloed him and disarmed him, charged him with carrying a weapon in town, and escorted him to the recorder's court in the Gird Block.

Wyatt caught up with them there. The courtroom was full and bustling with people waiting on Judge Albert Wallace—Virgil had gone to find him. When Wyatt finally located Morgan he sat beside him, facing Ike who sprawled on another bench as if trying and failing to get comfortable. Ike had a handkerchief pressed to a wound on his temple which was still bleeding bright red, and there was a sour stink about him that spoke of a lengthy acquaintance with liquor. Surly scowls on both Ike and Morg's faces indicated they'd been arguing, but they now seemed to be waiting on Wyatt.

He took a breath and addressed Ike firmly. "You've been threatening my life, and the lives of my friend and my brothers, and I want it stopped."

Ike stared at Wyatt with a hundred replies roiling across his face, but he voiced none of them. He simply turned away, angry and dissatisfied, as if there could be no answer, not in that time nor in that place.

This glimpse of an unexpected complexity or two in Ike Clanton had Wyatt surging to his feet, his fury spiked with a fear he could not and would not acknowledge. "You cattle-thieving son of a bitch—and you *know* that I know you are a cattle-thieving son of a bitch—you have threatened my life enough, and you have got to fight."

Ike had turned back to face him right away. "Fight is my racket!" he declared. "All I want is four feet of ground to stand on."

Morgan let out a laugh that sounded oddly liquid. "You shall have it."

Ike's attention snapped to Wyatt's younger brother. "If you fellows hadn't snuck up behind me like I was a dog gone feral, I'd have furnished a coroner's inquest for the town."

"I'll pay your fine," promised Morgan, "soon as the judge appears, if you'll fight me after."

"If I had a six-shooter now, I would make a fight with all of you!"

At which Morgan held out Ike's own pistol, and Ike got up to claim it—but one of the deputy sheriffs came between them, declaring that he would not allow any fuss.

Wyatt knew, at some deep level, that he himself should be the one counseling calm. But this had gone too egregiously far already and must be ended. "Where will you fight?" he muttered under his breath while the three of them stood close.

"I'll fight you anywhere or any way," Ike retorted with a hectic kind of happiness.

It was probably as well that Virgil returned in that moment—along with the Judge, who proceeded to fine Ike twenty-five dollars on the weapons charge. Ike paid up with no hint of regret or repentance.

Virgil asked in his familiar reasonable tones where Ike wanted his guns left.

"Anywhere I can get them," Ike replied, "after how you boys have treated me this day."

There was no response from Virgil to this implied threat, but Wyatt felt a shrieking in his head like a steam whistle.

"Then I shall leave them with the barman at the Grand Hotel," Virgil said, before calmly walking out of the court carrying Ike's pistol and rifle.

Wyatt watched Virgil go, with Morgan tagging along after him. Ike also left, with a determined set to him that belied the fact that he hadn't slept the previous night and had instead apparently been taking a drink in every saloon in town.

One thing was certain: Ike's blowing and blustering could no longer be dismissed as all talk. Maybe it had been a mistake to ever think it could.

Wyatt walked out of the court and the cold slammed into him. It didn't cool him down any.

A moment later he found himself face-to-face with Tom McLaury, the younger of the brothers. Tom had his hands in his pockets, and it was too easy to suppose that when he withdrew them a pistol would come as well.

"Are you heeled or not?" Wyatt raised his left hand high to intimidate the man.

"No, I am not heeled," McLaury returned, starting to back away. "I've got nothing to do with anyone."

Wyatt followed him—and when Tom started freeing his hands, Wyatt slapped him with his left and drew his own pistol with his right.

"I'll make a fight with you anywhere," McLaury declared, as if the slap had stung hard.

"All right," Wyatt replied, "let's make a fight here."

But McLaury kept his hands steady in plain view, and kept his gaze on Wyatt's, with his breath even, not even glancing at Wyatt's gun. He wasn't going to make a move. Despite the fact that Wyatt was certain he could see a pistol jammed into McLaury's waistband, just over his right hip, covered by his coat.

"Jerk your gun and use it," Wyatt insisted.

Still nothing. It seemed that McLaury had enough self-restraint not to push it further.

Wyatt did not, though he didn't want to shoot McLaury. Instead, he took his finger off the trigger and shifted his grasp on the gun—and brought it down hard on the side of Tom McLaury's head, just under his hat.

McLaury dropped to the dirt, his hat rolling off and coming to rest by the sidewalk. Slowly he gathered himself and started getting up to his feet, shaky but defiant.

Wyatt let him have it again, and this time McLaury was smart enough to stay down. Wyatt walked away.

He bought a cigar at Hafford's Saloon, clipped the end and lit it, inhaled the earthy rich smoke. He wanted it to ground him, as he stood there in the darkness of the quiet barroom—and after another couple of deep lungfuls it did. He should have arrested Tom McLaury for carrying a weapon within the town limits, but there had been one horrible moment in which Wyatt hadn't trusted himself. One moment in which he'd crashed to his knees in the dirt and hit the man again and again, deaf to the shocked protests of onlookers. Or had he…?

Wyatt took another draw on the cigar, and stepped back into the bright, cold light of early afternoon. For a moment everything seemed still and quiet, but then Wyatt slowly came to realize that people were starting to mill about as if sensing that tensions were building. It wasn't Wyatt's imagination—a faculty that Doc had always teased him as being nonexistent anyway. Men were asking each other what was going on, and answering with odd snippets of news or rumor, and then moving on to ask their neighbor if they knew anything more.

Beyond imagination or speculation, there was the hard fact that Wyatt saw Billy Clanton and Frank McLaury enter George Spangenberg's Gun Shop, half a block north of where he stood outside Hafford's on Fourth Street.

Wyatt didn't necessarily consider this a provocation, but it felt so ominous that he became aware of little else.

Frank's horse wasn't hitched, and she followed her master loyally, stepping up onto the sidewalk, perhaps wanting to get away from the growing crowds. This was against city ordinances. Wyatt found himself striding down there, grabbing the horse's reins, and trying to force her back onto the street. Frank came out of the shop, looking about as narrowly focused as Wyatt was, and he, too, grabbed the reins.

"You'll have to get this horse off the sidewalk," Wyatt said. He wasn't being petty, he reminded himself, and he wasn't wanting to provoke, but the planks of the boardwalks would not bear a horse's weight.

Frank didn't reply, but made himself known to the animal and shifted her back. Then he returned inside the shop, where Billy Clanton could be seen ominously loading his cartridge belt. Ike Clanton was there, too, seeming very sorry for himself; it wasn't entirely clear, but Wyatt thought Ike hadn't yet retrieved his weapons from the Grand Hotel.

Virgil appeared beside Wyatt, and they both watched the three Cowboys for a long moment. There was no question now that both Frank and Billy were armed and supplied with ammunition, and maybe the rest of them were, too.

In wordless agreement, the Earp brothers turned and retraced Wyatt's steps back down Fourth Street. Wyatt was aware of Oliver Storm Cloud amid the crowd, watching him gravely until Wyatt passed by and tore his gaze away.

Morgan met up with Virgil and Wyatt on the sidewalk outside Hafford's

Saloon. Virgil was his usual solemn self but also seemed troubled, while Morg mirrored his older brother's expression exactly. Wyatt stared at them, feeling much the same way, and understanding for the first time why some folk had trouble telling the three Earp brothers apart.

Virgil was carrying a double-barreled shotgun. When Wyatt lifted an inquiring brow, Virgil said gruffly, "Borrowed it from Wells Fargo."

You're expecting a confrontation? Wyatt silently asked, and Virgil nodded once.

Still, when Ike Clanton walked south down Fourth Street—seeming oblivious to the presence of the Earps—someone asked him, "What's the trouble?" and Ike replied, "I don't think there'll be any trouble."

The three Earp brothers exchanged looks part hopeful but mostly skeptical. Ike Clanton blew hot one moment and cold the next, and no one could ever predict what he would do. Soon both of the Clanton brothers and both McLaurys had entered the Dexter Corral on Allen Street; the Earps could watch the entrance from where they stood.

Doc Holliday joined the Earps—and before they could even exchange greetings, Johnny Behan showed up as well. "What's all the excitement?" asked Behan. It seemed his day was only just starting.

"There are a number of sons of bitches in town looking for a fight," Virgil replied, his steady tones sounding rougher than usual.

The Earps fell silent for a moment then, as they watched the Clantons and McLaurys cross Allen Street, with two of them leading horses, and enter the O.K. Corral.

"If they're staying in town, we need to disarm them," said Virgil.

Behan shook his head. "They won't surrender to you without a fight."

"I'm not looking for a fight, but they have talked about nothing else. They cannot be armed while they're in town—not when they're making threats."

"I will go alone," Behan said, surprising all of them, "and see if I can't disarm them."

The Earps and Doc stared at him, but maybe it occurred to all of them that there might be some use made of the county sheriff's otherwise questionable friendship with the Cowboys.

"All right," said Virgil. "That's all I want."

Behan nodded, and slowly but deliberately walked away down Allen Street, head down as if he were still thinking over the matter.

One of the town's wealthier citizens, the stockbroker William Murray, stepped up to talk to Virgil. "I know you're going to have trouble," Murray announced without preamble. "I can get twenty-five armed men together at a moment's notice to support you and your deputies."

Virgil exchanged a wary glance with Wyatt—who knew they were both thinking there was no point in provoking a fight or exacerbating the Cowboys' resentments if they didn't need to. Virgil told Murray, "As long as those boys stay in the Corral, or if they start riding out of town, then I shall let them be. It's only if they come out on the street again looking to stay, that I'll take their arms and arrest them."

"All right, then," Murray said, and he stepped away. For a moment, Wyatt wondered if he should regret this, but he and his brothers had never wanted a part in the Citizens' Vigilance Committee, and after all they couldn't trust in anyone's courage or judgment as implicitly as they did those within their own circle.

Another businessman approached them—John Fonck—offering ten men to assist the marshal.

Virgil replied in the same way: "I don't mean to bother them while they're in the Corral preparing to ride out."

"Why," said Fonck, "they are down there on Fremont Street now, in the lot by Fly's, and they're not going anywhere."

"Fly's?" Doc echoed, that being his boarding house—and it occurred to Wyatt that maybe Kate Elder was there that afternoon.

Which was a concern, but beside the point. It had been twenty minutes or more since Sheriff Behan had left, and the situation was obviously still unresolved. Virgil turned to Wyatt; they both knew they could wait no longer.

"You're armed?" Virgil asked Wyatt and Morgan. It was obvious that they were—they were both carrying pistols, each loaded with five bullets and the hammer on the empty chamber as was their custom—but that wasn't all Virgil was asking. His brothers answered in the affirmative.

Doc said, "You're not going to leave me out, are you?"

"This is none of your affair," said Wyatt, not wanting Doc to feel obliged.

"That is a hell of a thing for you to say to me!"

"It's going to be a tough one."

"Tough ones are the kind I like."

Virgil didn't take the time to formally deputize him, and perhaps wouldn't have anyway—but he handed Doc the shotgun. "I don't want to provoke any excitement going down the street with a shotgun in my hand. Keep it under your coat as long as you can."

Doc understood perfectly, of course, and gave Virgil his walking cane in turn.

Virgil grasped the cane in his right hand, his gun hand. "Doc, I want you to stand guard. Keep your distance while we disarm them. God only knows how many of their friends are hanging about."

"Yes, sir," said Doc.

Virgil looked from one to the other of them, and didn't seem to find them wanting. He nodded once with a dour kind of satisfaction. "Come along, then."

As the four of them walked at a steady pace down Fremont Street, Johnny Behan came running up. "I'm here disarming that party!" he protested to Virgil. "Gentlemen, I won't allow any trouble."

Virgil strode past him without breaking step, and his brothers and friend followed suit.

"For God's sake, don't go down there, or you'll be murdered!"

They continued on with Behan tagging along a short distance behind—and a moment later Wyatt, Virgil and Morgan were forming a loose line along one side of a vacant lot, and Doc Holliday was standing a few feet away from Morgan, still on Fremont Street.

Facing them in a group were Ike and Billy Clanton, Frank and Tom McLaury, and a friend of theirs who promptly backed away from the confrontation. Frank and Billy were openly armed with pistols, and the McLaurys were standing by the two horses which each bore a rifle in a scabbard on their saddles.

A moment froze silent in the cold air. Every man who could had a hand on his gun, or had already drawn, ready for what might come.

Virgil had lifted his right hand, brandishing the cane, his left hand open palm-out—demonstrably unable to fire a shot—and he called out in firm yet reasonable tones, "Boys, throw up your hands! I'm here to disarm you."

None of them obeyed. If anything, the Cowboys tensed even further. Was that aggressive enough in itself to provoke a response? They obviously meant to resist, but Wyatt wasn't ready to act quite yet... not quite—

Reading the shifting signs as closely as Wyatt did, Virgil cried, "Hold! I don't want that!"

Despite which, two shots were fired—Billy aiming at Wyatt but shooting wide, and Wyatt hitting Frank in almost the same moment.

At which more pistols were drawn, Virgil switching the cane to his left hand. After a brief pause another burst of shots was fired—Morgan, Doc with the shotgun, and Frank—and then all were firing as best they could. Wyatt stayed on Frank, the most dangerous of the four.

Tom McLaury was hit, and desperately trying to retrieve his rifle from a nervous horse. *Didn't he have a pistol before?* When the rifle remained stuck in its scabbard, Tom left it and stumbled off down Fremont toward Third Street, at least temporarily out of the fight.

Wyatt didn't have time to watch him—Ike Clanton blundered toward Wyatt, grabbing his left forearm in both hands, threatening to unbalance him. "Don't shoot! Don't shoot me!"

Wyatt struggled to throw him off. *He seemed unarmed at Spangenberg's.* "Go to fighting, or get away!"

At last Ike broke off and ran for shelter in Fly's boarding house.

Virgil had staggered for a moment as if hit—and now Morgan fell—but then both were up again and firing. Doc cried out as if hurt, but remained standing tall.

Frank, though crouching over a belly wound, grabbed a horse's reins and began making his way into Fremont Street, firing at the Earps and taking their fire until at last he was on the ground and done.

Billy was slumped back against the wall of Harwood House, obviously badly injured but still firing—until his pistol was out of bullets and he was too far gone to reload.

In the confusion, the fight took forever and yet was over in an instant. Later, Wyatt would be told it lasted thirty seconds or a little less, with thirty shots fired. He himself wasn't injured, but it was the grimmest half-minute of his life.

A shocked silence spread after the gunfire stopped, and people began slowly stepping forward to see what could be seen, do what could be done. Someone nudged the pistol out of Billy's hand and kicked it aside.

Then a steam whistle shrieked, and Wyatt started. But this time it was a mine sounding the warning. Too late to help, of course, but armed citizens came running to add to the chaos on Fremont Street.

CHAPTER SIXTEEN:

A CONSTRUCTIVE CITIZEN

Tombstone, Arizona;

October-November 1881

Doc could see that Wyatt was all right. Wyatt was his usual cool, collected self, and was moving freely—the only one unharmed of those who'd been part of the gunfight. His focus was on taking care of his brothers, who'd both been injured, and Doc wasn't needed just then, so he turned and made his way up to his room in Fly's boarding house.

Kate was there, standing betwixt door and window, caught between curiosity and self-preservation. "Doc," she said in thick tones, seeming relieved to see him.

Doc went to sit on the side of the bed, and for a moment the shock of it all vented in a burst of tears. "Oh, this is awful—just awful."

"Are you hurt?" Kate asked, coming close with her hands reaching out as if offering him comfort.

He discarded hat and coat, and loosened his shirt enough to see a mark across his hip where one of Frank McLaury's bullets had grazed him. "No, I am not." It was nothing, given what else had transpired.

Doc stood, poured out some water and cleaned the slight wound, set his clothing to rights, and then washed his face. "I have to go. Virgil and Morg were hit, and I need to help Wyatt."

"Yes," Kate said gently, escorting him to the door of their room. "Go and help Wyatt."

It was the first time in a very long while that she'd said Wyatt's name without resentment.

Virgil and Morgan were put to bed at Virgil's house, with Louisa taking care of them and the feisty Allie armed and ready to defend them against all comers. The brothers were both in pain—especially Virgil, though his injury was less serious—but Doc thought they should heal well enough.

He and Wyatt walked out that evening to try to discover what might happen next. The McLaury brothers and Billy Clanton had died of their wounds, and inevitably there was fearful talk about a mass retaliation from the Cowboys. Citizens belonging to the Vigilance Committee strolled about the streets, armed and ready, but in reality the town seemed to be carrying on as usual, if a little subdued.

The next day presented more of a challenge. The bodies of the three Cowboys were displayed in the undertaker's window under a sign reading *Murdered in the Streets of Tombstone*, and the funeral procession following them to the Boot Hill cemetery was by far the largest the town had ever seen—at least half as many again as had paid their respects to Marshal Fred White.

The gunfight would not be easily forgotten nor forgiven. And, Doc thought, probably neither should it be.

The coroner's inquest took two days to determine that:

William Clanton, Frank and Thomas McLaury, came to their deaths in the town of Tombstone on October 26, 1881, from the effects of pistol and gunshot wounds inflicted by Virgil Earp, Morgan Earp, Wyatt Earp and one Holliday, commonly called 'Doc' Holliday.

"Even you, Wyatt," Doc remarked, "could not state the obvious so clearly."

Wyatt remained grim. The Earps had of course hoped that the coroner's findings would declare their actions justifiable, which might have meant the end of the legal ramifications, but that was not to be.

It was hardly surprising that Ike Clanton was also expecting more. In response to the coroner's carefully non-partisan statement, on October 30th Ike Clanton filed first-degree murder complaints against the Earps and Doc, alleging they had acted with malice aforethought. This was a capital offence, that could mean their deaths if found guilty.

Judge Wells Spicer issued warrants for their arrests, though Morgan and Virgil were permitted to remain at home undisturbed. Wyatt hired Thomas Fitch as defense attorney for the Earp brothers, while Doc hired T.J. Drum on his own behalf.

A preliminary hearing began on October 31st, during which Spicer collected and considered evidence with the aim of determining whether the Earps and Doc should stand trial.

The hearing lasted a month, and for the first week Wyatt and Doc were released on bail. As the initial damning testimony was heard, though, the prosecution asked that bail be revoked—and Wyatt and Doc spent the following sixteen days in jail.

Unfortunately for Doc, Tombstone now had its own jail; a small wooden affair, with two cells behind iron bars. The sturdiness of the bars seemed ridiculous to Doc when he thought that even he could break through the planks forming the outer walls with a well-placed kick or two. Which wasn't the problem for a pair of honorable gentlemen. Doc and Wyatt would do their time. The problem was that the small wood stove in the far corner wasn't generously supplied, and what little heat it generated did nothing to prevent the bite of the cold night air.

Wyatt sat on his bed in the other cell, seeming comfortable enough with a blanket around his shoulders. He was watching Doc, who despite the early hour had not scrupled to climb into his own bed and burrow under the covers. It must have been obvious that Doc was shivering. It was a wonder he didn't set the whole building rattling.

"Harry," Wyatt said to the undersheriff who was guarding them, "I'll stay here. You don't need to keep an eye on me. But take Doc to a room at Mrs. Woods' boarding house."

"I'm all right," Doc declared. It wasn't as if his teeth were chattering.

Harry Woods—himself in two coats with a shawl wrapped snug around his shoulders, and sitting hunched over the stove—bestirred himself. After a long moment, he said, "I can't do that, Wyatt." They didn't need to ask why. Everyone remembered all too well what had happened with Luther King making his escape from Woods' custody, and now he must play it strictly by the book. Another pause lengthened before Harry offered, "Guess I can go fetch another blanket."

"No, then," Wyatt replied, standing and gathering up his own pair of blankets. "Just let me in there with him, and we'll share."

A moment's consideration, and then Harry came over to unlock the door to Wyatt's cell and then Doc's. He didn't lock them again, perhaps thinking that Wyatt might want to retreat to his own bed at some stage. Then Harry returned to settle into his chair by the stove, turned away far enough to allow for some privacy, but not so far that he wouldn't catch any untoward movement in the corner of his eye.

Not that Doc was moving. He was lying frozen in place, struck more by wariness than the weather now. Wyatt was efficiently arranging his blankets over Doc and tucking them in, and then he stood for a moment.

Doc belatedly began shifting back in the narrow bed to give Wyatt room to join him—but Wyatt had other ideas. "Come this way," he said, beckoning with one hand. "It's colder by the wall."

Once Doc had turned onto his side as close to the edge of the bed as feasible, Wyatt put his hands on either side of Doc and sprang over him, then got under the blankets—and was not shy in hauling Doc back into his top-to-toe embrace. "All right?" Wyatt murmured, settling his head beside Doc's on the pillow.

Doc could feel his friend's breath on the nape of his neck, and already the coldness that had taken hold of Doc was edging away from Wyatt's warmth. "Mmm, yes," he replied, "I thank you," while silently reflecting that really his own dear Wyatt had *no* idea.

CHAPTER SEVENTEEN:

WHISKEY WISHES

Tombstone, Arizona;

November 1881

Johnny Ringo had been abandoned. He'd spent weeks riding in the wilderness, gallivanting under the stars, sleeping in what shelter he could find, drinking whiskey and meandering about, and asking the few people he met if they'd seen anyone matching Lucian's description. None of them had, of course, though most of them obligingly puzzled through their memories. The son of the Devil did not reappear, nor did he seem likely to. Johnny never felt nor even glimpsed those hints of a presence he'd had before, those flares and glimmers of light that teased with the notion they might coalesce into a presence…

He never gave up on his quest, but eventually Johnny found himself in Tombstone again, and the place felt bewilderingly overwrought. Three of the Cowboys had been killed in a shootout with Doc Holliday and the Earps. Three of Johnny's… acquaintances rather than friends, he supposed. Frank McLaury had always been doomed to such an end, but Johnny felt a pang for Billy Clanton who at nineteen was in many ways still just a boy. If he would grieve for anyone, though, it might be Tom McLaury, who had been quiet and intelligent, handsome, and a more reasonable man than most, who had taken care of the business side of things at the McLaurys' ranch.

There was a trial going on—or a preliminary hearing, anyway—though he'd heard that the defendants were out on bail. Ike Clanton was going about the town declaring that the Earps and Holliday would be hung— "and if the law don't oblige, we'll hang 'em ourselves."

Johnny didn't join in the noise, but instead found himself wending his way over to Fly's boarding house and climbing the stairs to Doc's room, thinking that at least Johnny could wait for him there, and maybe in the meantime enjoy the comfort of a proper bed for the first time in weeks.

But Doc's woman Kate Elder was there instead. When she opened the door to his knock, she fixed Johnny with a sharp, knowing glance, but then took a step back and welcomed him in. "Mrs. Holliday," he said, taking off his hat.

"Mr. Ringo," she responded, with a slightly mocking tone for these formalities, which almost made Johnny smile. Yes, they could deal honestly together.

He stood there in the largest open space in the room with his hat in both hands, and he did *not* glance at the bed, while she closed the door.

"What can I do for you?" Kate asked, taking a step or two closer but no more than that.

"I guess Doc knows what Ike Clanton is saying."

"Threatening to hang him, legally or otherwise?" When he nodded, she continued, "Yes. But go talk to him if you want. Not now—they'll be in court—but this evening. As of last night, they're holding Doc and Wyatt in jail."

Johnny took a breath to speak, but then paused. The situation was impossible, but if Doc knew what was going on, then it wasn't as if he couldn't take care of himself well enough. It wasn't as if Johnny could do anything to help.

"What is it?" Kate asked. "Do you know something more? Something specific? You should go talk to him."

"I can't," he said.

She looked at him shrewdly. "Because of Wyatt...?"

Johnny wasn't entirely sure what she meant, but it was indeed because of Wyatt, so he settled for nodding—and she nodded, too. Perhaps they were both all too aware of Doc's loyalties, or more to the point his loyalty, singular. Perhaps they both wished it were otherwise.

A thoughtful moment stretched, and then Johnny said, "Doc will be all right where he is, but maybe you shouldn't be staying here. Ike will be keeping an eye on this place for when Doc's released—and it all happened right next to this building, didn't it?"

"Yes, it did."

"Not that Ike has even a line of poetry in his soul, but that would strike him as fitting."

"To ambush Doc here?" Kate shivered. "I saw him that morning, you know. I was looking through the photographs in Mr. and Mrs. Fly's studio, and Ike Clanton came through with a rifle, asking for Doc."

"The only thing on Ike's mind right now is revenge, and it won't be pretty."

Kate's expression grew troubled, and she turned away. "I want to go back to Globe, Mr. Ringo, but I have no money. I had seventy-five dollars, but Doc lost it playing faro."

Johnny's brow rose in surprise at Doc having such bad luck at cards and being so unchivalrous to boot, but there was an obvious solution to the problem. All Johnny needed for himself now was cheap whiskey, and he had plenty of money for that. He delved into his pocket and peeled off fifty dollars in bills. "Take it," he said, holding it out to her, "and take care."

She didn't say anything, but she took the money and shook his hand, and her eyes gleamed in gratitude.

It was the one useful thing he did while in Tombstone. Otherwise, he drank whiskey, sitting on Doc's old seat at the bar in the Grand Hotel. Not that even Doc Holliday would be reckless enough to venture into Cowboy territory these days, surely. Doc had chosen a side, men were dead, and there could be no more fraternizing across the lines that had been drawn—or indeed etched.

Johnny stayed where he was, though. It had worked once, waiting here for Lucian, and though he knew it was hopeless now, still he stayed. In the evenings, the glow of the lamplight would gently taunt him with memories of his demon lover, and the only response left to him was to take another drink and sink lower and lower into dreams…

Chapter Eighteen:

Threats, Assaults and Braggadocio

Tombstone, Arizona;

November 1881 – January 1882

After a couple of weeks, the tenor of the hearing changed yet again, and the defense lawyers successfully requested the release on bail of Wyatt and Doc, with two of the most powerful businessmen in town acting as sureties for them. Wyatt began feeling more confident of the outcome.

Nevertheless, the three Earp brothers and their wives—along with the once-more solitary Doc Holliday—moved into adjoining rooms at the Cosmopolitan Hotel for the sake of security and solidarity. "Is Kate still at Fly's?" Wyatt asked Doc as they stood together in the hallway outside their rooms in the darkest hours of the night. "She'd be better off here."

Doc shook his head, just once, and seemed to be contemplating the intricate pattern of the carpet runner. "Went back to Globe while you and I were in the hoosegow, with nary a message left for me."

"Oh," said Wyatt, wondering why he wasn't aware of it if Doc and Kate had had one of their bust-ups during these past days in which Wyatt and Doc had hardly ever been apart. No one in the vicinity of an argument between Doc and Kate could possibly not notice.

"She'll probably write." Doc didn't seem convinced or even very concerned. After a moment he lifted his head and looked at Wyatt. Doc's expression was neutral, though he seemed to be waiting for something.

Words filled Wyatt's mouth, weighed down his tongue. He almost asked, 'Will you be warm enough on your own?' but of course Doc would be. There was no lack of creature comforts at the Cosmopolitan. Wyatt wasn't fool enough to question the matter. But still they both stood there, waiting.

Until at last Wyatt simply nodded and said, "Goodnight, then," and Doc murmured, "Goodnight, my friend." Wyatt turned away and headed for his own room, his own bed, and he held Mattie in his arms all night long instead.

Feelings in the town remained tense and were growing troubled. Wyatt was all too aware of the Grand Hotel—the haunt of the Cowboys—standing firm against the Cosmopolitan across the width of Allen Street.

The last testimony in the preliminary hearing was given on November 29th, and Judge Wells Spicer only made them wait until the following afternoon for his decision. He came down firmly on the side of law and order. Wyatt's sense of relief related more to the fact that Spicer considered the Earps' actions to be appropriate in the circumstances.

> *I cannot resist the conclusion that the defendants were fully justified in committing these homicides; that it was a necessary act, done in the discharge of an official duty.*

The only criticism Spicer had was for Virgil, who had *acted incautiously and without proper circumspection* in *calling upon Wyatt Earp and J.H. Holliday to assist him in arresting and disarming the Clantons and McLaurys.* Testimony had detailed Doc's quarrel the previous night with Ike Clanton, the *hot words* exchanged by Wyatt and Ike that morning, and the *difficulty* Wyatt had had immediately afterwards with Tom McLaury. Virgil must have realized that Wyatt and Doc's presence when confronting the Clantons and McLaurys could well be provocative. However, Spicer concluded,

> *I can attach no criminality to his unwise act. In fact, as the result plainly proves, he needed the assistance and support of staunch and true friends, upon whose courage, coolness and fidelity he could depend in case of an emergency.*

The case was presented to a grand jury in mid-December, but the jury did not see fit to indict the Earps and Doc, so the matter would go no further. Wyatt felt that Virgil and his deputies had been vindicated, that the confrontation had been unfortunate but necessary—and most of the townsfolk seemed to concur.

But Ike Clanton, of course, was more furiously resentful than ever, and young Billy Clanton and the McLaury brothers had had many friends among the rustlers and ranchers who felt likewise. The town of Tombstone seemed more settled than it had been for a long while—but discontent still lurked in the countryside surrounding it and at times made its presence felt. Threats were still muttered, anonymously or thirdhand, but Wyatt was inclined to dismiss them. A judge had declared that the Earps and Doc had acted lawfully, and that must be enough for all.

Soon, however, even the judge himself was threatened, in an anonymous letter that Wells Spicer asked the *Epitaph* to print along with his response. The author of the letter recommended that Spicer depart for *a more genial clime, as you are liable to get a hole through your coat at any moment.* Spicer responded that *fight is not my racket*, but they knew where to find him should they want him.

Everyone knew where to find the Earps.

Even the new President of the United States, Chester Arthur, was aware of the Cowboys and he raised the issue in his first State of the Union address.

> *The Attorney-General calls attention to the disturbance of the public tranquility during the past year in the Territory of Arizona. A band of armed desperadoes known as 'Cowboys', probably numbering from fifty to one hundred men, have been engaged for months in committing acts of lawlessness and brutality which the local authorities have been unable to repress. The depredations of these 'Cowboys' have also extended into Mexico, which the marauders reach from the Arizona frontier. With every disposition to meet the exigencies of the case, I am embarrassed by lack of authority to deal with them effectually. The punishment of crimes committed within Arizona should ordinarily, of course, be left to the Territorial authorities; but it is worthy consideration whether acts which necessarily tend to embroil the United States with neighboring governments should not be declared crimes against the United States.*
>
> *It seems to me that whatever views may prevail as to the policy of recent legislation by which the Army has ceased to be a part of the posse comitatus, an exception might well be made for permitting the military to assist the civil Territorial authorities in enforcing the laws of the United States. This use of*

the Army would not seem to be within the alleged evil against which that legislation was aimed. From sparseness of population and other circumstances it is often quite impracticable to summon a civil posse in places where officers of justice require assistance and where a military force is within easy reach.

The report of the Secretary of the Interior, with accompanying documents, presents an elaborate account of the business of that Department. I ask your careful attention to the report itself.

Wyatt read an account of the speech in the *Epitaph*, and felt the whole thing keenly.

The Cowboys themselves seemed to pay it no mind.

Virgil had only just walked out of the Oriental Saloon onto Allen Street, late on the night of December 28th, when Wyatt heard four or five shotgun blasts from close by. He ran outside to find Virgil staggering back toward him, hunched over with one arm hanging loose, and dark wet patches on his black coat that meant blood.

There were cries of "Head them off!" and a few citizens running past them, so Wyatt concentrated on Virgil. "Can you make it to your room?"

"Yes," Virgil hissed in an answer more determined than certain, and he began lurching in that direction.

Wyatt supported him as best he could, and called to the nearest passers-by, "Fetch the doctor!"

"Which one?" was the witless response.

"Both of them!"

A short but agonizing while later Virgil—only recently recovered from the bullet wound he'd received in October—was stretched out on his bed at the Cosmopolitan with Drs. Henry Matthews and George Goodfellow in attendance, and the faithful Allie at his side.

Shotgun pellets had hit Virgil's back and thigh, and shattered his left elbow. There was talk of the amputation of that arm, to which Virgil was vehemently opposed, and the doctors didn't manage to sway either Wyatt or Allie to their view of things. Still, an operation was required in order to remove the fragments of bone. All in all, the prognosis did not look good.

In a quiet moment before the doctors began their bloody work, Virgil drew Allie close with his good arm; she tucked her head in against his shoulder, and he pressed a kiss to her hair. Wyatt watched the warmth of their mutual devotion with something like envy in his breast.

Then he turned away, and went to send a telegram asking to be appointed deputy U.S. marshal in order to bring justice for Virgil.

With a feeling of inevitability, the new year began with the Sandy Bob stagecoach to Bisbee being held up and sixty-five hundred dollars in cash stolen from the Wells Fargo box despite Charlie Bartholomew riding shotgun.

The very next day, the stage coming in from Benson was also held up, this time earning the robbers little more than bragging rights—but that may have been riches enough when one of the passengers proved to be Wells Fargo chief detective James Hume, coming to Tombstone to deal with the ongoing stage robberies.

Hume talked first with Marshall Williams, at length, and then Hume asked Wyatt to meet with him in the Wells Fargo office. "I want to be frank with you, Wyatt," Hume said as he closed the door firmly behind the two of them. "Anything we say here will remain in confidence, unless we agree otherwise. All right?"

"All right," Wyatt responded. It was how he usually operated, after all.

"We're closing down the Bisbee office," Hume announced with no further preamble while they were still on their feet. "If Wells Fargo wanted to lose that much money, there are far less dangerous ways of doing it than working the Tombstone-Bisbee route."

"And this office?" Wyatt asked.

"Will remain open." Hume sat behind the desk and indicated Wyatt should sit opposite him. "Not that I'm overly fond of Tombstone, as you know—but I might be here a while anyway," Hume muttered, "trying to make sense of Marshall's bookkeeping. For my sins," he added, pushing aside a hefty ledger and other paperwork. Then he leaned forward into the cleared space to ask, "How's your brother? How's Virgil?"

"Recovering," Wyatt replied, "or starting to, anyway. We'd feared the worst."

"I'm glad to hear he's mending. You Earp boys were made sturdy."

"He kept his left arm, but he's lost the use of it."

Hume nodded, and left a sympathetic pause before asking, "You attribute the shooting of your brother to this same group of cattle rustlers and stage robbers—the Cowboys?"

"Yes," said Wyatt. "The shots came from a half-built place across from the Oriental Saloon on Allen Street. Virgil saw Frank Stilwell going in there just as he stepped outside. You'd remember Stillwell's awaiting trial for the September hold-up of the Bisbee coach."

"I remember."

"We found Ike Clanton's hat—with his name in it—at the back of the building, as if he'd dropped it while running away."

"The older brother of Billy Clanton?"

Wyatt confirmed this with a nod. "There are two older brothers, Ike and Phin. We've had more to do with Ike, but they both have reason to hate us. There's also been talk about Curly Bill Brocius being involved."

"All of them 'Cowboys'?"

"Yes, sir."

Hume was making notes in a small bound book that he'd taken out of his coat pocket. When he was done, he took a deliberate breath and then asked, "Who do you think responsible for these two stage hold-ups?"

Wyatt took a moment for thought, but he was too cautious to name names without good reason—Pony Diehl, for instance, had been mentioned in connection with both the assault on Virgil and the Bisbee hold-up, but Wyatt wasn't sure of Diehl's guilt—and in this climate any careless spark might set off a flash and a half of lightning. "It's not clear yet," Wyatt replied in measured tones. "We're investigating."

Hume put his pen down, and closed his book though he kept a firm hold on it. Wyatt had formed the impression that the notebook never left Hume's immediate possession, and he wondered what other combustible notions had been recorded on its pages.

The Wells Fargo detective had sat back in his chair to coolly consider Wyatt, and now at last he said, "If you'll form a posse and ride out to arrest these men—for the shooting, for the hold-ups—Wells Fargo will fund your expenses. Does that sound like something you can do?"

Could he...? Hell, there'd be nothing he'd like more. Wyatt's heart thudded once, hard. "Yes, sir, it does."

"Good man," said Hume. They stood and shook hands on it.

New management was taking over the Oriental, which made it convenient for Wyatt to sell his gambling concession at the saloon. A secure amount of readily available cash seemed far more useful now than the distractions of earning an income.

He began thinking about the membership of his posse, too. Morgan would ride with him, of course, and Doc would always be at Wyatt's side— and he had no argument with solid men such as Dave Neagle, Fred Dodge, Marshall Williams, Bob Paul. But perhaps the time had come to look beyond the townsfolk, the lawmen, the citizens.

Perhaps it was time to seek men who had the right principles but were patterned more on Doc Holliday than Wyatt Earp. Wanderers such as Sherman McMaster; men who were adventurers by nature, such as Turkey Creek Jack Johnson and Texas Jack Vermillion.

Virgil was maimed and in pain, and would be confined to his bed for months yet. It was time for Wyatt to respond to this attempt at assassination in ways that the Cowboys would understand.

CHAPTER NINETEEN:

BROKEN-MINDED

Tombstone, Arizona;

January 1882

Everything was gone from him, everyone was gone, and Johnny Ringo had nothing left but whiskey. Or maybe there was one more thing left to do.

He was weaving unsteadily through the sauntering crowd on Allen Street, questing for a fresh bottle of liquor, when he saw Wyatt Earp and Doc Holliday approaching together, walking shoulder to shoulder—or, rather, first he saw their souls. Wyatt's was upright and true, as unimaginative and solid as the man himself, and Doc's soul was more decorative and mysterious but standing tall beside his friend's. Johnny fancied that if he put this into words, Doc would see it immediately, and he'd share that slow, secretive smile of his with Johnny, while Wyatt would not comprehend.

And then maybe Doc would ask Johnny about his own soul, and by now Johnny had forgotten what it even looked like, it had been so long sundered from him. While Doc's soul was not only firmly affixed to Doc but also tethered to Wyatt's now, as if the two would never be broken apart, and this—if he hadn't been convinced of it before—proved that Doc had no further interest in Johnny. Not that their encounters were ever affectionate, but despite Doc having heard all Johnny's secrets, there had been a sympathy in Doc, and a wish for his welfare, that Johnny had found nowhere else.

Everything and everyone was gone from him. But there was one more thing to do.

"Let's end this!" Johnny cried out to Wyatt Earp. "Let's finish this now." His hand on the pistol tucked into his waistband, just in case his intent wasn't clear.

"You've been drinking, Ringo," Wyatt replied, already turning away in dismissal. "Go sleep it off, and we'll talk tomorrow."

"No, I'm ready now. Let's play for keeps."

Some of the folk nearest them had paused to watch, and started drawing back to give them room. Others, walking past beyond them, seemed unaware that anything was happening at all.

Doc had stepped forward, no doubt intentionally half-sheltering his friend. "You and I have nothing to lose, Johnny, so it's easy to play for keeps."

"Let's do it, then."

"The thing I like about Wyatt, though," Doc mused, hand on the pistol in his gun belt, but pondering slow as if he had all the time in the world, "is that he has *everything* to lose—and he still plays for keeps."

Johnny stared at him, wondering if Doc could possibly know how provocative he was being. Probably. He very probably did. Johnny firmed up his grip on his pistol. "Come on, Holliday. I know you're not all talk."

For a moment there was a hint of a familiar appreciative smile on Doc's lips. "You are right about that, pilgrim."

"Let's have it out here and now."

And for a moment… for a moment they were on the brink… and Johnny had no doubts, no regrets, no wishes for an end any different from this…

But a weighty hand grasped Johnny's right arm above the elbow and made it impossible for him to draw—and Johnny saw Wyatt grasp Doc's arm a moment later likewise—and the chance fell apart and was lost in the cold, light air.

An encounter that might have been superb out there on the street now turned trivial. It was James Flynn who'd stopped Johnny, wearing Virgil Earp's town marshal badge. Johnny and Doc were arrested for disturbing the peace, and fined thirty-two dollars each. It was all very gentlemanly—when Johnny couldn't find even twenty dollars in his pockets, Doc stepped in with a murmured, "If you'd be so good as to allow me…" and he paid the full amount on Johnny's behalf.

Johnny would have hated him then if he'd had the verve, but his head ached and his soul yearned, and maybe he was matching Doc's civility when he forbore to mention gifting his own funds to Doc's woman, or more likely Johnny was just too reduced to even speak anymore…

He noticed Doc palming a folded bill as their business in court was concluded, as if to discreetly pass it over with a shake of Johnny's hand—but Johnny shrugged and turned to go, saying over his shoulder, "I got enough for a bottle of whiskey."

"Pilgrim…" Doc sighed. "Why do you drink so much?"

Johnny didn't have the energy left to take umbrage, but he was curious, so he turned back and retorted, "Why do you?"

"Self-medication. Haven't you noticed all consumptives are drunks or laudanum addicts? But for you, it's… despair. Isn't it?"

He would have laughed if he could. "I'll see if there's an answer to that in the next bottle."

And Doc quietly farewelled him with a wish: "May you find truth and beauty at the bottom of it."

A day later—or two days, or three, Johnny couldn't tell—he was brought in by the law again, this time for holding up a poker game in Galeyville. He had a vague memory of the occurrence, or at least could imagine it, and he couldn't deny it sounded like him. Apparently he'd gotten away with over five hundred dollars! Which would have been riches enough to sustain him in style for a year or more, though where the money was now was anyone's guess. Johnny shrugged, and let Deputy Sheriff Billy Breakenridge escort him to jail.

"You pleaded not guilty when Dave Neagle arrested you for this, back in November," Breakenridge tried reminding him.

"Did I?" he responded, astonished. Even if he'd committed the crime, he had no memory of any consequences. Unless maybe… Johnny frowned, reweaving the tale in his head… and eventually decided maybe the least said, the soonest mended. "Well, I'll stick with not guilty, eh?" he said with the friendly smile that Abe Franklin used to provoke in him. Franklin… Galeyville… Lucian abandoning him… Maybe there was something to this hold-up story after all.

Breakenridge remained unmoved by the smile, unamused by Johnny's honest confusion. "You've been out on bail these past two months. You haven't forgotten that, have you?"

It was true that Johnny wouldn't want to forfeit any bail money… He wondered if that's where the five hundred dollars was now, being held for him, and therefore whether he could recover it. That would buy him enough whiskey to drown in…

Breakenridge locked him in a cell, and said nothing more. Darkness followed day, and it was bitterly cold but that wasn't why Johnny was shaking. They brought him food and drink—better food than he'd eaten in a long while, but not enough drink, never enough drink. The process of sobering up wasn't pleasant.

Johnny remained silent as much as he was able. But the next time it was daylight, and he felt the return of his wits or at least enough of his wits to begin making some kind of sense, he asked for paper and pencil. They brought it to him readily, and he sat against the wall, flattening the paper against one thigh propped up, and he began pondering on or at least trying to find words for Doc Holliday's soul.

Righteous

He'd thought that before. He'd even said it out loud to Doc himself.

Doc was a Southern gentleman, and he had the soul to suit. He hadn't lost it, or forfeited it, or bargained bits of it away. Other people, Johnny suspected, would be surprised to hear this, would never believe him.

Whole. ~~Integral~~. An integrity in form and purpose.

That was the thing he was thinking about now, wasn't it? Fully formed and yet—

> *Whole in its own right*
> *yet also completed by another. The man beside you—*
> *Unaware. Righteous, too, but ~~innocent~~ ~~ignorant~~ naïve*

Johnny growled in frustration. The words weren't flowing as they used to do when he had an idea to be captured, an image clear in his mind. Usually, by the time he got to writing it down, the draft was already polished into perfection.

At least that last word was the right one. Would people be surprised to hear that Wyatt Earp was naïve…?

Two ~~whole~~ complete souls, but each more complete in partnership

His guts stirred sourly, and Johnny wondered if his own resentment was hobbling his mind.

You love him with everything you are,
and he hardly knows the first thing about it.
Does he?

There.

He was done. Not the poem, which had finally staggered into a moment of clarity, but Johnny himself. He was done, and his pretensions to versifying were over.

He let himself fall loose, rolled the back of his head against the wooden walls, seeking the sharpness, the precision of pain. He let the paper and pencil go.

But then, after a moment, his gaze was snared by the inadequate words he'd written, and he knew he couldn't bear for them to be read by anyone at all, himself included.

He grabbed for that sheet of paper and crumpled it, tore it into a few pieces—and then began chewing and swallowing them, one at a time.

The other men in the jail looked at him as if he'd gone mad.

And maybe even Johnny knew by then that they weren't wrong.

A couple of days later he was sober and bored enough to have arranged bail. He had to move. The unlooked-for seclusion had been welcome for a while, but now he needed to be out under the cold, high skies and journeying, it didn't really matter to where.

What had prompted him onto his feet and out of the door was the talk he heard about Wyatt Earp leading a large posse to find and arrest Ike and Phin Clanton, and Pony Diehl. Chances were that Johnny's friends would not surrender peacefully, and maybe the Earps were more than ready to take advantage of even a hint of resistance. Disaster loomed. So Johnny hired a horse from the Dexter stables and rode out to warn them.

When he finally found them, days later, he was dizzy with hunger and thirst. But not so reduced that he didn't realize they were laughing at him. Johnny propped himself up on a chair in the corner of a dim room, head back against the adobe wall, and he drank the over-watered whiskey they gave him.

Ike was hooting. "We didn't rob no stagecoach! They're gonna look like fools, bringing us in." Everyone thought this was the funniest thing.

"Harassment," Phin added, "of the worst kind. It'll be clear for all to see."

Was stage robbery what this was about, though? Johnny wasn't so sure. "The attack on Virgil Earp," he said. "They want you for that. Don't they?"

A snort from Ike. "Botched that one! Have to go back and finish the job."

"Who will?" Johnny persisted. "You?"

The others looked shifty, sliding their eyes away. Apparently Johnny wasn't to be favored with straight talk, and they didn't hear or trust what he was trying to tell them. Instead they laughed and made a display of bravado. As if he were just anyone.

"And then Morgan next," someone muttered, and the pack of them all chortled low in their throats. Someone else added, "Worst thing we could do to Wyatt…"

"Well," said Johnny, "last I heard the Earps were in Charleston. They might find something there to bring them this way. I just wanted to make sure you know."

"We already knew," Phin announced in a condescending tone.

"We ain't giving ourselves up to the Earps!" Ike declared. "Wyatt's got thirty men or more with him. No telling what they think they can get away with."

Johnny frowned in puzzlement. Didn't more men mean cooler heads, less personal fear, and therefore a greater chance of being dealt with fairly? But it seemed Ike felt overwhelmed and outnumbered.

"We've sent messages," Phin informed Johnny. "The sheriff's sending Charlie Bartholomew and Spence and a couple of others. We'll go into town with them, and we'll get this sorted out."

"We'll make the Earp boys look like idiots," Ike added with great anticipated satisfaction. And they fell to talking amongst themselves.

It was clear Johnny wasn't wanted or needed even by the men he'd once thought of as friends. He sighed and hauled himself to his feet, and snared a half-full bottle of whiskey on his way out of the door.

"Johnny!" came a call from Phin. "Johnny, wait," he said, following John outside. "You're in no condition to go anywhere right now."

"I'll be fine," Johnny replied, saluting him with the bottle. "Just got a powerful thirst, is all." He took a mouthful and scrambled clumsily onto the horse. Phin stood there watching him go.

Partway back to Tombstone, Johnny was met by Jack Jackson, who told him his bail had fallen through or some such thing, and Johnny was considered an escaped prisoner. Johnny shrugged and took another swig of liquor. What did he care, really? He had nothing to do, nothing to be, and he could just as well do and be that in jail as elsewhere.

When they got back there, Johnny handed over the empty bottle and walked into the cell. The narrow bed beckoned. He didn't even bother taking off his boots, but fell facedown along it and descended heavily into sleep.

CHAPTER TWENTY:

BLOOD AND THUNDER

Tombstone, Arizona;

February-March 1882

Pony Diehl and Ike and Phin Clanton at last appeared in court to answer for their attack on Virgil. Wyatt sat in the courtroom, grim-faced, while Sherman McMaster testified that he'd spoken to Ike about the assault, and Ike had grumbled about having to return to Tombstone and 'do the job over' seeing as Virgil's wounds weren't fatal. The prosecution presented evidence, including Ike's hat being found at the scene of the shooting.

Ike claimed that he'd lost his hat some days before and couldn't imagine how it had ended up where it had. And then the defense lawyer brought on five or six of the Cowboys who all swore on the Bible that Ike Clanton and the others had been in Charleston on that day. It was arrant nonsense, of course, but the judge was left with no alternative but to set the defendants free for lack of clear evidence against them.

Judge William Stilwell—no relation to Frank Stilwell, who Virgil still swore he'd seen moments before the shooting—spoke with Wyatt the day after the hearing, just the two of them in the judge's chambers. "These men have such a contempt for the law," Stilwell opined, while pouring himself a brandy, "that they think nothing of lying under oath to provide their friends with an alibi."

Wyatt politely refused the offer of a drink. He'd have thought the judge would be outraged by this reflection. Instead, it sounded as if Stilwell had accepted this as an unwanted but undeniable fact. Wyatt took his time pondering this, but he couldn't draw any conclusion other than, "While I'm a lawman I'll never quit trying to bring them to justice. The charges will have to stick one day."

"I believe you," said Stilwell, sitting across the desk from Wyatt and considering him solemnly.

"They tried to kill my brother—and Virgil, he's the best of us Earps—but if they came after *any* lawman, any law-and-order man—"

"I know." Stilwell nodded. "But they're going to keep coming after you, Wyatt—you and your brothers. And they'll always have friends willing to perjure themselves—and more—to protect them."

Wyatt had an idea of where this was going, but it was still shocking to hear such talk from a judge. And Wyatt knew he himself wasn't always the shrewdest, so no doubt it was best to have it said plain. He waited for Stilwell to explain further.

"You'll never clean them out this way, Wyatt," Stilwell continued at last. "For those few men who pride themselves on being so far outside the law, perhaps justice can only be found outside the law, as well."

Which was plain enough even for Wyatt.

He didn't immediately reach for his gun, though. Instead, Wyatt went back to the hotel, hunted up pen and paper, and he wrote out a message for Ike Clanton.

> *Tombstone, February 1st, 1882*
> *Mr. Isaac Clanton, Grand Hotel, Tombstone*
> *Sir:*
> *There is no profit in rehearsing the great harm that has been done since summer when last we spoke as one man to another. It is in your interest and mine, in the interest of our families and of this community, for you and me to ensure that no further harm is done. I propose we meet once more and talk with a view to reconciling our differences and putting our animosities behind us. If we cannot forgive, nevertheless we can choose not to seek vengeance. I do not ask for your friendship but for your word as a gentleman that you will no longer seek to injure my family and friends, and I offer you my word likewise.*
> *Respectfully,*
> *Wyatt S. Earp*

The words poured out of him and through the ink, fully formed, and when he reread it, Wyatt was satisfied. He folded the sheet of paper and took it to Doc at the Alhambra, to ask for his opinion—Doc having had *far* more schooling than Wyatt.

Doc took his time reading the message while Wyatt stood by him. When he handed it back, he said in his slow Georgian drawl, "It is perfect. It cannot be improved—certainly not by me."

Wyatt tucked the message away in his coat pocket and nodded his thanks. He didn't leave right away, though, as it seemed clear that Doc had yet more to say. Eventually Doc looked up directly at Wyatt and said, "I suspect your olive branch will be wasted on its recipient, Wyatt. Even if the man in question has a sense of honor, it is barely a sliver of a thing, and I don't know that it can be relied upon."

He shrugged. "Figured I have to try, anyhow."

"And I love you for it," Doc declared, his gaze all aglow.

Wyatt didn't say anything more, but he took the warmth of Doc's regard back to the hotel with him and all the way up to Virgil's room.

Virgil likewise approved the message, though he immediately suggested an addition. "Offer him your word, Wyatt, that's done well—excepting only your sworn duty as an officer of the law."

Wyatt nodded in acknowledgment of the point. "I've followed the law as best I could, Virgil, you know that. But to say so in this letter… Ike would take that as a threat, and he'd call it persecution."

The brothers shared a sigh, and Virgil said, "Send it, then, and I hope he appreciates the gesture."

Wyatt went down to reception, and asked one of the boys working at the hotel to deliver the message at the Grand across the street. Then he went back up to Virgil's room and settled in to wait for a response, sitting in a chair placed by the bed where Virgil lay stretched out with his head propped up on pillows.

Allie soon excused herself: "I'll go sit with Mattie, Wyatt, if you'll stay with Virgil a while."

"Take a rest," Virgil said fondly to his wife, "if you can. You've earned it, nursing this cranky old man every hour of the clock."

Allie snorted, and glanced at Wyatt—perhaps reflecting that she'd rather have cranky than stubborn—before making her way out of the room and shutting the door behind her. Not that either of the brothers were cross-tempered that day, but Wyatt was gloomy right enough—maybe more like cross-grained—and it was probably clear that he wanted to unburden himself to Virgil.

They sat in silence for a while, until at last Virgil prompted, "Out with it, then! Something's chewing you up."

Wyatt grimaced but finally said, "I was talking with Judge Stilwell—"

Virgil echoed the grimace. "I don't like them going free either, Wyatt, but the judge didn't have a choice."

"No, I see that—but he told me *I* have a choice." Wyatt let out a sigh. "There were the Clantons and Pony Diehl organizing it so that they came into town with Charlie Bartholomew instead of us… and I shrugged when I heard of it, because if they wanted to turn themselves in, they hardly had anything to fear from *us*…"

"Damn straight," Virgil muttered.

"But then the judge is telling me, in private, that justice will never be served while they have friends enough to lie for them—and maybe we should have just shot them after all, and left them out there, and have done with it."

Virgil stared hard at Wyatt, and Wyatt didn't flinch. "The hell you say…"

"I swear it, Virgil, that's what he said. I wanted to be sure, so I let him keep talking until I was. Judge Stilwell saw this playing out just as Ike feared it would."

A silence stretched between them as they each pondered this unwelcome notion.

Until a knock sounded at the door, and Wyatt went to answer it. The boy who'd taken the message for him was there, shifting nervously from one foot to the other. "Well?" said Wyatt, holding out his hand in expectation. "You have a reply for me?"

"I do, sir. But he didn't write it down."

"Go on, then."

"He said, sir, 'Absolutely not. Not ever.'"

Wyatt glanced back at Virgil, wondering why he'd thought there could be any other outcome. He turned back to the boy, and clarified, "This was Ike Clanton himself? I bet he used some words you aren't repeating."

"Yes, sir." The boy was beset by a grin that he tried to suppress. "And *yes*, sir."

Wyatt gave him a couple more coins and sent him on his way. Then he shut the door, feeling as if he had aged ten years in as many hours. He slumped down in the chair at his brother's side, and they were both silent again for a while—until at last Wyatt blurted, "What are we doing here, Virge? I don't even know what we're doing here anymore."

"It's not like you to feel sorry for yourself, Wyatt."

"I don't. It's not that."

"You did the right thing, trying for a truce with Ike. He's the idiot for refusing."

"I know, Virge." He scrambled within himself for the right words. "It's more than that. It's… We've worked hard, we've done our duty as lawmen. It's been tough going. But what have we achieved?"

"Wyatt, you know it hasn't been for nothing."

"When even a judge is saying we need to do more? To go beyond the law to put things to rights?"

"Wyatt—"

"And maybe you don't hear what people are saying, up here in your room—"

"I read the papers! Even when Allie tries to hide them from me."

"Half the people in town don't support us, Virge. Half of them are questioning us."

Virgil nodded, but said, "You always get that with this job, Wyatt. You're always going to displease some people; you're always going to hear complaints. We wouldn't be doing the job right if everyone liked us."

"It wouldn't bother me if it were only one man in ten who complained, Virge—and it's not even that they support the Cowboys and their friends instead. There's a whole lot of people here who don't like *us* any better than *them*."

At last Virgil didn't argue back, but instead pondered Wyatt and what he was trying to say.

"I thought… I thought when Wells Spicer found that we acted lawfully back in October, there would be an end to it. People would accept his judgment and things would settle down."

Virgil nodded. "But things haven't settled."

Wyatt sighed, and thought some more, but he could no longer resist the conclusion that had barely even formed in his mind before now. "Maybe the people would be better off without us here."

This seemed rather a shock to Virgil—either the idea itself, or that it was Wyatt voicing it. "*We're* not the problem!" he blurted.

"No," Wyatt agreed. "But maybe we're exacerbating it."

They talked back and forth and through the matter for another hour or more, and Virgil consulted with Allie, but the decision had become clear to Wyatt and eventually Virgil agreed.

Wyatt was in fine letter-writing fettle, so he was the one to draft their joint resignation as deputy U.S. marshals.

Arizona Territory's U.S. marshal, Crawley Dake, refused to accept the Earp brothers' resignations, though he did appoint Jack Jackson as an additional deputy in order to appease the louder grumblings.

Meanwhile, Ike Clanton obviously wasn't in a mood to let things be. He swore out another murder complaint regarding the deaths of his brother Billy and the McLaurys—this time in the town of Contention, seeing as the case in Tombstone hadn't gone his way. Sheriff Behan announced he would arrest Wyatt, Morgan and Doc and escort them to Contention for the hearing in mid-February—Virgil still hadn't left his bed, so naturally was excused from appearing in court. Wyatt didn't fear the legal outcome, but he was haunted by the notion that Ike wasn't done yet.

Contention was eight miles from Tombstone—eight mostly empty miles in which anything might happen. Indeed, the murder complaint could have been sworn with the sole purpose of luring the Earps and Doc out of town so they could be ambushed by the Cowboys. Behan laughed off this idea, so Wyatt figured he couldn't rely on the sheriff or his deputies to protect them, not if there were a serious attack—they'd likely be outnumbered, for a start. So Wyatt went looking to recruit their friends to accompany them, and he began at the Wells Fargo office.

"Marshall Williams?" echoed James Hume. "I'd like to know where he is, too. You don't know, I take it?"

"No."

Hume considered for a long moment, but apparently decided he could talk freely to Wyatt about his suspicions. "It seems he's left town." Hume added with a gesture toward the files and ledgers, "It also seems the Wells

Fargo accounts don't add up."

Wyatt took a breath. "Not due to poor bookkeeping?"

"If he were better at bookkeeping, he might have covered his tracks, but no—it looks as if he's 'borrowed' over two thousand dollars of Wells Fargo money. And when I was purchasing supplies yesterday, I was given to understand that he has other debts in town."

"Hell," said Wyatt under his breath. How had he misjudged Williams so badly? And even if Hume's suspicions were wrong, or could be explained and dealt with, Marshall Williams had gone, anyway, and that meant one friend less for the Earps.

Thankfully there was no ambush on the way to or from Contention, perhaps because of the show of strength from the defendants. There was no new evidence for the prosecution to present, and the judge considered that the lengthy hearing before Wells Spicer had been appropriately thorough, so the second murder charges against the Earps and Doc were dismissed. The only problem remaining was that Wyatt knew very well Ike would remain dissatisfied and would be racking his brains over what to try next.

Wyatt didn't sit around waiting to find out, but got back to business.

Charlie Bartholomew had charged three men with the robbery of the Bisbee stagecoach in January: Pony Diehl, Charles Hawes and Al Thibolet. And Wyatt would dearly love to bring Pony Diehl to justice.

He formed a posse that included Morgan, Doc, Texas Jack Vermillion and Sherman McMaster, and they ended up splitting into two groups, one to work along the Mexican border and the other through San Simon Valley. They all returned to Tombstone empty-handed, but at least had some good news there.

Virgil had left his bed at last, and was even managing to take a daily constitutional along the sidewalk on Allen Street—just to the corner of Fifth and back, and wrapped snug against the cold—but it was something.

"Get the old man well again, soon as you can," Wyatt overheard Morgan telling Allie.

"And don't you think I'm trying?" she retorted in her fullest Irish brogue.

Morgan put an arm around her shoulders and squeezed. They all loved Morg, and let him get away with such familiarities. "I'm sure you are," he said fondly. "I just think… it's time to get out of here, that's all."

Allie nodded, and answered in tones that lacked her ironic bite, "You won't get any argument from me, Morgan."

Wyatt took that away with him to ponder. Maybe he'd kept them all here long enough, wanting to prove a point. Not that Virgil could have traveled anywhere after he was shot, but maybe Wyatt should now take the cue to quit being so obstinate. He was beginning to suspect, after all, that this situation in Tombstone was never going to be properly resolved. So maybe there were times when it was the work of the strong man, the righteous man, to turn and walk away.

And the feeling persisted that the longer they stayed, the more likely it was that something would happen, something bad. It was as if the town itself was holding its breath. It began to seem as if there were always someone treading quiet and close on Wyatt's heels.

On an afternoon in the middle of March, Wyatt happened to pass by Briggs Goodrich—one of the lawyers, along with his brother Ben, who had represented various Cowboys in court, including Ike Clanton. The Goodrich brothers were decent and professional men, even if they voted on the other side of the chamber than did the Earps; Wyatt took the opportunity to speak to him.

"I think they were after us last night," Wyatt said. Goodrich needed no explanation of who 'they' and 'us' were. "I felt as if I were being watched, as if they were waiting on a chance—and I'm not the imaginative sort."

Goodrich remained appropriately solemn, though a corner of his mouth quirked at this last declaration.

"Do you know anything about it?" Wyatt asked.

"No," Goodrich answered, just as directly. "But I wouldn't ignore your instincts, Wyatt. You Earp boys should take care to protect yourselves."

Wyatt sighed, and pondered for a moment. He'd been hoping to have his fears dismissed, or at least to be reassured. "I haven't seen anyone in particular from that crowd in town these past few days…"

Goodrich also paused—before saying very evenly, "I think I've seen some strangers here that might be after you."

"All right." It would make sense on the part of the Cowboys not to tip off the Earps with any familiar faces. "Thank you, Briggs," Wyatt said heavily, offering his hand.

After a firm handshake, but before Wyatt could turn to go, Goodrich announced, "I have a message for you from John Ringo."

"Ringo?!" Wyatt blurted in surprise. "What would *he* have to say to me?"

"To you Earps—and to Doc Holliday," Goodrich said, as if that helped explain the matter. Wyatt just stood there dumbfounded, until at last Goodrich continued, "John Ringo wanted you to know that if any fight came up between you all, he wanted nothing to do with it. He is going to look out for himself, and anybody else can do the same."

Wyatt hardly knew what to think about that, but maybe Doc would have a better idea. "Well, all right," Wyatt said. "Thanks!" They shook hands again, and parted.

"I should have known I would find you here," said Doc, knocking the excess raindrops off his hat and sitting opposite Wyatt at the small table. "Without your patronage, this place would be forced to close over winter."

Doc was exaggerating, of course, for the ice cream parlor also did a steady trade in homemade candies, and Wyatt was hardly the only person who indulged. "Mrs. Crabtree has also done her part," Wyatt remarked.

A quirk of Doc's mouth and a lift of his brow seemed to imply that he had taken this to indicate more than Wyatt intended—but in the end Doc simply said, "Morg said you were looking for me."

"Yes." Wyatt took another spoonful of ice cream and pondered its cool sweet smoothness, before relaying the message from John Ringo. An uncomplicated smile grew on Doc's face as he listened. "So?" Wyatt prompted once he was done. "What does he mean by it?"

For a moment Doc seemed almost to hug himself in pleasure, but then his focus turned back to Wyatt. "It means that the most dangerous gunman associated with that riffraff has retired from the fight, and we've nothing to fear from him."

"Good," said Wyatt. "As far as it goes."

"But it also sounds as if he's warning us," Doc continued, "that the rest of the rabble aren't done yet."

"Yes." Wyatt sought a moment's solace at the bottom of his glass bowl.

Once he was done, he ventured, "There's something personal for you in this with Ringo."

Doc took a breath, and turned his face away for a moment's reflection. Eventually he said in easy tones, "We happened to meet up before all this. Before Tombstone." His glance at Wyatt shied away, and he said half-wistful and the rest ironic, "Two lost souls in the wilderness…"

It appeared there would be no further explanation, though Wyatt couldn't help but mutter, "Not so long ago he was aiming to shoot us down on Allen Street, and now he's warning us that others might do so…"

Doc didn't seem overly concerned. "There's a play opening tonight at Schieffelin Hall—*Stolen Kisses*."

"It doesn't seem wise—"

"It's a comedy, Wyatt. Aren't you in need of a laugh just now? Morg is, anyway! He and I already decided to go."

"John Ringo, of all people, takes the trouble to warn us, and you—"

"You can't all hide in your hotel rooms forever, Wyatt. Even Virgil is up and about now! Morgan needs an outing, and I'll be there to take care of him. Ringo might have stood down, but I haven't."

So, Wyatt could impose the authority of an older brother on Morgan and keep him confined, or he could let Morg and Doc have an hour or two of fun, and do what he could to protect them. "I'll meet up with you afterwards."

"You want to be out half the night in this weather?"

"Yes."

Doc took him at his word, and blessed Wyatt with a warm smile. "We'll meet up with you afterwards, then, and I for one will be glad of it."

As it turned out, Doc was the one who elected for an early night once the play was done, and he walked off down Fremont Street to his boarding house with a happy grin on his face. Morgan was in high spirits and in no mood to settle yet, so Wyatt—and a friend and fellow theater-goer, Dan Tipton—escorted Morg to Campbell & Hatch's for a game of billiards.

Morgan and Bob Hatch settled into a game at a billiards table toward the back of the room, and Wyatt sat in one of the chairs lining the wall to watch them. The pair were both excellent players, and the game didn't take long to conclude. Bob had won, but it was a close fought thing.

"Come along, Morg," said Wyatt, "it's time to turn in."

"One more game," Morgan pleaded in response. "I don't want for anything else."

Bob Hatch had already set it up, so Wyatt shrugged. And it was just as Morg leant down to take his first shot—

Glass panes in the back door shattered—Morg lurched forward with a cry—and something thumped into the wall above Wyatt's head.

General dismay, and Morgan not the only one groaning with pain. Hatch and Sherman McMaster ran for the back door to try to grab the culprits, so Wyatt headed for his brother. He heard others heading out front to go find a doctor.

But it was immediately obvious there was little hope. The bullet had gouged right through Morgan's torso, and the wound was too horrendous for them to be able to do much to stop the bleeding. Wyatt and their friends carried Morg over to rest on a couch, so at least he'd be comfortable.

"Lay me out straight, Wyatt," Morgan said, "and take off my boots."

"You are straight, Morgan. Just as straight as you can be."

"Then my back is broken."

Wyatt knelt on the floor beside him, holding his hand, until at last the doctors came and Wyatt gave way. Allie had brought Virgil and helped him into a chair, and there was Louisa already quietly, helplessly weeping, and then Doc arrived in a fine fury of grief, so Wyatt dealt with them and explained the little he knew.

The doctors soon concluded there was nothing to be done, and offered a dose of morphine to ease his pain—but Morgan refused. "I want to be clear for this." He was only thirty, and had approached life with the enthusiasm of twenty. Death, it seemed, he would face square on with an older man's wisdom.

Louisa sat with her husband, as was her right, but Morg beckoned Wyatt close again for a whispered exchange. "Do you know who did it?"

Wyatt knew well enough—or at least where to start—even though McMaster had indicated with a discreet shake of his head that the gunmen had escaped for now. "Yes," Wyatt firmly said to Morgan. "And I'll get them!"

"That's all I ask. But, Wyatt—be careful—"

He affirmed this with a nod, and then sank to sit on the hard floorboards to be near Morgan while not crowding out the others. An older brother shouldn't have to lose the younger ones, nor should a brother have to lose his sisters. Martha, in birth order immediately before Wyatt, had died as a child, as had their baby sister, Virginia—and now Morgan, Wyatt's next youngest brother and everybody's favorite, dear affable Morgan would join them.

Just before midnight, lying there in the heart of his family and friends, Morgan's last breath sighed away into peace, and the new day began without him.

CHAPTER TWENTY-ONE:
ONE OF THEM

Arizona;

March 1882

Doc stuck close by Wyatt's side, entirely at his disposal. It was Sunday, March 19th—Wyatt's thirty-fourth birthday—and the man's sole concern was caring for his younger brother and sending him off on his last journey, and packing up Virgil and the women to go, too. They were to seek peace and safety with the Earp parents in Colton, California—while Wyatt stayed behind in Tombstone and sought justice, and Doc of course stayed with him.

Barely twelve hours after poor Morgan had died, his coffin was loaded onto a wagon, and Doc and Wyatt and their friends saddled up and escorted him to Contention, which had at last been reached by the railway down from Benson. They were a solemn procession, with none of the bravado they'd shown last time they rode out this way, just over a month ago, to attend court. It had seemed only reasonable to expect an ambush then; an ambush now while they were disarmed by grief would be the most reprehensible of crimes. Nevertheless, Doc would put nothing past Ike Clanton and his cronies, who already believed that the Earps were acting beyond the pale. Doc therefore kept a discreet watch on their surrounds—which Wyatt acknowledged with a brief nod, before turning to face front for the rest of their ride without even a glance elsewhere. Wyatt was fearless, but he wasn't impractical nor was he reckless with the lives of his friends.

The coffin was to rest overnight at the train station. Doc sat beside it to keep Morgan company, and with another nod this time of farewell, Wyatt turned away to head back to Tombstone with the rest of them.

The night was long and quiet, and gave Doc plenty of time to think of Morgan Earp and yet he wasn't done by dawn and maybe he never would be done. Much as Doc admired Virgil and adored Wyatt, it was Morgan with whom he'd rubbed along best. Morgan who was ever ready with a bright smile and a great guffawing laugh, who enjoyed Doc's company with no quibbles or reservations. Doc loved Wyatt—but Doc had never had to worry about embarrassing Morgan, who would always take his part in any disagreement. Everybody liked Morgan… Doc had assumed until a day or two ago that even the Cowboys bore Morgan no ill will but saved all their hatred for Morg's older brothers. Doc had been tragically wrong about that, but there was no denying Morgan was the family favorite, and the most popular among the Earps' friends, and his carefree, happy nature had won him the sweet, beautiful Louisa… If any of them were going to die in this ridiculous confrontation, if nigh *all* of them were going to die, it still should have been Morgan who survived.

Well, the confrontation between the Cowboys and the Earps was petty no longer. Doc had understood with barely even a glance from Wyatt as he sat on the floor by his brother's body, and above them Louisa wailed in grief: it was time to put an end to this, in terms that would be deeply felt. Revenge had an ugly tone to it—but not when it was justice.

Once the railway station was staffed again, Doc let himself doze away the morning hours slumped in his seat with his feet up on another wooden chair. He was woken by the return of the wagon from Tombstone, this time driven by Wyatt and containing Virgil, Allie, Mattie, Louisa and enough of their belongings to see them through. Virgil was none too happy about leaving, but someone needed to escort Morgan and the Earp women to safety—and while Wyatt was doing what had to be done, he wouldn't want to be worrying over another beloved brother who was still too badly hurt to be sure of protecting himself.

When the train arrived, and all the passengers and goods had been disembarked, they took Morgan aboard and everyone in the vicinity paused for a few moments with their hats off and their heads bowed. Then Allie helped Virgil aboard, the luggage was loaded, and Mattie and Louisa were settled in the carriage with Virge.

Doc turned away with a last shake of Virgil's good right hand and a tip of the hat to the women. But when Doc stepped down off the train, Wyatt restrained him with a touch of his arm and led him a few paces out of earshot. "We're going, too," Wyatt announced.

"To California?" Doc blurted in surprise. "Of course we're going," he equably agreed in the next breath. Anything Wyatt needed…

"As far as Tucson, anyway." Wyatt wasn't about to smile, but for a moment he appeared less somber at Doc's display of loyalty. Then he grimly explained, "I've had telegrams. Frank Stilwell has gone up to Tucson, and Ike Clanton's there, too, and they're watching the trains coming in. They've got to be wanting to finish off Virgil."

Doc swore under his breath and grasped Wyatt's shoulder for a moment. "Let's go, then!" Anything at all…

Sherman McMaster and Creek Johnson climbed aboard, too, and the train whistle sounded as they left Contention behind, the train slowly pulling away with a regular *chuff chuff chuff* of steam, like a gruff heartbeat.

The train stopped as scheduled in Tucson to allow the passengers to take an evening meal. Doc and Wyatt greeted the local deputy U.S. marshal on the platform, and then escorted Virgil and the Earp wives to Porter's Hotel, where they ate. Doc was surprised to find himself hungry, so he was happy to dig into a plate of roast beef with potatoes and gravy.

All seemed quiet as they made their way back toward the train just after seven p.m., and helped Virgil, Allie, Mattie and Louisa onboard. But then McMaster strode in from a forward carriage, wanting to confer with Wyatt and Doc. "Passenger saw two men lying on a flatcar up near the engine," he said, low but urgent, and indicating the second set of tracks running alongside.

Wyatt had disappeared out a door on that side of the train before McMaster had even finished speaking, and Doc saw a hint of Wyatt's shadow as he flitted by below the windows.

"Didn't get close enough to look," McMaster was left to explain to Doc. "Didn't want to warn them."

"Good man," Doc said—and then he was off after Wyatt as quick as he was able, stumbling along between the two tracks with McMaster following close behind.

The twilight was deepening, but Doc could make out Wyatt's silhouette a carriage-length ahead. He was slightly crouched as he went, but the gravel crunching under each footfall soon alerted the two watchers.

Both of them sprang to their feet, stared for a moment at the approaching figure—jumped down from the flatcar and *ran*. One of them disappeared into the gathering darkness, but the other made the mistake of turning his head to look back—

He shouted incoherently, and froze—shifting only to face the threat, his hands up as if wanting to ward off some horror. "Morg!" he cried out.

It was Frank Stilwell. Wyatt didn't pause or falter, but ran at him directly with his long loping strides, shotgun held ready, low down at his waist.

"Morg!" Stilwell cried again.

Wyatt was upon him, and Stilwell clutched at the shotgun—but he didn't have a chance to try pushing it away—Wyatt let him have both barrels, and Stilwell collapsed in a mangled mess at Wyatt's feet.

Doc caught up with Wyatt as he was about to take off after the other reprobate. "Don't," said Doc, anticipating an ambush. "It's too dark now for hunting."

"It was Ike," Wyatt said as if his throat were raw. "Let me after him."

There was a sudden burst of gunfire from the center of town, a street or two away, and people crying out, apparently more in wonder than fear. A strange golden glow arose—not flickering, like fire, but steady and unending. It seemed like a portent, even to Doc, as if the earth had cracked open and a glimpse of hell shone through.

"You've got this bastard," Doc reassured his friend as the gunfire and cheering continued; God only knew what was happening in town, but they were well out of it. Daring to lay a hand on Wyatt's shoulder, Doc concluded, "That's a hell of a reward for one night's work."

After a moment, Wyatt nodded, and with a shriek of the whistle, the train began to roll forward with a slow *chuff… chuff… chuff…*

Wyatt walked alongside it, looking for Virgil—who was standing in a doorway, looking for him. The brothers stared gravely at each other and lifted a hand in farewell. "One for Morg," Wyatt called to Virge as the train began to pick up speed. "That's one for Morg!"

Doc kept a careful eye on Wyatt as he finally stopped at the edge of the light thrown from the railway station and watched the train depart. Doc wouldn't put it past Ike Clanton to fire on him from the shadows like the coward he was.

McMaster was wary, too, and restless on his feet, but he took a moment to murmur a query to Doc: "Why did he call on Morg? Stillwell, I mean. If he was pleading for mercy…" Sherman trailed off.

"Guilty conscience," Doc replied, as Wyatt finally turned and started making his way back toward them.

"D'you think?" McMaster pondered this for a moment. "Am I gonna be calling out the name of every man I killed when I die? Might take a while!"

Doc huffed. "No…" He almost did laugh then, his gaze always and forever on Wyatt. "Haven't you noticed how the Earp men look so alike? Frank Stilwell thought that was Morgan's ghost seeking vengeance."

"Ah…" McMaster sighed. "That was proper justice, then."

No one had come to investigate the shotgun blast, so Wyatt turned away, conveying with a shrug that he considered they were free to go. The four of them—Wyatt and Doc, Sherman McMaster and Turkey Creek Jack Johnson—started walking along the tracks back toward Benson, until they reached Papago Station after ten miles or more. No one was talking much, though there was a sense of grim satisfaction of work done and an equally grim anticipation of more work to do.

While taking a brief rest at Papago, they heard a train approaching from Tucson, and were able to flag it down. It was a freight train, but the engineer reluctantly let them find a makeshift seat in one of the half-empty carriages. Indeed, Doc fancied it would be difficult to deny a request from this well-armed group, so somber in appearance and yet so polite.

Doc curled up as comfortably as he could and managed to grab some sleep, anticipating long hard days and restless nights ahead. He woke to find the train pulling into Benson. They disembarked and waited for the first train to Contention—where, after a brief pause to break their fast, the party gathered their horses, and then they rode back to Tombstone.

It was early afternoon on March 21st, a mere two days and some hours since Morgan Earp had been killed. The world had shifted a massive way on its axis since then.

Frank Kingsbury, manager of Tombstone's telegraph office, brought a telegram to Wyatt as the four men rode up to the Cosmopolitan Hotel. Wyatt dismounted and read it, then passed it to Doc wordlessly. It was from Tucson, asking Sheriff Behan to arrest the alleged murderers of Frank Stilwell.

The wanted men handed the telegram back to Kingsbury—and he, being a friend and admirer of the Earps, waited on a response. The usually stoic Wyatt grimaced for a moment, but then all he said was, "We'll be leaving town again just as soon as we're ready." Kingsbury nodded, tucked the message away in his jacket pocket, and strolled off along Allen Street and turned down Fourth.

Wyatt looked from one to the other of them. "You're not obliged to ride with me," he said, "but the job's not done yet."

"I'm with you," McMaster said.

"Just try leaving me behind!" Creek protested.

Then Wyatt met Doc's steady gaze, and he nodded in response. Nothing need be said. Anything… Always.

It was almost dark by the time the four of them gathered in the lobby of the hotel, and were joined by Texas Jack Vermillion. They were all armed and ready—and as they were starting to head toward the double doors onto Allen Street, Johnny Behan finally appeared, telegram in hand.

"I want to see you, Wyatt," he said.

Wyatt didn't break stride. "You may see me once too often, Johnny," he replied in an even tone that told of rage suppressed.

Doc and the others followed him, simply ignoring Behan and his deputies Neagle and Breakenridge. None of the Earp party bothered even glancing at the sheriff let alone threatening him or his men—why would they need to, when Behan apparently couldn't even summon the nerve to try making an arrest?

Wyatt stopped on the sidewalk just beyond the doors, however, and let his companions pass by before half-turning and saying, "I will see Bob Paul."

And with that promise of a future reckoning still resounding, Wyatt Earp swung up onto his horse. A few concerned citizens of good standing stepped forward and offered help or expressed their support, all of which Wyatt acknowledged with grave courtesy. Then he rode out of Tombstone with

Doc beside him and his other loyal friends following close behind.

They left a clear trail and camped no more than a couple of miles outside town, where Behan could have found them if he'd wanted to. Wyatt, never talkative beyond his family, hardly spoke a word that evening. Doc sat quiet beside him, while the others took turns keeping watch, and after a while Wyatt stretched out on his bedroll with a blanket covering him from top to toe, and perhaps he managed to exchange his thoughts for less troublesome dreams.

The coroner's inquest on Morgan's death was held early the next morning in Tombstone, and they all knew that Marietta Spencer would be testifying against her husband Pete and his cronies.

Dan Tipton rode out to join Wyatt and Doc and the others once the inquest was over. Barely pausing to dismount and nod a greeting, Tipton announced, "They're charging four men. Pete Spencer—"

"In jail already," McMaster observed. Most of them had heard that Spence turned himself in for the sake of the dubious safety to be found under the care of the sheriff.

"Frank Stilwell—"

"Already dealt with," said Doc.

"Indian Charlie—"

"Who?" Doc asked.

"A man part Indian, part Mexican," Creek explained, "name of Sais. Florentino Sais, or something like."

McMaster said, "I've heard of him. He used to run with Guadalupe Celaya. Nasty piece of work, and I don't suppose he's changed any."

"And Frederick Bode," Tipton finished; "a German citizen. Spencer's wife only knew him as Fritz—or 'Freetz'—but someone else identified him."

Wyatt immediately asked, "*That's* the four? What about Hank Swilling?"

"No mention of him," Tipton said with a shake of his head. "You were expecting—?"

"I heard…" Wyatt thought for a moment, and sighed. "I heard that a few days before, Spence and Swilling were talking together when Morgan walked past—and Spence said, 'That's him, that's him!' so Swilling started after Morg to get a good look at him."

They were all silent for a long moment, until McMaster finally concluded, "That's pretty damning."

Wyatt turned back to Tipton. "What about Ringo and Curly Bill? Any mention of them?"

"Oh, not Johnny Ringo," Doc blurted—and then he came nigh to blushing for the first time in *years* when the others all turned to stare at him. "Ringo tried to warn us, Wyatt! You told me so that very same day. He said he'd have nothing to do with any fight between us and the Cowboys."

"And then Morgan was killed!" Wyatt retorted. "Isn't that enough to make you think twice about taking his word? What if he wanted our guard down?"

Doc opened his mouth to reply, but decided he had nothing purposeful to say and closed it again.

"What about Curly Bill?" Wyatt persisted. "Have you got anything to plead on his account?"

Doc just shook his head mutely, and Tipton ventured, "There was nothing said in court about either of them, Wyatt—or elsewhere, far as I know."

A moment dragged by, and then Wyatt said in something approaching his usual businesslike tones, "All right. Anyone have an idea where Sais or Bode can be found?"

Creek said, "Indian Charlie works in Pete Spence's logging camp, up in the Dragoons. Chances are we'll find him there."

Wyatt nodded decisively. "We'll start with him, then—as soon as you're ready, gentlemen."

They rode east toward South Pass in the Dragoon Mountains, finding the logging camp easily enough. Near a small cabin was a corral where mules would be held—but it currently contained a few head of cattle, which was unexpected for the lumber business, unless the owner had a side interest in rustling… Seemed they were in the right place.

A group of workers were not far off the road, gathered around a fire waiting on a pot of coffee to boil—mostly Mexican, by the looks of it, and Sherman McMaster spoke Spanish fluently so he took the lead. "Ask them about Hank Swilling," Wyatt insisted.

After some back-and-forthing, McMaster announced, "They have nothing to say about Swilling, but apparently Indian Charlie is working on the slopes above the road, a short way back toward Tombstone."

Wyatt nodded at the workers and said, "Gracias," before turning his horse and leading the way back along their own tracks.

They soon caught sight of a figure making his way down toward the road as if to meet them—but when he saw the six armed men riding in his direction and paying close attention to him, he dropped what he was carrying and started running back up the slope.

It was useless, of course. The posse turned off the road and cantered their horses up through the sparse trees. Soon enough the lone man heard them close behind him, and he stumbled to a stop, turning around with his hands in the air.

"You're known as Indian Charlie?" Wyatt demanded. The conversation proceeded clearly enough, with McMaster helping where he could.

"Sí, señor."

"Your name is Florentino Sais?"

The fellow didn't say anything, but his expression stiffened, which was confirmation enough.

Wyatt asked, "You know why we're here?"

Sais stared back at him, and again he nodded. Doc could see it plain on his face and in his stance—not guilt, perhaps, but a sorrowful kind of foreknowledge that hardened into resentment. Sais knew exactly why Wyatt Earp was there. There was an old pistol jammed into the back of his trousers, but Sais was wise enough to keep his hands at his sides and open. Doc kept a careful eye on him.

Wyatt dismounted, and took a step or two toward Sais, his bearing confident but not yet threatening. "Did you shoot my brother Morgan?" he asked directly.

"No, señor," Sais replied with a shake of his head. It seemed to be the plain truth.

Wyatt considered him for a moment. "Do you know who did?"

Sais let out a sigh, and his gaze fell away to one side. No doubt about it: he already knew that one way or another this would lead to his own death. "Sí," he replied. "Mr. Stilwell was there, and Curly Bill, and Mr. Swilling."

"Frank Stilwell, Curly Bill Brocius, and Hank Swilling?" Wyatt confirmed.

"Yes, sir."

"Not Pete Spencer?"

Sais shook his head. "Spence didn't shoot. He didn't even draw his gun. The other men did."

"How do you know that for sure?"

Another sigh, and Sais raised his gaze again. He was not one to shirk from the truth—that much seemed certain. "I was there that night, at the back of the saloon. I was keeping watch for them."

Wyatt stared at him hard. "That's all? Just standing watch?"

"Sí."

After a long moment, Wyatt turned away, and stepped back toward his horse. Perhaps he would let the fellow be in return for his information. Doc might not have granted Sais such mercy, but he admired Wyatt for being so inclined.

Sais's expression had just begun to shift from despair to wary caution— when Wyatt turned back. "Let me ask you something," he said in a more reasonable tone. "What did my brothers or I ever do to you? Why would you be part of a thing like that—ambushing a man and shooting him in the back?"

"It wasn't what you and your brothers did," Sais immediately returned.

"You agree we'd done nothing to harm you? Certainly not Morgan!"

"Sí. It was about the other men, who are my friends. They did plenty— *not* to harm me, lo entiendes?"

Wyatt cast a glance around him at Doc and his other friends all waiting there ready to follow his lead. "I guess I can understand that," Wyatt muttered—though Doc knew it wasn't as if Wyatt would ever ask any of them to shoot a man in the back, not even now, sorely provoked as he'd been.

Sais, however, had relaxed too far and now made a mistake. He shrugged, and said, "De todas formas—"

"Anyhow," McMaster quietly supplied.

"—Curly Bill paid me. He paid me twenty-five dollars. Just for keeping watch for a little while."

Fury visibly cut through Wyatt like a lightning strike. "That's all my brother was worth to you?" he snarled. "Draw! Draw, if you're a man."

And Sais did at last reach behind him for his gun—but even as he lifted it shakily in Wyatt's direction, Wyatt also drew, and a moment later Sais was sprawled back on the ground with two wounds weeping a deep red.

It was clear the business was done, but Doc drew his own pistol and fired into Florentino Sais's thigh and torso. Wyatt turned to look at him askance even as he was holstering his own gun, and Doc shrugged. "No need for you to carry the full burden, Wyatt."

"Doc," Wyatt said—but then he stalled.

"Come on," Creek muttered. "Let's get out of here before they come to investigate."

Wyatt mounted again, and the six of them rode west, following the road that led back to Tombstone.

The party swung south of Tombstone itself, while Dan Tipton was sent into town to tell James Hume at the Wells Fargo office where Florentino Sais's body could be found. Dan was also to gather what news there was, and collect the proceeds of a loan Wyatt had organized. They planned to meet up again at the Cottonwood Springs waterhole in the Whetstone Mountains—west and slightly north of Tombstone, where they'd see the backs of any posse heading toward the South Pass in the Dragoons. Meanwhile, they could camp at the waterhole, and decide what to pursue next.

It was a hot day, and for a long while it seemed as if the only thing moving in the country was the five men and their horses. Doc unforgivably found himself being lulled into a doze by his horse's slow, relentless gait. Everything was quiet, and no one spoke but for a few directions shared in desultory tones. Until they reached the top of a rise which hitherto had hidden the waterhole from sight—

Wyatt reined in his horse so sharply that it reared with a loud squeal of protest. McMaster turned to shout a warning to the rest of the party—"Curly Bill!"—and Doc in his sleepy befuddlement turned with the others and sought shelter.

With a mix of pride in his friend and shame for himself, Doc saw that Wyatt had stood his ground while the rest of them retreated. He'd dismounted while his horse bucked and snorted in fear. Bullets flew by him—surely he would be hit! But the Cowboys' gunfire was so wild that it dissuaded even Doc from returning to Wyatt's side.

Wyatt was cool enough to take careful aim, and blasted first one barrel of his shotgun into his target and then the second. Doc guessed that was the end of Curly Bill Brocius. Then Wyatt was reaching for the rifle affixed to his saddle, but despite the reins being wound firmly around Wyatt's arm, the horse would not stay still long enough to let him retrieve it—a queasy memory surfaced of Tom McLaury in much the same predicament.

Texas Jack Vermillion was the one who finally responded—digging in his heels and forcing his horse forward again despite its nerves.

After some fumbling while reaching for one of his six-shooters, Wyatt returned fire—seeming to find another target before laying down general coverage. Wyatt's long coat blew back once, twice, with the impact of bullets. Doc watched in horror.

Texas Jack's horse went down, and he struggled to haul his leg out from under it, at last rolling up to a crouch with his Winchester ready in both hands.

The two men were obviously outnumbered, though, and at a distinct disadvantage. Soon they were retreating behind the cover of Wyatt's horse—though when Wyatt tried to remount there was a heart-stopping moment when a bullet clipped the saddle horn sending splinters flying—and another moment almost comic when he found his cartridge belt, loosened while riding during the heat of the day, had slipped so low as to restrict the use of his legs.

Doc huffed a humorless laugh, and at last broke out of his stupor—though by the time he met up with them, Wyatt was securely on his horse again, and Texas Jack had leapt up behind him.

The group of them urged on their horses and dashed off the narrow track for the nearest accessible ridge, and then paused to take stock of the situation once well out of sight.

"Nine of them!" Wyatt exclaimed as he dismounted with none of his usual grace. "Eight now, and one of them hurt."

"Are you hit?" Doc asked, rushing to help his friend while McMaster crept back to the ridgeline to keep watch. "Where are you hit?"

Wyatt looked quizzically at his own left hand, and flexed it as if to check that it was in working order. Then he sank to the ground and crooked a leg to examine the heel of his boot, part of which had been shot away. It was only after he'd taken off the boot and felt about his foot that Wyatt seemed to realize he was unharmed.

Doc had been examining the holes in the skirt of his coat. "How were you not hit?" he asked in wonder.

Wyatt stared back at him, steady but as if that steadiness could not be relied on. "I got Curly Bill, Doc. Almost blasted him in two."

"That's good, Wyatt," Doc murmured while the others also praised him. "That's good." He had a hand wrapped around Wyatt's wrist, and was deeply unwilling to let go.

"And Milt Hicks—I think I hit him in the arm." A shudder ran through Wyatt as if he were shaking off a bad dream. "Sherm, are they coming after us?"

"No," McMaster replied. "Looks like they're dealing with Brocius and tending to whoever that is. One of the Hicks brothers, you say? Guess they figure we won't be back right away."

Doc still sat there staring at his friend, wondering how he hadn't been shot. Now Doc thought about it, Wyatt had been the only one of them uninjured back in October, as well.

Wyatt offered him a small smile. "I'm all right, Doc. Just numb—my hand and my foot were numb, from the impact I guess, and I thought I'd been hit but I wasn't. Are you gonna start talking about ghosts again?"

"It wasn't *me* thinking you were a ghost, back in Tucson!" Doc protested.

The others had drawn away to at least make a show of minding their own business, or to join McMaster in watching the Cowboys. Nevertheless, Wyatt spoke in low confidential tones: "I swore an oath to Morgan, to see justice done. No bullet's gonna harm me till that's finished, Doc."

Which sounded like an awful risky attitude to Doc no matter the righteousness of the cause, but he retorted, "That's good, then!" and finally he let his friend go.

A short while later, one of the Cowboys cantered off down the track, apparently paying no attention to where Doc and Wyatt and their friends were sheltering. "Do they even guess we're here?" Wyatt asked McMaster.

"I reckon not," was the reply. "They had someone keeping lookout for a while, but he quit already. And that rider didn't even throw us a glance."

"Gone to get a wagon for the two men dead or injured, I guess," Texas Jack said.

Creek urged, "We should charge them while their guard's down. There's only six left to make a fight of it."

Wyatt shook his head. "If you're hungry for a fight, you can go get your fill. I'm staying here."

"Why stay?" Doc asked. "What do we do here?"

"Wait for Dan," Wyatt replied evenly. "Then we'll go find another place to camp."

"All right," said Doc, and he settled in for the duration.

An hour or more later, a wagon was driven up to the rise above the waterhole, and Curly Bill's body, wrapped up in a blanket, and the wounded Milt Hicks were loaded up and taken away. Two of the other men accompanied them, which left four of the Cowboys at the waterhole—but Wyatt still wasn't inclined to take advantage of their numbers in an attack.

Dan Tipton finally showed up as the sun was westering and twilight was beginning to creep across the lower ground. Texas Jack had been sent down the trail to head him off, but must have failed, for Jack rejoined the party just as they were watching Dan ride toward the waterhole, relaxed and obviously expecting to find his friends there. Doc supposed they could have called out to him, but no one did, and after all it would have provoked the fight that Wyatt wanted to avoid—and with the unsuspecting Dan in the middle of it, too, unprotected by any righteous oath.

Luckily, Dan was quicker to deal with the surprise than his friends had been. They watched him raise a hand in greeting and call out something friendly. The Cowboys had all drawn on him, but after a query was answered to their satisfaction—Dan must have invented some brief story to explain his presence—the guns were holstered, and Dan was invited to join them at the campfire.

Doc and Wyatt and the others watched in bemusement as Dan Tipton enjoyed a supper and conversation with their enemies. And then, once the moon had risen, Dan apparently refused any urging to stay for the night, and he rode back down the track, letting his horse pick out the way.

The Earp posse saddled up and quietly rode down to meet up with Tipton—who was warier this time, or was feeling spooked, for he drew on them as they approached. "It's us, Dan," Wyatt called in low tones.

A pithy curse or two dropped into the darkness and then the group were gathered together again. "I'm almighty glad to see you, Wyatt," Dan continued in a more civilized manner. "All of you? They were talking as if they'd shot up a dozen men or more, and I saw Texas Jack's horse lying there—"

"All of us," Texas Jack replied from where he was seated behind their leader. "No real harm done, though none of us can make out how they missed Wyatt. He's a powerful tall target!"

Doc cut through the humor. "What did you tell them?"

A sharp moment of silence—before Dan answered equably, "Why, nothing to the point. Said I was looking for three mules that escaped."

"That's good, Dan," said Wyatt. "That's good."

They wound their way into a dry arroyo nearby and set up camp for the night. They had barely enough fresh water for the men, and only a little for the horses, but it was too late to go looking for another waterhole.

"So, I was in town longer than I liked," Dan said once they were settled. "The sheriff detained me. Said you'd all resisted arrest the other day at the Cosmopolitan."

The rest of them exclaimed in protest at this, politely or otherwise, and of course Dan had heard the story in full a few times already.

"Exactly," Dan continued. "I said you were all the honorable sort, and was he sure he'd made it plain that you were arrested—"

"What did he say to that?" Sherm asked.

"He didn't have an answer! There are witnesses saying the same, too. And then I pointed out that I wasn't even there. He said something about me aiding and abetting, and strode off, but after a while Deputy Billy came to show me out. Anyway, Wyatt, Behan's not gonna give up on the whole thing, but he can't charge you with resisting."

"Not yet, anyway," muttered McMaster.

He was answered with a few wry huffs.

"I heard that Fritz Bode and Hank Swilling are in custody now, too, along with Pete Spence. I confirmed it with Mr. Hume. I don't know if they turned themselves in, or they were just happy to go when arrested, but you've put the fear into them, Wyatt. That's not nothing."

Wyatt pondered on this for a long moment, and then lifted his head. "What else?"

Dan sighed. "You won't like it!" But he just spat it out rather than make them wait: "The charges for Morgan's murder have been dismissed for lack of evidence."

A low groan wrenched through Wyatt, though all he said was, "Can't say I'm surprised."

"Those three are staying in jail, whether it's for other charges or they're asking for protection. But I don't reckon anything's gonna come of it for Morgan's sake."

Wyatt nodded grimly. Then he turned to his bedroll and stretched himself out, and they didn't hear anything more from him until morning.

In the cool early light, Wyatt was of a mood to quietly share his thoughts with Doc. Not that he seemed to mind that the others were all nearby, slow in waking up and going about their business, but neither did he seem aware of anything much outside his own ruminations and Doc's willing ear.

"Frank Stilwell and Curly Bill are dead; that's justice done for Morg and for Virgil. Sais is dead, too—and I almost wish he weren't. I lost my temper. It was just the thought of the twenty-five dollars…"

"Understandable," Doc murmured. He was watching Creek build up the small fire while Texas Jack brought out a slab of bacon for carving and frying.

Wyatt might not have even heard Doc, except a one-shouldered shrug contested the point.

"Sherm has since told me Sais was a murderer," Doc added. "He and a compadre were wanted for killing two deputy U.S. marshals."

Wyatt shot him a sharp glance, but was obviously not reconciled. "Didn't know that at the time, Doc. I just lost my temper."

Doc lay a gentle hand on Wyatt's shoulder, wishing he could give absolution. "That's so, but there were two souls glad of you bringing justice, and no doubt more."

Wyatt didn't remark on this. Eventually he continued, "I don't care about Spence if he didn't do the shooting; and Swilling and Bode are in jail. Not that they'll be there long, but I can't touch them, and I won't. I'll leave them to the law."

Doc nodded. Not that he cared for the Swillings and Bodes of the world, but he knew Wyatt must draw the line somewhere on this side of chaos, for his own sake if no one else's.

"So that's all I can do for poor Morg," Wyatt concluded. For a long moment his stoic mask failed, and Doc saw the darkness newly etched by grief across his countenance.

"I know you felt," Doc offered, "the affection of a father for Morgan, even though there was only four years between you. I know you felt a responsibility for him."

The old Wyatt emerged for a moment with a wry grimace. "I was the man of the house at twelve, when my father and Virgil and the rest went off to war. Morg *was* my responsibility, and I never forgot it." He paused for thought, and then added, "There was the farm, of course, and my mother and sisters—and Warren, too, though he was always cussedly wayward even as a child. But Morg got himself lodged somehow in a particular place in my heart."

"Which makes *me*," Doc replied, "the wicked uncle! Just as affectionate, of course, though *far* more likely to lead the young fellow astray…"

Wyatt smiled, just slightly, for the first time in days and he even reached out a hand to prod against Doc's arm. But when he spoke again it was of serious things. "I'm not finished yet for Virgil. Pony Diehl was at Cottonwood Springs, too, and he got away."

Doc turned toward the others. "Dan, was Pony Diehl at the camp last night?"

"No," Dan replied with a shake of his head.

McMaster said, "He went off with the wagon."

"We can follow them," Doc said to Wyatt. "They'll be expecting us, but we've ridden into worse situations."

The others indicated their willingness to stick with them, but Wyatt's head was down as if he wasn't convinced.

"And then there are the Clantons," Doc continued. "I would put any money you like on Ike having been there when Virgil was shot. We may as well do the job properly."

"I don't disagree," Wyatt finally said. "There's Phin Clanton to consider—though Ike's fool enough to find a bad end under his own steam. But we'll need to find them first, and they'll have gathered their friends around. How many men are we prepared to fight, to get through to the Clantons?"

The party was silent for a while. Creek shared out the bacon on slices of bread, and they fell to eating. At last, when it came time to start packing up camp, Doc asked, "What's next, then, Wyatt?"

And Wyatt replied, "I'll head for the Sierra Bonita ranch. I want time to think, and Henry Hooker will have the latest news." He looked around at each of the others, and added, "Be glad of your company, if you're still willing."

Naturally, they all were.

CHAPTER TWENTY-TWO:
MYSTERIOUS ATTRACTION
Arizona;
March-April 1882

The gates to the compound of the Sierra Bonita stood wide open, and Wyatt led his men through early on the morning of March 27th. Henry Hooker, dressed as usual in a suit and bowtie like the Eastern gentleman he'd once been, approached them with a warm greeting. "Welcome! Come on in, all of you. I hoped you'd find your way here, Wyatt."

Some of Hooker's men came forward to take their worn-out horses and started leading them to the stables. But Wyatt didn't want to ask for hospitality and help under false pretenses, so he stood by his horse with the reins firmly held, and said, "Morning, Henry. You heard Morgan was killed, just over a week ago?"

"Yes, I did." Hooker had about twenty years on Wyatt, and as was the way of things had known his own griefs. His expression was one of profound sympathy. "I'm right sorry for it, Wyatt, and for Virgil being hurt so badly."

Wyatt nodded an acknowledgment, and continued, "You know what I've been doing since then?"

"Seeking justice," Hooker replied in even tones.

"I've killed three men, and wounded another. All of them known to be involved in ambushing Morgan and Virgil." Wyatt paused for a moment, conscious of his own friends at his back and Hooker's ranch-hands waiting a discreet length away. "One of the dead men was Curly Bill Brocius."

Hooker gazed off into the distance, perhaps seeing the dark blue silhouette of Mount Graham against the sky, perhaps not. Finally, his mouth quirked, and he turned back to say, "Wyatt, if you knew what trouble Curly Bill and his gang of rustlers have caused me and mine, you would forgive me for being tempted to smile at your news." He reached to grasp Wyatt's shoulder and shook it in reassurance. "You're doing good work, Wyatt, and there's more to be done. When you're finished, if there are any charges to be answered, I'll get you pardoned!"

Wyatt couldn't help but grimace at the thought, but it was honestly meant, and would probably come to seem very welcome in time. He nodded again, trusting that Hooker could read his gratitude well enough.

"Here, let my men take care of your mounts," Hooker continued, gesturing one of them forward, "and let us give you breakfast. We can talk more about the news once we've got a pot of coffee in us."

"Sounds good," said Wyatt, handing over the reins and letting himself be led into the ranch house, with his friends following.

The others tucked energetically into the generous hot breakfast, but Wyatt was too distracted to feel much hunger. Instead, after a few mouthfuls of food he drank a mug of coffee, and then a refill, while contemplating an issue of the *San Francisco Daily Examiner* of a few days before. There was an article on page two that Henry Hooker had pointed out to Wyatt. The headline would have grabbed his attention without such a prompt.

> *THE COWBOYS.*
> *What Wells Fargo's Detectives Know About Them.*
> *THE EARPS AND THE CLANTONS.*
> *A Denial of the Statement that the Earp Boys are Thieves and Gamblers—Doc Holliday.*

Wyatt glanced at Doc, but instead of commenting set himself to reading. The article began:

> *The feud between the Earp brothers and the Arizona Cowboys has naturally attracted a great deal of attention, and there is a general desire on the part of the public to know something of the causes which have led to the killing of so many men.*

To this end, an *Examiner* reporter had interviewed Wells Fargo officials *who have had personal and practical experience with the rough element of Arizona.* The reporter wrote that the Cowboys were a gang of about seventy-five men under the leadership of Ike Clanton, and enjoying the support of an unnamed official.

The majority of the best citizens of Tombstone, however, are in favor of the Earps, who have incurred the enmity of the Cowboys simply because they refused to allow them to have their own way when they came to town on a protracted spree, Virgil Earp being Marshal of the place. Wyatt Earp is represented to be the brains of the Earp confederacy—

Wyatt huffed in wry humor, and skipped the summation of his history and credentials.

Doc Holliday, although a man of dissipated habits and a gambler, has never been a thief and was never in any way connected with the attempted stage robbery when Philpot, the stage-driver, was killed.

The article attempted to set the facts straight about various events that had been misrepresented, and then returned to the present situation, reporting that Wyatt and his men had refused to be arrested by Sheriff Behan—this time clearly named.

Wyatt Earp has said that he would never surrender to Sheriff Behan, because he believed that if he was once in his power without arms, the Sheriff would allow the Cowboys in the jail to murder him.

The article concluded:

Which party will come out victorious in the conflict it is difficult to tell, but that there will be more bloody work in Arizona, from the well-known desperate tangle of the contending parties, there can be no doubt.

Wyatt paused on that thought, and then handed the newspaper over to Doc. Having thought he himself appeared impassive, Wyatt was surprised when Hooker declared, "Yes, I was astonished, too."

"Why is that?" Doc murmured absently while reading.

"Wells Fargo stating their current business so clearly," Hooker replied. "Not that they operate in the shadows, but they prefer to keep a dignified silence even at the worst of times."

Wyatt cleared his throat. "I guess we have Jim Hume to thank."

"I guess you do—"

Doc let out a loud guffaw. "Dissipated habits! But I never was a thief… Most obliging."

Hooker shot Doc an amused glance, but then turned back to Wyatt. "They've backed you unreservedly, and that really is astonishing—thoroughly deserved as well, of course. They obviously value you, and they valued Morgan for being dauntless and reliable." Hooker took a breath, and said, "I'm backing you, too, Wyatt, if it still needs saying. Whatever me and mine can do to help, you just say the word."

Wyatt nodded, and this time tried to ensure his gratitude was plain for all to see. "Thank you. There's no one in the Territory whose opinion I value more."

And yet once Henry Hooker had gone to rustle up another pot of coffee, Wyatt found his gaze wandering toward Doc, and when Doc's mouth quirked in a smile, Wyatt's heart warmed.

The Sierra Bonita Ranch—named for the beautiful mountains to either side of its location in Sulphur Spring Valley—had been founded ten years before in wilder times. The ranch house was built of solid adobe bricks around three sides of a large square, and it faced inwards with no windows in the outside walls. The only way in or out was a fortified door in the fourth wall which completed the whole. In the early days, the trouble came from the Chiricahua Apache, but now the cattle raids were more likely carried out by the Cowboys.

"You can stay here, whether it comes to a fight or not," Henry Hooker said to Wyatt.

One of Hooker's men had ridden in at a gallop to announce that a large posse led by Sheriff Behan was only a few hours away, heading in the direction of the Sierra Bonita though they didn't seem to be in a great hurry.

The sun was already westering. Wyatt shook his head and said, "I'm grateful for the offer, but we'll pack up and make our stand elsewhere."

"I mean it, Wyatt. No one has breached these walls yet, and if the Apache couldn't, then Behan is hardly likely to succeed."

"It's not your fight, sir."

"Wyatt, it has been my fight for as long as I've been here."

"Thank you, but this skirmish we'll make ours. You and your men don't deserve to take any hurt for it. Later, perhaps, we'll leave the battle to you."

Henry didn't argue any further, but simply shook Wyatt's hand and asked what supplies were needed.

The six of them—Wyatt and Doc, Sherman, Creek, Texas Jack, and Dan—made camp on the crown of a hill about three miles north of Hooker's ranch. They didn't light a fire that night, but then neither did they try to hide. It wasn't that Wyatt wanted to fight another lawman, but he wasn't going to run from a confrontation with Behan. He certainly didn't trust Behan enough to turn himself or his men over to Behan's care, and he suspected Behan was—for different reasons—even more reluctant than Wyatt to make a fight of it. So Wyatt sat and waited, and they all took turns keeping watch.

The sheriff's posse arrived at Hooker's ranch early the next morning—fourteen or fifteen of them, from what Creek could see through his spyglass. "Including a fair few of his Cowboy friends, from the looks of it," Creek added. "Phin Clanton, I reckon... unless that's someone else riding his horse. Yeah, that's Ike beside him. John Ringo."

Wyatt cast a sharp glance at Doc. "So much for Ringo declaring this isn't his fight."

Doc didn't say anything in reply, but a thought sparked within him and he seemed to both frown and smile.

Creek concluded, "Not a crowd Henry Hooker will be happy to find on his doorstep. But they're heading inside."

Honor demanded that hospitality be offered, but once Behan and his party had broken their fast and watered their horses, they saddled up to ride out. "Guess we can expect them soon," Sherm remarked.

Wyatt and the rest readied themselves, making sure they had guns and ammunition to hand, and a sturdy tree or rock to shelter behind. Wyatt stood clear, a pace or two in front of the others and his hands empty, still wanting to settle this without any further harm done. The six of them watched in a silence so deep that Wyatt could hear Doc's breath steady and quiet in his usual rhythm. It calmed him.

For a few minutes it seemed as if Behan and his men were going to circle the hill, perhaps knowing a better approach to take to the summit, perhaps wanting to surround them… But then it dawned on Wyatt that the group was simply riding past, without so much as glancing in his direction.

"What the deuce?" someone muttered, and then they were all standing in plain view, watching the posse ride off further northwards. Wyatt looked around at his companions, but none of them seemed to have any better idea than he did about what they'd just witnessed.

The hoof-beats eventually faded away into the distance. And then Creek holstered his gun, and asked, "So, what's next, Wyatt?"

"We stay here," Wyatt replied. "They'll probably come back this way, and I don't want to involve Henry Hooker in a fight, no matter how willing."

"All right." And they settled in for the duration. It must have been apparent that Wyatt was inclined to be quiet, because the other four withdrew a little and talked amongst themselves while taking care of the horses and the necessities of the camp. That left Doc to keep Wyatt company, and he seemed to understand that Wyatt needed time to mull things over.

Not that he made any headway, for his thoughts circled around and around. All Wyatt knew was that the job wasn't done yet, even though the hot urge for vengeance had subsided. He needed to work out what to do next, and what to do for these men who'd stood by him loyally and selflessly. It was a righteous cause, but in following Wyatt they had made an enemy of the county sheriff.

All this while, Doc sat by him, almost close enough for Wyatt to feel his warmth, and he pondered his own thoughts or perhaps didn't think at all. Eventually, when the interruption of a meal seemed imminent, Wyatt turned to him and asked in tones intended for only Doc to hear, "What do you make of Ringo riding with Behan?"

Again, that spark lit Doc from the inside, but he lifted his brow quizzically and said, "I can't explain it."

Wyatt almost challenged him: '*Can't* you?' But instead he asked, even quieter, "Does he owe you, then, or feel an obligation? Would he hold them back from harming you?"

The spark became a glow, though Doc shook his head in denial. "A kind notion, Wyatt! And Ringo knows me well enough to calculate that the worst harm they could do me is to hurt you. *But*," Doc forged on without allowing a response, "I doubt that's it. If it were another man, I might suggest he sought the safety of numbers—"

Wyatt knew enough to finish the thought: "—but that's not Ringo's style."

"Exactly." Doc sighed out a breath. "Maybe it's as simple as him feeling short of friends, and they asked him to join them. Maybe that's all it is."

Though a soft smile never quite left Doc's lips. Wyatt nodded, having to accept this mystery whether it originated in Ringo's motivations or Doc's reactions—or in both.

Behan and his posse rode past again two days later, on the Thursday. Again, if any of them had bothered looking up they'd have seen Wyatt and his men—who had the benefit of higher ground, but were outnumbered by more than two to one. The sheriff could have made a fight of it if he'd wanted to, and he must have had exactly that in mind when he recruited the Cowboys who were guaranteed to be ready and willing to fight anyone aligned with the Earps.

It made no sense, unless it was all of a piece with Behan's cowardice and incompetence. Wyatt was amazed that one of the Cowboys didn't pick up on their presence and force the issue—the Clantons and John Ringo were perfectly capable of it, and he was sure they weren't the only ones.

The posse rode into Hooker's compound and dismounted, and men came forward to take care of the horses. Creek was watching the interactions through his spyglass, and after a minute or two erupted in laughter. It took him a few gasping breaths before he could explain why. "Hooker just pointed up here, pointed right at us, giving them directions—and Behan is staring off at Mount Graham as if he don't have the first clue what Hooker's talking about."

The others all enjoyed the humor of this, but Wyatt couldn't even raise a smile. There was still work to be done, and Behan seemed determined to— to *thwart* him, if not directly oppose him. Wyatt had never felt so frustrated.

He sat down to wait. And when Behan finally led his group southward, perhaps returning to Tombstone, Wyatt gathered his gear and took his men back to the Sierra Bonita.

"Did you see the class of men Sheriff Behan is riding with these days?" Hooker demanded as he came striding up to Wyatt.

"I did," Wyatt replied calmly.

"Rustlers and ne'er-do-wells, the lot of 'em. He had one sworn deputy with him. *One!* The rest were, like as not, looking around to learn how best to steal my cattle."

"I've brought this trouble to your door, Henry."

Hooker took a deep breath and somewhat calmer said, "Don't you mind about that, Wyatt. You and your men are welcome here. Come on inside, now. There's coffee brewing."

"Thank you," said Wyatt. He and Doc accompanied Hooker to the house, while the rest of Wyatt's men went to help the ranch-hands with the horses and their gear.

"Did you hear that Bob Paul was planning to join Behan's posse?" Hooker asked once they'd settled around one end of the long table.

Doc frowned. "Why would he? He's a friend of Wyatt's!"

"My guess is he wanted to make sure you were brought in safely, Wyatt, if you were of a mind to be arrested."

"It's true that I trust Paul, and I plan on answering to him." Wyatt glanced at Doc for his confirmation. "I told Behan as much, when we left Tombstone."

"I remember." Doc turned back to Hooker. "All right, then—so why didn't he?"

Hooker leaned in to tell them with obvious relish, "Bob Paul was so disgusted with Behan's choice of companions that he refused to ride with them. Said it was clear that Behan wanted to provoke a fight, or even a murder, and he'd have nothing to do with it."

Wyatt nodded. In many ways he was pleased that Paul had retired from the fray, and was leaving it up to Wyatt to work out when and how to come in. Not that Wyatt knew the answer to that himself yet, but he appreciated that it was his decision to make.

After a silence, Hooker asked, "What do you need, Wyatt?"

"Time," he responded without even thinking about it. "Time and peace."

"That I can give you."

Wyatt and Doc took the offer of a bedroom in the main house, while the others elected to join the ranch-hands in the bunkhouse. Doc, who was inclined to be garrulous, managed arrangements and tended conversations so as to let Wyatt remain quiet. Wyatt had rarely felt so grateful.

Later that evening, as the two of them were stripping off their outer clothes on either side of the bed, Wyatt cleared his throat and said, "We'll have to move on. At least for now."

"I know," said Doc in easy tones.

"Do you mind?" Wyatt blew out the remaining lamp, and they each climbed in under the covers. "We were building a life there in Tombstone."

"No, I don't mind. Any losses are more than outweighed by my gains." A silence stretched, and a sleepy twilight had begun creeping up on Wyatt when Doc finally added, "I have to thank you, Wyatt. It's a long while since I've done anything… useful."

He murmured a wordless response, and let the twilight take him away. The two of them were lying there in the big double bed with enough room to be quite separate, and Wyatt felt blessedly comfortable in all manner of ways. He felt better still, though, when he half-woke in the darkness of the small hours, to the sensation of Doc pressed close down his back with an arm curved protectively around Wyatt's waist, just as Wyatt had held Doc in the jail in Tombstone, wanting to share his warmth with his friend. It wasn't that Wyatt's body needed the care, though, not this time. It was the ache in his soul that Doc was easing.

'I have to thank you…'

They settled into the Sierra Bonita for the time being. Sherm, Creek, Texas Jack and Dan spent their days working alongside the ranch-hands, though they came to the house for the evening meal as often as not. Wyatt remained quiet, keeping his own counsel with Doc always at his side as silent reinforcement. The two of them rode out to nearby watering places each day and kept watch for anyone coming or going. Hardly anyone did, and no one nefarious; the region's rustlers seemed to either be riding with Behan or choosing not to attract attention.

One day a messenger arrived at the ranch bearing a thousand dollars in cash for Wyatt as a 'loan' from one of Tombstone's leading businessmen, E.B. Gage, to cover the posse's expenses. It was understood, however, that the money needn't be repaid. As Wyatt took up the parcel of dollar bills, something shifted within him, and he began to feel less stuck.

The next day he and Doc rode to the Fort Grant army camp, nine or ten miles north of the Sierra Bonita, in the hopes that Wyatt could find a notary public. When he did so, he signed his remaining property deeds over to his sister Adelia, and put them in the mail.

Colonel James Biddle came to greet them and warn Wyatt that he knew of the outstanding warrants for arrest in the matter of the murder of Frank Stilwell. "I'm going to have to detain you, Wyatt," he explained, "but come and eat with us first."

At some stage during the meal, Colonel Biddle excused himself from the table—and he never returned. When Wyatt and Doc were done eating and went outside to smoke a cigar, they found their horses watered and groomed and waiting for them. Doc shrugged at Wyatt. "Blame me for leading you astray, if you like, but I believe we're being invited to resist arrest."

"I'll tell them you galloped out of here, and I felt obliged to chase you down."

"Ah…" murmured Doc with a glint in his eye, "what with me being a wanted man and all… But what are you going to do with me when you finally catch up?" he added. "That's the real question!"

They rode out of camp at a leisurely pace, and no one tried to prevent them leaving. Wyatt sighed a silent 'thank you' for Colonel Biddle.

When they returned to the Sierra Bonita, it was to find that Wells Fargo had also sent Wyatt a thousand dollars in cash, with a verbal message that it was to cover expenses and was strictly off the books.

Hooker was contemplating something while he considered Wyatt during dinner that night. Eventually he casually mentioned, "The Arizona Cattlegrowers Association offered a thousand-dollar reward for Curly Bill Brocius. You've seen that the newspapers are debating whether he's alive or dead—those lowlifes must have buried him out there on unhallowed ground and left it a mystery. But, Wyatt, I take your word for what happened."

Wyatt paused for a moment's thought, but the substance of his answer wasn't in question. "A lawman can't claim a reward for doing his duty, Henry," Wyatt said steadily, though he knew well enough that he had pushed and perhaps passed the limits of what he could do while bearing a deputy U.S. marshal's badge. "And I won't take a reward for keeping my promise to Morgan."

"I understand," said Hooker, not taking any offence.

Wyatt met his gaze. "But you can tell them that if they want to pass you the money to help cover all you've done for us, I'd appreciate it."

Hooker nodded in gentlemanly acknowledgment, and they let the matter be.

"There's unfinished business," Wyatt murmured that night while Doc held him close in the dark.

"What's that?" Doc gently replied.

"Ike and Phin Clanton are still out there." Wyatt sighed. "I feel as if I'm finished, but I know that the task is not yet done."

Doc tightened his arms around Wyatt for a moment but remained quiet. He was being unusually reticent these days, as if determined to let Wyatt work things out for himself.

"But if they're riding with Behan," Wyatt continued, "then it won't be just you and me against the two of them. They'll make a real fight of it, and if they can they'll involve more than the Cowboys."

"True."

"I hate Behan, and I don't much care for Woods or Breakenridge, but Neagle's a good man—and anyway, they all wear the badge, whether they deserve to or not." He sighed again, but what had seemed a conundrum before was now clear as day.

It became clearer still the next afternoon when news arrived that Frank Stilwell's older brother had come to Tombstone to settle Frank's affairs.

"Not *the* Comanche Jack Stilwell?" Creek exclaimed when Hooker raised the subject over dinner.

"The same," confirmed Hooker. "He's scouted for the army in every state and territory this side of the Mississippi."

"He was the hero of the Battle of Beecher Island," added Sherm.

"I never believed they were related, when I heard talk of it," said Texas Jack. "I figured Comanche Jack was more likely to be kin of the lawyer-man."

"It makes you wonder," Doc remarked in his Southern drawl, "if he had any idea of what his baby brother had become."

Hooker nodded. "Comanche Jack is law-and-order all the way. He might be in for some nasty surprises."

Wyatt remained quiet, but after the meal was done he convened a meeting of his men in the ranch house's courtyard. "We've done what we can," he announced. "It's time to walk away."

"But the Clantons…?" Sherman McMaster asked.

"If the sheriff and his deputies are standing with them, I'm not prepared to go through them to get to Ike and Phin."

"They're not the sort," observed Doc, "to avoid justice for long, whether legal or poetic."

"And I'm not prepared," Wyatt continued, "to fight Comanche Jack Stilwell. No doubt he'd feel obliged to take the part of his brother against me, but under any other circumstances we'd stand together."

"All right," said Texas Jack. "What next, then?"

"Henry Hooker is going to talk to Governor Tritle about a pardon. Wells Fargo will back him, and it might go all the way to the President—he's made his views clear on the Cowboys. But until those arrest warrants are dropped, we need to leave the territory." Wyatt looked around at these men who'd stuck by him despite the losses involved, when so many wouldn't. "We'll head for New Mexico—we'll ride to Silver City to begin with. Eventually I'm thinking Colorado. You might have your own plans, but you're welcome to join me for as long as you like."

There were nods and shared glances, and a speculative light in their eyes. Except for Doc who stared quietly at Wyatt.

"The problem is," Wyatt continued, "we'll all need to start again. A new life in a new place—but we'll each have a stake to use in doing that. Some men, important men, have been grateful for what we've done. Maybe they can't always announce their support, but they've sent help just as practical— or more so. I'll divide up the money we have left, divide it up evenly, and that should be enough. If we use it wisely, it should be plenty."

There were appreciative murmurs, and the other four each shook Wyatt's hand before heading for the bunkhouse. Doc didn't say anything, but simply accompanied Wyatt to the room they shared.

"Did I make sense?" Wyatt asked as he lay there held safe in the dark.

Doc huffed in humor. "Of course you did, Wyatt. Perfect sense."

"I haven't talked that much for… hell, I can't even remember. Since Morgan died, I guess."

"That's not so long ago," Doc murmured, his tones wistful with grief.

"It feels as if a lifetime has passed since then. Midnight struck, and the world changed."

Doc reached a hand to soothe across Wyatt's hair. "True… and poetically expressed."

Wyatt thought of ten different things he wanted to say, but eventually settled for asking, "Where's Kate?"

A shrug was the response, and though Doc still held Wyatt as close as ever he withdrew a little in spirit. "Oh, back in Globe, I imagine, or perhaps she's off on another adventure."

"You don't know?"

Doc's tone turned somewhat sharper. "She left Tombstone while we were in jail in November, Wyatt, if you recall. She left without a word, and I haven't heard from her since, nor tried to contact her."

"All right," Wyatt murmured, and he fell silent.

After a while Doc calmed again, and he tightened his arms around Wyatt. "I'll stay with you, my friend, if that's what you're asking. At least— until you remember who you are."

"What…?" he asked on a breath.

"And then I'll pack you off to California to go pick up your wife—if she'll still have you."

Wyatt was all out of words. He was so used to everyone dismissing his wife—except for Allie, of course. He'd come to believe he'd chosen poorly, and that Allie was being contrary.

"There's more to Mattie Blaylock than might appear," Doc scolded him—though being gentle about it. "There's more to all of us than anyone else knows, and sometimes we're a mystery even to ourselves."

He was out of breath as well as words, and could only listen.

"I think… I think that an acquaintance of mine might say our souls are always larger than us. And we all have a soul, Wyatt. Mattie has a soul, which you can love."

Doc stroked Wyatt's hair again, and he lay still for it, and it eased him, when if this had been anyone else Wyatt would have bristled.

"But you, Wyatt," Doc continued, "*you* are soul-sized. You'll remember that one day soon. You always knew who you were, Wyatt."

"No," he replied hoarsely. "I'm not the man I thought I was. Not the man I wanted to be."

Doc clutched him close with his limbs and his self and his—his soul.

"Not with all I've done," Wyatt persisted, "since the world changed."

Doc's face pressed against Wyatt, and perhaps for a moment his mouth blessed him with a kiss where Wyatt's blood beat strong in his throat. "Yes, you are, Wyatt," he insisted. "One of the things I love you for is that you've always known your own mind. You put that aside for a little while, for good reason."

"Yes?"

"Now let some time pass, and you'll remember once more." Doc was still wrapped around him, holding him safe and promising, "I'll be with you until you do."

CHAPTER TWENTY-THREE:

SUPPOSE, SUPPOSE

Arizona and Beyond;

July 1882

One thing… One more thing left to do. It was already as hot as if he were in hell, and the whiskey burned his gullet as if it were flames.

"Johnny Ringo!" someone called, and he slurred around, finding himself on a horse, sitting upright more or less in the saddle. "Ah, Johnny," the voice said, softly chiding, and John managed to focus well enough to recognize Billy Breakenridge. "Where are you going?"

"G-G-Galeyville," he managed, after a few attempts at getting his tongue to cooperate. He looked about him and figured he must be in the Dragoon Mountains, which was at least the right general direction if he'd been coming from… had he been in…? Tombstone. Yes. He thought so.

"I'd take my hat off to you if the day weren't so hot," Breakenridge was saying. "I've never seen anyone so drunk and not passed out!"

Johnny proffered the bottle of whiskey, and when Breakenridge demurred Johnny reassured him, "I got more!" brandishing the full bottle he'd found—thank God—in his saddlebag.

Breakenridge took a mouthful of liquor, but it wasn't to Billy-boy's taste, and he handed the half-empty bottle back right away. "Johnny, you shouldn't be out here drinking like this on such a hot day."

"Going to Galeyville," Johnny insisted, having mastered those hard Gs and trying to get the horse moving again. It stood there stubbornly.

"Why Galeyville?"

"Why not?" he countered with a hoot of laughter. Which was unanswerable, really.

"Come back with me to the Goodrich ranch," Billy asked. "At least wait until sundown to continue your journey."

An invitation… not that he fancied Billy nor cared enough to try to comprehend him, else Johnny would have chanced his luck a long time before… but any company was good company when a man had been so thoroughly abandoned… Doc Holliday had left the territory now, and Johnny heard he'd traveled up half the country to colder climes… Joe Olney had been ready to betray a friend to his death, so Johnny wondered if he himself had ever understood *anyone*… and as for Lucian, he'd vanished as if he'd never existed at all, which maybe actually he hadn't…

"John, please," Billy said, leaning in to insist on his attention—but when Johnny reached to grasp his hand, Breakenridge recoiled. As if Billy had anyone better—or anyone at all!

The horse deigned to walk on at last, and Johnny celebrated by downing a goodly portion of whiskey, and if he heard an exasperated "Johnny!" called after him he didn't pay it any mind.

Later that afternoon… was it the same afternoon? It must have been. Later that afternoon Johnny found himself lying stretched out on the sunbaked soil, and he figured he must have made camp for the night because his feet were bare, but even he could see it was a wretched place to spend the night, and anyway the sun was hardly even westering yet.

Johnny forced himself to sit up, and he looked around for the horse, and then he looked around again. The sun was heavy on him as if fate-laden. The horse must have wandered off, and gone quite a ways as well because the scrubby trees were sparse here and Johnny should have been able to see her. If she'd gone in search of water, it was worth trying to track her… Well, he'd have to find her anyway. Johnny had his guns and his hat, but no coat and no boots and most importantly no whiskey…

He didn't get far with the ground scorching his feet, he wasn't so drunk that he couldn't feel the pain of every step. So he sat down and tore strips off his undershirt to wrap around his feet as makeshift protection. The sun beat down, drilling into his poor head, and his tongue was thick with thirst. He stumbled on…

But it was useless… it was useless. He found trees, and a creek, it must be Turkey Creek, he knew where he was now, but where there should have been water there was sand. Where there should have been dwellings nearby there was desolation. The horse had been smarter than him, obviously, and had gone elsewhere. The heat was unbearable, even sitting in the crook formed by the intertwined trunks of two big old black oak trees, not enthroning him but cradling him up off the ground… The creek was dry, and while he knew the Sanders ranch shouldn't be far away it was too far for him, and no doubt the Apache would discover him long before the Cowboys did, if any of them even thought to try finding him at all.

Well, he had his guns. And there was just one thing left to do. There had always been this one thing, his father had been the first to show him the way, and the wonder was that John had deferred it until now.

Johnny Ringo lifted his pistol and pressed the muzzle against his temple—and his hand clenched as if it knew as well as he did that—

It was done.

At first there was nothing, and that was fine, he'd wanted nothing. But then he became aware that the nothing was actually darkness, and then he realized he felt cool, which would have been so very welcome if only he hadn't been wanting an end to everything.

He groaned, and opened his eyes, and found himself in… air. That's all he could see or feel, he was drifting through the air, and it wasn't unpleasant and at least he wasn't thirsty anymore, but any moment now he would remember who he was and why he had sought nothingness so desperately, and what unfathomable misery he'd felt.

He groaned and curled up into as tight a shape as possible, hoping only to disappear—but it was no use. Johnny Ringo was himself again, nothing more and nothing less, and he was all alone with nothing to distract him from how unbearable his life had become.

He groaned, and hung there hopeless in the emptiness, wanting naught but nothingness. Instead, the air about him grew damp and white and textured as if he were in a cloud, and then it tinged blue, and swiftly became a pure clear blue as if he were above mountains. The air passed him, or he passed by, traveling somewhere he didn't know.

And then there were indeed snow-shrouded mountain peaks far below his feet, and steep valleys, rocks and trees, and then wooden buildings of soft, worn gray. He found himself over a balcony, outside a window, still a long way off the ground, and after a while he figured he must be meant to see what was inside.

He didn't go in, though he sensed he could. He drifted closer to the glass and peered through the lace curtains, focusing in and further in until he could clearly see—a hotel room which had reveled in better days but was still richly comfortable. And there was a bed, and resting within the bed was Doc Holliday, and lying asleep within Doc's arms was… Wyatt Earp.

Johnny scowled and yanked himself away. He'd been wanting peace, and instead he was given this vision to plague him. Was this, in fact, hell? The tenderness on Doc's face, the kindness with which he held his friend. It didn't even look as if they'd had sex. Had they had sex or not?

He pushed close again and considered the pair. If Doc had ever held Johnny like this… If he had ever truly cared for him… Bitterness exploded where Johnny's heart had been… He hadn't even known what he wanted, until now when it was too late. Or maybe…

Maybe it had always been too late. For Johnny. But not for Doc—and not for Wyatt, either, if he could receive this gentleness whether or not he felt it himself.

Johnny sighed, and calmed… the bitterness fell away, and eventually the envy evaporated, and he found instead an acceptance that seemed almost a blessing. He pushed in again, wanting to dwell on that perfect contentment evident on Doc's face, in his posture, in every part of him… but something caught Johnny's eye.

He turned, but it was only a shabby old gray rag caught on the balcony railing, maybe a well-worn shirt plucked off a washing line by a breeze, and blown about until its tattered remains ended up here. A waft of air set it to dancing, and Johnny drew close, curious despite himself. It wasn't…

It couldn't be… Could it? His soul, which he hadn't seen for so long he'd almost forgotten he even had one. Who'd have thought?

Johnny eased closer, and reached for it with one hand and then two. At first it seemed snagged on a splinter of wood, but then it was in his grasp as if returning home. He held it for a while in wonder, and brought it to his lips before tucking it away within his shirt against the skin over his heart.

Maybe he had hoped in these moments to find himself in an embrace, with Satan's son his own to enjoy for all eternity in heat and flames… but this was better. This was so much better. A day blessed with cool sunlight, and a gentle dance of the rare blue air… and what was left of him wafted apart and was released at last into peace…

Epitaph:

Here Lies One Whose Name was Writ in Blood

Denver, Colorado;

May 1885

Doc had heard they were in town, so he dressed in all his finest gear, and walked down to the Windsor Hotel on Larimer Street. The opulent lobby was quietly bustling with guests and staff. Doc paused to await the attention of one of the latter, and looked about him with some curiosity. Alas, the stakes were a little too high for him here in these threadbare times, but no doubt there were guests who'd appreciate the thrill of daring the rougher gambling halls and—

And then he saw him. Him!

Wyatt Earp, who'd seen Doc, too, and was standing from a sofa, stepping away from a small, convivial group, to come and meet Doc halfway across the lobby. As tall and as handsome and as striking as ever. "Doc!" he exclaimed on a breath, reaching to shake Doc's hand, and then not letting go but instead clasping that hand firmly in both of his.

"Wyatt," he murmured in reply, unable to repress a giddy glowing smile. "What a delightful sight you are."

"Three years," Wyatt was saying. "It's been three years."

That familiar piercing Earp stare was examining Doc from top to toe, and Doc didn't want to think too hard about what Wyatt would see—a much thinner man, his hair paler, and his face gaunter as his final illness busily made its mark. Instead, Doc examined Wyatt just as closely, and was pleased to find him as strong as he'd always been, with his familiar upright yet easy posture. He was dressed as a gentleman, in a fine yet understated way in elegant grays, having eschewed his lawman's choice of a dramatic black suit and hat.

"I'm so glad to see you again, Wyatt," Doc said—a redundant remark if ever there were one.

The usually impassive Wyatt smiled, and avoided making some remark on Doc's health or appearance by tightening his grip on Doc's hand and then saying, "Come and meet the others."

"Wyatt—" Doc managed as Wyatt finally let him go and began leading him over to the intimate setting of sofas which bore three people all watching their reunion while pretending to discretion.

"I know," Wyatt replied with a flash of those blue eyes over his shoulder, "but just say hello first. Tom Fitch is here—you remember, from Tombstone."

"Ah, yes," Doc replied distractedly, He was grateful for the prompt, for it took him a moment to recall the lawyer who'd so ably defended the Earp brothers before Judge Wells Spicer.

"Look who I found!" Wyatt announced to his companions.

And then Doc was bending over Mrs. Earp's hand, murmuring "Charmed, my dear!" and casting her a wicked smile, and then nodding politely to Mrs. Fitch, and shaking Fitch by the hand with a "Splendid to see you again." A few minutes of polite chatter, during which the only information Doc attended to was that Wyatt and his wife were running a saloon called the Fashion in the little silver mining town of Aspen up in the mountains.

"Will you excuse us?" Wyatt was saying, no doubt sooner than he should have but the others all nodded and smiled with fond indulgence. Doc offered them a slight bow and turned away before they could glimpse the tide of emotion swelling within him.

Wyatt invited Doc to a quiet corner of the lobby, and they settled opposite each other in the luxurious chairs. A waiter followed them over and undertook to bring them a pot of coffee. Soon they were catching up with each other on what had happened since they'd parted three years before, and then began asking after shared friends and family.

Virgil and Allie Earp were in Colton, California, where Virgil had interests in racehorses and politics, and was talking of opening a private detective agency. Wells Spicer had returned to the wandering life of a prospector in Arizona and Mexico, forever chasing that elusive gleam of silver or gold. Bat Masterson had been a constable in Trinidad, Colorado for a year, and was now in Dodge City trying out a new career in journalism, but talking of coming to Denver. Bob Paul was still serving as sheriff in Pima County, Arizona—and had once attempted to extradite Doc from Colorado to finally stand trial for the murder of Frank Stilwell.

"Bat Masterson saved me from that fate," Doc said, "for which I have *you* to thank, Wyatt."

"I asked him to help," Wyatt acknowledged.

Doc huffed a laugh, which turned into a cough. When he could he remarked, "Bat certainly didn't do it for love of me!" And they were both laughing then, at this whole unlikely friendship of theirs, the righteous lawman and the disreputable gambler, the taciturn rock and the loquacious river. No one understood it or approved of them. Maybe even Doc himself didn't quite understand. But it had been the most precious thing in his life.

Eventually they grew serious again, and Doc quit coughing long enough to observe, "One way or another, I wouldn't have survived a return to Arizona."

Wyatt nodded grimly, and said, "You heard that the Clantons are still operating as they always did?"

"Regrets?"

"Many." Wyatt shrugged. "But I can't change what happened, and I don't know that I should have done anything different."

"Did you hear…" Doc murmured. Then he swallowed down a sudden unexpected welling of grief and had to start again. "You heard that John Ringo died?"

"Yes." Wyatt waited for Doc to say something more, but finally prompted, "Ruled a suicide, but wasn't there some mystery to it?"

Doc nodded. "Ringo was found the next day, but his horse had run off with his boots and coat, and wasn't found for two weeks or more. Which explains some things but not others. He was wearing his cartridge belt upside down, and I heard he was partially scalped."

"Exit wound?"

"In a different location." Doc let Wyatt ponder that for a moment before saying, "There was some talk of him being murdered—by Buckskin Frank Leslie, for instance."

Wyatt glanced at him sharply. "Do *you* believe he was murdered?"

Doc let out a sigh. "No."

"I never went back there, Doc."

"I know," Doc reassured him with a slight smile. "I know it wasn't you."

"Do you…?" Wyatt seemed puzzled by this assertion, almost as if he'd imagined the notion so often that he himself half-wondered if it were true.

"I have to conclude that he put an end to his own life—or to be more exact, his own torments. And if anyone's to blame…"

"Doc—"

"I chose you over him, Wyatt," Doc said very directly, "and while I can't wish it otherwise, there are nights when he haunts me."

Wyatt returned his gaze, not flinching from all these unspoken truths. "Regrets?" he asked in gruff tones.

"Many," Doc replied, "but I wouldn't change a thing." And after a moment he quipped, "It's just as well my conscience isn't any more tender than it needs to be."

And Wyatt regarded him steadily, not fooled in the slightest.

They talked of less delicate or difficult things for a while, but eventually it was time for Doc to take his leave. So many hours had slipped by as they'd sat together that the upper reaches of the room were shrouded in twilight. "It will be a long time before we meet again," Doc said. There were tears glistening in Wyatt's eyes, and to Doc's astonishment one spilled over and ran down his cheek. "A drop of saltwater! Worth more to me than diamonds."

They stood—and then were in each other's arms, Wyatt holding on so tight that Doc feared—or wished—that he'd be crushed and there'd be an end to it.

"There, now… Let me go, Wyatt." Once Wyatt had done so and Doc had regained his tentative balance, he asked, "Make my excuses to the others. You understand… I always made an awkward bow." They began walking through the foyer together, until Wyatt had escorted him past anyone Doc might have to acknowledge.

"God bless you and keep you," Wyatt managed in tones thickened by grief.

"Goodbye, old friend," Doc replied. And he gathered the last tatters of his dignity about him and walked unsteadily out into the cold empty world— with embers of love glowing in his vitals that would warm him through the little while he had left.

◆

Historical Notes

My love of the American Old West belatedly began with the film *Tombstone* (1993); I walked out of the cinema enthralled by the Tombstone story, by the intriguing friendship between Wyatt Earp and Doc Holliday, and in particular by Johnny Ringo as portrayed by Michael Biehn. Fan fiction ensued, and soon proved not to be enough; I made a start on this novel, writing almost half of it before eventually setting it aside.

Living in Australia in those pre-internet days limited my research. I ordered some books via Amazon, and happily devoured *And Die in the West* by Paula Mitchell Marks (1989). I hardly knew anything about John Ringo, though, other than a brief *Encyclopedia Britannica* entry—which, frankly, proved to be wrong in some fundamental aspects.

All of which is to explain that my initial take on John Ringo was created out of whole cloth, and I made some choices that I probably wouldn't make today. When I finally picked up this novel again in early 2020, I had the benefit of the biographies written by Jack Burrows and David Johnson, and I rewrote accordingly. Still, the resulting character no doubt reflects this patchwork of literary history, and none of these fine scholars is in any way to blame for my imaginative use or abuse of their material.

More broadly, while I endeavored to stay true to the Tombstone story, there are complex strands of history leading into and out of The Gunfight, involving a cast of thousands (well, hundreds), with many contemporary accounts in direct conflict with each other, and subsequent interpretations heading in several directions at once. Inevitably I had to pick and choose which elements of the story to use, which to streamline or ignore, which characters to conflate, and so on.

For example, at the outset I was absolutely determined to include all six of the Earp brothers, but ended up ignoring Newton and James, and only briefly mentioning Warren. I'm not the first to focus on Virgil, Wyatt and Morgan, and I probably won't be the last!

Also, I decided to focus on Wyatt's relationship with Mattie Blaylock rather than Josephine Sarah Marcus. While Wyatt apparently first met Josie at Tombstone, I feel their story belongs to the post-Tombstone years. I wanted to give Mattie her due, and I also wanted to focus on Wyatt's relationship with Doc.

Otherwise, I ignored various people such as Milt Joyce and Billy Claiborne, and I only included Bat Masterson in the Dodge City chapters. Conversely, I included a few fictional characters in order to address certain themes. You can find more details on all these in my List of Names.

Historically, there were other stage robberies, other prison escapes, other posses, other tribes. I mention the Chiricahua Apache but not Geronimo, nor the White Mountain Apache and Nakaidoklini. In smaller matters, I ignore some details such as Tombstone's town marshal being renamed 'chief of police' in April 1881. I introduce Johnny Behan as a (fictional) deputy sheriff of Pima County in anticipation of his (historical) appointment as sheriff of Cochise County. I include Doc in a posse he wasn't actually part of, to further explore his commitment to Wyatt.

I trust that none of these or similar choices detract from the essentials of the history (or indeed the story).

Regarding the direct quotations, I've included some from historical sources, either excerpts or in full. The following are all genuine, with only minor tweaks for readability: the coroner's verdict on The Gunfight; Wells Spicer's judicial decision concluding the preliminary hearing; Chester Arthur's State of the Union address; and the Wells Fargo interview published in the *San Francisco Daily Examiner*.

However, I myself composed Wyatt Earp's letter to Ike Clanton sent in February 1881. There was indeed such a letter, an offer to try to reach a peaceful agreement which was ignored by the recipient, but as far as I'm aware we don't possess a copy, nor do we know its specific contents. I hope I've done justice to Wyatt's direct yet dignified style.

LIST OF NAMES

Chester A. Arthur (1829-1886), President of the United States 1881-1885.

Ed Bailey (fictional?), gambler. No one has found any evidence substantiating Wyatt Earp's anecdote about Bailey's fatal dispute with Doc Holliday in Fort Griffin, Texas—and Kate Elder denied it. The story itself was probably invented by a *San Francisco Enquirer* reporter rather than Wyatt.

Moses Baird (1850-1875), involved in the Hoo Doo War, friend of John Ringo. The attack on Baird (fatal) and George Gladden in 1875 brought Ringo and others into the conflict, seeking vengeance.

Charlie Bartholomew, lawman, shotgun rider for Wells Fargo in Arizona.

John Behan (1844-1912), lawman, politician, businessman, Cochise County sheriff, friend of the Cowboys.

Frankie Bell, dance hall girl, sex worker in Dodge City.

Colonel **James Biddle**, commanding officer at Fort Grant, Arizona Territory.

Celia Ann **"Mattie" Blaylock** (1850-1888), sex worker, seamstress, common-law wife of Wyatt Earp.

Frederick "Fritz" Bode, outlaw, Cowboy.

Ned Boyle, bartender at the Oriental Saloon in Tombstone, witness of events leading to The Gunfight.

Billy Breakenridge (1846-1931), lawman, Cochise County deputy sheriff, friend of the Cowboys.

"Curly Bill" Brocius (William Bresnaham, 1845-1882), outlaw, gunman, rustler, Cowboy.

Guadalupe Celaya, rebel and outlaw leader in Northern Mexico.

Jim Chaney, involved in the Hoo Doo War. Paid by John Clark to lure Moses Baird and George Gladden into an ambush; Chaney was killed in September 1875 by John Ringo and Jim Williams in retaliation. Ringo was arrested and charged with murder, but the charges were eventually dropped due to the prosecution being unable to make a case.

Ah Chum **"China Mary"** Sing Lum (1839-1906), businesswoman in Tombstone.

Billy Claiborne (1860-1882), cowhand, miner, Cowboy. Mentioned in this novel as "the friend" of the Clantons and McLaurys in the vacant lot (Chapter 15).

Joseph Isaac **"Ike" Clanton** (1847-1887), ranch-hand, rustler.

Newman Haynes **"Old Man" Clanton** (1816-1881), rancher, rustler, patriarch. Father of: Phin Clanton; Ike Clanton; Billy Clanton.

Phineas Fay **"Phin" Clanton** (1843-1906), ranch-hand, rustler.

William Harrison **"Billy" Clanton** (1862-1881), ranch-hand, rustler.

John Clum (1851-1932), Indian agent for the San Carlos Apache reservation, first Mayor of Tombstone, founder and editor of the *Tombstone Epitaph*. Married to **Mary "Mollie" Ware** (1852-1880).

Scott Cooley (1845-1876), involved in the Hoo Doo War, former Texas Ranger, outlaw.

Annie Leopold Crabtree, common-law wife of Jack Crabtree in Tombstone. The 1926 estate case of nationally popular actress Lotta Crabtree included a claim from her niece Carlotta, daughter of Annie Leopold and Lotta's brother Jack Crabtree. Wyatt testified in support of the status of Annie and Jack's common-law marriage, mentioning that he met Annie Crabtree at Tombstone's ice cream parlor. Wyatt Earp's declaration that he liked ice cream is thus part of the legal record. (Unfortunately for Carlotta, the court decided she could not prove her parentage, and so she did not receive an inheritance.)

Jim Crane, outlaw, highwayman, participant in the attempted robbery of the Benson stage in March 1881.

Charles "Sandy Bob" Crouch, stagecoach operator in Tombstone.

Crawley P. Dake (1836-1890), U.S. marshal for Arizona Territory 1878-1882. He appointed Virgil Earp and later Wyatt as deputy U.S. marshals, and supported them throughout their service.

Private **Mervyn B. Davis** (c.1845-1912), Texas Ranger, newspaper correspondent.

Charles Ray **"Pony" Diehl** (c.1848-c.1888), outlaw, rustler, Cowboy. Charged with robbing the Bisbee stagecoach in January 1882.

Fred Dodge (1854-1938), gambler, lawman, friend of the Earps. He later revealed he'd been working undercover in Tombstone for Wells Fargo, but the Earps didn't know that at the time.

Thomas J. Drum, lawyer, U.S. Court Commissioner, defense attorney for Doc Holliday in the preliminary hearing following The Gunfight.

Marietta Duarte, married to and witness against Pete Spencer. Neighbor to the Earps in Tombstone.

Morgan Earp (1851-1882), shotgun rider, lawman. See also: Louisa Houston.

Virgil Earp (1843-1905), lawman, businessman. See also: Allie Sullivan.

Wyatt Earp (1848-1929), lawman, sometime pimp, gambler, gunman, shotgun rider, businessman, prospector. See also: Aurilla Sutherland; Mattie Blaylock; Josephine Sarah Marcus.

Earp family: father **Nicholas Porter Earp** (1813-1907); mother **Virginia Ann Cooksey** (1821-1893). Half-brother **Newton Jasper** (1837-1928) from Nicholas's first marriage to **Abigail Storm** (1813-1839). Brother **James Cooksey** (1841-1926); *Virgil Walter Earp* (1843-1905); sister **Martha Elizabeth** (1845-1856); *Wyatt Berry Stapp Earp* (1848-1929); *Morgan Seth Earp* (1851-1882); brother **Baxter Warren** (1855-1900); sister **Virginia Ann** (1858-1861); and sister **Adelia Douglas** (1861-1941).

Kate Elder (Mary Katherine Horony, 1850-1940), sex worker, businesswoman. Lover of Doc Holliday.

Andrew Felter, justice of the peace in Tombstone.

Thomas Fitch (1838-1923), lawyer, politician, defense attorney for the Earps in the preliminary hearing following The Gunfight. Married to **Anna Mariska Shultz**.

C.S. "Buck" Fly (1849-1901) and his wife Mary Edith **"Mollie" McKie** Goodrich (1847-1925), photographers, proprietors of a boarding house on Fremont Street in Tombstone.

James Flynn, lawman, deputy town marshal under Virgil Earp in Tombstone, and appointed town marshal when Virgil was incapacitated by injuries.

John Fonck, former lawman, now businessman in Tombstone.

Eddie Foy (1856-1928), nationally popular entertainer.

Abraham Maurice **"Abe" Franklin** (1857-1932), storekeeper, businessman, friend of John Ringo.

"**Major**" **Frink**, cattleman, with a ranch near the McLaurys in Arizona Territory. Identified in scholarly tomes as either "John Randolph Frink" or "Edwin B. Frink"; the *Arizona Weekly Star* (Tucson, 13 October 1881) mentions him as "R. Frink", so probably the former? Apparently "Major" was a nickname rather than a formal rank.

E.B. Gage, miner, prominent businessman in Tombstone, friend of the Earps.

George W. Gladden, involved in the Hoo Doo War, friend of John Ringo. In 1876, Gladden was sentenced to 99 years in jail for murder—the only such conviction during this violent feud. It seems he was pardoned in 1884, but didn't live much longer.

Dr. **George Goodfellow**, medical practitioner in Tombstone. Not coincidentally, he "developed a reputation as the United States' foremost expert in treating gunshot wounds" (Wikipedia).

Ben and **Briggs Goodrich**, brothers, lawyers, hired as attorneys by Ike Clanton inter alios.

Richard **"Dixie Lee" Gray**, outlaw, Cowboy, killed in Guadalupe Canyon Massacre; older brother **John Plesent Gray**.

Louis Hancock, farmhand, John Ringo's shooting victim in Safford, Arizona (Chapter 8).

Billy and **Ike Haslett**, brothers, ranchers. Billy Leonard, Harry Head and other Cowboys were sent to kill them over a land dispute. Instead, the Hasletts killed Leonard and Head, and in retaliation were killed by Jim Crane.

Bob Hatch, co-owner of Campbell & Hatch's Saloon and Billiard Parlor, friend of the Earps, witness to The Gunfight and to Morgan's death.

Charles Hawes, Cowboy. Charged with robbing the Bisbee stagecoach in January 1882.

Harry Head, outlaw, highwayman, participant in the attempted robbery of the Benson stage in March 1881.

Bob Henderson, miner, chicken rancher, friend of Pete Spencer. A correspondent from Bisbee later wrote, "Bob, by the way, is our only colored citizen—an enterprising and useful one he is, too" (*Tombstone Epitaph*, 22 July 1882).

Milt and **Will Hicks**, brothers, outlaws, Cowboys. (Some sources identify the injured Cottonwood Springs/Iron Springs shooting victim as **Johnny Barnes**.)

Higgins (fictional), small rancher selling off his cattle and goods before leaving Pima County. (I invented the name though the situation was common enough.)

Dr. John Henry **"Doc" Holliday** (1851-1887), dentist, gambler, gunman. See also: Mattie Holliday; Kate Elder.

Martha Anne **"Mattie" Holliday** (later Sister Mary Melanie, 1849-1939), cousin to Doc Holliday, correspondent, nun, inspiration for the *Gone with the Wind* character Melanie Hamilton.

Holliday family: father **Henry Burroughs Holliday** (1819-1893); mother **Alice Jane McKey** (1829-1866). Henry's second wife was **Rachel Martin** (1843-1921). Adopted brother **Francisco Hidalgo** (1835-1873); sister **Martha Eleanora** (1849-1850); *John Henry Holliday* (1851-1887).

Henry Clay Hooker (1828-1907), prominent businessman, founder of the Sierra Bonita ranch (the first and eventually the largest ranch in Arizona Territory), friend of the Earps.

Louisa Houston (1855-1894), common-law wife of Morgan Earp.

George Hoy (?-1878), cowhand, would-be gunman in Dodge City, badly injured during a shootout and later died of his wounds. He was probably in his early 20s. Hoy is the only man Wyatt Earp is known to have killed other than during The Gunfight and the Vendetta Ride—and it might not have been his bullet that hit Hoy, though Wyatt took responsibility for the death.

James B. Hume (1827-1904), miner, lawman, chief detective for Wells Fargo.

John Henry **"Jack" Jackson**, law-and-order man, eventually appointed deputy U.S. marshal in Arizona Territory.

"Turkey Creek" Jack Johnson (c.1847-c.1887), cowhand, friendly with the Cowboys, later aligned with Wyatt Earp and may have acted as his informant.

Harry Jones, Cochise County deputy sheriff.

John Keats (1795-1821), English poet of the Romantic era.

Annie Kee (fictional), laundress.

Luther King, participant in the attempted robbery of the Benson stage in March 1881. It was rumored that he was murdered by the Cowboys soon afterwards for informing on the other three highwaymen.

Frank Kingsbury, manager of the telegraph office in Tombstone. Someone in the telegraph office deliberately delayed delivery of the telegram to John Behan about arresting the Earp posse for the murder of Frank Stilwell. I haven't found a scholarly tome yet that identifies the person, but it feels odd not to use a name in a novel for this minor key player. Humble apologies to the memory of Mr. Kingsbury if I have mistakenly maligned him.

Billy Leonard, jeweler, outlaw, highwayman, participant in the attempted robbery of the Benson stage in March 1881, friend of Doc Holliday.

"Buckskin" Frank Leslie (1842-c.1927), scout, businessman, adventurer, gunman. There was some talk that Leslie killed John Ringo, but this has been discounted.

Lucian (fictional), a mystery, a distraction…

Dr. Thomas **"T.L." McCarty,** doctor, druggist in Dodge City.

Robert Findley **"Frank" McLaury** (1849-1881), small rancher, rustler.

Thomas **"Tom" McLaury** (1853-1881), small rancher, rustler.

Sherman McMaster (1853-1892), former Texas Ranger, sometime Cowboy, later aligned with Wyatt Earp. There is speculation about him working undercover for the Rangers while with the Cowboys, and acting as an informant for Wyatt.

Josephine Sarah Marcus (1861-1944), common-law wife of Wyatt Earp. While Josie and Wyatt no doubt met each other in Tombstone, there is no evidence that their partnership began there. Historically, Josie is the "Mrs. Earp" in this novel's Epitaph.

Bartholomew **"Bat" Masterson** (1853-1921), lawman, gambler, journalist; brother **Ed Masterson** (1852-1878), lawman in Dodge City.

Dr. **Henry Matthews,** medical practitioner in Tombstone, and Cochise County coroner.

John Meagher and **Joseph Mellgren,** businessmen, co-owners of the Alhambra Saloon, acted as surety for Doc Holliday when arrested.

Ed Mitchell, cattle rustler in Texas.

William Murray, stockbroker, businessman in Tombstone.

Dave Neagle, Cochise County deputy sheriff.

Joseph Graves **"Joe" Olney** (alias Joe Hill, 1849-1884), involved in the Hoo Doo War before moving further west, cattleman, rancher, friend of John Ringo. Married to **Agnes Jane Arnold** (1850-1887); they had five children, who fondly remembered Ringo as "Uncle John". I conflated one of the Olney children with **Mary Hughes**, who hero-worshipped Ringo. Mary was actually the 11-year-old sister of **Jim Hughes**, who had a ranch in New Mexico and was aligned with the Cowboys.

Tom Owens (fictional), troublemaker in Dodge City.

George Parsons (1850-1933), diarist. Mentioned in this novel as "the citizen" at the McLaury ranch (Chapter 15).

Robert Havlin "Bob" Paul (1830-1901), lawman, Pima County sheriff, friend of the Earps.

Lance Perkins, Cochise County deputy sheriff.

Eli **"Bud" Philpot** (1853-1881), stagecoach driver in Tombstone, shooting victim during attempted robbery of the Benson stage in March 1881.

Hank and **Len Redfield**, brothers, ranchers, friends of the Cowboys. Aided the highwaymen following the attempted robbery of the Benson stage in March 1881.

John Ringo (1850-1882), cattleman, gunman, outlaw, Cowboy.

Ringo family: father **Martin Ringo** (1819-1864); mother **Mary Peters** (1826-1876); *John Peters Ringo* (1850-1882); brother **Martin Albert** (1854-1873); sisters **Fanny Fern** (1857-1932), **Mary Enna** (1860-1941), and **Mattie Bell** (1862-1942).

Peter Roerig, miner, shooting victim during attempted robbery of the Benson stage in March 1881.

Dave Rudabaugh (1854-1886), outlaw in Kansas and elsewhere.

"Indian Charlie" Florentino Sais, logger, outlaw, Cowboy. Incorrectly named "Florentino Cruz" in the *Nugget* and the *Epitaph* following Morgan Earp's death.

Ed Schieffelin (1847-1897), scout, prospector, founder of Tombstone.

Charley Snow, ranch-hand, outlaw, Cowboy.

Son of the Devil (fictional), demon.

Pete "Spence" Spencer (Elliot Larkin Ferguson, 1852-1914), former Texas Ranger, outlaw, Cowboy, domestic bully. Charged with robbing the Bisbee stagecoach in September 1881. See also: Marietta Duarte.

Wells Spicer (1831-c.1885), journalist, lawyer, justice of the peace, prospector. Conducted the lengthy preliminary hearing after The Gunfight in Tombstone.

Frank Stilwell (1856-1882), outlaw, Cowboy, businessman, sometime Cochise County deputy sheriff. Charged with robbing the Bisbee stagecoach in September 1881.

Simpson **"Comanche Jack" Stilwell** (1850-1903), army scout, lawman, hero, brother of Frank Stilwell.

William Stilwell (1849-1928), lawyer, justice of the peace. No relation to Frank Stilwell.

Oliver Storm Cloud (fictional), friend of Wyatt Earp in Dodge City and Tombstone.

Alvira **"Allie" Sullivan** (1849-1947), waitress, seamstress, common-law wife of Virgil Earp.

Aurilla Sutherland (1848-1870), married to Wyatt Earp in Lamar, Missouri. Died ten months after their wedding, along with their unborn child.

"Indian Hank" Swilling, outlaw, Cowboy.

Al Thibolet (or Tiebot), Cowboy. Charged with robbing the Bisbee stagecoach in January 1882.

Dan Tipton (1844-1898), sailor, miner, gambler, affiliated with the Earps. Tipton was a part of Wyatt Earp's Vendetta posse; I conflated a couple of other posse members with him for the sake of simplicity.

Frederick Augustus Tritle (1833-1906), Governor of Arizona Territory 1882-1885.

Gregory Vaughan (fictional), schoolteacher in Tombstone.

John Wilson **"Texas Jack" Vermillion** (1842-c.1911), soldier, lawman, outlaw, aligned with the Earps.

Albert Wallace, lawyer, justice of the peace in Tombstone.

Corporal **J.W. Warren**, Texas Ranger.

Fred White (c.1849-1880), lawman, first town marshal in Tombstone.

Jim Williams, involved in the Hoo Doo War. John Ringo and Williams killed Jim Chaney in September 1875, in retaliation for the ambush of Moses Baird and George Gladden. Williams was killed by a mob in September 1876.

Marshall Williams, Wells Fargo agent in Tombstone. ("Marshall" was his given name; he wasn't a marshal.)

Harry Woods, politician, Cochise County undersheriff, owner and editor of the *Tombstone Nugget*. Luther King escaped custody from the sheriff's office on his watch. (One source has King being held at a boarding house in Tombstone run by **Mrs. Woods**; I combined the two stories.)

All these… and a variety of Texas Rangers, county sheriffs and deputies, deputy U.S. marshals, town marshals and deputies, citizens, townsfolk, lawmen, outlaws, soldiers, livery men, farmers, cowhands, cattlemen, ranchers, Cowboys, challengers and wannabe gunmen, Lakota, Chiricahua Apache, bartenders, hotel managers and staff, punters, card players, miners and prospectors, &c.

LIST OF BOOKS

Allen Barra, *Inventing Wyatt Earp: His Life and Many Legends*, University of Nebraska Press, Bison Books edition, 2008.

John Boessenecker, *Ride the Devil's Herd: Wyatt Earp's Epic Battle Against the West's Biggest Outlaw Gang*, Hanover Square Press, 2020.

Jack Burrows, *John Ringo: The Gunfighter Who Never Was*, University of Arizona Press, paperback edition, 1996.

William Cronon, George Miles, and Jay Gitlin (editors), *Under an Open Sky: Rethinking America's Western Past*, W.W. Norton & Company, 1993.

Chris Enss, *According to Kate: The Legendary Life of Big Nose Kate, Love of Doc Holliday*, Twodot, 2019.

Jeff Guinn, *The Last Gunfight: The Real Story of the Shootout at the O.K. Corral – And How it Changed the American West*, Simon & Schuster Paperbacks, paperback edition, 2012.

Robert V. Hine, John Mack Faragher, and Jon T. Coleman, *The American West: A New Interpretive History*, Yale University Press, second edition, 2017.

David Johnson, *John Ringo, King of the Cowboys: His Life and Times from the Hoo Doo War to Tombstone*, University of North Texas Press, second edition, 2008.

Ann Kirschner, *Lady at the O.K. Corral: The True Story of Josephine Marcus Earp*, Harper Perennial, 2014.

Steven Lubet, *Murder in Tombstone: The Forgotten Trial of Wyatt Earp*, Yale University Press, 2004.

Paula Mitchell Marks, *And Die in the West: The Story of the O.K. Corral Gunfight*, University of Oklahoma Press, paperback edition, 1996.

Gary L. Roberts, *Doc Holliday: The Life and Legend*, John Wiley & Sons, 2006.

Casey Tefertiller, *Wyatt Earp: The Life Behind the Legend*, John Wiley & Sons, 1997.

Roy B. Young, Gary L. Roberts, and Casey Tefertiller (editors), *A Wyatt Earp Anthology: Long May His Story be Told*, University of North Texas Press, 2019.

ACKNOWLEDGMENTS

Thank you kindly to:

Bruce Dettman for the conversations which helped brighten my pandemic isolation, and for sharing his own writings on Tombstone, The Gunfight, and Doc Holliday (and to Gary L. Roberts for having kept a copy of the latter).

The Arizona Historical Society, and particularly Perri Pyle, for chasing down some details for me.

Jane Elliot, a good friend and an author of excellent Westerns, for casting a sharp eye over my manuscript.

Mags Kulbicka for making my dreams come true with her beautiful illustrations.

Dianne Thies for the wonderful cover design.

Sue Laybourn for giving the text a very necessary polish.

Please don't blame these fine folk for the weirdness or queerness of my Wild West tale. (However, my sister Bryn, the dedicatee, can probably be held to account for much of it!)

About the Author

Ordinary people are extraordinary. We can all aspire to decency, generosity, respect, honesty – and the power of love (all kinds of love!) can help us grow into our best selves.

I write stories about 'ordinary' people finding their answers in themselves and each other. I write about friends and lovers, and the families we create for ourselves. I explore the depth and the meaning, the fun and the possibilities, in 'everyday' experiences and relationships. I believe that embodying these things is how we can live our lives more fully.

Creative works help us each find our own clarity and our own joy. Readers bring their hearts and souls to reading, just as authors bring their hearts and souls to writing – and together we make a whole.

I read books, lots of books, and watch films. I admire art, and love theatre and music. I try to be an awesome partner, sister, daughter, friend. I live an engaged and examined life. And I strive to write as honestly as I can.

I have lived in two countries – England and Australia – which has helped widen my perspective, and I have travelled as well. I love learning, and have completed courses in all kinds of things. My careers have been in Human Resources, and in eLearning and training, so there has always been a focus on my fellow human beings and on understanding, conveying, sharing information.

Knitting gives me some down time and the chance to craft something with my hands. Coffee gives me stimulation and a certain street cred. My favorite color has segued from pure blue to dark purple, and seems to be segueing again to marine blues.

I think John Keats is the best person who has ever lived.

And that's me! Julie Bozza. Quirky. Queer. Sincere.

If you want to know more, please do come find me at juliebozza.com and libra-tiger.com.

TITLES BY JULIE BOZZA

The Butterfly Hunter Trilogy:
    Butterfly Hunter
    Of Dreams and Ceremonies
    Like Leaves to a Tree
    The Thousand Smiles of Nicholas Goring

Novels and Novellas:
    The Apothecary's Garden
    The Definitive Albert J. Sterne
    The Fine Point of His Soul
    Homosapien … a fantasy about pro wrestling
    Mitch Rebecki Gets a Life
    A Night with the Knight of the Burning Pestle
    A Threefold Cord
    The 'True Love' Solution
    The Valley of the Shadow of Death
    Writ in Blood

Stories and Anthologies:
    Call to Arms
    A Certain Persuasion
    Crisis at Christmas
    An English Heaven
    Heroines
    Love in Every Stitch
    No Holds Bard
    A Pride of Poppies
    Rock Paper Water